Acclaim

"*Forsaken Oath*...is infor and few can portray it better than V.S. Kemanis. Highly recommended." — *San Francisco Review of Books*

"Besides being a well-written novel with interesting characters and strong narrative impetus, [*Homicide Chart*] is a law buff's delight, with intelligent discussions of unusual legal situations and excellent courtroom combat. Kemanis is an excellent writer." — *Mystery Scene Magazine*

"Riveting reading... V.S. Kemanis's compelling legal thriller *Deep Zero* distinguishes itself with its powerful blend of vivid writing, legal expertise and insight, and finely and compassionately drawn characters." — *Foreword Reviews*

Thursday's List is "engaging and thought-provoking... Well written, with a plot that...will keep you captivated..." — *The Kindle Book Review*

"Kemanis writes in a precise prose that elucidates the stakes of the cases while delving into the interior lives of her characters... [*Seven Shadows* is] a finely crafted legal thriller." — *Kirkus Reviews*

"*Power Blind* has everything a legal mystery should have: characters you care about, ethical conundrums, ripped-from-the-headlines legal issues, a compelling subplot, page-turning excitement, and an author who clearly knows her way around a courtroom... [A] well-crafted and timely novel." — *USA Today* and *WSJ* bestselling author Amy M. Reade

Homicide Chart is "a page-turner, expertly written and well crafted, deftly plotted with characters that portray real, human emotions... Kemanis is a writer of high caliber worth noting, and this is a novel well worth reading." — *The U.S. Review of Books*

Forsaken Oath "really shines. A powerful book..." — *Mystery Sequels*

Power Blind is "an engaging read, with plot twist after plot twist that will keep readers guessing... Cinematic in nature, the novel's complex plot lines will remind readers of some of television's greatest legal dramas." — *The U.S. Review of Books*

In *Thursday's List*, "Kemanis draws on her experience as a prosecutor at the county and state levels and brings her personal knowledge of the investigation process into the story. Her overall attention to detail makes the work a true page-turner." — *Kirkus Reviews*

In *Seven Shadows*, "tension mounts and leads to a climactic confrontation that is surprisingly different from what one might expect. Kemanis has created an engaging plot on which to build her narrative—one chock full of technical legal expertise. Yet it is the emotional tributaries that flow from that plot that give this story a greater sense of literary weight." — *The U.S. Review of Books*

"In *Homicide Chart*, V.S. Kemanis weaves three separate plot lines into a compelling tale. Her characters are well defined, very authentic, painted with a deft hand. This is Ms. Kemanis' real talent. She makes us care for the characters." — *Online Book Club*

Forsaken Oath is "clever, immersive... Kemanis, a talented weaver of scene and exposition, keeps the reader engaged with each new twist and bit of evidence." — *Kirkus Reviews*

Power Blind "is a family saga, mystery, and legal tale all rolled into one... The author did a fantastic job drawing me into the story through compelling observations, descriptions, and dialogue... Frankly, there is a lot to like in this one." — *San Francisco Book Review*

"Kemanis writes in a style that adeptly dramatizes legal arguments while also finding moments of stark lyricism... [*Deep Zero*] is a well-drawn legal thriller." — *Kirkus Reviews*

In *Deep Zero*, Kemanis "vividly portrays the difficulties of balancing the intricacies of the practice of law with the intimacies of the practice of parenthood. Her principal players seem particularly real... This is a confident author as at home with courtrooms, legal briefs, and summary judgments as she is with bedrooms, term papers, and adolescent anxiety." — *The U.S. Review of Books*

"*Forsaken Oath* is a terrific legal thriller, written by a prosecutor who knows her way around the legal trenches. Kemanis's expertise brings wonderful authenticity to a twisting plot." — Allison Leotta, author of *The Last Good Girl*

Also by V.S. Kemanis

Dana Hargrove Legal Mysteries

Thursday's List
Homicide Chart
Forsaken Oath
Deep Zero
Power Blind

Story Collections

Dust of the Universe, tales of family
Everyone But Us, tales of women
Malocclusion, tales of misdemeanor
Love and Crime: Stories
Your Pick: Selected Stories

Anthology Contributor

The Crooked Road, Volume 3
The Best Laid Plans
Me Too Short Stories
Autumn Noir

Visit
www.vskemanis.com

November 2025

Seven Shadows

a Dana Hargrove legal mystery

V.S. KEMANIS

Cover art by Roy Migabon
Paperback cover design by Valdas Miskinis

ISBN-13: 978-0-9997850-5-8
ISBN-10: 0-9997850-5-2

℞ **Opus Nine Books**
• **New York** •

"Only curiosity about the fate of others, the ability to put ourselves in their shoes, and the will to enter their world through the magic of imagination, creates this shock of recognition. Without empathy there can be no genuine dialogue..." —*Azar Nafisi**

.

CONTENTS

SPIN

Friday, May 1, 2015

A BEAUTIFUL DAY for a guilty verdict.

Warm, but not too. Even better, no wind to ruffle clothing or hair.

Early this morning, News 7 reporter Tanya Jordash aggressively staked her claim to the prime spot in front of that art deco ziggurat, the monstrous Manhattan Criminal Court building. Hours of waiting, and now, her crew carves a pocket-sized stage of light for her. Tanya shines in chiseled perfection between the two gray obelisks at the south entrance—the pillars of justice. Scattered around her, reporters and crews from competing news services settle for the outskirts.

She takes a final look at her notes. In the studio, "Special Report" scrolls across the bottom of the screen. Tanya lifts her head to the camera lens. Cue.

"We're live here at the criminal courthouse, where Suzette Spinnaker is on trial for the murder of her boyfriend and business partner, Connor Davidson. Just minutes ago, the jury came in with a verdict—and it isn't what the legal experts predicted."

Tanya's articulate painted mouth is alive with practiced inflection, milking the suspense for all it's worth. Behind the camera crew, a throng of onlookers ogles her. She feeds on their energy but otherwise ignores them. For now.

"This day marks the beginning of the end for Suzy in her dramatic downfall, from millennial millionaire to convicted killer. The jury has approved her final deal: Suzy will be trading in her gems and designer duds for an orange jumpsuit."

Tanya doesn't need to remind her audience of the backstory. The public is already swimming in Suzy's morass, emblazoned on every screen for months now. Suzette Anne Spinnaker, a child of privilege, reared in an upper-crust suburb by a two-percent family. Near genius, golden voiced, sparkling, gorgeous. Envied. Homecoming queen and valedictorian of Scarsdale High School in 2004, graduate of MIT in 2008. Sophomore year of college, she met Connor Davidson. Together, they developed a tech startup, affectionately named Video Junkie. Fun and user-friendly, their software supported easy uploading of video clips from digital cameras to personal computers or websites, with SEO maximization. They successfully marketed their product to students on campuses nationwide.

Connor was the first to be done with it. Too much work. MIT was tough, and their pet project even tougher. At the ripe age of twenty-two, he was ready to graduate from MIT and retire at the same time. He convinced Suzy they should cash in and lead the high life.

The impatience of youth, even for geniuses, is a sure catalyst for sabotage.

They sold Video Junkie to a company called Viral Images for ten million and believed they had it made for life. It was 2008, in the infancy of the smartphone, people still using video cameras, the video explosion on social media yet to come. If Suzy and Connor glimpsed the slender orange glow on the horizon, they failed to imagine the nuclear brilliance behind the curve of the earth.

What did it matter? Nothing, at first. They were too busy spending their money. Not bothering to get married, they set up house together—or rather, houses. They hosted all-night parties with celebrities in their Upper East Side townhome. Spent summer months at their beach estate in the Hamptons. Enjoyed shopping sprees on Madison Avenue. Went skiing in Vail, strolled the Champs-Élysées, and yachted in the Caribbean.

So much to do, no time to notice the silently rolling snowball. Expanding on their baby, Viral Images was stealthily growing into a billion-dollar business. Within a few years, everyone was making home videos on their cell phones. Cute cats and dogs, garage bands, dancers, vocalists, child prodigies, artists, chefs, athletes, kamikaze stunts. Inspirational stories: acts of heroism, miracle remissions from cancer, new gizmos to conquer physical disabilities. People were thirsty for Internet exposure. Promising viral fame, VI acquired personal videos for relative pennies. VI understood the power of click bait and banked on the typical video junkie's tolerance for brief detours on the way to a fix: advertisements.

Meanwhile, Connor and Suzy weren't complete fools. They took some efforts to preserve and grow their funds, playing the stock market. But they played it badly. Suzy woke up one day to find her bank and trading accounts nearly empty.

One by one, the people in her life disappeared: Suzy's personal assistant, her housekeeper, the cook, driver, and bodyguard. Glamorous friends of the leisure class were suddenly "busy," never available. When all the human buffers fell away, Suzy found herself alone with Connor. Living with him became a real drag. Their Hamptons estate was in foreclosure. The Manhattan townhome was next to go. They moved into a tiny rental on the Lower East Side.

Impossible to ignore, VI's mushrooming business model dominated the trade news. Suzy realized she'd missed out big time, and she blamed Connor. Alcohol and idleness made a winning combination for loosening her memory. Wasn't it Suzy's idea from the start? Didn't she do all the hard work on Video Junkie? And Connor squandered it.

The fighting began. Nights of drug and alcohol use became daily abuse. Words became fists and boots. Finally, they had the blowout to beat them all, the fatal assault on Thanksgiving, 2014. They were home that night, both on the outs with their families, not invited to anyone's holiday dinner. Suzy smashed an 8 by 10 picture frame with her favorite photograph of the two of them: Connor tuxed, Suzy gowned, beaming, fancy, on the town. The jagged glass ripped their image asunder and yielded a convenient murder weapon. She grabbed the glistening shard, squeezing deep cuts into her own hand as she swung it wildly, slicing Connor's jugular.

An accident? Heat of passion? Or intentional killing? At trial, Suzy claimed self-defense. She took the stand and told the jury, "I didn't mean to kill him." But the forensic evidence proved otherwise. The medical experts agreed. She'd inflicted two deep stab wounds in his chest *after* she sliced his neck. Connor's heart was already pumping the life out of him when she continued her attack. Didn't stop to save him. Couldn't or wouldn't stop. Had to go all the way. The extra wounds proved her intent to kill, so the legal experts said. But *they* weren't deciding this case. Suzy's fate was up to twelve residents of New York, a city well known for its compassionate citizenry.

Tanya looks directly into the camera lens. No need to consult her notes again. She has this. "Judge Dana Hargrove gave the jury three choices. She asked them first, was it self-defense? 'No,' the jury replied. Second choice, was it murder? Did Suzy intend to kill Connor?"

Guilty.

What's that? Did someone say, "Guilty"? Tanya blinks. Her eyes flicker toward a movement in the crowd. A heckler?

It's only a fraction of a second, and Tanya doesn't skip a beat.

"To the charge of murder, the jury said, 'Not guilty.' Connor's mother cried out in anguish. The victim's family, his parents and brother, have attended every minute of the trial. This is *not* what they wanted to hear. But it wasn't over yet. Judge Hargrove gave the jury a third choice. Was it manslaughter? Was Suzy only trying to inflict serious injury? To that one, the forewoman said, 'Guilty,' loud and clear."

It's murder!

Now she knows she heard it. Tanya's eyes dart to the same spot in the crowd. Is that the man? He's half hidden, on the outskirts, wearing a scowl. A perfect "everyman," angry, quick to speak out, a prime candidate for her "Person on the Street" segment. She'll grab him in a minute. She's almost done now.

"Tonight, Sweet Suzy gets her first taste of lockup. She's been free on bail, but that's over, now that the jury has spoken. What will her sentence be? Judge Hargrove was once known as a tough prosecutor but has lightened up since she assumed the bench. Her younger sister, Cheryl, is now the tougher Hargrove on crime." Tanya's mouth curls in a little smile at her own cleverness. "As we speak, the actress is next door in the DA's office building, filming another episode of *Plain Justice*."

"Cheryl, love you, baby." Not the same man. A jokester on the other side of the crowd.

Tanya talks over him. "Will the judge go light on this one? Sentencing is scheduled for June first, and Suzy could get anywhere from five to twenty-five years for taking Connor's life."

"Give 'er twenty-five!" Laughter. Tanya can't tell where that one came from.

"We'll have more for you this evening at six o'clock. This is Tanya Jordash, News 7, reporting live from Manhattan Criminal Court."

The camera cuts off, and Tanya undergoes an instant personality change. Her smooth perfection is gnarled with rage. She turns to the audio engineer and screams in a whisper, "Don't tell me you aired all that shit from the crowd?" Heckled. Made a fool of. Fears she won't admit out loud.

The engineer's face barely registers shock and confusion before Tanya morphs back into her lovely TV persona. Her accusation vanishes. "Live" is live, and there's nothing she can do now. The crowd is breaking up, and Tanya needs to grab a few onlookers for her Person on the Street segment. She'll interview as many as she can; they'll edit the footage before six o'clock.

She spots that scowling everyman on the edge of the crowd. He's shaking his head, inching away. Quick! She nods to her cameraman, starts walking, and he follows.

"You, sir!" She's coming up fast, thrusting the microphone in everyman's direction. "What do you think of the verdict?"

But she's too late. The man has already swung around and given her his back. Before she can blink, he lopes around the corner of the courthouse, taking uneven, wolf-life strides.

The perfect victim turns his back on Tanya? How dare he. But she doesn't waste a moment in finding another. Plenty to choose from. She moves, and her camera guy follows.

"What do you think? Should Suzy get the max?"

The man smiles and plays to the camera while skewering Suzy with his draconian prediction of her fate. This man isn't shying away from a chance at fame and glory on the six o'clock news. Will his interview with the stunning Tanya Jordash go viral?

Around the corner, on Hogan Place, Tanya's "everyman" keeps moving, relieved to have ducked the cameras at the last minute. Bad luck to be standing next to a wiseass who kept yelling at the reporter. A close call, and now, he keeps his eyes open for other risks. The streets around the courthouse are jammed with cops and prosecutors. He walks down the short street, sandwiched by two buildings that hold the Hargrove sisters. Although wary of the risks, he's not done for the day.

He puts his hand inside a jacket pocket and fingers the edges of the folded papers he placed there. This can wait. He turns another corner, walks a full block, finds a quieter spot, and lingers. He'll turn back in a few minutes, looking for one Hargrove or another. If not them, the people they work with. He might see something new. But he suspects that, whatever he sees, it will only confirm what he already knows and understands.

1 » CUT!

A BEAUTIFUL DAY for an arrest. And the end of a season. The third.

Assistant district attorney Jed Markham stands in the boss's office, trying to explain himself. Bureau chief Blaire Kendall, sitting behind her executive-grade desk, slowly rises in a beautiful swell of controlled anger. "You know that isn't true, Jed." He's been dishing out nothing but bullshit. She levels a discerning eye and picks up the damning report with a flourish.

ADA Markham withers under her glare. "But...but I didn't—"

A flat palm cuts him off. She shakes her head, circles the desk, advances on shapely legs in dangerously high heels. Jed staggers backward, unaware of the muscle behind him—Blaire's handpicked men from the DA's squad. She nods. "Take him."

One of the law men grabs Jed's shoulder. The other applies the cuffs as Jed whimpers a final hangdog cry: "Blaire! I-I'm sorry."

Her eyes gleam softly with emotion. She's not without feelings for her one-time top attorney. Her ex-lover. "No one is more disappointed than I am, Jed."

The camera moves in for a closeup.

"No one."

Pause. A moment. A subtle roll of warm memory crosses her

face. Ten years of close collaboration, hard-fought cases against the toughest bad guys in Gotham. All of it: over. Like this.

"Cut! That's a wrap!"

The stillness erupts into a din of voices and laughter. In this borrowed office, six crew members and four actors return to the real world. Everyone is smiling, Jed a little less so. Played by actor Donald Livingston, the character Jed Markham will not be returning for season four of *Plain Justice*. In his zealous pursuit of an organized crime lord, Jed has tampered unforgivingly with the evidence. He's destined to spend years behind bars while his OC target goes free—for now. All to pique the viewer's imagination. In season four, scriptwriters will have fun pursuing the criminal kingpin.

Unlike Donald, Cheryl Hargrove has no immediate need to sell herself. A week ago, she found out that the show has been renewed. Always a relief. And so far, there's no apparent jeopardy to her career. Cheryl can do a few more seasons of *Plain Justice* and end on a high note, without serious threat of permanent typecasting. She's already shown her versatility. Attorney Blaire Kendall is the most straitlaced, serious character she's ever portrayed. In the early years, her twenties to mid-thirties, she sang and danced on Broadway, followed by a transition to television. Into her forties, she played small roles of every stripe, comedies and dramas, until she landed this leading role. In the New Golden Age of Television, opportunities abound. At forty-seven, Cheryl has no intention of aging out in the role of Blaire Kendall, bureau chief in the Manhattan District Attorney's office.

Does she owe Dana for her role in *Plain Justice*? Not directly, but it's no secret that the producers had an attorney like Dana in mind as the model for the series. Cheryl's family connection gave her an edge.

After the final wrap, the cast and crew linger. As always for Cheryl, a job completed and well done gives rise to a mix of emotions. She's grown close to these people. Their energy and talent are overwhelming, addictive. But it's time to go.

She has a few more laughs with the DP and the gaffer, and they part ways. Over in a corner, Donald is happily chatting it up with the investigator who cuffed him. Cheryl sees him, isn't ignoring him, but first, she needs to find her cell phone and make a call.

Mario is on standby in the streets of New York. He answers on the first ring.

"Ms. Hargrove. What's your pleasure?"

"We're wrapping up. Can you be out front in fifteen?"

"Sure thing. I'll text you the spot. It could be a block south of Hogan Place. There's a mess of news vans out front."

"Dana's case?"

"Yes. The verdict just went live. Not guilty of murder, but they got her on manslaughter."

"Interesting. Okay, I'll look out for your text."

"I can't leave the car. Don't come down alone."

"I'll be okay—"

"That's an order!"

"Yes, boss."

With a smile, Cheryl ends the call. Blaire Kendall has the DA's squad at her back, but Cheryl Hargrove has her own personal muscle, a driver-turned-bodyguard, Mario Donatelli. Strangely fatherly at age twenty-five, Mario is always looking out for her. Even during his off hours, spending time with his girlfriend Angela or lifting weights in the gym, he's on call, tuned into Cheryl's schedule and her need for protection. She could be cynical and say that he's motivated by the generous salary she pays him, but she knows his dedication runs deeper. They've always kept a professional distance, Mario in the driver's seat and Cheryl in back, but it's no barrier to the personal affection that's grown from their daily interaction.

Most of the time, Cheryl considers herself just another person on the street. It drives Mario crazy, but she likes to remind him that her fans are very respectful. Sometimes she gets no more than a doubletake (*hmm, that woman looks just like that actress…*), and other times she gets an awestruck request for an autograph.

Celebrityhood. A chimera. A superficial, temporary state. Her passion is acting. Her joy is being part of a team, a cog in the production of a gripping drama that people enjoy. But glitz and glamour? She'd rather not worry about dolling up every time she leaves the house. For now, people say she looks fabulous *au naturel*. She doesn't mind looking at herself in the mirror. But how long will that last?

She packs up and turns to go. Full makeup will remain on her face until she gets home. Caitlin has started to notice and gets a kick out of watching Mommy wash it off.

Just one more goodbye. She knows how hard it is for Donald to leave the show. Hard for her. In real life, Donald and Cheryl are the closest of colleagues, enough to rival Jed and Blaire. They even had a brief real-life affair during season one—for the sake of adding realism to their on-screen chemistry, they like to joke. But it was just that. Brief, with no aftertaste of bad feeling. They are the best of friends.

Cheryl and Donald hug tight and pull back, still in each other's arms, eyes glistening. "I'm worried about you," she says.

"No need. My agent is on the job. Scripts are waiting to be read."

"I'm talking about when they send you up the river. Our bad guy got the word to his soldiers in the pen. They're sharpening their shivs for you."

"Very funny, Blaire. You forget. I'll have a lot of time on my hands, thinking about you."

"Oh, yeah?"

"Time for plotting revenge. Better watch your *own* back

when I get out!"

"How 'bout this?" She gives him another squeeze and a kiss on the cheek. "I won't run when you come after me."

Donald roughs up her hair. "Go home, Miss Perfect."

"Same to you."

A thought crosses her mind, an invitation home. After all, according to Mario, she needs an escort down to the street. Why not ask Donald to get in the car with her as well?

But, just as quickly, the thought evaporates. Where did *that* come from? Not a good idea. Not what she wants. They say their goodbyes, and Cheryl enlists a starstruck, twentysomething PA to accompany her out of the building.

And so begins a month-long break before the next shooting schedule. Cheryl looks forward to leisurely days with her daughter. A worry-free time to relax. Maybe. There are issues. And work has always been the best way to avoid those issues, or at least to forget them for long stretches of time.

This is one trait the Hargrove sisters share: a craving for punishing, long hours on the job. Hard work makes the world go away. Cheryl's hard work, because she dwells in the realm of fiction and imagination; Dana's hard work, because the reality of court cases belongs to the litigants. Real people and situations inspire television drama. Real people and situations are the actual stuff of legal disputes. Immersion affords complete escape.

But when the hard work is done, the awakening may come as a shock, whether rude or pleasant, depending on the circumstances. The world of *Plain Justice* isn't Cheryl's, and the world of *People v Spinnaker* isn't Dana's.

Real life awaits.

The crowd in front of the Criminal Court building is breaking up. Gawkers and camera crews feed the usual rush hour snarl. Mario, at the wheel of the Town Car, jockeys for position. The Channel 7 News van noses out and blocks the lane.

Mario leans on the horn. "Tanya Jordash. Princess of Manhattan!"

"You think they'll loop it again?" Cheryl presses a button, turning on the TV screen in the seatback facing her. She punches through the channels.

"We'll be lucky if they *stop* looping it."

"Here we go. Complete with a new courtroom sketch." Suzy Spinnaker, rendered in oil pastels, teeters shamefully under sagging shoulders, head bowed, avoiding the eyes of the forewoman announcing the verdict. Sitting above them, a black-robed Judge Hargrove, stern and smart in her RBG-like lace collar, directs her full attention to the jury. Suzy is history, this picture says.

"I still can't get used to Dana in those glasses. You should see this sketch, Mario. They cover half her face." Huge lenses, heavy black frames, almost a caricature.

"Blind justice," Mario quips. He's powerless to escape the gridlock in front of the courthouse where Jordash said, less than an hour ago…

"…*trading in her gems and designer duds for an orange jumpsuit.*"

"I know what you mean about Tanya. I'm turning this off." Click. "Can't stand to watch her."

"Get lost!"

Still angry at Jordash? Cheryl looks up. No. Mario is waving his hand dismissively at a man in the street, gazing intently into the Town Car. Cheryl says nothing. The man can't see much more than shadows through the tinted windows, and she doesn't like to encourage Mario's opinion that rabid fans are constantly pursuing her. Mario loses him by nosing into the next lane and moving a couple of car lengths.

"Did you call Renee with our ETA?" No poetry intended.

"Yup." Mario glances at Cheryl in the rearview. "She's cooking. Says she'll have family dinner ready at six thirty."

Family of two, Cheryl and her five-year-old, Caitlin. Would've been a family of three, if only Hunter were the kind of man to...

Don't go there. Hunter is *not* family. If anyone could claim family status it's Renee: nanny, housekeeper, and personal assistant extraordinaire. But Renee isn't the kind of person to demand special status. Tonight, as always, she'll graciously fade into the woodwork during dinner and soundlessly clean up afterward before she goes home, lending tacit support to the mother-daughter reunion. Cheryl has been staying in the city all week during this final push to get the season done.

Perpetual bonding, separation, and re-bonding. That's the family norm ever since *Plain Justice*.

Cheryl checks her cell phone for the time. More than twelve hours since her alarm sounded in the pre-dawn darkness. A long day, an exhausting week, with the promise of a perfect ending. Dinner with Caitlin, a bedtime story, and after that, they'll both drift off to never-never land until at least seven in the morning. When they awaken, the sun will actually be up! No more pitch-black mornings for a long time.

The Town Car creeps and halts. "We'll be lucky if we make it home in time for dinner," Cheryl says. "Rush hour on Fridays is always the worst."

Mario glances at the GPS on his dash. "Red lines everywhere, but it loosens up after the George Washington Bridge."

"Great," she mutters, low and gravelly.

Nothing to do but sit and wait and decompress. She can't read in the car—it makes her sick—and she has no interest in TV or surfing the Net. Her thoughts are too private to include Mario in conversation. Driver and celebrity fall into their respective, inner worlds.

Outside her tinted window: chaos. Pedestrians and vehicles jam the concrete grid, darting and weaving in a miraculous dance of avoidance. They've all erected invisible shells. Don't touch. Get back. Stay away. She doesn't regret for a minute that she's headed north for an uninterrupted month in the suburbs. This town isn't going anywhere. It will be here when she needs it. Dana and Evan want it more than she does. Let them have it.

Let us all have what we need, the best of both worlds. This was the reasoning Cheryl, Dana, and Evan adopted when they rearranged their lives in 2013.

At the time, Dana and Evan were undergoing big changes. Their nest was empty. Their older child, Travis, was in his final year at Cornell, and Natalie was starting freshman year at Vassar. Dana finished her term as Westchester County District Attorney and was elected a trial judge in New York County. Evan gave up fulltime litigation to teach law at NYU, retaining partner status at his firm on a reduced schedule. They weren't crazy about a long commute from suburb to city. Wishful thinking: tap their heels three times and materialize. Not possible, so maybe, they should move to Manhattan. Their hearts brimmed with lingering fondness for the city.

Middle-age crisis? A fantasy of youth and vigor? Dana and Evan told exciting stories of the early days, their tumultuous beginnings in the battleground of criminal justice and their fateful meeting in the Manhattan DA's office, collaborating on a memorable case. Maybe they could do it again—allow the city to grab them, to challenge and excite them—before it was too late.

But a few things stood in the way. Money and Natalie. A married couple in their fifties could hardly enjoy the Big Apple squeezed into a cramped walkup. They needed spacious, respectable digs. To do that, they'd have to sell their home at a good price. Natalie, the sentimental family member, protested vehemently. "Give up our house? Mommy! Daddy! You can't sell our *house*.

What about my friends? Where will I *go?*" Starting college was stressful enough, but losing her home? Her sacred retreat during school breaks? "You'll stay with us, of course," Dana told her. "In the city." Natalie would have none of it.

Enter Cheryl, favorite sister, sister-in-law, aunt. The new money bags, the new mommy, the beautiful family glue. She'd been living in her Upper East Side penthouse, raising toddler Caitlin with loads of help from Renee. Cheryl wasn't happy with this, didn't want to raise a city child. She dreamed of a backyard and a neighborhood. Something like the Hargrove-Goodhue home on Dovecote Lane, a quiet cul-de-sac. A well-maintained, three-bedroom colonial on a private acre with an expanse of green lawn in back.

The next step was easy. Cheryl made an offer they couldn't refuse. Dana and Evan turned that money into a down payment on their own apartment in the city—not nearly as grand as Cheryl's penthouse, but spacious and airy at the top of a new doorman building on the West Side, their old neighborhood. Cheryl kept her penthouse for the times she needs to stay over for work—and for parties—and for everything else Manhattan is good for, Caitlin's cultural education.

The best part of the arrangement is Cheryl's generous open-door policy on Dovecote Lane. The extended family is welcome "home" at any time. Travis and (more so) Natalie drop in during breaks from school. Dana and Evan come up when they need fresh air and trees. Full family get-togethers are better than ever. Cheryl has made everyone extra comfy by expanding the house with a new addition: two extra bedrooms and baths, an enlarged family room, and a wraparound backyard deck.

It works for everyone.

That reminds her. She wants to confirm Dana's plans for the weekend.

It's going on five thirty, but the judge is probably still in her office. Cheryl calls Dana's mobile number, gets voicemail, and clicks off. She knows her sister too well, her annoying habit of turning off the ringer when deep in thought about some arcane point of law. She'll try Dana's private line on her office phone. She presses a number and, too late, realizes she pressed the wrong one. She has both of Dana's office numbers in her contacts, the private one that only Dana picks up and the one that goes through the gatekeeper. Never mind. She loves the gatekeeper, Henny.

On the first ring of the office number, he picks up. "Chambers of the Honorable Dana Hargrove. How may I help you?"

"Hello, Henny."

"Thought it was you." Henny knows Cheryl's number—and Cheryl—very well. But, on instructions from his boss, he never deviates from a formal greeting when answering the office phone. Dana has set the tone for her professional enclave, placing a premium on decorum and civility. Better to be too reserved at the outset, with the option of loosening it up, instead of the other way around. Let the guard down at the wrong moment and, well, familiarity can be misinterpreted, and people may be offended.

In this moment, familiarity is fine. Cheryl and Henny are good buddies.

"Is your boss keeping you late on a Friday night? Let me set her straight!"

"No problem here, girlfriend. My party days are over."

"Even married people like to party, Henny."

"Yeah, well Reggie won't be home for a while, so I'm happy to serve Her Honor for another half hour at least."

"I heard about the verdict. Court is closed, and your day should be over."

"It never stops. There's always something around here that needs to be done." A diplomatic reference to his boss's workaholic tendencies. "Let me get the judge on the line," he says. "I'm sure she wants to speak to her baby sis."

Henny puts her on hold, and ten seconds later, Dana comes on.

"Am I talking to Blaire or Cheryl?"

"ADA Kendall is happily on sabbatical, for a month anyway."

"Congratulations."

"Thanks. I'm exhausted. On my way home now, and I just saw that throng outside the courthouse. Were you surprised by the verdict? Everyone said it would be murder."

"Everyone wasn't in the courtroom. The defendant took the stand and impressed the jury. Her story about self-defense might have been a drug-induced fantasy, but she convinced them that she didn't intend to kill her boyfriend. She's charismatic. The jury liked her."

"That's a role I haven't played yet: the charismatic, wasted drug addict."

"She's only twenty-nine and still very beautiful. Really smart. Articulate. A young person can bounce back from alcohol, drugs, and hard living."

Said by a woman of fifty-three to her little sister, age forty-seven. "There was a time I thought that twenty-nine was over the hill," Cheryl recalls.

"On your twenty-ninth birthday?"

"Maybe."

"Youth is wasted on the young, as they say. I wouldn't want to be twenty-nine again for anything, even though I'm *exploding* right now from another hot flash." Cheryl hears a rush of breath, "phew," and a rustle of paper. Dana is fanning herself.

"The things Mom didn't tell us."

"Painful but quick. Watch out. They're coming your way. Runs in the family."

"You're making this up. You just need some country air. Are you and Evan still coming up tomorrow?"

"You bet. I want to see that little cutie of yours. It isn't Hunter's turn to have her, is it?"

A pregnant pause.

"Cheryl?"

"Caitlin's with me tomorrow and every day after that, until she's at least eighteen."

"Let me guess. Problems with Hunter again."

"He's being impossible. I'm keeping him away from her. He doesn't have any rights anyway."

"Of *course* he has rights."

"We never got married."

"He's the father. You can't change that now."

Cheryl falls silent again and notices Mario's eyes flicker up to meet hers in the rearview. How can she argue about rights with a judge, for Christ sakes? They've had this conversation before. The father's name, Hunter Merrick, never made it onto the birth certificate, but as Dana likes to point out, it doesn't matter. Apparently, something as little as a name on a piece of paper isn't needed to prove fatherhood in a court of law. Although biology is on Hunter's side, DNA alone isn't always enough either. The in-between stuff is much messier, everything that would emerge if they ever fought it out legally. The history of their relationship… Cheryl doesn't want to think about it right now.

"Something happened last week. I'll tell you later, Dana. I know you're busy."

"Tomorrow. Promise."

"I don't want to ruin the weekend."

"You need to deal with it—for Caitlin."

Cheryl knows this better than anyone. She resists the urge to make a snappy comeback. It's maddening the way Dana is usually right, and always has been, from the day Cheryl moved to Manhattan, age nineteen, fresh from the Jersey suburb where they grew up. Eyes wide on Broadway. Auditions, double shifts at the diner slinging hash, men on the weekends. Lots of men, maybe too many back then.

All that has changed, but Dana is still looking out for her sister. Lectures, warnings, and advice. Trying to run her life? Cheryl could resent her for it—if there hadn't been those times in the past when Dana saved her from disaster.

Sisters. A complicated package, the good and the bad, mostly good. Dana. Fair and giving, practical and strong, dependable and committed. Uber responsible and borderline controlling, but not even close to running Cheryl's life. The sisters' choices and pathways couldn't be more different. Dana *is* the law, but so much more.

"Okay, Dana. We'll talk. I promise."

"You have options, you know. I just want to help."

"I know. I know."

They end the call, and magically, traffic is moving. A promising sign? Freedom is what Cheryl wants. Release from this crowded, suffocating box, into the fresh air. Freedom from him, her mistake. Wrong word. Together they made Caitlin, the joy of her life.

On her left, the Hudson River flies past her window as they speed up the West Side Highway. Why must every fight be against the current?

"I'll bet the good judge can help," Mario says.

Just what she needs. Wisdom, from a mere kid of twenty-five. She can't blame Mario for doing his job, looking out for her security, but she'd rather change the subject.

"The good judge and her husband are coming up tomorrow, so I won't be going out. Take the day off, Mario. Spend some time with Angela."

"Thank you. I will."

"Tell her I didn't steal her boyfriend. I don't want her pissed off at me."

He chuckles. "That could never happen. Angela adores you."

A moment of silence. But then, he just can't turn it off. "Make sure you keep the house armed, especially at night."

"I will," she says, knowing she won't. She doesn't like to set the house alarm. She's tripped it accidentally more than once, summoning local police to her door.

"And think again about installing that video surveillance system."

"Yes, Dad." He's been pushing it for a while now, even got quotes and specs for her to consider.

"It's just, you know…"

Cheryl laughs. "It's okay, Mario. I know you worry about us. That's why I hired you."

With instinctual flow, acting fast, Mario zips around another laggard in the fast lane.

"Not to mention, I like the way you drive."

2 » *HYPOTHETICALS*

PROFESSOR GOODHUE SCANS the sea of young faces in the lecture hall. Seventy law students are fanned upward in tiered, semicircular rows. Nimble fingers ripple on laptops and tablets as he speaks. Facial expressions complete a spectrum of emotion, thought, and attitude. Worry, fatigue, concentration, zeal, self-doubt, confidence.

Today, the worried looks predominate. Next week is the last class of the term, followed by a week-long study period and final exams. The reckoning. Can they apply what they've learned about criminal procedure to hypothetical cases? Arrest, indictment, plea, trial, evidence, verdict, judgment, sentence, appeal. Today, Evan is wrapping up…

"Post-conviction motions. Otherwise known as," in his gangster voice, "'My appeal was denied. Wha' do I do now?'" Evan clicks the mouse next to his laptop. "Answer. Become a jailhouse lawyer." A black-and-white film clip jumps alive on the wall behind him. Music fills the room. Elvis twitches and gyrates with fellow inmates around the cellblock in *Jailhouse Rock*.

Seventy millennials laugh and hoot at this relic from the last century.

"Sorry, fellas," Evan says to the dancers on the wall. He clicks the mouse and they disappear. "Rock 'n roll won't set you free. You'll have better luck spending some time in the prison law library." He turns to the class. "By the way, you'll need to know *all* the New York statutory grounds for post-conviction motions. The final will have one short essay question on this subject."

Groans.

There's only so much Evan can do to lighten the mood of law students, especially this close to finals. He keeps trying, invested in the belief that a little jollity is an antidote to brain freeze—the bane of law student existence. Now, two years into his new life as a law professor, Evan is still perfecting his schtick. His signature.

Criminal procedure is his favorite class, and these bright twentysomethings are his favorite students. Most of them, anyway. His eyes flick up to a dim corner at the top of the room. When did that boy sneak in? Prescott Covington slouches and stares hard at the professor. Evan refuses to engage. He'll deal with Prescott later.

With a quick look at the roster, Evan confirms where he left off on Wednesday. To minimize student humiliation, he uses a modified version of the old-school Socratic teaching method. Students aren't singled out at random, by surprise, but given advance notice of their "day," so they can be extra prepared.

His teaching style has rewarded him with a special nickname: "Professor Softie." Grinning students have confessed it to his face. He hopes—no, he *knows*—that the nickname has *nothing* to do with the extra five pounds above his beltline, where his love of food doesn't quite succumb to his intense exercise regimen. "Softie" is a term of endearment, much like the other nicknames he's overheard in the hallways: "Professor Cornball" and "Professor Sunshine." Are these cracks about his sense of humor or vague allusions to his completely bald, fifty-eight-year-old head? He doesn't mind. They treat him with respect and affection, and he loves these kids back. Gives them tough love. They know that he's never soft on things that matter, curriculum and grades. He sets a high bar, tough but fair. Grade inflation helps no one.

Bending the rules helps no one. That's why Prescott is *not* going to get his way. *Deal with that later.*

The next person on the list is ready for her day. She's sitting up tall and alert in the front row. He turns his attention to her now.

"Ms. Yearling."

"Yes."

Advance notice is no cure for the nerves. She hears her name and, reflexively, her hand jerks on top of her open textbook, sending it dangerously close to the edge of the desk. Quickly, in a fumbling save, she centers it on the table.

The class doesn't notice. Evan has distracted them with a simultaneous click of the mouse, projecting an image on the wall behind him. A ten-dollar bill.

"Imagine this," he says to Alison Yearling. She's one of his brightest students and can nail anything, but he starts off easy, posing a hypothetical similar to a case in their assigned reading. As he recites the "facts," he paces slowly in front of the room, head bowed in thought. "Your client, let's call him Jonny Convict, is in the fifth year of his life sentence for a murder he says he didn't commit. You now have two credible witnesses who can give Jonny an airtight alibi. These witnesses did *not* testify at Jonny's trial." Evan looks up at Alison. "What are the statutory grounds for post-conviction relief here?"

She hesitates a moment and says, "It depends."

"Oh? This calls for a nuanced analysis?"

"I need a few details. Isn't that what the law is all about?"

Laughter.

"Right you are, Ms. Yearling. What do you need to know? Fire away."

"Was I the trial attorney?"

"What, you don't remember?"

More laughter.

"Sorry, I've had so many cases since then…"

"I see. You're in high demand. No, you were *not* the trial attorney. You are a pro bono attorney with an innocence project. Jonny's trial counsel was Legal Aid."

"So, these alibi witnesses are new to me. But I'm wondering, did Jonny know about them during his trial?"

Evan makes a face of comic bafflement. "Your guy doesn't know his own friends?"

A few giggles.

"You didn't say they were his friends. They could be strangers who saw him somewhere other than the crime scene. Maybe they just found out that Jonny is in prison and they've come forward."

"Hmm, possible. Yes. Let's say that these two people work at a casino where Jonny was gambling on the night of the murder. Jonny's trial attorney nosed around at the casino but didn't have the resources to make a complete investigation. Came up with nothing."

"Okay. I'm not going to claim ineffective assistance of counsel because the attorney made reasonable efforts."

"Sounds right to me."

"But…she probably *would* have found those witnesses if she'd had enough time and money. Under the statute, this wouldn't be considered newly discovered evidence."

"Also sounds right."

"So, I'm going to argue actual innocence. Jonny is innocent and should be released from prison."

"Hmm. You know what, Ms. Yearling? I really don't care if your client did the murder or not."

A few "boos" from the audience.

Evan shrugs and glances around the room in mock surprise. "Where does the New York statute say that you get out of prison if you're actually innocent?"

Alison smiles knowingly. "It doesn't say that exactly, but there's a general provision against violating constitutional rights. Under that section, the Appellate Division held that it's unconstitutional to imprison an innocent person."

"Really? When did the court say that?"

"Last year."

"And that case would be…"

Alison smiles and glances at the face on the ten-dollar bill. "*People v Hamilton*."

"By the way, class, I'm not bringing my slides to the final exam."

He hears a couple of playful protests.

To Alison: "How does *People v Hamilton* apply to Jonny's case?"

"We have two credible alibi witnesses. That's enough to prove his innocence by clear and convincing evidence."

Evan nods. "I'll take that." He slaps the podium and starts pacing again. Everyone waits. Alison is smiling, relaxed, off guard when Professor Softie suddenly turns to her with a warning. "Not off the hook yet, Ms. Yearling."

Alison's face scrunches briefly in consternation.

He grins. "It's just that you're doing so well. I have one more hypo for you. A small twist of the facts. Let's say that Jonny didn't have a trial. His attorney negotiated a deal for the minimum sentence. Jonny just had to admit the murder and plead guilty. Now, what do you say?"

"I would still argue it's unconstitutional to lock up an innocent person."

"Maybe so, but how can you prove that Jonny's innocent? He swore in open court that he was guilty."

"But he only wanted to avoid the maximum penalty."

"Ah hah. I see what's going on here. You're an anarchist, Ms. Yearling. You want to undermine our criminal justice system."

"No…"

"Well, you seem to be okay with allowing Jonny to swear to whatever *facts*," (with air quotes), "may suit his needs. Plead guilty to get a good deal, then swear innocence just to break the deal and get out of prison."

"Innocent people like Jonny end up in prison when the odds are stacked against them. He *had* to admit the crime just to get the deal. It's almost like duress."

Evan's been having fun, but he backs off as devil's advocate. "You make good arguments on *moral* grounds, counselor, but let's consider the *law*."

A few giggles. Evan looks out into the room: "You notice a little incongruity? I save that issue for debate in my small seminar on policy. Law and morality: where do they intersect? Where do they diverge? But right now, we're looking at the language of CPL article 440. Where does it say you can get out of prison on the ground of actual innocence after you pled guilty?"

"It's not in the statute—"

But her voice is lost under the students' reactions to Evan's click of the mouse. Splashed on the wall behind him, in vibrant color, is an enormous enlargement of the face of a Bengal tiger.

Alison smiles. "It's still an open question in New York, but there's a trial court that applied the rationale of *People v Hamilton* to a guilty plea case. The court considered the defendant's actual innocence claim and held that she couldn't prove her innocence by clear and convincing evidence."

"And the name of that case is… Drumroll please."

"*People v Tiger*."

"Excellent, counselor. Well done."

"I'm off the hook now?"

"Swimming free. I have another hypothetical, but I'm not going to lay it on you. It involves, heaven forbid, an unethical defense attorney, something you will never be in your future career."

Evan's eyes roam the room. "I'm throwing this out to the class. Anyone who thinks they know the answer, raise your hand."

A few of the more eager, overly confident students perk up in their seats. These are the kids that love to engage. Everyone else shrinks a bit, impossibly trying to hide in plain sight.

"At the hearing on Jonny's post-conviction motion, the judge credits the testimony of the two alibi witnesses and vacates Jonny's conviction. The prosecutor appeals the order and loses. Jonny is out, free as a bird. Then, uh-oh, the prosecutor learns that Jonny's attorney was a fraudster who paid those two witnesses to lie. My question to you: Can the prosecutor appeal *again* and throw Jonny back in prison?"

Evan points at a raised hand. "The prosecutor already appealed and lost. There's no way to appeal again."

"Interesting point," Evan says. "How do we get around that?"

Another student raises a hand. Evan points. "Move to reargue the appeal. Either that, or at the same time, also move to reargue the hearing court's order."

"Sounds like a plan. What about—"

"And cite *People versus Pineda*," blurts a voice from the top of the lecture hall. "Your *wife* had no problem keeping that defendant in prison."

A jolt to the gut. The gall of that kid! The room is silent. The other students know better than to make light of this.

Evan lifts his focus to meet Prescott's shining eyes and sees misplaced self-confidence along with something new. Contempt. His comments imply a chilling invasion of privacy. The case he cites isn't in the assigned reading. He had to dig deeply to find something marginally related to the class assignment but intimately related to Evan's wife, Dana.

There's no way he can ignore Prescott now. "Interesting case but completely off point."

"It has the same issues. There was a crooked attorney and perjured testimony."

"That case has *nothing* to do with my procedural question. The prosecutor discovered the fraud and informed the court *before* its ruling on the post-conviction motion. The court never had to consider the correct procedure for undoing an order based on fraud."

That'll shut him up. Evan turns away. He can't look at Prescott again. Quickly, before another word can be said, the professor dives into the rest of his lecture. He paces the front of the room as he talks, head down, glancing up now and then at students in the first few rows only. He keeps at it until the end of class, when he looks at the wall clock and says, "Our time is up. Next week, for our final class, I'll summarize the material we covered this semester. Have a good weekend."

Scraping chairs, a growing din of voices. Evan ventures a glance to the top corner of the room. The chair is empty.

As the lecture hall clears, Evan ducks under the podium for his laptop case, still feeling, oddly, the heat of watching eyes. He stands, turns, and sees the Bengal tiger, majestically reigning from on high.

Click. The tiger disappears.

Professor Durst slows down and flings a comment in Evan's direction as she passes him in the hallway. "Did you hear? The Spinnaker verdict just came in. Guilty, Man One."

"Thanks for the heads-up."

"We'll talk," she says over her shoulder and keeps walking.

It's one of their usual truncated communications, Evan coming out of class, Amelia rushing to hers. He continues down the hall to the stairwell and goes up one flight, from the second to the third floor of Vanderbilt Hall. Office hours until six, then home.

On the third-floor landing, he opens the stairwell door, turns into the hallway, and—

"Professor Goodhue."

—jumps an inch. Prescott is blocking his path, arms crossed over a tattered, Black Sabbath T-shirt. The boy is a few inches taller than Evan's five ten, but his slouch brings them eye to eye. The unmistakable gleam of contempt is now softened with a touch of insecurity. It's not so easy to be badass when the professor faces you, two feet away.

Evan's senses are on high alert. He takes a step backward. Prescott exudes the odor of roiling anxiety and poor hygiene. For a second, it's just the two of them, alone, locked in a vacuum, but then the volume rises. Two chattering students move into Evan's peripheral vision and pass them by.

"I was just coming to your office."

With anyone else, Evan would extend an invitation to walk with him down the hall to his office. He stands his ground. "I don't think there's any point to it. I've said all I need to say."

They've already had three private meetings, each one starting out calm and rational, gradually building, changing tone. Prescott, irritatingly persistent, growing volatile and dark. Evan, controlled and even-keeled, his rising alarm well hidden under a calm veneer. He isn't going to do this again.

"You can tell I'm studying the material," Prescott says.

Researching Dana's old cases?

"I can take the midterm and the final on the same day."

"I've already registered your incomplete in the dean's office."

"It's unfair," the boy protests in a louder voice. A head turns toward them. Another passerby.

More than fair, Evan could respond. Should be an "F" instead of an "I" after Prescott blew off the midterm and the makeup exam. No legitimate reason for missing the midterm in the first place, and then some BS excuse about not getting the e-mail about the makeup, despite proof that the message was delivered. Didn't read his e-mail, more like it.

This is not the kind of behavior that makes a good lawyer. This lack of diligence. He needs to learn this or, as bright as Prescott is, one day he'll be facing the attorney grievance committee, defending himself against client complaints of neglect.

"I gave you two opportunities. And you still have a chance to redo the course next term. I'm not going over this again."

Prescott stands frozen, momentarily tongue-tied, his face contorted with effort.

"Now, please excuse me." Evan passes him, takes three steps, and hears at his back, "I'm going to appeal this!"

Evan doesn't turn around. He nods and raises his hand briefly in acknowledgment. *You do that.* Keeps walking.

At his door, fumbling for his key card, Evan risks a darting glance to the side under his brow. Prescott has disappeared into the stairwell. The key card slips. *Damn.* Almost falls before he lifts it to the card reader. With a "click," he's in, letting the door slam behind him. Sets his laptop case on the desk and plops into the deep, upholstered chair he likes to use for thinking.

Can't get over why that kid rattles him.

Evan takes a glass-half-full view of the world. In all his years as a litigator, a profession based on conflict, he negotiated with, confronted, outdid, or becalmed difficult people of every stripe, relying on his strengths: optimism, amiability, compassionate insight, and good judgment. Rarely, did anger rear its head. He's feeling a little bit of that now.

Family always comes first for Evan. Anyone who so much as hints at a negative sentiment toward his wife or children is a person to boil the blood. What did Prescott mean by his snide comment: "Your *wife* had no problem keeping that defendant in prison"? A sneering emphasis on the word "wife."

Evan clutches the armrests and lets his eyes roam the office. Law books, wilting coleus plant on the windowsill, a framed photo of black-robed Dana at her swearing-in ceremony. He visualizes the incomplete lesson plan for the last day of crim pro, lurking under the screensaver on his computer. Hard-working students, nervous about the final exam, are likely to start knocking on his door at any minute.

Move on. Not much can be done. Evan already toyed with the idea of having Prescott banned from the law school building. When he looked into it, he found that Prescott is otherwise in good standing, on track to pass his other courses. Apparently, crim pro is the only class he's having trouble with. *Lucky me.* Evan can always call campus security if the boy ever makes any *real* trouble, but what is there, really, to pin on him now? A raised voice. A look in his eye. Persistence. A few emotional outbursts.

Unpleasantness. No calling in life is entirely free of it. Evan's desire to minimize unpleasant confrontations is one of the reasons for his life change, the switch from litigation to teaching. Dana thinks the main reason is something else. A nostalgia of sorts. After decades battling attorneys and judges, the law school days of yore compare favorably, with the help of an imperfect memory. A rosy-hued idyll. Halls of ivy, an exciting immersion in theory and intellect. Bright young minds. Travis.

That's what Dana suggested, without saying it in so many words. Their son is a reminder of times gone by.

Quite "coincidentally" Evan's desire to teach developed when Travis expressed an interest in law school, two years ago, during his junior year in college. Yes, Dana would say, their son was the catalyst for Evan's reimagining of this blissful new life. At first, Dana was skeptical of Evan's desire for a career change, before she came around entirely and lent her full support.

He remembers their first conversation about it.

"Travis will make an excellent lawyer," Dana said, "but we should warn him. Law school is hell, don't you remember?"

"Not at all, Dana. Not for me. Actually, I've been thinking of applying for a teaching post."

Her eyes opened with a look of mild surprise. "Law? I can't see you being tucked away in academia. You like to be in the thick of things. With real people."

"Students aren't real people?"

"You know what I mean. The real stuff. Resolving conflicts. Casebooks and lectures are tedious. You'd have to interrogate students, make them squirm. It was hell, you remember."

"I don't remember it that way. And now that we *know* what happens in the real world... Now that we know so *much*, it isn't the same. All that anxiety is gone. With all our experience, we have something to give back. You, as a judge. Me, as—"

A babysitter of the likes of Prescott? Is that what this is coming to?

Unpleasantness, yes, but very little of it. Most of the students are great. Travis is the greatest of all—although Evan will never get to teach him directly.

Here lies the true coincidence. When Evan and Travis were simultaneously applying to several law schools, NYU made offers to them both, and they both accepted, failing to tell each other until after the fact. NYU didn't know their connection because the faculty search and student admissions committees are independent bodies. Evan considered backing out. Despite no factual basis, would there be an *appearance* of nepotism? He raised the concern with administration, and they ironed it out with a single requirement. Travis may never take one of his father's classes.

Fair enough.

Evan still enjoys the thought of Travis being in this building at the same time, learning the law. He loves (maybe more than Travis) when they bump into each other, or when he surreptitiously spies his son in the distance, talking to other students. He's thankful for every opportunity to snag Travis for a quick lunch at their favorite sandwich place near Washington Square Park.

Evan credits Dana's "nostalgia" theory as one of the motivations for his change-of-life plan. He doesn't mind. What's wrong with wanting to be closer to your son? He remembers joking, "So, you're accusing me of a midlife crisis?"

They laughed, but of course, there's always some truth in every jest.

And what of *Dana's* midlife crisis? Evan doesn't go to that place in his mind very often. When he does, he's baffled. He doesn't quite understand whether something is happening to them or what it might be. They're different, the way they are together. Is it him or is it her going through a mysterious something?

Like right now. Nostalgia. He remembers his early days at the law firm, Dana still an assistant district attorney. They were in their thirties, newly married, no longer working for the same employer. Something would happen at work, and he'd just pick up the phone and call. Something would happen during her day, and *she'd* just pick up the phone and call. Almost every day. Even if it wasn't a momentous something. This habit continued into the following years, when the children were babies, and then in grade school and high school. Added to the challenges of their jobs were the challenges and joys of parenthood. Always juggling, always planning. A team.

Sure, there were hundreds of missed calls and messages. They were busy. But they always found a way to talk. Too impatient to wait until evening when they got home, worn out from a long day.

Dana, his confidante and legal advisor.

Evan, her confidant and legal advisor.

"Love you," the last words most often spoken before they ended their calls.

He'd like nothing better right now than to call Dana and talk. Just talk. About his confrontation with Prescott. About her jury verdict in the Spinnaker case.

It will wait.

Evan pulls out his cell phone and types a text message to which the judge may, or may not, respond. *Heard about your trial. C U for family pizza night.*

Will she smile at this? When the kids were still home, Friday nights were always family pizza night. Everyone was too exhausted from the long week to do anything but decide which of the Goodhues was responsible for ordering the pizza and picking it up or having it delivered. Those days seem like ancient history.

Evan is surprised when his phone vibrates almost immediately. *Mm. Delish. Lot to talk about.*

A sudden burst of happiness. In a few hours they'll be home, together, and decide what to do about dinner. It won't be pizza.

He has ten seconds to enjoy the feeling before a knock sounds at the door. A student has come to pray for guidance from Professor Goodhue.

3 » NEST

A TUG ON her knee. "Tug." Funny.

Another tug. That's what they used to call her nephew, a name made from his initials, Travis Ulrich Goodhue.

Heavenly to be curled up, so warm and soft. A shake on her arm. *Mommy.*

An exhale, a child's breath on her face. "Mommy, wake up." Cheryl opens her eyes. Two liquid pools of brightness stare back. Caitlin's head is turned sideways, up against the pillow, inches away.

"Good morning, sweetheart. Come here." Caitlin climbs up, and Cheryl puts an arm around her. Ahh. Nothing like a cuddle with a pajama-clad five-year-old, still warm from bed. Sweet smelling nape, the baby-soft hair all messy.

But Caitlin quickly loses patience with the arrangement and jumps down. Another tug on her mother's arm. "Come on. Let's go see Renee."

"Renee went home last night. You remember."

"Oh. Okay. I'll get the cereal." She's already walking to the door.

"Maybe I should teach you how to make coffee," Cheryl calls out after her. She lifts her head and squints against the sunlight streaming in the window. The bedside alarm says ten after seven. *Argh.* A couple more hours would be nice, but this is a lot better than four thirty.

She throws on a robe and goes downstairs to the kitchen, where Caitlin is moving on efficient little legs. Two cereal bowls, two spoons, and the Cheerios box are already on the table. Caitlin opens the refrigerator door and says, "I can't reach the milk." Cheryl wonders how her daughter reached the cupboard with the bowls, then she sees the dishwasher open, the rack partially pulled out.

Cheryl gets the milk, puts it on the table, and says, "Don't you want something better? Some eggs and toast?"

"Renee does that. She's not here, so I'm helping."

"That's very sweet, Caitlin. I appreciate it, but I can make the breakfast for us."

"You don't have time. Aren't you late?"

"No, I'm not."

"I thought you have to hurry."

"Not today."

Caitlin is mixed up, and why shouldn't she be? A surge of heart weakens Cheryl in the knees. She drops into a kitchen chair, trying to hold back tears.

Caitlin's face scrunches up with the effort of rearranging her assumptions. Suddenly, she brightens. "You're staying home?"

"Yes."

Caitlin runs up and throws her arms around her mother's neck. "You're staying home!"

This is what it's all about. "Yes, yes! Today, and all month long, my love. It's me and you, for a whole month."

Caitlin pulls back and looks in her mother's eyes. "Then why are you sad?"

"I'm not sad. I'm happy as a clam. So happy, I could cry."

"Do clams cry?"

"This one does."

Caitlin breaks the embrace and goes to the refrigerator door.

"Okay. So you can make me some eggs. I like scrambled."

"Yes, ma'am."

Dana wakes up feeling tired, despite a full eight hours in bed. Hot and cold, covers thrown off and pulled on again. A drenching sweat at two in the morning. Up for a change of nightie, then a full hour staring into the dark before sleep takes her again.

When she enters the kitchen, Evan is bright eyed and perky, sipping his coffee. "How'd you sleep?"

"Just great."

"Counting my bruises now." He looks at his arms and picks up his shirttail, pretending to examine himself. "Not enough for the battered husbands' shelter today."

Always so damn cheerful. Dana ignores the teasing and goes for the coffee pot. Her condition isn't a joking matter. "I had a nightmare," she says. "Actually, a morning-mare."

"What about?"

"One of those dreams that mimics what you're doing in the moment. Suzy Spinnaker was in her jail cell on a cot—"

"Mimicking our bedroom, the jail cell…"

"…but then," ignoring Evan, "Suzy morphed into Anneke and was mumbling in Dutch. She tried to scream but couldn't because the sheet was twisted around her neck. Then *I* tried to scream, but my throat was closed, like a hand was pressing on my neck. I woke up all tangled in the sweaty sheets."

Anneke, their Dutch au pair when Travis was two, comes to mind in times of stress. Her involuntary trip to the Manhattan Detention Center, "the Tombs," is hard to forget.

"Wasn't me," Evan says.

"What wasn't you?"

"Defending myself. With a hand on your neck."

"You were sleeping like a baby. Didn't notice a thing."

"Guilty as charged."

Maddening. Always so well rested, as jolly as Santa every morning.

Dana takes a few sips of black coffee and makes toast with jam. She sits across from Evan at the kitchen table. They eat in silence, reading the paper. She's pretty much talked out after last night. An unusual night for them, somewhat reminiscent of their early days, two hours of continuous communication. They dined at a neighborhood restaurant, their conversation flowing with the aid of a good bottle of cabernet. Drained it. Which reminds her. Alcohol makes the hot flashes worse. Best to stay away from it. Coffee also, for that matter, but how can anyone give up coffee?

Last night, they shared their respective work-related dilemmas. Evan's: Whether to punish an obnoxious slacker, a child of privilege, with an "I" or an "F." Dana's: Whether to sentence a young woman, fallen from privilege, to a term of five or fifteen or twenty-five years.

The comparison: Damage to a grade point average versus decades in a prison cell.

Evan voiced a precise, unyielding opinion of the Spinnaker case. "Sounds like the evidence fully supports a murder conviction," he said before their second glass of wine. "It's a mercy verdict. She looks sweet, so the jury felt sorry for her."

"I don't agree. The evidence raises a reasonable doubt on her intent."

"Stab someone in the neck? Deliberately slice the jugular and then keep stabbing? In your DA days, you'd be arguing clear intent to kill."

"She'd been drinking and taking pills…"

"But no intoxication defense, right?"

"True. She said it was self-defense. Her story doesn't jibe with the physical evidence, but it was a domestic situation. Passions were boiling. It's unclear whether she intended to kill him.

Besides that, she's not a threat to the general public."

"Only to her future boyfriends."

"I'm thinking of going middle of the range on this."

"Fifteen years? For murder? The jury already showed her mercy. If they'd come in with the correct verdict, she'd be looking at twenty-five to life."

Twenty-five to life. The words float in the back of Dana's mind this morning as her eyes graze the surface of a newspaper story about the crumbling New York City subways. Maybe Evan has a point about Spinnaker, and maybe his work-related stress is just as valid as hers, but... Doesn't he see the contradiction? He's fine with twenty-five instead of fifteen for Suzy, but *not* fine with an "F" instead of an "I" for a sniveling complainer.

And what's this? Her mind jumps to a new thought, an impression from last night, a snapshot of Evan's face as he described that student. Pressley or Prescott. Dana wasn't paying proper attention, foggy from the wine, and maybe she was too caught up in her own dilemma to understand the full extent of his. Now it comes to her. Is there something a little *off* about this kid? Does Evan feel threatened in some way?

She glances at her husband, nosed into the sports section. It's early in the baseball season, and the Yankees are winning. What could be more important on a Saturday morning? They'll talk about this later. She doesn't want to spend another minute thinking about law students or Suzy Spinnaker. One nightmare is enough.

Dana closes her section of the paper and stands up. "I'm going to get ready. Let's leave in an hour."

He nods. Evan is on board, he always is. On weekends, he can stay home for hours on end, or come along for a change of scenery. He's fine either way. Dana is usually antsy to get moving. Everything about this stage of her life comes with a big dose of urgency. She can't stand to sit in this apartment with Evan all day.

It's akin to the feeling she had before they moved back to the city, the dread of whiling away the hours together, stagnant, in their childless suburban home.

The move to the city was the right thing. She likes this neighborhood and their apartment, its spaciousness and convenience. She has no regrets about her career track, her ascendency to the bench, accomplishing the goal she strived for. She wouldn't want to be a judge anywhere else but in this vibrant city, a melting pot of every kind of human being on earth. For a job this demanding, they just can't be living in upper Westchester anymore. The commute would be unbearable.

But still, the trade in living arrangements with Cheryl has an odd, other-worldly feel to it. There are times, and today might be one of them, when she walks in the front door of that white colonial on Dovecote Lane and thinks, "This is *my* house." She can hear the young voices of Travis and Natalie and their school friends, echoing in the halls and inside every room. Many of the framed family photographs still hang on the walls. Dana usually avoids looking at them. The images of those times long past make her sad.

An hour after breakfast, they throw their overnight bags into the trunk and hop in the car. Evan drives. Dana sits quietly, gazing out the window all the way up the West Side Highway.

When they breach the county line, the scenery is verdant, the trees plentiful. Evan starts to hum a pleasant tune. A few minutes later, he just can't help himself. He glances at his wife and says, "You okay?"

His question, a recent favorite, cracks her fragile shell. Of course she's okay. Why wouldn't she be? She turns to him and puts on a smile. The love in his eyes is tinged with a look she's come to think of as bafflement. Or maybe it's disappointment? The look of a kid who's picked last for the team.

He may have a reasonable doubt, but her intent is *not* to

confuse or disappoint him. If he's feeling these things, his reaction is incorrect. None of this is about him. If it's about anything, it's about her. The world looks different to her than it did ten years ago, or even two years ago.

She adds an affirmative nod to her smile.

"How 'bout I call Tally and see if she decided to come?"

"Sure," Dana says, and turns to look out the passenger window again.

Evan presses a button on the steering wheel and says, "Call Natalie." Three rings blast from the speaker on the dashboard, and their daughter picks up in the middle of the fourth.

"Hi, Daddy."

"Good morning. How's everything in Poughkeepsie?" Like a train conductor, Evan stretches out the first syllable, "Poe," for a second or two.

"Awesome. I'm eating breakfast now. Yogurt with strawberries."

"Good old college days. Breakfast at ten."

"It's all that late-night studying, you know."

"Right. I remember. I used to study *every* Friday night too."

"Very funny. You just gave me an example for my term paper. How a person's background affects their perception. You're perceiving me through the lens of your own life experiences."

"Really? So, how's this for a life experience? Eighteen years of living with Natalie Goodhue before she abandoned me for college."

"Yeah, and for me, it's nineteen years of listening to Evan Goodhue's jokes. That's how I *know* that you really believed I was studying last night."

Evan laughs. Dana smiles at the trees rushing past her window.

"So, with all that studying under your belt, do you have time to drive down to Dovecote today and see the old folks? And that cute little cousin of yours."

"I'd like to. I really, really would…"

"I believe you, based on my life experiences. I also believe that you're about to say you aren't coming."

"Someone just invited me to a party, and I'd really like to go. It starts at six."

"Ah-hah. She *does* go to parties."

"If I come down, I'd only see you for about two minutes before I'd have to drive back."

"More than two minutes, but I see your point."

"Don't worry. There's only a few weeks until you'll be seeing me every day and telling me to bug off." Natalie has an internship lined up in the city and will be moving in with them for the summer.

"No way will I ever tell you to bug off."

"I love you too, Daddy. Say hi to Mommy for me."

Dana turns her head to the left and says to the dashboard, "I'm right here, sweetheart."

"Oh. Hi."

Awkward that Dana didn't make her presence known or that Natalie didn't guess it. "We're in the car, driving up to Cheryl's now," Dana says. Her eyes sting. What is it about today? Not so long ago, when Natalie was in high school, they were in the habit of daily phone conversations. Dana would be at work or in the car, and Natalie would call on a whim, to say whatever popped into her head. Today, Natalie still sounds so young and achingly unaware of what's to come. Everything that will happen. Everything that *could* happen between the ages of nineteen and fifty-three.

Their au pair Anneke was only nineteen.

But her mind strays. Dana's unsettling dream has put her on a roll of comparisons. On one side are young adults from humble or impoverished beginnings, like Anneke and many defendants Dana prosecuted. On the other side are kids born with silver spoons in their mouths, like Evan's student and Suzy Spinnaker.

And where does Natalie figure into this array? A child attending Vassar on her parents' dime, raised in a stable home, lawyers for parents, not wealthy but financially secure. A child of privilege. But also, a child of depth, compassion, and good works, insightful, with so much to give and wanting to give it. They've done some things right, haven't they?

"Sorry I can't come," Natalie says. "Have a good time. Give Aunt Cheryl and Caitlin hugs for me."

"Will do," Dana says.

After goodbyes, Evan signs off and says to his wife, "She sounds good."

"Yes, she does."

"She's not the little girl we used to know. The social butterfly. I wasn't going to say it out loud, but I'm glad she's going to a party tonight. She's become almost too serious."

"Mm-hmm," Dana says absently.

"So focused, this early in her college years. I wasn't like that."

Dana nods in agreement. They've discussed this many times.

Natalie's focus (obsession?) with human perception dates from age thirteen, when she was summoned to testify in a criminal case. She agonized over giving a true picture of the incident, worried about the details that had slipped her mind and the accuracy of the details she did remember. Over the years, she has awakened to the layers of separation between her observation of that traumatic event and the jury's understanding of it. In college, she's exploring those layers.

Observation: Affected by light, angle, perspective, and distance from the subject.

Perception: Colored by the witness's personal background and prejudices.

Memory: Morphed by repeated mental reliving of the event until what's recalled are the recollections of images with the greatest emotional impact.

Outside influences: The edited memory further shaped unintentionally by the suggestions of investigators, their wording, tone, inflection, innuendo, and unstated assumptions.

Communication: The witness's word choice and the imperfection of language adding more layers of distance between the event and the (now altered) memory of it.

Juror understanding: Witness testimony interpreted through the filter of the jurors' personal backgrounds and prejudices.

Natalie can get frantic if she thinks too hard about all this. What is real? Is *anything* real? Now in her sophomore year of college, she's on a personal journey as much as an academic one in her chosen field of cognitive science. She has an urgent need to get a grip on the nuances in perception and memory that baffle her.

How much of Dana's own angst about witness testimony has she communicated to her daughter over the years? She ponders this, briefly, but says nothing more to Evan about it. She agrees with him that, today, a social event with college friends is a better choice for Natalie than a family get-together.

Ten minutes to destination, Dana pulls out her cell phone. "I'll give Cheryl a heads-up we're almost there."

"Okay. Should I get Mom now or in a little bit?"

Dana freezes, her finger hovering over Cheryl's avatar. Evan notices the hesitation. "You remember. Mom wants to come see us."

"Yes, fine, but…" She forgot all about it and needs a moment to prepare for the humming, singing, and chattering that Evan's eighty-six-year-old mother will add to the gathering.

He tests her with a tentative suggestion. "You'd rather not." He often tiptoes around the subject of Brenda, and although his intention is pure, his insecurity annoys her. Dana's parents died within a year of each other, her mother from cancer in 2012, and her father from a heart attack in 2013. Evan seems to be worried that any mention of Brenda is a reminder that he still has a living parent and she does not.

"No, of course it's okay."

"She can be too much."

"Evan. I adore Brenda. You know that." And she means it.

"She adds a different dynamic."

"I was just thinking when the best time would be. Now or later." Dana needs to have a private talk with Cheryl, which already involves a detour around Evan and Caitlin.

Three heartbeats of silence.

"Tell you what," Evan says. "I'll drop you and go over to Mom's for a while. She needs help with her finances and paperwork. I'll bring her over in a couple of hours."

"Sounds like a good plan."

He glances at her with a knowing smile, no longer the kid picked last. "You can have some sister time without the annoying, hovering husband."

That's what twenty-seven years together looks like.

"Thanks, Evan." Dana taps her phone. "Cheryl? We're almost there. Here's the plan…"

Caitlin is climbing on the massive play structure in the backyard while the sisters lounge on the deck, sipping iced tea.

Cheryl gazes lovingly at her daughter and says, "Don't you wish Mom and Dad were here to see this?"

"She's a dream. A little firecracker too. Brings back memories. Here you are with a five-year-old, and I've been empty nested almost that long."

"I'll be a hundred and two by the time of *my* empty nest."

Dana smiles to herself. Embellishment and drama. That's her little sis, the actress.

"Look, Mommy!" Caitlin is at the top of the slide, preparing to launch a backward descent.

"We're watching," Cheryl calls out in a singsong voice.

The girl seems to be a risk taker, like her mother. "Doesn't that make you nervous?" It's been so long, Dana can't remember if her kids ever did stunts like this.

Cheryl shakes her head. "She's an expert. And I installed state-of-the-art cushioning underneath." Caitlin makes it down successfully and turns to them with a gleeful smile, arms raised in victory. Cheryl yells, "Woohoo!"

On the side table between them, Cheryl's cell phone rings. She looks at the display and says, "Hunter. Again."

"Answer it. You'll only make it worse."

"Don't want to—"

"Talk to him. Then *we'll* talk." Dana wiggles her hand at the phone to encourage her. Cheryl picks it up and walks away.

"Auntie Dana! Look!"

Caitlin is now hanging upside down by her knees from the top bar.

"Nice, honey. Be careful."

Dana's eyes are glued to the little girl, as if something could happen if she shifts her gaze. On the other side of the deck, Cheryl is talking on the phone. "No. Absolutely *not*."

Caitlin the acrobat reaches up, grabs the bar between her knees, and…

"That did *not* work last time."

…flips her legs off the bar, hanging by her hands with her legs overhead, parallel to the ground. "Look, Auntie!" Her voice is muffled under the pretzel-twist of her scrunched chest.

"Be careful!"

"Not *here*."

Dana stands up. Should she…

"Monday morning. I'll come to *you*."

…run? Grab her?

Cheryl's eyes go there. "Caitlin!" She dashes to the play structure, arriving the moment her child untwists and safely jumps down. "Ta-da!" Arms overhead.

Dana drops into her chair. *Really.* Cheryl delivers belated warnings as the exuberance slowly fades from Caitlin's little face. The girl dutifully climbs on a swing and starts pumping conservatively, not daring to soar—just yet. Cheryl returns to the deck.

"You heard all that, I'm sure," she says.

Dana assumes she means Hunter. "It didn't sound good."

"I'll pay him a visit on Monday, when Renee comes to watch Caitlin. I'm not giving in to him. I'm sick of his games. You know what he wants. He has *no* interest in being a father."

Dana has a different impression, but perhaps something has changed. Cheryl will have to fill her in.

Caitlin is the product of a brief romance when Cheryl was forty-two, still feeling her way into a television career, the future uncertain. Husbandless and childless, healing from a recent break up, Cheryl was starting to panic about her ticking biological clock. An adoring aunt to Travis and Natalie, she longed for a child of her own. She met Hunter, a screenwriter, on the set of an episode he'd written, in which she had a small part. Soon after that, Cheryl was offered a leading role as an assistant district attorney in a prospective series. Hunter was excited for her and tried to wrangle a job on the writing staff. But the pilot didn't sell, and the show wasn't produced. Cheryl produced Caitlin instead. As her belly grew, Hunter was the one to panic, mostly about his flagging career. Cheryl's own career languished for a few years after Caitlin's birth, but gradually regenerated. Small roles, and finally, the big break. Another pilot for a legal series, and this one made it. *Plain Justice.*

"I don't know what I saw in Hunter."

"I do." Dana remembers the single occasion when she and Evan went out to dinner with Cheryl and her new beau. Hunter had big ideas and talked nonstop, mostly about the film and television industry. He was edgy, quick, fiery. (A bit manic?) He had a charming chivalrous side and was intensely romantic, in the habit of bestowing constant attention on Cheryl. Little back rubs, whispers in the ear, kisses on the cheek. Cheryl often went for guys like this, never marriageable. In a way, he reminded Dana of one of Cheryl's first boyfriends in Manhattan, the proverbial tall, dark, and handsome sort who had one significant flaw: an association with a narcotics cartel.

Cheryl shakes her head. "The rat disappears when I'm five months pregnant and shows up when our child is four years old. 'I want to see her. I'm her father.'"

"If you didn't want him around, the time to deal with it would have been last year, when he first showed up. I thought you wanted to help them build a relationship. You said he was quite tender with her."

"It was pure fantasy. I totally blew it, letting him see her."

They both gaze out into the yard, where Caitlin is sedately swinging, humming to herself, no longer trying to impress the adults. In her own little world.

"It's not wrong to want the girl to know her father," Dana says.

"It *is* wrong with *this* father. At first, we didn't see much of him, but the more money I make, the more often he comes by. He shows up unannounced, sometimes when I'm at work and Renee is here. He calls all the time, and now he's demanding overnights with Caitlin. Says he needs money for a 'decent' house, a nice place for her to stay. This is all about money, Dana. He's staying at his brother's house. He's broke. He has no credibility in the industry. And then, last week..." She sighs deeply. "I didn't tell you about that one."

"What happened?"

Cheryl's eyes fill with tears. "I was in the city. He showed up here and wouldn't leave. Renee called me and I sent Mario. When he got here, Hunter was holding Caitlin, and she was screaming bloody murder, trying to get away. Mario had to physically separate them and throw Hunter out of the house. Now Mario wants me to install video surveillance and keep the house alarm on at all times."

"Do what Mario says."

"Live in a prison?"

"It's a security system. Not a prison. And don't visit Hunter on Monday."

"I have to. I said I would. Just now, on the phone. If I don't go, he'll get crazier."

"Okay, well, make sure Mario is with you. Tell Hunter, in a calm voice, that he *has* to stop his unannounced visits. You're filing a proceeding to terminate his parental rights and getting a protective order." The system can be made to work for Cheryl's situation, Dana thinks, even though it's the opposite of the typical case that lands in court. Usually, an unwed mother, penniless, abandoned by the child's father, petitions to declare his paternity, to get him to pay support. Along with the financial obligations, the father has visitation rights. Cheryl doesn't want or need anything from Hunter. And his visits with Caitlin have now taken a bad turn; they could be damaging to the child's emotional health. "It can be done. I'll help you."

Cheryl wipes an eye. "Thank you, Judge Hargrove." She wipes the other eye. "You're so lucky to have Evan. You don't know how lucky."

Dana thinks about her strained conversation with Evan at breakfast. Her annoyance. Her fleeting wish, almost, that he wouldn't be here with them today. "He's a good man. So simple and happy all the time." Her voice is flat but fails to disguise a hint of mockery.

Cheryl turns and stares at her sister. "*What* is going *on* with you?"

Dana feels the heat and averts her eyes. "I'm just saying, you shouldn't downplay the advantages of being single. Twenty-seven years with one person has its challenges too."

They're quiet for a moment, so quiet they can hear Caitlin out in the yard, gently humming "Row, Row, Row Your Boat" in time with her ladylike swinging. A robin hops here and there on the lawn, pecking for worms.

The sun is warm, the breeze fragrant with honeysuckle. Did Dana really mean what she just said about Evan? Should she blame their recent lack of intimacy and her change-of-life symptoms, the physical discomfort? Or is there an actual, founded desire lurking in the depths? A desire to just pick up and *go*...

Cheryl, aghast, is still staring at Dana. "'Simple' is the *last* word I'd ever use. How about 'highly intelligent and devoted.' And yes, 'happy.' What's wrong with that? Evan has such a wonderful disposition, unlike his *wife*. At times."

A lump forms in Dana's throat. She lifts her glass, the ice cubes tinkling. She takes a sip of tea, sets the glass on the side table, and glances up at her little sister, a woman who leads the exciting life of a television star. An illusion. A dream. Cheryl's reality is a life of responsibility for that beautiful little girl, a responsibility Dana understands well, even if time has eroded the sharp edges that used to cause moments of panic at the overwhelming meaning of parenthood.

So simple and happy all the time. Suddenly, Dana wishes that Caitlin would be taken by a simple, irresistible impulse to run to her, to jump up on her lap. To give her auntie a big hug.

A dream.

With shame, Dana casts off the weight that darkens her mood. It's a beautiful day to love and be loved. Evan, Travis, Natalie. Her family, her big loves.

She clears her throat. "Forget I said that about Evan. I didn't sleep well last night."

"Pardon my saying, but you just need to get you some."

Dana gives an embarrassed laugh. "It hurts. Something else our mother didn't tell us."

"Oh, *please*..."

"Don't worry. There are ways to work around it."

"We'll have that conversation some other time."

"Five or six years from now. Actually, the insomnia is the worst part of this stage of life, and the stress at work doesn't help. I had a tough week. Difficult cops and lawyers in my court. A young woman, who might not be a threat to *anyone* at this point, is going to prison for years or decades. I'm the one who makes that decision. It's my call." She sighs deeply. "There are times when the system seems broken or inadequate to me."

"Well, don't let the system break entirely before I file my lawsuit. And don't offend all those *difficult* people in law enforcement. I might need a few good cops to put Hunter in line."

Dana reaches over and pats her sister's hand. Looking out into the yard, she sees Caitlin jump down from the swing in a sudden, frantic hurry, acting on an impulse. She's running fast and hard and here she comes now, up the steps onto the deck, running, breathless, because she needs a hug.

Not from her aunt, but from her mother.

4 »   DESOLATE

SOLITARY CONFINEMENT. ISOLATION. Segregation. SHU: Special Housing Unit. Keeplock. The Box. Hold down. Lockdown. The Hole. Behind the Wall. Disciplinary Confinement. Tier III. S-Block. Death Row. Protective Custody.

A Check In, is what she is. Or would have been, if the warden, or whoever, hadn't decided it for her. Suzy's a media case, the girl everyone loves to hate. The suburban princess, unschooled in street smarts, doesn't know how to protect herself. Not a good candidate for Gen Pop. That pretty face, her only currency, would be mauled before she makes her next public appearance on the first day of June.

Yesterday morning, going into hour fourteen of the crazies, she started this game. She's been playing it off and on, when needed, whenever the walls of her cement square creep inward. Inching. This torture chamber is hungry for a tight sandwich of compacted flesh. Strong language, spoken into the space, is her defense against impending suffocation. The words come into her head and spill out of her mouth, terms she heard in cop shows or read in crime novels. Decades of entertainment before *she* became the entertainment, a star in her own reality show.

Everyone watching her. *The Truman Show*. What a great movie that was. Connor caressed her arm and neck as they laughed through it, sitting in the mini movie theater of their

Hamptons estate. They had wild sex afterward on the cushy carpeted floor between the five-seat front row and the screen. Blew the sky off as they imagined being watched.

Who's watching her now, in The Big House? Do people still call it that? If they do, this isn't exactly it, not yet. What would you call this? The Little House? Rikers Island is anything but. More like The Little City, walled off from Suzy's view. They haven't given her a tour of the cell blocks, the dining hall, or the yard, and maybe never will. After June first, she'll be headed Up the River to The Big House.

B.H. Big House. Bedford Hills. It matches. She isn't sure but thinks that Up the River refers only to Sing Sing, on the Hudson in Ossining. The women's prison, B.H., is also Up the River, but east, in the middle of Westchester County, strangely situated in intimate proximity to the exclusive Bedford neighborhood of movie stars like Michael Douglas, Catherine Zeta-Jones, Richard Gere, and Glenn Close. Famous alumni of Bedford Hills Correctional Facility include Kathy Boudin and Jean Harris. The prison's newest renowned inmate, Suzette Anne Spinnaker, will be checking in for twenty-five years, where she will be slowly forgotten by the time of her release at the age of… She ticks it off: fifty-four.

It's hour thirty-nine, by her calculation. She's a goddamned MIT graduate, for Christ sakes, so the math must be correct. A little while ago, Correction Officer Reilly, the nicer one, plump and motherly, delivered the corn flakes and told her the time. Seven in the morning, Sunday morning. That makes it the middle of hour thirty-nine. Tick-tock. The uneaten, milk-swollen corn flakes grow fragrant in the corner.

The remnants of Suzy's freedom vanished on Friday at 4:35 p.m., marked by the bronze hands of the huge wall clock in the courtroom. Her attorney valiantly argued to keep her out. Not guilty of murder. Doesn't that say something? Rays of light and hope streamed down on her when the forewoman said, "Not guilty." Darkness descended a minute later. "Guilty" of manslaughter. The jury got it wrong, her attorney argued. "We have strong grounds for appeal. My client isn't a flight risk and bail should be continued." Judge Hargrove didn't buy it. Suzy is in for a minimum of five years, up to a possible twenty-five, so she might as well get started now. "Bail revoked. Defendant is remanded. June first for sentence." Bang of the gavel.

Bitch. Take another life, why don't you? The first life was taken by mistake, by accident, in defense... Suzy knows this in her heart, if not in her mind, as she sorts through the foggy images from that night.

She'd taken her usual prescriptions. It was Thanksgiving, and no one wanted Suzy or Connor at their dinner table. Not her family. Not his family. Her low mood was worse than usual, so she took a double dose of the meds for depression. A mistake, maybe. An hour later, she felt antsy, hyper, speedy, in need of something to counteract it, the pills for anxiety and panic attacks, swallowed with a couple shots of tequila. She was a bit down when Connor came into the living room and offered her a few lines of coke. It sent her off on a jag about the holiday. Connor started in on her. "Look at you," he said, grabbing the nape of her neck, spinning her around to face a mirror. "Why would anyone want to see *you*?"

She imagines, now, that there must have been a bruise at the back of her neck. Her hair would have covered it. She forgot to tell the cops to take a picture because she didn't feel any physical pain. She wasn't even aware of her hand, gushing blood. She was feeling only the hurt in Connor's words.

He wouldn't get off his refusal to accept the blame. Back in 2008, she didn't want to sell, and she told him so. He pressured her into the deal. Squandered their opportunity and never admitted his responsibility. When their money was gone, she became the target of his constant needling. He blamed her for their poverty, as if he wasn't the one who loved to party and drive fast cars and take private jets. As they argued, she repeated what she'd said a hundred times. "I didn't spend ten million on my own!" He refused to see. They started knocking each other around, banging into things, her body numb, objects falling, breaking, that picture frame...

She rubs the scars on her hand where the glass cut deeply. So much blood on her hand, her face, her clothes, his chest, his neck... Her mind is on the tip of seeing his neck again, reliving the moment of realization, the impossibility of undoing the damage—but it won't go there.

The images superimpose into a blur. Only one thing is certain, the most important thing, and the jury confirmed it. She never meant to kill him. The jury must have rejected the testimony of that so-called expert who said there was evidence of repeated stabbing *after* the fatal slice. Intentional stabbing, the prosecutor argued.

I'd never do that, Connor. Never. She's convinced herself of it.

His life is gone, and isn't that enough? The first life, not taken intentionally, but the second life, or a big chunk of it, will be taken deliberately by that woman in a black robe. Blind justice. It's blind, all right. Judge Hargrove wasn't there to see what happened, and she isn't here now, to see what it's like, living the first thirty-nine hours in solitary.

Hash Marks, Tally Lines, Notches Etched on the Cell Wall, thirty-nine of them. Maybe it's premature to start scratching now. What is the prisoner protocol for making those marks? Probably months or years, not hours, but Suzy wants to know how many hours are in twenty-five years. She starts the calculation, and the numbers set her mind adrift, back in time to her junior year of college, to that house full of students. Connor wasn't one of her housemates, but he may as well have been. He was always there, working with Suzy on their baby, the tech startup, Video Junkie. What an amazing feeling, counting their new subscribers as the list grew. They had a beer party after the first hundred. An all-night blowout after the first thousand. *My business partner. My lover. Never would I do that.* The house, she remembers, was dim, dirty, a mess. A typical student abode, a place of energy and unsullied futures. She felt happy in her own room, although it was just as small and even dingier than this.

Suzy tilts her face up to the weak morning light, trickling down from a dirty window, high on the narrowest wall. To her right, over the sink, a tin square reflects her distorted, wavy image. A nonthreatening, impossible-to-kill-yourself piece of crap meant to be a mirror. No glass shards here. Why put a mirror in a jail cell at all? To give the solitary resident a companion? How sweet. *Me, myself, and I.* Maybe this is the only cell with a mirror. They've awarded her the luxury suite, VIP accommodations, fit for any bankrupt millionaire who kills her business partner-slash-lover. Slashed her lover. You'd think they wouldn't give a mirror to someone like Suzy.

When Video Junkie reached thousands of subscribers, Connor was done with it. "I'm not working on this anymore. Let's shop it around." Suzy loved the work. She wanted to keep perfecting the program, upgrading it with new features, basking in the adoration of their fans. She loved their subscribers, so many video artists. There was a lot of junk video too, for Video Junkie. But she liked to think she was, in a way, a patron of the arts, helping filmmakers upload their creations to YouTube or their websites in those clunky days of yore, when people were still using digital cameras.

Hard to remember what it was like, now, in the age of easy iPhone videos, instant uploads to Facebook and Instagram, the promise of Internet fame from virtual content gone viral. In 2008,

Suzy saw it coming, didn't she?

"Twenty-twenty hindsight," Connor mocked her on the night he died. His life taken, accidentally, unintentionally.

The company Viral Images also saw it coming, she understands now. But Connor was impatient. "Ten million. We aren't going to get any better than that." He dragged her to the attorney's office, where she signed on the dotted line. So easily, she gave up her baby for adoption and adaptation into a slick commercial enterprise, a billion-dollar enterprise.

Suzy plunks down on the cot, rolls onto her side, and curls up in a ball, trying to erase the world. It isn't even eight o'clock yet, and she's exhausted, going into hour forty.

Abandoned. Alone. At the height of their wealth and party days, Suzy and Connor had plenty of "friends," some more aptly described as "groupies." The number gradually dwindled, then plummeted, on a graph roughly the same as their diminishing financial holdings. Family was the last to fall.

No Thanksgiving dinner, and no family since then. Her parents and sister didn't attend the trial. No Spinnakers to even out her side of the courtroom, across the aisle from Connor's family, his sobbing mother, stoic father, and angry brother. Her family support consisted only of Dad's money: drug rehab and a white-shoe lawyer for Suzy, bail of a half million posted. Bertrand Spinnaker was shamed into this financial help by the extra press coverage. Clean up his daughter for her trial. Give her a well-respected, dignified attorney. Avoid the humiliation of Suzy's pretrial incarceration at Rikers.

Well, she's in this stinking hole now, but Dad should be okay with it. The jury has spoken, and his bail money has been returned. She was a good girl, attended every court date.

Would anyone in her family visit her now, here, in The Little City? Would they drive Up the River to The Big House, anytime in the next twenty-five years?

Suzy closes her eyes and wonders if it's true, that you can get any kind of intoxicant you want in prison. Something to look forward to. That, and meetings with her lawyer to plan her sentencing hearing and her appeal. Will Dad keep picking up the tab?

At two in the afternoon, Suzy gets a surprise. A correction officer, the one who's not as nice as CO Reilly, opens the door and says, "You've got a visitor." Critical, judgmental eyes flit up and down the length of Suzy, burning through the baggy jumpsuit.

"Who is it?"

CO Slits-For-Eyes doesn't answer. She twitches a finger, and Suzy follows, wondering who her visitor could be. Not Mom or Dad. Maybe it's her sister, Nadia, or her former best friend, Candy, dressed down for the occasion. Designer jeggings, perhaps, and a not-very-formfitting top, falling nicely over the hundred-dollar bra. No way. Suzy can't imagine Nadia or Candy setting foot in this place.

The CO takes Suzy down a long hallway of closed doors, solitary cells. They turn into a small vestibule, and into another hallway, and then a larger corridor, the CO using her key card for each new entry. They pass a few people on the way. Their rubber soled shoes squish on linoleum. Distant, echoing voices float on the stale air, laced with a whiff of industrial grade ammonia. They enter a long room with a table running the length of it, divided down the middle by a thick plastic panel, scratched and discolored with age. Visitors on one side, prisoners on the other, speaking through perforated, round disks in the middle of the plastic. The dozen or so people in the room create a low din.

The CO indicates a chair. Suzy's visitor already sits on the other side.

Double the surprise. It's Flagg. She supposes she should be

grateful but feels something else. Uncertainty. Suspicion.

A couple of Suzy's friends attended a day or two of her three-week trial. R.T. Flagg was one of them. Sophomore year at MIT, Flagg was Connor's roommate. When Video Junkie was new, Flagg started bugging them about wanting to contribute, to be a co-founder. Suzy rebuffed him, Flagg got over it, and the three became a tight trio. In the big money days after graduation, Flagg was more than happy to share in the spoils, carousing with Connor and Suzy in their penthouse and the finer establishments of Manhattan. One night, when the booze was flowing and money was getting tight, Suzy accused Flagg of freeloading. It turned ugly. After sobering up, she apologized, and they were good again. Flagg continued to cling to them as the days grew darker and their funds dried up. By then, he was making plenty of his own money as a trader on Wall Street and didn't need theirs to have a good time.

But… Did he ever treat them to anything more than a fifty-dollar meal? Cheapskate.

Suzy last saw him in the courtroom on the day she testified, less than a week ago. Despite her preparation, she was nervous on the witness stand, not sure if the nerves were adding to, or detracting from, what she wanted the jury to see. Her true self. Not a lie. Isn't that the sign of an innocent person? A cold-blooded killer would have nerves of steel, would lie and believe in the lie.

Heeding her attorney's advice, she was cautious and frugal with her words, an exercise more difficult than skating on thin ice. Her attempts at accuracy weren't painting a clear picture. The state of her memory made it impossible to be precise. Connor *did* grab her neck. He *was* physically stronger, that much was real. When she glanced into the audience and saw Flagg's expression, she couldn't be sure what he was thinking. His eyes were dull, black pebbles, emotionless. Maybe he was putting on an act, an effort to look neutral as the best way to help her.

She'll find out now.

Taking a seat in the plastic chair, she says, "R.T." It's a greeting he won't like. Suzy is one of the few people who knows why he rejected his given names. As a boy, Richard Theodore was embarrassed whenever people called him Dick or Teddy. Ever since MIT, he's used the initials, as needed, for official purposes, omitting them in every social context. He introduces himself, simply, as Flagg.

"I'll ignore that," he says with a smile, trying to make it light, but his remark comes off as snide. "It's good to see you too."

"Sorry. I should've said thank you for coming." She eyes the part of him she can see: a button-down collar, light blue, a precision haircut against an incongruous two-day stubble on his cheeks. No doubt he'll shave closely tomorrow morning, before heading to his six-figure job.

"It's an adventure getting in here, I'll say that." He glances right and left, indicating the questionable company of correction officers and visitors on his side of the partition.

"You wouldn't like the *other* route into this place. It's even more of an adventure."

He doesn't say anything to that. Perhaps he thinks she's referring to killing someone as the ticket for entry. Instead, she's alluding to the route she took last Friday on the bumpy, diesel-fumed Correction Department bus from the courthouse in lower Manhattan to Rikers Island, where she was treated to up-close-and-personal handling for checking her in. "I doubt you had to go through a strip search," she says, as a point of clarification.

He snickers, a reaction that tells her how much he doesn't understand. His next question is a trite, expected one, his face not much warmer than it was in the courtroom. "How are you holding up?"

"How do you think? It sucks in here."

"I can't imagine."

Of course, he can't.

He notices her lack of response, and possibly the glare. Fills it with, "Don't give up hope," in a flat tone, like he's reading a train schedule. "You have an excellent lawyer. He'll make a good argument at your sentence hearing and on your appeal."

Pablum. Is he mocking her? "Thanks for the encouragement, but a 'good argument' doesn't cut it." She sounds as angry as she feels.

"What do you want me to say? I heard that Judge Hargrove is light on sentencing, and you're lucky to have her on your case. But I also heard she used to be a prosecutor who liked to recommend the *max* in her homicide cases. It could go either way."

Suzy is starting to boil. "What *are* you, Flagg? A robot? I'm dying in here."

"False hopes aren't going to help. You want me to say everything will be okay? Put my hand on a Bible and lie? *Some* people can do that, but I'm no good at it." He pauses and stares at her hard. "I figure it's better to be realistic."

"If you're being realistic, you should notice that all of this is *wrong*. I shouldn't be in here."

His lips press together tightly until they almost disappear. Oddly, despite the foggy plastic, or maybe because of it, Flagg's features come more distinctly to light than she's ever seen them in the decade she's known him. His face is narrow, and his forehead and chin recede slightly from a long nose, the tip of which is pinker than the rest of his skin. Like a snout.

"So, it's wrong for you to be in here," he mocks. "Let's tell Connor and see what he thinks. Is he still alive? Maybe you didn't kill him. Or do you mean that you killed him, but you shouldn't be punished for it?"

Suzy is about to explode but feels the presence of CO Slits-For-Eyes at her back, begging for any excuse to get rough with an irate prisoner. She keeps her voice under control. "What's this all about, Flagg? The party days are over. I gave and gave and gave to you, and you still want something from me. What did you come here for, anyway? To torture me? Believe me, this is enough torture for anyone."

He sits up taller and takes a righteous tone. "I came here to get the truth."

"You heard the truth from me. In the courtroom."

"I *heard* the fantasy of a drug addict who murdered my best friend." His snout jerks toward her in a hungry attack. "I hope you *rot* in here." Just as suddenly he pulls back and darts away in a feral scurry toward the guard at the visitor exit.

Suzy is frozen to her seat, staring at the vacant square of space behind the thick plastic. She's in a bubble of silence, the volume slowly rising on a murmur of a dozen voices surrounding her.

A hot hand grabs her shoulder. Slits barks a command. "Time to go, sweetheart."

5 » HUNTER

MARIO DOESN'T ALWAYS like it, but he does what he's told by the person who writes his paycheck. He'd like to be in complete control of every situation involving Cheryl's safety, but she's strong willed and free spirited. You could even say she's rash and careless, living in denial of reality. A dangerous combination of qualities for a celebrity. "I'm just a person," she says. She walks around in the open and is genuinely surprised when people stare at her in awe or approach her for an autograph. He hopes the day never comes when one of those "fans" on the street turns out to be not so friendly.

Following orders doesn't mean complete subservience. Mario freely expresses his strong opinions, and Cheryl listens, before she lays down the law. Occasionally he says something that sticks, but if she orders him to keep out of sight, he remains vigilant, ready to act.

On Monday at 9:45 a.m., Mario is ready to go. Cheryl kisses Caitlin goodbye and hands her off to Renee. It's a fifteen-minute drive to her ten o'clock appointment with Hunter. On the way over, Mario eyes her in the rearview mirror and asks, "Is anyone else going to be in the house?"

"Not at the moment. His brother and sister-in-law are both at work."

"Then I'll come inside with you and stay in the hall, by the front door."

"You will not. Just wait outside. I'll be only ten minutes, twenty minutes, tops."

"Not a wise plan. Not after the last time."

"That was different." Cheryl is looking out the window, avoiding Mario's eyes. A sure sign that some of what he's saying is hitting home.

"I had to peel your little girl out of his arms and push him out of your house."

"Why do you think I told him not to come over?" She flashes Mario a look. "I'm keeping Caitlin out of this."

"And walking into the fire yourself. He doesn't give up easily, but, okay, I'm ready for him. I've been pumping extra iron." Mario doesn't doubt his physical superiority over that sorry excuse for a man.

"I've known Hunter for six years. Maybe he's a little manic at times, but he's never raised a hand against me."

"There's always the first time. People snap. He's the type. I've seen it before."

"Mario, enough. You're not coming in, okay?" This time, she levels a stare at him, but her lips curl up in a little smile when she says, "I know you're *dying* to find out every detail of my private life, but you're not coming in."

He returns the smile. "Yes, ma'am. Understood." He concentrates on the road, and they're silent for the last five minutes of the drive.

Mario has never been to Hunter's house, or rather, Hunter's brother's house. His GPS takes them to a quiet neighborhood of nearly identical boxes on quarter-acre lots. Halfway into the block, he pulls into a driveway. Maybe Cheryl is right. The man wouldn't dare act up in this little house, where the neighbors could easily hear a scream or peer into the windows if they really wanted to.

Mario stays in the driver's seat as Cheryl scoots out the back. She leans in through the open door to give a final word. "Twenty minutes, tops," she says. "If I'm not out by then, you can ring the bell."

Second thoughts? Mario gladly receives this revised instruction. He nods and sets a timer on his cell phone. Maybe he'll keep the engine running.

He watches as she walks up the short footpath, rings the doorbell, and waits. A minute. No answer. Her allotted time with her ex-boyfriend now stands at nineteen minutes. She presses the bell again, waits another minute, presses it twice in quick succession, glances at Mario, and shrugs. She raises a fist to the door, poised to knock. The door swings open.

There's the asshole now. Hair pushed up on one side. Ripped jeans. Shirtless. How did this loser ever rate with Cheryl Hargrove? Unbelievable.

The timer has ticked down to seventeen minutes and seven seconds. A magical number. Mario doesn't like this at all.

They sit on the deck facing that huge backyard, Caitlin on his lap, patting the top of his sun-drenched, dark hair.

"Just like mine," she says.

"Because I'm your daddy."

The doorbell chimes.

Caitlin grabs a lock of his hair and tugs on it hard. "No, you're not," she says in her mother's voice. The doorbell sounds again. She jumps down and runs away, laughing.

Two chimes in quick succession. The person at the door is getting impatient.

Hunter jerks awake and sits up in bed, sweating. His vision is layered with cobwebs. There, on the bedside table, he makes out a slender rectangle of black plastic. Touch. Light. Three minutes after ten. *Shit*. Forgot to set the alarm.

The new meds are to blame. His doc keeps playing around with the dosage, partly in response to Hunter's dismal track record with his medication. He conveniently forgets to take the capsules, preferring the crystal-clear highs that his own unique body chemistry produces. When he's clear headed, the ideas gush forth in an uncontrolled geyser of magnificence, and he can write and write and write.

Hunter is convinced of the brilliance at his core, even if his manic energy has produced (mostly) rejected works. His few successes, in the year he first met Cheryl, held the promise of greatness to come. He was on a roll then, but she distracted him. His writing suffered. She was offered a lead in a prospective series, did the pilot, and he was considered for the writing team. But the show never got off the ground. Times got bad, fewer pitches and sales, infrequent successes, glaring failures, a doctor's visit, the shock of a diagnosis, bipolar, a flip-flop of medicated and nonmedicated existence.

This has been the pattern for more than five years: a non-medicated belief that he'll make it big as a screenwriter, long dry spells, poverty, resolutions to accept treatment and to restart his career as a freelancer. A few boring, low-paid magazine articles. Travelogues. Book reviews. Men's fashion copy. A relapse into nonmedicated bliss, manic energy, nonstop ideas, new screen-plays, perhaps a sale, a bit of money, the hope. Again.

His latest resolution is only a week old, made on the day that Cheryl's big bruiser tossed him out of her home. The next day, he went to the doctor, who prescribed a new pharmacological cock-tail for him.

None of this can be explained to Cheryl, just now, as she impatiently waits for him at the front door. In a fog, Hunter gropes along the floor and finds his balled-up jeans. Pulls them on. He's now fully aware that his armpits and breath are not the sweetest they could be. But last time he saw her, his best-groomed state failed to work any magic, so what does it matter? She's here to deliver an ultimatum, that much is obvious. She has the decency—and the moxie—to come here and do it in person.

He's not about to give up. Last year, when he met his daughter for the first time, everything came clear: *She's mine.* The dimpled cheeks, the hair, and the shape of the nose match his own at that age. He has his own kindergarten photos to prove it. Does he love his little girl? Who knows? Give him a chance to find out.

This desire has possessed him with an urgent determination to make up for lost time. He's pushed Cheryl too far, and now, any bit of progress he made is shot. She isn't going to forgive him after all.

He's not proud that he left her, but those were hard times. No steady work for him or Cheryl, as they watched her belly grow. He remembers, and regrets, that he suggested an abortion early on. Thank God she didn't listen to him.

And he's not proud that he stayed away so long. She doesn't know how difficult it was to make that first contact after so many years. Damn gutsy on his part, but she doesn't give him credit for that.

On the surface, the justifications for what she's about to do are solid. He told her to abort, said he didn't want to be a father, left when she was pregnant, stayed away for years. She'll point to these mortal sins and say they're unforgivable. Her ultimatum will be neatly packaged, supported with unassailable righteousness. But Hunter can see through these excuses. His mistakes are long past and deserving of forgiveness, especially from someone like Cheryl, a woman he once thought of as having a big heart. The circumstances have changed. *She* has changed, and maybe he is the only person who can see it. Is she blind to her new self? It's glaringly obvious to him.

This is all about money. My poverty compared to her new status as a multi-millionaire. Well, then, share some of that, Cheryl. You have enough to go around.

But she's already made it clear that this isn't about to happen. Okay. He can accept it. Let her be stingy. There's nothing wrong with him wanting to show Caitlin a real life at her impressionable age. The child should come visit her daddy in this little shithole of a house. Let her experience some family tension, an uncle who's so fed up that he's about to kick his freeloading brother out on the street. The little princess lives in a false world of perfection. A Disneyland life. The glamorous mother, the babysitter, the housekeeper, the big backyard. The driver-bodyguard. The exhaustively vetted playmates.

Some of these thoughts, and the anger they evoke, are bubbling up as Hunter walks to the foyer, turns the deadbolt lock, and swings the front door wide open. He's no longer so taken with the beautiful Cheryl Hargrove that he doesn't see her muscleman a short distance away, sitting in the Town Car with the engine running. Hunter is forewarned to keep his anger under control.

Cheryl flashes one of her sardonic smiles. She's confident in her mission and isn't about to be swayed by anything that comes out of his mouth. The sexual tension that once dominated their relationship is completely absent and so far in the past that he wonders if it ever existed. She strides into the foyer in her designer athletic shoes, white Capris, and a bright pink jersey. Pink never looked so powerful.

She eyes his hair and face and chest. "Rough night last night?"

"Sorry. My alarm didn't work."

"All that partying can take it out of you."

He shakes his head. "You don't know me, Cheryl Hargrove. Don't know me at all." And, indeed, she doesn't. He was diagnosed a month after he left her, never told her about it, and has no plans to tell her now.

"Whatever. You can go back to bed in a minute. We can talk right here if you like. I just have a few things to say, and Mario is waiting."

Hunter pushes the door closed behind her and says, "Don't be that way. Come in and sit down."

She glances around. She's been here once, many years ago, for dinner with his brother and sister-in-law, before she was pregnant. Hunter notices the little scrunch of her nose, a sign of distaste. For him? For this modest, working-class abode? He interprets it as some of both.

But then she surprises him. "All right," she says, and walks into the living room. She avoids the small couch, no bigger than a loveseat, where he might sit next to her. She goes to the La-Z-Boy chair instead. He sits across from her on the couch, facing the living room window.

"You really scared Caitlin last time."

"Let me set you straight. You weren't even there."

"I heard plenty about it."

"You heard from your babysitter and your muscleman. They both overreacted."

"They both said that Caitlin was screaming and trying to get away from you."

"Children cry. I was holding her. I was comforting her, and your nanny, Renee, tried to take her away. She panicked and made it much worse. Children pick up the vibes of the people around them."

"You're such an expert on children."

"You weren't there to see it. Renee was frantic. When she called that tow truck of yours, things really got out of hand. Those two could terrorize anyone, especially a little girl."

"Listen, Hunter. No, hold on a minute! Renee knows the difference between comforting my child and frightening her."

He shakes his head. "She couldn't tell you if this is New York or the Land of Oz. I'd get a new nanny if I were you. She completely lost it. I wasn't going to hand Caitlin back to that hysterical twenty-year-old."

"Twenty-seven."

"Whatever. Between a babysitter and the father, there's no contest."

"You're not Caitlin's father."

He laughs and stands up. "So, you're going with a new story? We all know how you like men."

"That's not what I meant."

"I don't care how many men you slept with. Take a look at that little girl's face. She's mine. I'll spit in a Petrie dish right now for you."

"Wouldn't do any good. You're not her father legally. I've looked into it. DNA doesn't matter if you abandon a child and do nothing to show that you're her father."

"I'm showing her now."

"You disappeared when I was five months pregnant and didn't show up until last year. That's abandonment by any standard."

"But you've let me back in."

"For a few visits, half of them uninvited."

"Ten or more."

"Five or six, and I see now it was a mistake." The fire in Cheryl's eyes softens. A new tactic. "Hunter, sit down." The voice is gentler. He sees the switch, the acting. It's method, like she's on script, under the lights. He sits down again, just to humor her. "*My* mistake," she says. "I realize that now." Suddenly humble and magnanimous, deflecting the blame away from him.

"I'm listening." He'll pretend for a while, even though it's bullshit. Something catches his eye. He glances away from her face to a flash of movement outside the front window. A head.

Dark eyes. The goon. *I see you.* The eyes are there and gone in a flash. Surreal. Hunter has never been watched like this in his life, but he isn't going to complain. What would it get him? She's being sweet. He'll be sweet too.

"When you called last year, it set me off into a fantasy. Wouldn't it be nice to be a family? Wouldn't it be nice for Caitlin to have *two* parents? But we aren't together, Hunter. We can't expect a four-year-old to understand that a man who suddenly appears out of nowhere is her father. We're confusing her. It's my fault that I gave in, but it's time I fix my mistake. This isn't good for her. We should be thinking of what's best for Caitlin. She's the most important person here."

"But it's *not* a fantasy. She *does* have a father."

"A biological father. We've identified you to her. On some level, she understands who you are. She'll understand better when she's older. But you can't force a relationship out of that."

"*You* wanted us to have one. You let me into her life, and we've started a relationship."

"A bad one, the way it went last time. You came over uninvited, forced yourself on her, and terrorized her. She kept pulling away from you and you kept chasing her down and grabbing her and shoving Renee aside."

"They're feeding you lies. Your babysitter and your goon. They're dictating your life."

"No, they're not. I'm listening to Caitlin. She doesn't want to see you again. She told me. She was shaken up. That night, she pleaded with me. 'Tell him to go away,' she said. I can't let you back into my house." Cheryl has been wringing her hands, her voice intensifying. She tones it down again and reinjects the sweetness. "I'm asking you, Hunter. Please, please, don't come to my house, ever again."

"You can't shut me out. I'm not going along with this."

She rises from the chair and takes a defiant stance, hands on hips. "Then I'm not asking you. I'm telling you. Don't *ever* set foot on my property again."

He stands up quickly, and the floor slips away. He's floating and dizzy with anger or the meds or both. Does she notice? But it's over in an instant. He steps toward her, asserting his physical advantage, at least six inches in height. "I have a right to see my daughter. Tell your driver to bring her over here for a visit."

She smiles and crosses her arms. "Why would I *ever* do that?"

The disdain is sickening.

"Yeah, why would you ever let her see a stink hole like this? If you weren't so attached to your money, you'd give me your spare change for a decent place to live."

"This isn't about money. I gave you a chance. You blew it. I have to protect my child."

"Protect your castle, more like it. And the little princess in it. She lives in a bubble with pink dresses and lollypops and filet mignon for dinner."

Cheryl gives him a scathing look. "We're through here." She starts for the front door.

Hunter follows her. He isn't finished. "The perfect little world! *That's* what you're taking care of. Not a little girl. You can't keep me away from her."

In the foyer, Cheryl stops and turns to face him. "I asked nicely. You won't listen."

"You call that nice?"

"So, I demanded, and you still won't listen." She backs up, getting closer to the door. "Let me tell you how it's going to be. *This* is what's going to happen."

He grabs her arm.

"Get your hand off me!"

The door flies open.

* * *

Five minutes after Cheryl walks into that house, Mario is still sitting in the driver's seat, drumming his fingertips against the dash. Yes, he follows orders. He will not go inside. But nothing was said about what he could or couldn't do *outside* the house.

And what are the rules in case of emergency? He takes it as implied that he's free to ignore any orders that contravene his better judgment in situations calling for the protection of life and limb.

When the timer shows nine minutes remaining, Mario gets out of the Town Car and walks slowly up the footpath to the front door. He hears nothing to suggest an emergency. No raised voices, no sounds of a struggle, no cries for help. Is he letting his imagination run wild? No way. Anything could happen. That man isn't to be trusted. A stinking lowlife with a delusional claim of entitlement.

The footpath takes Mario past the living room window. He glances in and gets a picture, enough to understand the position of his charge. He sees the back of Cheryl's head, Hunter sitting across from her. Hunter's eyes flick up and meet Mario's. A fraction of a second. A warning.

Watch out. You're no match for this.

Mario continues to the front door and puts his ear to it. A small house made of ticky-tacky, muffled voices within. He wonders if... Touching the door latch, pressing it down, he's surprised to feel the give. Hunter left the door unlocked after letting her in.

Mario pushes the door, gently, slowly, until it's cracked open an inch. He stands at the opening, still outside, still no violation of Cheryl's orders. He can hear their voices at low volume, but clear enough to understand what they're saying.

She's being nice to him, and what does she get? A demand for money? Unbelievable.

The voices get louder, the exchange more heated, accusations flying about lollypops and filet mignon.

Cheryl is walking toward the front door.

"Get your hand off me!"

Mario pushes in, the door narrowly missing Cheryl's back. With a single, open-handed shove, he sends Hunter stumbling backward, nearly falling, catching himself against the wall.

Arm around her shoulder, Mario guides Cheryl out the door, her head twisted back to glare at her stunned ex. "I'm taking this to court!" she's yelling. "I'm suing your ass!"

"Let's go." Mario nearly lifts her off her feet to get her outside. He slams the door behind them, not bothering to give Hunter a second look. Will he follow them out to the car? Let him. He doesn't know half of Mario's strength.

But Hunter doesn't dare show his face again. In the car, pulling out the driveway, Mario hears a sniffle in the back seat. A minute later, he dares to meet her eyes in the rearview mirror.

She smiles wanly and says, "That wasn't twenty minutes." He can see the trace of fear under her unconvincing show of authority.

He winks and says, "Sorry 'bout that. Guess I have to fix my timer."

6 » MEMORY

NATALIE AND COURTNEY sling their backpacks over their shoulders, clear their dirty dishes from the table, and walk out of the dining hall. It's a beautiful evening, a delicious breeze sweeping their cheeks. Their stomachs are full. Not ideal conditions for doing what they know they must do: hit the books. Finals are two weeks away.

"I can't face the library right now," Courtney says. "Let's sit outside for a while."

"Maybe for five minutes."

"Half an hour. At least. You've already been good today. You don't need another brownie point."

"Food has got nothing to do with studying. And now you made me think of brownies. I might go back and get one." Yes, Natalie has been good. She stays on this side of the line between solidly healthy and plump by abstaining from desserts and playing intramural sports. It's a challenge, given her love of food and the slow metabolism she inherited from her father. Travis lucked out with the tall-and-thin genes of their mother. He can eat like a horse without consequence.

Natalie turns around and pretends to head back to the dining room. Courtney holds out a hand to stop her. "No sugar, girl. It'll make you crash when we finally get to the library."

"Ha ha. Thanks for this teaching moment, Professor Mendel." A reference to the nutrition instructor. Natalie's best friend and roomie, Courtney, satisfies her fascination with the human body by taking courses in biology, physiology, and nutrition. "You stick to the body. I'll stick to the mind."

"Good advice. I know just what our bodies need right now." Courtney turns her head sharply to the right, ponytail bouncing. "Here. Stop here." She points to a blank spot on the lush, green lawn.

"Only if I can play Professor Sturges while we sit. I'll think up an example in memory and cognition. That way, I'll feel like I'm studying."

"Whatever."

They throw their backpacks on the ground and settle in, not far from the walkway, happy for this bit of contact with nature. Their blue jeans are already smeared with grass stains from many previous sprawls on the lawns at Vassar.

Students come and go, walking toward and away from the dining hall. "There's Monica and Trish," Courtney says. They wave at the two girls as they pass by.

"We never asked Monica what she thought about Saturday," Natalie says. "Hey, that gives me an idea."

"For what?"

"Let's talk about the party. It'll be a good exercise in memory."

Courtney rolls her eyes.

Natalie thinks hard for a minute, calling up images of Saturday night, a party at a house off campus. She and Courtney arrived about six o'clock. The evening started out well, everyone having a good time, about a dozen boys and girls, mostly fellow sophomores. They barbequed hot dogs in the backyard. No one of drinking age, of course, but why would that stop the host from serving beer? With a donation jar alongside. Dave something. Natalie didn't know the boy and never found out his last name.

Mutual friends had invited her. "We're going over to Dave's house tonight," they said. "Want to come?"

Natalie debated whether to go to the party or to Aunt Cheryl's. She loves family get-togethers in her childhood home, but there would be plenty of time for that this summer. The invitation to Dave's party was tempting, and at the back of her mind was the thought that, maybe, she'd meet someone new. She doesn't worry much about her arid love life, but invitations to social events remind her of the void underneath the surface of her daily preoccupations.

Dave's house was medium-sized, a family home, not a rental for college kids. Natalie guessed he lived there with his parents, but she saw no one over the age of twenty. The crowd of kids gradually swelled, and after dark, three older boys walked into the backyard together. Natalie didn't recognize them from campus.

And then: Déjà vu all over again.

One of the boys confronted Dave and started a ruckus, triggering flashbacks of another night, long ago. Eighth grade. Natalie was at her friend Samantha's house for a "sleepover," but they didn't get any sleep that night. The house was huge, a McMansion. The parents were away when Sam's older brother came home with his rowdy friends, making trouble. What happened next awakened Natalie from her stubborn hold on childhood, her state of blissful (delusional?) normality. That night marked the beginning of her confusion and questioning, the self-analysis, the need to know what's real and what isn't. Repeatedly, she replayed the scenes in her head as she described them to investigators, to a grand jury, to a judge and trial jury. The experience sent her on a quest for understanding. How does the mind process what the eyes see? How do perspective and memory and communication change an event into something that, maybe, never happened?

How horrible is *that*?

To describe something to people—jurors in a criminal case—when you're not sure what's real and what isn't. When you suspect that your thoughts and words are changing the event. Unnoticed forces distort your perception. The effects of perspective and light and personal background and assumptions. Alertness and fatigue. Shock and trauma. Later, the lapses in memory, only the remembered parts replayed in the mind. The interrogators' questions and body language shaping your responses. Your choice of words to describe what you saw. The chosen words sticking in your mind, repeated, reinforcing the inaccuracies.

How horrible is *that*? To testify, under oath, to a complete distortion of memory!

Natalie brings it to mind now, Saturday night, and the altercation at Dave's house. "Altercation." Already she's characterizing it! She could find ten other words for it, and the image would be different.

Right after they left the party, she and Courtney briefly talked about what had happened. Mostly, they were glad to get out of there. In the days since, they have, undoubtedly, thought about it a number of times, focusing on different details, whatever made the most impact on them individually, personally.

A minute ago, when their two friends walked by, Natalie was reminded that she saw Monica at the party, on the fringes, standing right behind Dave. Does Courtney remember? Natalie recalls, first, what the troublemaker said, second, Dave's face, third, Monica's reaction. How to describe it? Her eyes widened in a sort of slow-moving shock, followed by an odd little laugh. Monica must have been drunk, but she had sense enough to step away, like the rest of them. Natalie, with a tumbler of Coke in hand, reacted quicker.

"Saturday night."

"What about it?" Courtney speaks lazily. She's already in a

daydream, resisting the call of duty. Study. Must study. Not.

"Let's compare what we remember. It's a good example of how we process perception, cognition, and memory."

"Maybe it is, but right now, I'm perceiving the fragrant flowers and the green grass. I'm perceiving that I feel too good to be trying to remember what I was perceiving a few days ago."

"I won't ask you anything too difficult. Just close your eyes and imagine you're in Dave's backyard when that big jerk started yelling at him…" Natalie cuts herself off. "Jerk." "Yelling." Her words are painting a picture. But she has to say *something* to identify what she's talking about.

"Yes, I do remember perceiving that big jerk."

Repeating Natalie's words! Reinforcing the image. Is the picture skewed or accurate? He was big, no doubt about it. Several inches taller than Dave, and muscular, his broad chest and tatted arms on display in a body-hugging tank top. By then, it was dark outside in the backyard, so how could they see him? They were caught in a bright circle from the floodlight on the back porch. Dave was talking to a girl when the intruder, with his friends tagging along, staggered up to him. Monica was standing behind Dave. Natalie and Courtney were a few feet away, in front, and to the side, of Dave.

"Okay, so you remember the boy. Can you describe him?"

"Big guy. When he came over, the air kind of moved around us."

Interesting. A tactile perception. "What else?"

"I don't know."

"What about his hair and clothes?"

"You could tell, he thought he was body beautiful."

Doubly interesting. Courtney answers a question about physical appearance with a comment about his thoughts. An assessment of his personality, really. How does she know about his self-admiration? A combination of things: his clothing and hair choices, actions and words. Her own assumptions and experiences. She's making a judgment and stating an opinion, not objective facts. "You don't remember anything about his hair or clothes?"

"He didn't have much hair. And I think he was wearing cargo shorts. What else would you like to know, Professor?"

Natalie remembers long pants and plenty of hair, but it was pulled tight in a ponytail at the nape of his neck. Even though she works hard at being accurate, she doesn't want to assume that she's right and Courtney's wrong. "Who was standing around us before he came up?"

"How do I know? I was talking to Tanner. I don't remember anyone else. I don't even remember where *you* were, exactly."

Makes sense that Courtney would forget Natalie in favor of Tanner, a boy she has a huge crush on. "I was standing on your left," Natalie reminds her. "Tanner was on your right."

"Whatever. All I know is, that jerk came up and ruined everything. Tanner was acting interested in me for once. Didn't you see? I was having a good makeup and hair day."

If there's anything about Courtney that annoys Natalie, it's her occasional lapse into superficiality, a tendency she probably learned from her mother. Luckily, Courtney isn't annoyingly superficial every day, and when she is, Natalie's extra grateful for her own mother: the lawyer, the judge, the rational intellectual. And more than that. A wise person who cares about deeper things.

Maybe Courtney's mother has those qualities too, but not from what Natalie has seen, the couple of times she visited their family. Courtney's mom fussed over her daughter's appearance, suggested different clothing and hairstyles, and pushed her to say whether she was dating or attracted to anyone. A bubbly, juvenile voice, her eyes lined and mascaraed. So different from Natalie's mother, who offers positive support and unpressured guidance about physical appearance and relationships. Judge Hargrove. Tough and strong, but in a warm way. A contradiction? It used to confuse Natalie, but not anymore. She still calls her mother "Mommy" and hears her voice in her head. Mommy loves to talk about ideas, school, and work, less about clothes, hairstyles, and social events. She's never coy or flirtatious. But…is it possible? Maybe she acted that way around Daddy when they were young. Hard to imagine.

"So, you don't remember what I was doing, but you must have heard… Forget I said that. Just tell me everything else you remember about what happened. The boy, what he said, who else was there." Open-ended questions. Not that Courtney *must* have heard or seen anything, even though Natalie is thinking that anyone with eyes and ears would have noticed who was standing nearby and, generally, what was said.

"Tanner was talking about the camping trip he's taking this summer when I felt the air moving, like 'whoosh,' and a loud voice like, 'This is all you have, dude?' Tanner stopped talking and stopped looking at me. He turned to see what was going on. That scary guy was leaning into Dave's face, complaining about the 'lame' beer and screaming, 'Where's the real booze?' Tanner didn't speak another word to me. He was going to break up the argument, and he started to, but that jerk's friends stepped in first."

Tanner, the would-be hero.

Natalie doesn't remember it quite this way. Tanner, with Courtney clinging to his arm, backed away from the chaos like everyone else. And the troublemaker's friends didn't break it up. They were laughing drunkenly on the side while three of Dave's friends came to the rescue, pulling the belligerent muscleman away. He cursed like a madman but, luckily, he and his friends left the party without causing any more trouble.

"I know," Courtney says. "You're going to say that my perception and cognition and memory are all screwed up. Right, Professor?"

"Not at all! That's just it. That's why this is so interesting. It's all valid, everything I saw and everything you saw. We just have to figure out the million things that affect our individual perception and description."

"Meaning that *your* perception is different from mine. You don't remember it that way."

Natalie doesn't want to nitpick. That isn't the point. "I remember it almost the same. Maybe a few little things are different, but that's how it always is. If we were in court, the jury hears the different versions and pieces it together to find the truth. A bunch of little differences aren't going to affect the verdict." Hopefully. But that's what Natalie has always wondered. Did anything she said change the outcome from what it should have been? Anything that was different from what anyone else said about that night at Samantha's house?

Oh, this is impossible!

"You should go to law school like the rest of your family."

"No way. But maybe *you* should apply. You have the name for it, Court."

"Very funny. And it's Courtney or Cee Cee to you," says Courtney Corrente.

Become a lawyer? Natalie's not interested. But it's a Goodhue family joke that, one day, she'll show up as an expert witness in one of their cases. She'll have a PhD in human memory and cognition, not to mention her intuitive acumen in the area of eyewitness perception. The lawyers will give Dr. Natalie a long list of variables affecting the perception of a key witness, and she'll opine, to a high degree of scientific certainty, whether the testimony of that witness is accurate. Margin of error, X percent.

Hah. Science fiction. People mistake their strong opinions for facts. Opinions, based on distorted memories. There's no certainty in the search for "truth," whatever that is. Even if science could provide the answers, Natalie has no desire to set foot in a court of law ever again. She's not quite sure where her future is headed, only that she's driven to explore the mysteries of perception and memory.

She falls silent and relaxes back onto her forearms, backpack supporting her upper back, legs stretched out in front. Courtney closes her eyes, happy to be done with Natalie's mental exercise. It really is a beautiful evening. Minutes drift by, and Natalie is afloat in reverie.

Regret creeps in. She wishes now that she'd gone to Aunt Cheryl's house on Saturday instead of Dave's party. She thinks of her little cousin Caitlin, Travis, her parents, and Grandma Brenda, her only remaining grandparent. A memory surfaces of an afternoon last summer, the extended family together in the backyard at Dovecote Lane. A hazy, hot sun beat down on them as they sipped icy lemonade from tall, sweating glasses. Natalie closes her eyes against that warmth, feeling the all-encompassing brilliance of sun and love. But then, the sharp edge of a hardcover book intrudes, pressing into her back.

She sits up. "Come on, Cee Cee." Natalie grabs her backpack and stands up. "We can't daydream all night."

Courtney stretches her arms, yawns, and says, "You're a spoiler. But I love you." She sits up and grabs her backpack.

The path is quieter now. It's still early evening, one of those spring days that will last until eight o'clock, but the shadows are longer, the natural light dimmer. How long have they been lounging on the lawn? Five minutes has turned into an hour.

On the path, a man's voice emerges from the warm dusky air. "Hello, girls." A faceless voice. Chipper. "Got a minute?"

Natalie startles. She turns to face a stranger who stands directly behind them. How long has he been walking so close? Courtney turns around too, looking relaxed and open, willing to engage. They all stop.

In the three seconds before the man speaks again, Natalie's mental camera zooms in to record his details. Middle-aged, short hair mostly gray, deep-set eyes, a long, sharp nose. About her father's height, five ten, because her head tilts up at the same angle to meet his eyes. But leaner than her father. And another flash impression, undefinable: This man is pretending at happiness. His eyes have a vacant quality.

"Those backpacks look heavy," he says.

What is this? Natalie inches backward.

"You must be working hard."

Courtney answers cheerily, "Gotta study for finals!"

What is she thinking? Natalie gives the man a fake smile and gently tugs at her friend's elbow.

"Sorry!" The man laughs, all jovial, staring at Natalie. "Did I startle you? I just wanted to ask you a few things about this college. How do you like it? My daughter is a junior in high school and she's thinking of applying here."

"It's a great place," Courtney bubbles. "She'll like it."

"But the classes are hard, aren't they? The profs really put the pressure on you."

"Yeah, we have a load of work—"

"If you want more information," Natalie cuts in, "you can go to the administration building." She points, very businesslike. "But the office is probably closed now."

"Yup, I already checked, and it's closed, but what can a working man do? This is the only time I can visit."

"Too bad," says Courtney.

"It's open on the weekends." Natalie is suspicious. She's aware, suddenly, that no one, other than this stranger, is in their immediate area.

"I'll try to come back then. Thanks for the info, girls. Good luck with your studies."

The man is smiling, the eyes vacant. He doesn't move.

Courtney giggles and says, "Thanks."

Natalie nods curtly with a flat-palmed wave of the hand and turns to go. She sets a brisk pace for them as they walk away.

Down the path, Courtney rasps, "Hold up!" Natalie slows a bit and glances back over her shoulder. The man is gone.

"You're acting all scared or something," Courtney says. They continue walking at a relaxed pace.

"I thought he was a little strange."

"He seemed perfectly nice."

"Did *your* dad ever come here alone when it's almost dark and ask two girls what they thought of Vassar?"

"No, but that man said he couldn't come any other time. What if he's a single dad, just doing some legwork?"

"Sure, but…" Natalie stops dead. Maybe this is another study in perception. She could ask Cee Cee what she remembers about the man's face, the way he stood, what he said, his tone of voice, his gestures, his body posture, the intensity of his gaze, those eyes…

How does anyone ever know anything?

Frozen to the ground, Natalie is a new marble statue on the college campus. Her friend stands, very alive, next to her. A few seconds pass, maybe more, and then Courtney surprises her. She grabs Natalie's shoulders and pulls her in for a hug. "Stop scaring me, girl," she whispers in her ear. Gently pushing away, she says in a louder voice. "I know what you need."

"What?"

"A few hours with inanimate objects. Books. Words on paper."

Natalie shifts her heavy bag to the other shoulder. Says nothing.

Courtney takes Natalie's elbow and gets them walking again. "No people. Abstract concepts. Our own little academic worlds."

This is the Courtney that Natalie loves.

They are not alone, she sees now. Other students, normal people, walk by, knowing where they need to go. Lights have come on along the path. There's only a little way to go. Natalie is comforted, almost, as they walk into the light cast from the windows of the Thompson Library. The Gothic structure, a daily part of Natalie's life for almost two years, has lost the creepiness it once held when she was new on campus.

So anxious to get back to studying a minute ago, Natalie now feels a different, pressing urge. She pauses outside the tall doors.

"Wait a sec. I think my phone is buzzing." Fingering the outside pocket of her backpack, she pulls the flap up from its Velcro strip and takes out her cell. Looks at the screen. "You go ahead. Save me a seat. I have to make a call."

Courtney looks askance at her friend. There was no audible buzzing, and maybe Natalie's face still isn't back to normal. But in the well-traveled, illuminated area outside the front doors of the main library, there really is no reason to worry. She says, "Sure," and goes inside.

Natalie checks the screen again. No calls or texts have come in.

There was a time in her life, not so long ago, when calls and texts were constant. That era started the moment she got her first cell phone in middle school and continued all through high school. Of course, most of the calls and texts originated from her own phone, not from Mommy's or Daddy's, but she always had the feeling that her parents were happy to hear from her, ready to talk. If they were busy, they would call back the minute they were free.

She always made more calls to Mommy than Daddy. Doesn't make sense. *He* was the one who seemed more ready to respond, to drop everything to talk to his daughter.

The pattern changed the minute she moved onto campus,

freshman year, and it mystified her. She persisted, and they responded, but the calls were shorter and the time it took for them to return her messages grew longer. The contacts gradually dwindled. Now, nearing the end of her sophomore year, Natalie has come to realize what a huge commitment it must have been for them to respond to her constant needs. Such busy, important people.

All her own problem, right?

Yes, her parents are important in the world. She doesn't use it as a bragging point or a badge for herself, probably because the shock of learning it is new to her. She'd like to know more about them, her own parents, and now they don't want to talk.

Her finger hovers back and forth over the two numbers with their two little round photos. Favorite photos, but dated. Her parents look older now, especially when standing in harsh sunlight.

Natalie chooses one and touches the screen. Three rings, and it almost rolls to voicemail, then connects.

"Hello, sweetheart," her mother says. A nice word, but the voice is distant, like so many other times when Natalie has called this year, many of those calls ending after only a few words. "Can I call you back?" her mother will say. "I'm in the middle of something right now." After they hang up, maybe she calls back, maybe she doesn't.

"Hi, Mommy. Are you working late? Did I interrupt anything?"

"No." This word comes over loud and distinct, as if her mother has just arrived on the scene, fully present. Amazingly, she seems almost attentive tonight. "Not busy at all right now. I don't start a new trial until Wednesday. I'm sitting in the living room, reading a novel. How are you? Ready for finals?"

"Just going into the library now to hit the books."

"I know you'll do well."

And that's just it. Mommy knows she'll do well, or rather, she has this opinion, and maybe it's a big reason that Natalie tries so hard. She can think of nothing to say in response, but mothers know that children can't say anything to a statement like that. Do you thank your own mother for the compliment? Do you agree and say that, yes, you're sure you'll do well? Mommy fills the blank spot by changing the subject. "How was your party on Saturday?"

"It was okay," Natalie says, surprised to feel her voice breaking up. It wasn't okay at all, and now the emotion is rising into her throat, threatening to choke her.

In the silence, her mother says, "Natalie. Is everything all right?"

Things aren't exactly all right, and she could blame it on that incident with the man, the stranger, but she's convinced that he has nothing to do with the lump in her throat. There's no reason to mention him to her mother. It's not the man at all that's causing this. It's her, all her, and how she reacted. Courtney's intuition is valid. Natalie overreacted. Panicked like an idiot. The conversation with the man was nothing more than what it was on the surface, and this means that everything Natalie obsesses over, day in and day out, everything she studies and seeks to understand, might be worthless. Is that possible? A waste of time. People should talk, should connect, should live. She felt it a moment ago in Courtney's hug, the caring and closeness.

How can she possibly say all this to her mother right now?

Anger and longing mix dangerously, but she will not cry. She takes a deep breath and steadies her voice. "Everything's fine, but the party was no fun. I wish I'd gone to Aunt Cheryl's instead."

Now it's her mother's turn to be silent.

"To see all of you," Natalie adds. "I miss you."

She imagines she can hear her mother breathing. She sees her face. The words, said in a husky voice, are exactly what she wants to hear. "I'm glad it's almost summer, and you'll be here with us. I've missed you too."

7 »   LETTERS

MONDAY WAS QUIET for Judge Hargrove, with only a few attorney conferences on her court calendar, and today will be the same. Time to regroup, to put Spinnaker out of mind, to prepare for tomorrow, the start of another high-profile murder trial: *People v Garth Underwood, M.D.* The forty-year-old orthopedist is charged with two counts of murder in the second degree, under a theory of depraved indifference. It's a case of first impression in New York.

In her office, door closed, Dana studies the case. Indictment, grand jury minutes, motion papers, witness list. She's skeptical of the legal theory. The District Attorney is really stretching the law on this one, inspired by a test case pending in California: *People v Hsiu Ying Lisa Tseng.* Pill mills. Patient deaths by overdose. But... What about the doctors' mental state? They didn't literally intend to kill their patients when they prescribed bottles full of painkillers. How about causation? They didn't literally put the pills in their patients' mouths.

The alleged acts of Dr. Tseng in California and Dr. Underwood in New York are horrific, Dana would agree, but does the evidence fit the crime charged? Murder. Really? The New York statute defines murder in the second degree differently than the crime of the same name in California. It's a tough standard. The DA must prove that Dr. Underwood utterly disregarded the value of human life, to the point of depravity and indifference, and committed reckless acts creating a grave risk of death. In defense, the doctor claims that the victims independently took their own lives, breaking the chain of causation. The DA replies that the overdoses were foreseeable and don't absolve the doctor.

Is this a game of semantics? Lawyers and judges agonize over words. Combinations of letters, shapes in black on white, define our daily lives and the consequences of our actions. Language can be crisp, rational, intellectual, and logical, unless it's inconsistent, impenetrable, and nonsensical. Words are powerful and limiting, inadequate, subject to misinterpretation, misapplication, and unintended consequences. Even the best-written statutes can't escape distortion from the subjectivity and human emotion that juries inject when they apply the law to the facts.

Another monkey wrench. The facts. State of mind is a "fact," but no one can possibly know what goes on inside another person's head. Dana will ask the jury to read the defendant's mind from his actions and the objective circumstances. Jury trials rely on the assumption that people have core similarities, that a "normal" law-abiding person can understand and discern the mental state of a "deviant" law breaker. A "depravedly indifferent" person. Words. The Underwood case isn't about a yes-or-no state of mind like intent to kill. Almost the opposite. The defendant is allegedly a species of sicko, a doctor who knows he's creating a grave risk that his patients—the "murder" victims—will take lethal overdoses and simply doesn't care if they die or not. Indifferent to it. Depravedly so.

Very difficult to prove, even by an experienced, topnotch prosecutor like ADA Sylvan Quince. His adversary on this case, Pamela Louise Grimes, is the best criminal defense attorney that money can buy. Dr. Underwood has plenty of cash to pay her bill. He's sitting on millions from his medical practice. Although the

DA filed a separate lawsuit to forfeit the doctor's ill-gotten gains to the state treasury, the civil arm of the trial court has thus far refused to freeze the doctor's assets. Why? Because it's presently impossible to distinguish the criminal proceeds from the legitimate income.

How much cash did the doctor make from patients who were simply buying illegal prescriptions, and how much did he earn from ethical doctoring? ADA Quince says there was none of the latter. The doctor was indifferent to his patients' health, didn't care if they lived or died, and was guided by sheer avarice. The ADA plans to prove it, and Judge Hargrove must decide whether to allow that proof.

First order of business tomorrow will be a hearing on the defense motion *in limine* to preclude evidence of Dr. Underwood's pattern of practice. Detective Aurelina Vargas is the lead investigator on the case, the main witness for the hearing. Dana and Lina have a history going back to the nineties. It will be good to see her again. The NYPD doesn't make them any smarter or more conscientious than Detective Vargas. She now works out of the Fifth Precinct, its headquarters only blocks from the Criminal Court building. The Underwood investigation fell to her because the medical office is located in the far northern reach of the Fifth, on Bowery near Houston.

Dana's ruling on the evidentiary issue is going to make or break the prosecution's case. If she permits only the evidence specific to the two victims, the jury is unlikely to find the defendant guilty of murder. A barebones case that the doctor prescribed lethal doses of painkillers for these two patients, who had no medical need other than narcotics addiction, will fall short of depraved indifference murder. It proves only that the doctor facilitated their drug habits.

But ADA Quince wants to introduce reams of evidence seized during a raid of Dr. Underwood's office, along with the testimony of a dozen witnesses who say that the clinic was a pill mill, nothing more. The doctor wrote thousands of prescriptions per year. Xanax, Oxycontin, Vicodin, Adderall. No medical insurance accepted. Cash only for a thirty-second consultation and prescription. Frequent repeat visits by drug-addicted patients for refills in stronger doses. No physical exams, no documented medical conditions or bogus diagnoses on patient charts. Law enforcement and the coroner notified the doctor, no less than ten times, that his patients had died from overdoses days after they filled their prescriptions. Yet, the doctor's prescribing practices continued unabated, resulting in the two deaths at issue in this case.

Depravity, yes, but also a slew of narcotics crimes. The defendant is on trial for two counts of murder in the second degree. Period. It violates due process to prejudice the jury against him with proof of uncharged narcotics crimes. That kind of evidence says, "Dr. Underwood is a very bad person, so let's convict him of murder." Can't do that.

But the law *does* allow exceptions. Of course. Every rule has exceptions. This one's called the *Molineux* rule after *People v Molineux*. The evidence is admissible if its probative value on an element of murder outweighs the prejudicial effect. ADA Quince says the evidence is relevant on the issue of Dr. Underwood's state of mind. It proves his awareness of the grave risk to his patients and his depraved indifference to it.

Another damned-if-I-do, damned-if-I-don't scenario.

Allow the evidence, convict the defendant, and an appellate court may reverse on the ground of undue prejudice. Exclude the evidence, and Dr. Underwood may go free. Or, more likely, the jury may convict him of a lesser-included offense that fits the facts. Reckless manslaughter. If that happens, the sentencing range is comparatively lenient: an indeterminate term as low as one to three, no more than five to fifteen, instead of a potential twenty-five years to life for murder.

Allow the evidence or exclude it—either way, Judge Hargrove's reputation is on the line, just like it is in the Spinnaker case. Suzy again. *Not now!* She pushes that case to the back of her mind. Sentencing is still a month away.

Dana looks up from the paperwork on her desk and takes off her oversized glasses. *Get your mind off Suzy.* A young woman, so intelligent, all of life ahead of her. Ruined.

Another young woman, intelligent, all of life ahead: Natalie. She hears her daughter's voice, that plaintive sound last night. *Mommy.*

When her second child went off to college, Dana was thrown into a period of reflection about their relationship. Was it time, finally, to cut the cord? To ease Natalie out of her clinginess? There was the usual parent orientation, where she and Evan heard the same pat phrases they'd heard when Travis started college. "Don't be a helicopter parent. Your child is an adult now." Pull back. Be confident that you've given her a moral compass and the solid judgment she needs to explore the world safely, to make her own decisions.

But at nineteen, Natalie still has a distance to go before adulthood. It was easier with Travis. Stubbornly independent from an early age, he rarely showed any vulnerability under his shield of maturity. He's now twenty-two, still so young, but much easier to think of as an adult than Natalie.

Pull back, they say. It's best. Easy to intellectualize. Dana took that advice, and now, she's not sure if it was entirely for Natalie or, in part, for herself. A defense. An adjustment to the empty nest. She's taken this adjustment harder than she admits to anyone. To herself. In rare moments, when her head is emptied of all thought of work, she misses the children. Achingly. There's a void where the energy of youth once filled their home. How could all those years be gone?

Last night, the longing in Natalie's voice served as a rebuke. They've addressed the clinging, and there's no going back. But what's wrong with closeness? The girl tugged at Dana's heart-strings, pulling out the buried thoughts. Dana is, very much, looking forward to Natalie's return home for the summer.

From her desk, the judge lets her gaze drift around her professional space. The aging Criminal Court building, completed in 1941, has its challenges, but her own space within it is ample. She's proud of her achievements, her framed diplomas and awards displayed against the dark wood paneling, the shelves holding lawbooks, photos, and mementos from her career. A few plants, credible fakes, because she always forgets to water. Cater-cornered to her is a small conference table with six chairs. Her view to the outside world is through a double window, the bottom half of one side dominated by an air conditioning unit. The window is perpetually dirty on the outside, and pigeons like to roost on top of the air conditioner, leaving filth and feathers. That's New York City for you, especially the government build-ings. External window washing is infrequent, mostly because it's a waste of time and money; the windows are quickly dirty again. She's on the thirteenth floor, but no matter, she isn't superstitious. The height gives her a good view of the other state and federal courthouses.

The window is on the outer wall to the right of her desk, and the door on the wall to her left goes to the antechamber, the work-place of her administrative assistant, Henny Versteeg. Two doors are on the wall she faces as she sits at the desk. The door closest to the outside wall opens into a private restroom. The other door, closer to the conference table, opens into a narrow passage. Turn left, and the passage goes past the windowless office of her law clerk, Zola Soyinka, and into the courtroom. Go right, and there's a door to a small robing room, which is attached to the restroom.

There's a knock on the door to the passage now. "Come in,

Zola," she calls out.

The young woman enters and says, "Good morning, Judge."

"Anything new on Underwood?"

Zola has already spent a full day researching the admissibility issue and is hard at it again this morning. "I just found a case that isn't cited by either party. It's close to our case, but..."

"Not exactly on point, I would venture to guess."

Zola hands her boss a printout and sits in one of the chairs at the desk. "Right, like the others I gave you yesterday. The closest case to ours, *People v Tseng*, is still in the pretrial stage and hasn't decided the issue. I found a couple of other recent murder indictments against doctors around the country, but this is a brand-new area."

Dana scans the page. "Interesting. This case supports the DA's position, but the crime is vehicular assault under a theory of depraved indifference."

"The court allowed evidence that the defendant ignored previous warnings and violations for reckless driving. The conviction was upheld on appeal."

"Good, this will help."

"I don't think I'm going to find much more on this issue. Do you want me to keep at it or go on to something else? The motions or that sentencing assignment..."

Not the sentencing! "Please spend the rest of today on Underwood. I want to make sure we cover all the bases. Tomorrow you can knock out a few of those motion decisions before you get back to Spinnaker." Last Friday after the verdict, Dana assigned Zola a monumental task, something to tackle little by little over the next month: a fifty-state review of sentences for female prisoners convicted of manslaughter crimes like Suzette Spinnaker's. Dana wants to know what everyone and her sister in the entire USA thinks about cases like this, whether there's a rough consensus among judges for the number of years a woman should serve for slashing her boyfriend and ex-business partner to death in a fit of rage.

An impossible assignment. A bit over the top? Dana was in a frantic, sleep-deprived state when she concocted it and now feels a bit mortified. Sentencing is the most difficult aspect of her new life as a judge, something she didn't anticipate after a decades-long career as a prosecutor. She soon discovered that recommending a sentence is a far cry from pronouncing the sentence. As a judge, she has the ultimate power to say what society thinks of a convicted felon's transgression. Sitting on high in a black robe, she's poised to slam the gavel down on a number. Her number. *This is how long I'm going to lock you away.*

Zola says, "Sure thing," her eyes betraying no awareness of her boss's inner turmoil. Dana hasn't confessed it to Zola, or even admitted it to Evan during their conversations about sentencing. But Evan probably knows what she's going through. In fact, she knows he knows, in the way a husband knows his wife, his closest companion for twenty-seven years. It's galling. Dana doesn't like to admit weakness to anyone, even to herself. She's keenly aware she didn't tell Evan about this absurd assignment, the fifty-state review. It hasn't come up in conversation. Maybe it just slipped her mind.

Perhaps her law clerk doesn't consider it absurd. A brilliant, recent law grad, Zola loves doing sociological surveys and discussing criminal justice issues like sentencing policy. She's determined and eager, unlikely to pass judgment on her boss. Still...

"I'm glad you mentioned the sentencing assignment, Zola. When you get back to it, I'd like you to limit your review to the tri-state region."

The internal phone line rings, and Dana picks up the receiver, thankful for the interruption. "Yes?"

"Judge, I've been opening the morning mail, and you might

want to look at this right away."

"What do you have?"

"A lot of letters about Friday's verdict, and one of them is very disturbing."

"Okay, come in." With a sigh, she hangs up. This case won't leave her be. "Stick around," she tells Zola. "Henny has something on Spinnaker to show us."

He walks in, hands the letter and envelope to Dana, and sits in the chair next to Zola.

Disturbing, indeed. Only a few lines are typed on the sheet of low-quality copier paper. From the look of it, the sender used an old-fashioned typewriter with a poorly inked ribbon. No salutation, no signature.

Suzy Suburbs gets Man One. Berto Barrio gets Murder.

The envelope is addressed to "Judge Dana Hargrove" at the courthouse, typed with the same typewriter. There's no return address, but it bears a postmark from the post office at Federal Plaza, a couple of blocks away.

Dana reads the two sentences out loud. "This is the work of some nutjob, or maybe it's material for a poetry slam."

"Sounds like a threat to me. And he was in our neighborhood when he mailed it." Henny gives a disapproving look and shakes his head. A slender man of dignified bearing, he sits in his signature posture, an upright spine, knees crossed, one hand resting in the palm of the other on his lap.

"Berto Barrio," Zola muses. "It sounds like a made-up name, especially since he gave Suzy a fake last name." She turns to Henny. "Barrio means 'the 'hood,' right Henny?"

"One of the nicer words for it. 'El Barrio' can also mean Spanish Harlem." Henny is their resident expert on the Spanish language. Despite the Dutch surname that came down to him from his paternal grandfather, Hendrik "Henny" Versteeg is three-quarters Venezuelan. He was born in New York and raised in a bilingual, English-Spanish home. "Slight possibility it's a real surname. Is Berto Barrio a defendant from a past murder case, Judge? From your DA days? This could be a disgruntled ex-con."

"Doesn't ring a bell."

"Whether the name is real or fake," Zola says, "he's sending a message about the criminal justice system. You know, white girl from the suburbs is treated nicer than Hispanic man from the 'hood. He's making the Spinnaker case an example of racial favoritism and classism. He's implying that the poor guy from the barrio got a raw deal just because of his ethnicity and poverty."

"Sure, I get that," Henny says, "but why would *anyone* need to make *that* point to Judge Hargrove?" He catches Zola's eye and they nod their agreement.

Dana smiles at Henny's suggestion and says, "Or to any of us?" She directs a warm look at each employee, in turn. Like her, Henny and Zola are people who consistently try to see essence and character first, remaining skeptical of assumptions rooted in physical characteristics or social categories. In an ideal world, this way of judging our fellow human beings would be second nature to everyone, but society hasn't yet evolved to that zenith.

An outsider walking into this office might notice a range of skin colors, from olive, to creamed coffee, to dark mocha. The person with the lightest skin, a woman in her early fifties, has dark hair pulled up in a twist, wears a well-tailored skirt suit, and sits in the position of authority behind a big desk. The person with medium-toned skin, a man in his thirties, has close-cropped hair and shiny shaved cheeks, wears skinny pants, a French-collared shirt, and a necktie decorated with drawings of Corgis (a tribute to his own Corgi, "Pooch"). The person with the darkest skin, a woman in her twenties, has African braids ending in a short natural in back, wears orange coral beads on her neck and ears, and dresses modestly in a white blouse and black skirt.

Just try to fit these people into boxes. Dana's law clerk and administrative assistant defy categorization. In the eighteen months she's known and worked with them, many interesting, outside-the-box things have come to light. Zola, the daughter of Nigerian immigrants, is a distant relation of Nobel Laureate Wole Soyinka, is a poet with literary pursuits of her own, is politically and socially liberal, and lives with her boyfriend Vadim, from a Russian Jewish family. Henny is politically and socially conservative on some issues, including criminal justice, and he married his longtime partner, Korean American Mun Han-gil (who goes by Reginald "Reggie" Moon) on the day that gay marriage was legalized in 2011.

Dana hasn't asked her staff, but she guesses that, if she solicited their opinions on the appropriate sentence for Suzette Spinnaker, Zola might say fifteen years, and Henny might say twenty-five.

The only box she has for these people is the colorfully gift-wrapped and beribboned box labeled "Excellence." Dana prides herself on having picked the best, although she doesn't always agree with their views. A judge should avoid hiring "yes-people." Divergent opinions and lively debate are essential. Zola and Henny are not afraid to speak up, and she listens. They're bright and loyal.

But not perfect. At the moment, they're being too nice to her. She confirms it with this involuntary mind-flash, her internal review of their physical and social attributes. Classlessness and color blindness are a fantasy. Dana is acutely aware of the class, race, and gender aspects of the Spinnaker case, and this kook, the anonymous letter writer, doesn't want her to forget them.

"I agree with you, Zola. Whoever wrote this wants to send a message about class and race. And I appreciate your concern, Henny. At this point, though, I'm not sure it's meant to be a threat or anything more than just an odd way of expressing an opinion about the case." She hands the letter and envelope back to him.

"Please make a photocopy of these for me and give the originals to Len." Captain Leonard Rankel supervises the court officers assigned to Judge Hargrove's courtroom and protective duty. "I'd like him to look into it."

"Okay. Is there any way to trace this back to the writer?"

"I doubt it. We can't track down every owner of an old Underwood typewriter." As soon as the name slips out, Dana notices the coincidence.

Zola laughs. "We should check Dr. Underwood's family history! Maybe he has a collection of old typewriters."

"I have a feeling the doctor has more to worry about than Suzy Suburbs and Berto Barrio at the moment."

"And, he'd have to hire someone to make the trip to the post office." Zola is referring to the terms of the defendant's pretrial release on bail. He's confined to home, wearing a GPS ankle bracelet.

"How about fingerprints, Judge?" Henny's brow is still etched with concern.

"We've handled this letter so much, there's little chance of finding usable prints on the paper. I'm more interested in finding out if Len recalls anyone suspicious in the courtroom during the trial. Like I said, I don't think this is a threat, but it's a good idea for Len and his staff to be on alert. And Zola, after you finish the Underwood research and get back to Spinnaker, maybe it's wise to search for the name 'Berto Barrio,' just in case I'm missing something."

"All right." Zola stands up, ready to get back to work.

Henny also stands, but hesitates. "Do you want to see the other letters, Judge? We got a nice little bunch. Half of them want you to throw the book at Suzy, and the other half are worried she won't fare well in state prison."

No way to avoid this case! For the next month, or maybe the rest of her life. "Do any of them claim to know the defendant personally?"

"Only one, and it's also a little scary. It's unsigned, anonymous, no return address. Three pages long. A male writer, I would say, from context. He claims to know Suzy and Connor very well from MIT, and in his opinion, in very graphic language, New York should reenact the death penalty for Suzy. At the very least, she should rot in prison for the rest of her life. 'Fry the bitch,' if I remember one of his choice phrases correctly." Henny's eyes dart from the judge to Zola and back again. "Excuse my French."

"His opinion won't get very far with me if he won't say who he is."

"Oh, but he's too important and powerful for you to ignore him. He insinuates it a hundred times in the letter."

"Okay, let me see that one, but start a file for the rest of the letters from the public. More will be coming in. I'll look at the file a few weeks down the road, *after* I've seen Zola's work on this."

"Good enough, Judge. But if I find any more threats—"

"*Cálmate*, Henny. I don't think either of these is a threat."

He does a doubletake and says, "I'm impressed with your accent."

"Better watch your cursing in Spanish around the judge," Zola warns him with a smile.

"You're mistaken, Zolita. I may quote, but I never curse."

8 » PARENTING

EVAN GAZES LONGINGLY at his son's choices: an eight-inch hero stuffed with meat and cheese, a bag of spicy tortilla chips, and a huge chocolate chip cookie. In front of Evan on their tiny two-top sits a bowl of leafy greens. A dab of balsamic dressing and shreds of assorted proteins provide the only fat calories.

Travis's cheeks bulge as his jaw works on an enormous hunk of sandwich. Evan stabs at a lettuce leaf three times, snags it, but makes his stomach wait. He has a chance to speak. "The last class of your first year. How does it feel?"

"Great!" The word is muffled by the food and a cacophony of sounds: scraping chairs, laughter and banter, clattering plastic trays, crinkling chip wrappers. They're squeezed into this typical New York deli, where mere inches separate the postage-stamp tabletops. Evan reins himself in, perched on a small, hard chair. Any quick jut of his left elbow to the side would risk hitting a plastic container on the next table. The pasta salad in that container is largely ignored by its owner, a young woman engaged in animated conversation with her companion. Her voice has an off-putting pitch.

This lunch spot is a favorite among NYU students. Evan is, possibly, the sole fossil in the room. Not quite. He spies, in a far corner, a relatively old person of forty-five or fifty, sitting alone, stoop-shouldered in a posture that reminds Evan of a predatory animal, protecting its kill. Or maybe the man needs protection from the onslaught of youth.

Evan has snagged his son for this lunch to celebrate their final classes of the year. Travis had his last torts class this morning, and Evan will give his final lecture in criminal procedure this afternoon. It's their only chance to meet for a while. Tomorrow, Travis will drop out of sight for a week-long immersion in the law before final exams.

The boy swallows and says, "How about you? Are you glad it's almost over?"

"It never ends, really. Give the exams, grade them, and then I supervise my summer interns."

"What're they going to be working on?"

"Updating the research on double jeopardy, my section of the crim pro treatise. And, of course, I'll be putting in more hours at the firm this summer." Evan is still a partner but with a limited role at Belknap, Rose, & Goodhue, P.C., where he's worked for twenty-five years. Has it been that long? Yes, he left the DA's office in 1990.

Travis says "Mm-hmm," around another mighty mouthful and makes garbled sounds which Evan interprets this way: "In your career, did you like crim pro or civ pro better?"

In his career. Past tense. Is Travis implying that what he's doing now, teaching law, isn't part of his career? No. A father knows that this is merely the way a twenty-two-year-old talks. "I'd have to say criminal procedure, even though I've spent many more years in civil litigation." He takes a bite of lettuce, with a piece of hard-boiled egg, and reflects on how he got here. Professor of law, a mentor to law students and to the young associates in his law firm. He happily relinquished the daily grind of litigation to them when he started teaching.

"Why?" Before Evan can answer, Travis asks, "Want some?" His father is eyeing his chips. "Go ahead." He pushes the open bag over. "Have a few."

Evan pulls out two curved triangles of tortilla bliss. "Does this mean you're prepared to feed your old man in his declining years?" He chomps down.

"It means you ought to order your own chips next time. You deserve it."

"Why, thank you." He's already swallowed. "They *are* delicious."

"But you didn't answer my question. Why do you like crim pro better?"

"Because it's rooted in bigger, more important issues. Constitutional rights. The two go hand in hand." Avoiding Travis's chips, he turns his head to the left precisely when his neighbor illustrates a comment by flinging her right hand, with plastic fork, up in the air. A broken piece of rotini flies from it and lands next to Evan's salad bowl. One glance, and he ignores it. "You'll be getting real hands-on experience with crim pro this summer at Legal Aid. When does your internship start?"

"Two days after my last final."

"Wow. Enjoy the two-day staycation. You're already living the life of a lawyer."

Travis nods and stuffs his mouth again. Father and son chew and swallow for a minute. Travis is deep in thought. Evan's heart swells with pride: What dedication and drive! Still unsure of his direction and the kind of career he wants, but that's only natural at his age. His eyes light up with genuine interest whenever he asks dear old dad to expound on his career in the law. Evan counts himself lucky to be included in his son's process of exploration and discovery.

This summer at Legal Aid, Travis will be learning criminal defense work. Evan hopes he'll also land an internship at the DA's office sometime during law school, so he can experience the world of difference on the other side of the courtroom. Stated starkly, the prosecutor's goal is to seek truth and justice, the defense attorney's goal is the client's, to be free of all charges. Temptations, pressures, and burnout can skew these goals, turning a prosecutor into a conviction machine, turning a defense attorney into a pure dealmaker looking for sentence "bargains," even for the innocent. Both barrels are infected by a few bad apples who can spread rot. Prosecutors who bury the truth and turn a blind eye to crooked cops. Defense attorneys who become embroiled in the criminal underworld of their clients.

Between the two sides, the lofty ideal of justice suits Evan better. He would advise any young attorney considering a career in criminal law, including Travis, to apply to the DA's office, and if accepted, never to betray the ethical high ground. Whether his son takes his advice is another matter. Travis has always been surprisingly independent in thought and action, but only after he's investigated all options. It's a quality that makes for a good lawyer, even if Evan doesn't always like the decision or outcome.

"So, is that the same thing?" Travis asks. "Since you like crim pro better, does that mean you liked being an ADA better than a civil litigator?"

A tricky question. If Evan agrees with him, it means that he's spent the bulk of his career doing something he likes less: civil litigation. But it's true. He was crazy about those years in the DA's office at the beginning of his career. Nowhere else is there a greater sense of purpose, helping to protect the city, showing compassion for the victims of violence, coming up with community solutions to crime. Nowhere else is the human condition more sharply in focus than in a criminal court, the place of high drama. Civil cases are important too, but how do you compare conflicts that are mostly about money with conflicts that arise from the deepest, darkest human drives and emotions?

And most important, the DA's office is where Evan met Dana, the woman who changed his life.

Should he admit all this to Travis and risk the consequences? Let's make the boy feel guilty. How do you tell your kid that you compromised your personal interests for him? For the family? After the first few years as an associate at Belknap & Rose, Evan thought seriously of returning to public service. But he and Dana had started a family by then, and New York City is an expensive place to live. Two government salaries are no match for a salary in the private sector. It could have gone the other way, Evan encouraging Dana to join a white shoe law firm. She would have done quite well. But he couldn't do that. She's the one with the deeper commitment to criminal justice and superior talent in that field. Evan made the compromise and stayed quiet about it.

Is he bitter? Resentful? Filled with regret? Not in the least. He's Professor Sunshine, perpetually chipper and optimistic. His nature isn't something he ever ponders because it's just that, his nature, easy and genuine.

A beautiful young man sits before him, unwrapping a huge chocolate chip cookie and balling up the plastic wrapper. He resembles his mother more than his dad. Three blinks of an eye have passed since Travis's question, enough time for Evan's blitz of conflicting thoughts on the subject. He answers, "Can't really compare apples and oranges. There's the good and the bad in both types of litigation. The fun parts and the not-so-fun. I've had loads of interesting cases. Criminal *and* civil."

Travis looks at him askance, like he doesn't believe it, but then his face changes suddenly. He rasps, sotto voce, "Dad!" Strangely, the exclamation point is whispered as his eyes dart upward to a point behind his father's shoulder.

Evan turns around and pulls back suddenly, involuntarily. Prescott Covington stands over him.

"Professor Goodhue."

"Hello, Prescott."

He looks more gaunt than usual. Sunken eyes peer out of

deep, dark pits of sleeplessness. His fist clenches a roll of white typing paper. "Eating lunch with your students now?" He tips his head accusingly toward Travis. "Can I get a lunch meeting too? I have my extra credit paper to show you."

Is Prescott hallucinating? What is this about an extra credit paper?

"When you see it, you'll have to let me take the final. The midterm *and* the final. I know more crim pro than any of your *star* students." Another accusing tip of the head.

"Prescott—"

"This is a private lunch," Travis cuts in. He's already sized up the intruder. "A *family* meeting." Travis bears his fangs, ready for counterattack.

"Oh, excuse *me*. You're the Goodhue kid."

A tense moment, speechlessness against the backdrop of deli sounds.

"Look, Prescott, I've already said what I have to say."

"Then…" He twitches and sweats, eyes flitting around the room. "Here!" The paper flies onto the table. "Just read it!" With that, he scurries away.

Travis eyes him warily as he leaves the deli. "Who *is* that, Dad? He's seriously disturbed."

Evan doesn't want to touch the rolled-up paper. It's dirty and stained. "He's not in any of your classes?"

"No."

"He's unhappy that I gave him an incomplete in crim pro. We won't worry about him."

"I'd worry. You should report him."

"I already have. To the university administration, at least."

"How about the police?"

"He hasn't committed a chargeable offense." As he says this, Evan internally debates the issue. Prescott is turning into a stalker. "At any rate, he's gone now."

Travis indicates the panel of windows behind his dad. "I saw him walk past the deli. He could be waiting for you outside, around the corner."

"We'll give him a few minutes to think better of it." Quick, change the subject. "We have a little more lunch to finish anyway."

"Want this?" Travis offers the last piece of cookie, all he has left.

"No, you go ahead."

He dispatches the piece in one big bite.

"How's Ginger these days?"

"Doing well. She likes her job, and she's really good at it."

"So, you've sat in on one of her group therapy sessions."

"Ha ha, Dad. No, I haven't. But you know her."

"Yes, I do have that pleasure." Travis has been going with Ginger since their senior year in high school. She's a child of a broken home, her father a recovered alcoholic, the time before he recovered not so fun for the family. The experience led her to major in social work in college and become a credentialed alcoholism and substance abuse counselor when she graduated. She works at a rehab center on the Lower East Side. A zealous, compassionate young woman.

"She's helped a lot of people already. She's totally into it and works long hours."

"More hours than a law student?"

"Yeah, she works just as much as I do. That's why…"

Travis falters and looks down at the table. The confident, self-assured young man is caught in an uncharacteristic show of hesitance or embarrassment.

"That's why…what?"

Travis clears his throat. There's no more sandwich or cookie to stuff into his mouth. "We're both so busy with work and school, it's hard to find time to see each other. She has a roommate she's not so crazy about, and I'm in the same situation, so, we were thinking..."

"That you might get married?" Travis looks up in shock. Evan's face is a picture of seriousness. "A wonderful idea. You're lucky to have her. Congratulations."

The color has drained from Travis's cheeks. He fell for it! Another uncharacteristic moment. Evan's kids are almost immune to his jokes. But he has underestimated the emotional significance of this subject. Travis and Ginger. Very important stuff. No joking matter.

"Just kidding, son." He gives Travis's forearm a reassuring squeeze. "It isn't 1944. People don't get married when they're twenty-two anymore. I know that."

"Yeah, well, it's more like we were thinking of finding an apartment together."

"Sounds like a wise plan. I know you've thought this through, and I'm all for it. And I don't think your mother will have any objection either."

Five minutes later, father and son get up and snake through the narrow passages between the little tables. The man in the corner eyes them from under his lowered brow as he hunches over the last bite of his high-priced meal. The top-heavy roll of white papers sticks out of the professor's jacket pocket, where they could easily get knocked out. The student who threw the papers on the table is too rash, the man thinks. *That's not the way to get what you want. Not the way to teach them.*

Father and son are about to exit the deli, when the man pushes away from the table and follows them. He already knows a lot about them. Professor Evan Goodhue, fifty-eight, happily married, well respected in the legal community. Travis Goodhue, older child, law student, early twenties, his whole life yet to be lived.

Envy tugs at the man's heart. He barely remembers his own father. His mother did all the heavy lifting in their family, for him and his sister. Never any chummy father-son lunches like this, no pillar of society to guide him. Still, he had a chance when he was young. He had everything it took to turn out just like this privileged young man, the pride and joy of Evan Goodhue and Dana Hargrove.

Outside the deli, they're half a block ahead. The sidewalk is jammed with students. Father and son brush shoulders as they walk and converse like good friends, comfortable with each other. Abruptly, Travis turns around, his eyes sweeping the area. *Does he think I'm following?* But then, he points diagonally behind him, across the street, like he's showing something to his father. They pause for just a moment and turn around again.

There's no reason the boy should know me.

At the next intersection, father and son cross the street, barely making it to the other side before the light changes. Cars push in, and the man must wait. He glances right and left, and there, down the side street, skulks that angry student who deposited the rolled-up papers on the professor's table. The Goodhue men walked right past the punk and didn't see him. He's in his own world, head drooped, talking to himself. Psycho maybe.

The light changes. The man crosses the street but doesn't see them anymore. He's lost them in the sea of kids clogging the sidewalk. Washington Square, NYU. Backpacks, laughter, brains, intelligence, privilege, future.

He knows where they've gone. They're headed for the law building.

Lawyers. Destroyers of life.

He doesn't care to follow them into the building. He's seen enough and knows all he needs to know for now. He might return later, or he might think about looking in on the girl with the rust-colored hair who works on the Lower East Side. The girl who looks like her name, Ginger, and who's so important to Travis and his family. She's one of seven on his list, the people essential to his greater plan. Beyond them lies an outer layer of others, the icing on the cake.

But right now, it's best to go downtown again and wait. There's no trial on, so they might have an early afternoon. He'll wait for them, and if he sees them, he'll try to read their faces. He needs to know if... Well, he just needs to know.

9 »   LATE

ZOLA STAYS ON after the judge pops in and says, "I'm heading out. Don't stay too late, now."

"I won't. Just finishing up. Goodnight, Judge."

"Goodnight. You want this open?"

"Yes, please." The judge gives a parting wave and leaves the door open. Zola's office has two doors, opening to Henny's office and to the narrow passage between the courtroom and the robing room. She keeps the door to the passage open. Otherwise, it's so stuffy in her small office.

Zola refocuses on her computer screen after a glance at the time stamp. Six twenty. In her windowless den, concentrating on her work, she tends to lose track of time.

Tonight, she can stay late. On Tuesdays, Vadim has class and doesn't get home until eight. He's in a part-time program for an LLM degree, taking evening classes after a full day of work with the Legal Aid Society. A rough schedule, God bless him. Vadim is Zola's law school sweetheart, the best part of those three years, and she plans to keep him. But she happily closed the book on academia for herself the day she got her JD in 2013. Vadim is getting an LLM because he plans to teach law one day.

Since it's after hours, Zola doesn't feel too guilty about straying from the judge's strict instructions to work only on the Underwood case. She *did* work on it all day, and at five o'clock, after exploring every possible avenue, she handed in her work product. There's nothing else to be found. When the judge said goodnight just now, perhaps she thought that Zola was tying up loose ends on Underwood or had moved on to whittling down the stack of pending suppression motions in other cases. Wrong and wrong again. That anonymous letter about Spinnaker has been at the back of her mind all day, and she can't escape its lure.

She's most curious about her boss's past cases as a prosecutor and as a judge. The actual assignment, a tri-state review of other judges' sentences, doesn't seem relevant or helpful. Every crime is unique. Every defendant is unique. A prison sentence should fit the specific case, so why is Judge Hargrove so interested in comparisons? It's insecurity, Zola senses, but she isn't going to say it out loud. She has enormous respect for her boss. Judge Hargrove runs her trials efficiently and is rock solid on the law: sharp, quick, knowledgeable, and confident.

But making a legal ruling during trial isn't quite the same as pronouncing sentence. Facts are infinitely variable; laws are indelible, black on white. A judge applies immutable principles to unique facts to decide the legal consequences. But sentencing statutes are flexible. Judges have a range of years to work with. More leeway. Discretion. Balance. Room for heart.

Come on, Judge Hargrove. Give it your heart.

The judge *does* have a heart, a very big one. She gives and gives and gives. Zola has felt the warmth of her heart many times, although it's not always immediately visible. When Judge Hargrove is troubled by a problem and wants an answer, she can become single-minded. The path is set, the blinders go on, the focus intensifies, and she comes across as stern and unyielding. It's part of being a judge, part of building a career in a field dominated by men, part of staying strong. Zola understands that outward appearances don't always tell the whole story of the inner plane. *Give it your heart, Judge.*

By now, Zola is familiar with the judge's former reputation as a prosecutor and how it has changed in the short time she's been on the bench. A softening. Zola likes to think that she's had some influence over the judge's sentencing decisions. Is it presumptuous for someone her age to think this way? Maybe so, but Zola isn't shy about letting the judge know her opinion when it comes to state prison sentences, especially for minorities and young offenders. Statistics on recidivism prove her right. There's little to no redemption or rehabilitation to be had in one of those concrete fortresses upstate. Check into the state prison system and you'll be schooled in the ways of hardened criminals. Cast your eyes on the color spectrum in the cell block and you'll find the darker brothers disproportionately monopolizing the real estate.

Alternatives to prison. Restorative justice programs. There's a movement afoot, and Judge Hargrove hovers on the threshold. She hasn't said as much to Zola, but it's evident in the amount of time she devotes to her sentencing decisions. And the judge's moodiness over it has been getting worse. After a slew of lower level felonies and back-page murders, she's hit with two crazy media cases in a row. Spinnaker and Underwood. The judge has been on edge, and next month's sentencing hearing is weighing on her mind. She puts on a neutral face, but Zola can see through it. She noticed it today, the moment the judge laid eyes on the Berto Barrio letter. A flicker of worry cracked her cool façade.

Two hours of legal research and googling have yielded nothing to indicate that ADA Dana Hargrove ever prosecuted "Berto Barrio." Zola gets the same results from searches for variants: Egberto Barrios, Roberto Barron, Heriberto Barrera, and many more. Berto Barrio was fabricated to make a point. What message is the letter writer sending? Throw the book at Suzy Suburbs. The jury already cut a deal for Miss Privileged, the white MIT grad, bankrupt multi-millionaire, party-girl, substance-abuser, boyfriend-slasher. Judge Hargrove should lay it on heavy or else...what? Does this mystery person have reason to believe the judge will go easy on a female defendant like Suzy? Something in prosecutor Hargrove's past might yield a clue.

A database with one-stop shopping would be nice. A single click to show all the cases ever prosecuted by Dana Hargrove, with details of how she handled them. But no such thing exists. Zola enters queries into the search engines of legal research sites to find reported trial and appellate decisions listing Dana Hargrove as the prosecuting attorney. She does the same for news services, looking for newspaper, magazine, and TV stories. In this way, Zola uncovers the bigger cases, the ones that attracted media coverage or had court decisions published in the case reports.

Of course, most of the defendants are male. Zola finds a few interesting cases with female defendants, one of them a shocker. In 1994, a young woman employed in the Hargrove-Goodhue household was arrested. Caused quite a media splash, with the ADA's name all over the news. But the arrestee was nothing like Suzy Suburbs, and she was exonerated, never prosecuted. Nothing about that case indicates that Judge Hargrove is likely to be sweet to Suzette Anne Spinnaker.

Here's another one, a 2001 case against a well-to-do female defendant, charged with murdering her husband. ADA Hargrove, then a bureau chief in the Manhattan DA's office, oversaw the prosecution and was vilified in the press for discrediting the woman's story that she was a battered wife. Ultimately, however, a very different truth came to light. The woman was convicted, and Hargrove's office recommended the maximum sentence. White female, privilege, money, murder. A closer case to Suzy Suburbs, but Hargrove can't be accused of favoritism. Far from it.

The same year saw another prosecution against a white female defendant, a former ADA who was, once, a colleague of ADA Hargrove. Motivated by jealousy and a larger plan to undermine the integrity of the DA's office, this woman falsified evidence in a failed attempt to free Ramón Pineda, a man Hargrove prosecuted. Again, there is no indication of favoritism or special treatment for that female defendant.

Now, here's one, maybe. In 2009, when the judge was District Attorney of Westchester County, she prosecuted two suburban white girls for cyberbullying and gave them a light touch, plea bargains with no state prison. But Zola finds good reasons for this treatment. The defendants were teens, classified as "youthful offenders" under the law, and the facts didn't easily fit any felony statutes. DA Hargrove's approach was reasonable, and a show of heart. But how can anyone compare that case to Spinnaker? The circumstances are completely different.

Nothing else comes to mind from Zola's time as Judge Hargrove's law clerk. She's been with the judge since her ascension to the bench in the fall of 2013. During that time, the judge has sentenced a handful of female defendants, all women of color, a few drug cases, a few larcenies, one assault. The woman convicted of assault could have gotten a sentence as high as seven years, but the judge gave her three. She listened to Zola's opinion on that one.

Give it some heart, Judge. Yes, even for the likes of Suzy Spinnaker. Zola comes out on the low end of the scale when she weighs the pluses and minuses. Suzy's crime was bloody and violent. She took a life. The life of a creep, some might say, but that's irrelevant. All lives have value, and Connor Davidson's family is suffering. Like many crimes, Suzy's was fueled by drugs and alcohol, and she has no good excuse for her descent into substance abuse. Unlike some defendants, Suzy had the smarts and connections to get help. Even so, she was at her lowest point, despondent, despairing, and broken. Connor's taunting provoked her. She acted in the heat of an argument, a convenient weapon suddenly at hand.

Bottom line, Suzy isn't likely to do something like this again.

Her crime was aimed at a certain individual under circumstances unlikely to be repeated. She's no real threat to society. Any punishment the judge gives her now is just that: punishment. Payback. Retribution more than rehabilitation. Suzy is already weaned from drugs and alcohol, and productive use of her intelligence could be wasted in lockup. Mental health and other programs are available in prison, but really, how much will she benefit after five years, or even one year?

What will society gain by paying for her room and board for more than the minimum term? Something intangible. A message, and not exactly the message that the anonymous letter writer intends. A statement about the value of life. Five years cheapens Connor's life. What's the right number? Ten, fifteen, twenty, twenty-five. As a measure of the value of human life, even twenty-five years is cheap. And why tick off the options in multiples of five? A pat, robotic, mathematical mantra divorced from emotion. That's why we do it. Remove the emotion, find some distance. Seven, twelve, eighteen, or twenty-two does it just as well. But to the person in the cell, twelve hits much harder than ten.

This is impossible! Zola does not envy the judge.

Her cell phone rings. She looks at the screen and answers. "Hi."

"Just leaving now," Vadim says. "What are you up to?"

"Thinking about murder." Zola gazes at the framed photo on her desk as she talks. A spring day in Central Park, Vadim's arm around her shoulder, white against black. Nothing is that clear cut.

"Nice. Should I be watching my back tonight?"

"Yes. You might get a back rub."

"Sounds good. I'll reciprocate. We both need it."

"You're giving me a reason to turn off this computer."

"Don't tell me you're still at the court."

"I got caught up in something."

"It's a quarter to eight."

"No *wahala*. I'm leaving now."

Before ending the call, they discuss what might or might not be in their fridge and remember the pasta leftovers from last night, more than adequate for a late dinner. Zola powers down, gathers her things, and heads out.

When do judges leave work for the day?

Not just any judge. *That* judge. The steamroller for "justice." The one who haunts the void of night and whispers in his ear at dawn. His constant companion. Not her exactly. Her ghost. A presence. A shadow over everything that his life is and isn't.

He first asked that question not long ago, when he was, at last, free to investigate, to find out everything else he needed to know. He made a prediction. *That* judge is more than a nine-to-five. She's the type to put in long hours, toiling away to save the city. Family and friends can wait.

Prediction confirmed. He's been watching her. Watching everyone around her.

At first it was a shock, seeing her again. The image in his head was slightly wrong, so he tweaked that picture, turned it into a double exposure, the younger woman overlaid with the older. Years change people, but not her. Not in any way that matters. Years change people, but not him. Not the part that's invisible to her and always has been. The part she doesn't care to see. That no one cares to see. The part that proves he feels regret, not just for himself. He's sorry for what happened, and there's no way to make amends. He could blame himself for everything, but that ignores what she did, her blindness to her role in ruining lives. His life.

Her boy, Travis. What is he? Twenty-two, twenty-three? The age of high expectations, a newly minted adult, everything ahead.

Unless everything gets ruined before it begins. He could tell that boy about a different kind of future, an unimaginable one.

The boy and his girlfriend are easy to watch. The husband too. And the sister, especially when she's in the city. She lives, he's discovered, in the judge's former home in Westchester.

But the judge isn't easy. He needs to be careful. She knows him. But mostly, he knows her. Very well.

Focused and vigilant, at a distance, he can pick up what he knows about her in the little things she does, the way she moves, her signature gestures. Still the same. A few weeks ago, as he peered around a corner, he saw her exit the courthouse and pause to speak to a court officer. There it was, her defining posture, the little show of authority. He remembers it. How he hates it. She leans forward at the waist, just enough to pierce the veil around a man's personal space, and she speaks her words with a flip of the hand, from palm down to palm up. In this way, she makes her indisputable point. "This is how it is." Or gives an order. "Now." With a false "please."

Other things. She still walks the same way, her head lifted and cocked, listening to her own thoughts. Her spine is a steel rod, her shoes always shiny new, a solid base for walking over the likes of him, defining the territory of righteousness. Still the same. She hasn't changed.

Most nights, she leaves through a back door of the court-house, the one reserved for judges and their staff. Most nights, her car is waiting there. An officer gets it for her and pulls up in front of the door.

Wouldn't that be nice? Oh, wouldn't it?

But there've been a few times when she pretends to be nobody. She uses the public door at the south entrance to the Criminal Court building and marches straight into the chaos, headed for the subway. She melts a path through the jam of courthouse visitors, the jurors and witnesses and cops and attorneys who were in her courtroom minutes before. The accused criminals she didn't incarcerate but nicely released on bail pending trial. Street people, janitors, food vendors, stenographers, bail bondsmen, court interpreters, and municipal clerks. She brushes shoulders with everyone, swinging her briefcase stuffed with papers that determine the fates of the unfortunate. Acting like one of the crowd. Who is she kidding?

By now he knows her court officers and the two people closest to her—the Randy Rainbow-type and the proud-faced sister, black as midnight. The outer circle, the icing on the cake. He knows their names. Captain Rankel and his underlings are more likely to use the public entrances to the building, but Versteeg and Soyinka always use the back exit for judges and their staff. He reads their faces when he chances to see them at the start or end of their workdays. *We're too important to mingle with the public. We work for Judge Dana Hargrove.* The steamroller.

Friday was a big day for them. For him. For the city, awaiting the verdict. He was outside most of the day, anonymous in the crowd. Too tricky to hide in plain sight at the back of Judge Hargrove's courtroom. He almost tried it once during the trial, took a seat in the last pew before the proceedings started. When she swished through the judge's door in her black robe, he realized his mistake, the risk to his greater plan. At the sound of "All rise," he slinked out in a hurry, behind the backs of the people in the audience.

On Friday, media vans and reporters clogged the area in front of the courthouse. He skirted the fringes and avoided the cameras when they got too close. He spent much of the day like this, waiting. He had the time, like every other day, hours to kill until midnight, when he goes to his minimum-wage job on graveyard shift, cleaning other people's messes at a homeless shelter. The place stinks worse than prison. He takes naps in the middle of the afternoon and hasn't slept more than a few hours a day in weeks because of his day job. The unpaid gig, surveillance. He waits and watches, ready to seize the right moment to claim his reward. That day will come.

In the hours before the verdict last week, his fingertips repeatedly sank into his jacket pocket for a reassuring touch, a mental count. He'd bought an old typewriter at a junk shop and used it to prepare a business-size envelope and three letters with different messages, each paper folded in thirds. His sister Graciela isn't aware that he has the old manual Underwood. He uses it when she's at work and then hides it and the stationery underneath boxes in the closet. Too loud to clatter on it when she's home, tipping her off to his activity inside the thin walls of the room that really isn't his room.

Nothing is his. It's a two-bedroom apartment, and the room he uses belonged to their mother. She lay dying in the bed for months, finally succumbing to the cancer in late 2014. Graciela is still grieving. She hasn't changed the furniture or bedding. It's washed, of course, and so are the curtains, but when the door is closed, the room still smells of their mother's sickness, the sour breath and sweat that penetrated everything.

He typed three messages for three possible verdicts. When the reporters announced the jury's decision, he knew which one to use. After ducking the cameras and loitering in the area, he lucked out and saw Cheryl Hargrove coming out of the building next door. Wasn't that sweet, seeing her in a position of helplessness? She was imprisoned in her Town Car, unable to escape the traffic jam as he stared at her through the tinted window. Something he can use later.

He could have followed that car for blocks while the driver tried to shoo him away. Instead, he found the right letter in his pocket, inserted it into the stamped envelope, sealed the flap, and mailed it at the post office a few blocks away. Slipped into an alley and tore up the other two letters. Almost threw them in a dumpster but thought better of it and took off walking for an hour, tracing a grid of rectangles of city blocks as he deposited one jagged bit of paper at a time into a dozen or more city trash receptacles.

They must have received it by now; a full weekend and two days have passed. Maybe he can tell by the looks on their faces. From five o'clock on, he loiters at various corners of the building and makes passes through the block near the judges' exit. If he lucks out, he'll time it right. The few times he's seen them, Versteeg is the earliest to leave, sometime between five and six. Then it's either Soyinka or the judge. They trade places on who leaves later in their competition for the Badge of Diligence, the Medal of Honor for Champion of Justice. Sometimes they finish in a tie.

Of course, it's impossible to keep continuous watch without being noticed. He knows enough not to get too close to the door, where the guard can see him. The NYPD and court officers own the neighborhood, popping up anywhere, anytime, unpredictably. He's back and forth for hours, and by seven thirty, he's sure he's missed them all. *I'll give it a few more minutes.*

At this time of year, the sun doesn't set until eight, but a premature dusk settles inside the caverns of city streets, under the shadows of tall buildings. Most ominous of all, the ziggurat of the Criminal Court building dominates the sky, carving out a solid city block of sorrow and despair. Quiet, empty, and gray, the city block awaits his final pass. A puff of warm breeze kicks up a swirl of dust and debris, the filter ends and candy wrappers from nervous cigarette breaks.

He's a hundred yards away when he sees her. The law clerk. She steps away from the door quickly and walks fast. He has a chance. She doesn't notice him.

She heads uptown at a clip, off to someone or something far more exciting than her day at the court. Petite and proud, bouncing along. Happy? He sees it in her walk and, oddly, in the brilliance of her white blouse against the gray light. She would blend into the dusk completely if not for that white beacon. He follows it, rushes and catches up, but still, she doesn't see him, focused on her thoughts and her joyous destination. Happy, even as she passes White Street and the little alley that leads to the Tombs where thousands of pretrial detainees and misdemeanants languish and suffer. A step past the Tombs, he's right behind her, close enough to smell the pungent apricot aroma of her hair product.

She must have seen his letter. Must have. He wants to know.

He coughs and whispers, changing his voice into a raspy hiss. "Berto Barrio!"

She startles, halts abruptly. He nearly rams into her back as she swings around to look over her left shoulder. But he's already passing her on the right, acting like nothing happened. He glances back and sees her turned around, searching.

Hah! She hasn't a clue it was him. Quickly, he faces forward again, before she can turn around and see him looking at her. In his loping, uneven stride, he rapidly puts distance between them.

He doesn't need to look back again, to see her face. He knows what she must be thinking: *An anonymous letter, and now this! That crazy name, whispered in the dark. Did I really hear it? Am I nuts? Is this real or imagined?*

It's real, baby. And this is only the beginning.

10 »   THERAPY

At SEVEN, GINGER answers her ringing cell phone. Travis has stepped outside the law library to make the call. He's been studying all afternoon, ever since he came back from lunch with his dad. Ginger suspects that, if she didn't exist, Travis would stay in the law library all night, nothing and no one to save him from his relentless drive.

She's not complaining. She admires her boyfriend's work ethic and has the same drive for her own work. Long hours and frequently changing shifts are her life, making it difficult to coordinate their down time together. This is a problem because of another drive they share. They *must* see each other. Have to have to have to.

Travis lives with a roommate in an NYU dorm, and Ginger lives with a roommate in Alphabet City. When they spend the night together, she prefers Travis's place, but it's unfair to constantly impose on his roommate, a law student who likes to study at home. The roomie is very tightly wound and difficult to tolerate, especially during finals, so Travis does most of his studying in the library.

Tonight, they will have to settle for a late dinner date. Ginger is scheduled to run a group therapy session from seven thirty to nine. "Is nine fifteen too late?" she asks. "Nine thirty if you want me to come up to you."

"No, I'll come down there. It'll give me a little break. I don't mind waiting until then to eat. I'll be up all night anyway."

"You have to get some sleep. You can't function like that."

"I'm good with four or five hours."

They decide on a favorite Mexican restaurant close to Ginger's work. They'll eat a high carb meal to fuel Travis's late-night studying and to satisfy her own, intentional void.

Ginger likes to go hungry into her group sessions. It gives her energy and a bit of desperation. The hunger brings her closer to her clients, into a mental and physical space that induces an awareness of abstinence and want. An urge that cannot be filled — for them, never, for her, temporarily. While experiencing this deprivation, she must remain calm and rational, focused and receptive. She's open but mustn't cross the line. She gives a bit of herself, but not too much, maintaining a professional distance.

She learned these techniques in college and clinical training, but the hunger tactic is all her own. She discovered it by accident one day when she was so busy she forgot to eat lunch. The hunger made her more effective during the session, and she stuck with it.

Ginger is the youngest counselor at RealYou, where she's worked since 2010, four years of college work-study, then fulltime since graduation. Six months ago, having completed the clinical hours for certification as an alcohol and substance abuse counselor, she started running her own groups. Her supervisor thinks she has natural talent for this work. Ginger would say it's simply her deep-seated desire to help. She's had some successes but hasn't been counseling long enough to know if they're long lasting, if her clients will stay sober for good.

After ending the call with Travis, her mouth is already watering at the thought of Mexican food. She walks into the group therapy room early, ready to receive her clients as they arrive, one by one. Tonight's session may be tough. A new group of alcoholics. These seven people, three women and four men, have recently detoxed and are taking one kind of medication or another, to block the craving for alcohol or to reduce the symptoms of withdrawal: insomnia, anxiety, restlessness, and dysphoria. A few of them are on Antabuse, a drug that will make them sick if they drink. She's read their files and is familiar with their backgrounds, their families, their stories.

Carly, Dieter, Reese, Inga, Marie, Jack, and Manuel. In their small circle, the seven faces display various levels of receptivity, from open to closed, warm to hostile. Carly is on the open-warm end, Jack, on the closed-hostile end. Their backgrounds span the spectrum from unemployed laborer to homemaker to corporate lawyer. The youngest is nineteen, the oldest is sixty-seven.

After a few icebreakers, Ginger leads them into the topic for tonight. Triggers. Each person has a unique trigger, a situation, person, or place associated with alcohol, inducing the craving. It could be an argument with a spouse, a social gathering where wine is served, or a tough day at work.

Gently, Ginger guides them. An hour into the session, the woman sitting to her left starts talking. Inga is twenty-eight, single, and works at the front desk of a high-end health club. She exudes health and vigor, despite her problem with alcohol. She's tried a hundred times to stop drinking on her own; this is the first time she's enrolled in rehab.

Inga recounts the triggering event that caused her relapse, a large family gathering. "I brought my boyfriend along. He's a weightlifter I met at the club. I guess I should call him my ex. It didn't last too long!" She laughs. "My family loves to drink. Half of them are high-functioning alcoholics. If you ask them, it's not a problem." She raises her eyebrows in subtle commentary. "My brothers and cousins were there. We always have a great time. And there's *always* drinking." She laughs again.

Around the circle, heads are nodding in silent support, even Jack's. The forty-five-year-old auto mechanic has been silent for the hour, except for a few words at the beginning of the session when they took turns introducing themselves. Since then, he's been gazing down at his feet or hands, intermittently looking up at Ginger when she speaks. He sits directly across from her in the circle. His face will pop up suddenly, projecting a tough, impenetrable expression. It's unsettling.

Inga continues. "My ex comes from a family of teetotalers, but he was having fun too. He had a couple of beers, I think, not enough for more than a slight buzz. I didn't remember much else about the last part of the evening. The next day, when my boyfriend was breaking up with me, he told me every detail of what I said and did. So embarrassing. Who would want to be with a girl like that?"

Ginger is turned toward Inga but notices Jack in her peripheral vision. He bobs his head subtly, keeping his face lowered, his eyes on his hands. Ginger says to Inga, "Being around friends or family you used to drink with is the number one trigger for many people in recovery."

Jack's head pops up. "Like *you* know anything about it," he mumbles. Ginger turns to him. Their eyes catch and hold. His smoldering hostility is palpable.

After an awkward pause, she says, "I'd like to hear you on that, but Inga has the floor. Let's give her a chance to finish what she's saying…"

"I'm almost finished," Inga says. "I just want to know what I'm supposed to do about this. Are you saying I have to avoid the people I love just because they drink?"

"The triggers are going to be out there. That's life. We're here to help you find ways to cope with these situations, so you can stay strong and not give in. But for now, at least during the early stage of recovery, it's usually best to avoid the triggers entirely."

"Like that's so easy," Jack cuts in.

Ginger faces him again. "Not easy at all."

"Like you know everything."

They stare at each other for two seconds. "Tell us what's on your mind, Jack."

"What's on my mind is that if I want advice on how to stop drinking, I'm not going to ask a little girl who looks like she never had a drink in her life."

"I'm sorry you feel that way."

"You're sorry."

"Yes. I'm sorry you're disappointed in what you believe to be my training and personal experience. But this group isn't about me. The group is here to support you and help you find your own solutions. What works for you has very little to do with me or my personal experience."

"Okay. So, it doesn't matter that you've *never* felt like you're going to rip your guts out if you don't get a drink. It doesn't matter that you never wanted something badly enough to kill for. You're still qualified to help me find a solution." His eyes burn with accusation and superiority.

So unfair, but she's dealt with people like Jack before. Not quite as hostile as he is, but still… She works at keeping her cool. "I understand your craving. I know how overwhelming it is. I *do* have alcoholism in my family, so I have that experience and perspective."

"From the outside. Watching other people. You call that experience? Watching so-called alcoholics while you sit back and judge them?"

A personal jab. He's really starting to bug her now. "There's no judgment here."

"Oh. *There* isn't." He mocks. "'I do have alcoholism in my family.' So, your mama or your daddy are into the bottle. You *know* about their overwhelming craving. You're a victim of those pathetic alcoholics."

"Leave the girl alone, Jack!" On Ginger's right, Carly is

smiling tightly and leaning forward in her chair, ready for the fight.

Carly's help is appreciated, but this is Ginger's fight. She's already donned her gloves. "Maybe you're not ready for this group, Jack. These people want to stay sober. I'm not sure that you do. This group isn't about some god or goddess of sobriety who can fix all your problems. This isn't on me. It's on you, and *you* have to want it." Maybe she should have eaten something before tonight's group. "What you get out of this therapy has nothing to do with me or my background. This group is about all of you," tracing their circle with an index finger, "not me," hand on her heart.

The minute Ginger hears the emphasis on "you, not me," she regrets saying it. Her tone is all wrong. She sounds like...

"Miss Holier Than Thou, thank you very much." Jack springs to his feet. "*This* is bullshit!" He turns suddenly, kicking over his folding chair in the process, and walks out.

Darkness has fallen completely by the time Ginger steps out the door. She's in her own world, feeling very down on herself, agitated and anxious, nose to the ground, not looking where she's going when —

"Oh!" She bumps into someone directly in her path. She looks up into the face of a man, half a foot taller than she is, and says, "I'm sorry."

What an odd face. Pear shaped with fat cheeks, unshaved, hardly any neck, a prominent, snout-like nose, distorted like she's viewing him through a peephole. Despite the warm weather, he's pulled the hood of his sweatshirt over his head. He gives her a small, intimate smile with shining eyes, implying that he believes she actually *wanted* to bump into him, to make the physical contact.

"It's all right," he says. "Excuse *me*." But he takes his time moving out of her way, casually stepping aside. She feels his eyes on her back as she walks away.

Just what she needs, another creepy middle-aged man to worry about. But, as she walks, her mind quickly erases the image of the stranger and goes into a replay of her exchange with Jack during the group session.

What *is* it about Jack that sets her off? She reacted defensively, condescendingly, as if she has the right to lecture a man old enough to be her father. He called it. She sounded like she was sitting in judgment of him. Maybe that's what she was doing all along while she tried to convince herself it was something else. At the very least, she handled the session all wrong. A counselor should never defend herself to the group. A counselor should never act like she's above the clients, like they're the ones with the problem.

She'll do better next time. She has to, even if Jack never returns.

But something tells her he might stick around, even though he isn't ready for treatment. He's found a place to vent his anger, to play the blame game. Someone is to blame for his inability to stay sober. Why not make it that fresh-faced girl, so proud of her little bachelor's degree and counselor certificate? The girl with no personal experience, who "understands" his craving and the devastation it has caused. Jack is on the brink of losing his job. He's divorced, the noncustodial father of two—facts that Ginger read in his case file. Of course, there's no reciprocity at RealYou. No case file on Ginger for Jack to study.

What is it about him that made her react that way? She's never done that before.

Ginger picks up her pace. The night is warm, and people are out on the streets. Once a high-crime neighborhood, Alphabet City is now gentrified, but Ginger can't shake the feeling of foreboding. She's already forgotten that man she bumped into on the street and attributes her uneasiness to the voice in her head, the man who's really bugging her. Jack. *This is bullshit*, he says, mocking her. Something about him is familiar, the short, compact muscularity, the square hands and fingers, the combative body posture. The intense energy and its potential for good, wasted on alcohol.

She speeds up. Almost there. *This is bullshit.* And it comes to her, the voice, the words, the body type, the refusal to see that he's hurting himself, hurting the people around him. Even his eyes are the same. Not the same color or shape, but they have the same hardness, the sickening self-assurance, sending a wordless message that he thinks he's right, when everyone else can see that he's wrong.

Her father.

But that was so long ago, the years and years of his drinking, when Ginger was still a young child. He's been better now for seven or eight years. He stuck with his recovery and has been a good father. Doesn't all that goodness make up for the bad? The early years have faded slowly in memory but will never be erased. Ginger has her own triggers, the reminders. In a flash, she's back there again, in her childhood bedroom, waiting and wondering how bad he will be when he comes home. The days and nights of second guessing him, the fear, longing, and frustration.

Jack is like her father in the days when he wasn't ready to make the change.

These thoughts carry her inside the door of the restaurant. She sees Travis beckoning from the table he's found next to the front window. He stands up when she comes over and kisses her on the cheek. They sit across from each other. The room is dim, half filled with diners, a lighted candle in the middle of each table. Travis's tired face is dreamlike. When Ginger was a teenager, she was obsessed with candles, loved to fill her room with little flickering flames of hope.

The waiter takes their order, and then she asks, "How's the studying going?"

"Okay, I guess. There's just so much to remember."

"You aced the first semester, so you're going to do well."

"It won't be easy."

"Easy-er if you would just ignore the taboo against taking your father's classes. That would be a couple of guaranteed A's."

"Hah! My dad would probably flunk me."

Ginger rolls her eyes up to the ceiling, smiles, and says, "Maybe your *mom* would, but not your dad."

They laugh. "How was your day?" he asks.

Ginger grows serious and opens up about her standoff with Jack during the session.

"Don't beat yourself up," Travis says. "The guy's an asshole. He doesn't know how lucky he is to have you for a counselor. Just forget about him and concentrate on the people who really want your help."

"I'll try, but it'll be hard to get him off my mind. The guy really bugged me."

Travis frowns and focuses harder on her. "Wait a minute. Did this guy creep you out? Are you afraid of him?"

"N-no…"

"I worry about you at that place, all those addicts."

"They're mostly good people."

"Mostly."

The waiter interrupts them, delivering their plates piled high with rice, beans, tortillas, cheese and meat. They dig in.

Cheeks full and chewing ravenously, Ginger glances out the window. Three people are talking and laughing as they pass by on the sidewalk. When the view clears, she sees him. There, across the narrow street, the man is loitering, staring into the restaurant. Their eyes meet. She quickly looks away, down at her food.

Travis, ever attentive to his love, picks up her vibe. "What is it?" He looks out the window, his eyes going to the same place across the street. His brow furrows. "Wait. Is…is that him?"

Ginger dares another glance. The man smiles and lopes away quickly, taking big, uneven steps. She shudders.

"Is that the guy from RealYou?"

"You mean Jack? No, it's not him. But I saw that man earlier, when I was leaving work tonight. I bumped into him by accident, on the street."

"That's sick. He was looking at you."

"Maybe looking at you too." Her eyes move, scanning every part of the street she can see. "He's gone now. I don't think we have to worry about him. He's just some homeless guy."

"No, he's a step up from homeless."

"A small step."

"He's not scruffy enough."

"Whatever. He *does* seem a little off. We'll keep our eye out for him."

"But, Ginger, this is so weird."

"What?"

"I think I've seen him before. This afternoon. Up by NYU. He was in the deli where Dad and I had lunch."

They're silent for a moment, thinking. Ginger says, "Then he's following *you*, not me."

Travis shakes his head. "Why would he? Maybe I'm wrong. He's wearing a hood now, so it's hard to tell. He looks like the guy at the deli, but I don't think he is."

They turn their attention to their plates and move their forks into position, ready for the next onslaught. But they hesitate. "You're sure he isn't the same guy?"

"Almost. Maybe. I'm going to walk you home, just in case, before I go back to the library."

She smiles. "I think *you're* the one who needs an escort. The guy is following you."

"It can't be the same guy. But what if it is?"

"I think all that criminal law you're reading is getting to you." She puts the next big bite in her mouth.

He sighs. "Everything will be so much easier when we have a place together." He fills his mouth and gazes into her eyes. She places her hand on his bare forearm and caresses it gently.

11 »   PILLS

Dana, BLACK ROBED and outwardly impassive, feels anything but emotionless as she presides over a pretrial hearing in *People v Underwood*. Intellectually, she knows that every case has at least two sides. A judge does not advocate for any one side or position. A judge remains open, listens carefully to testimony and argument, applies reason and the rule of law. There's no room for emotion in any of that. Or is there?

Maybe in a utopian forum, nestled on a fluffy white cloud under a cleansing, brilliant light. But down here on earth, Dana, like every other judge, can't stop her heart from beating when she assumes the bench. Judges are human too. Perhaps too human to live up to the ideal of blind justice.

What's wrong with compassion? Nothing at all. Everything about it is right, but a criminal judge's compassion should apply to all. Compassion for the victims, the victims' families, and yes, even for the accused murderer, a fellow human being.

Today, the blindfolded lady must balance the scales for the man sitting in the defendant's chair, on trial for depraved indifference murder. Two counts, corresponding to the numbered paragraphs of the indictment, an arrangement of black letters on white paper. One paragraph for each victim, the two patients he poisoned to death. Depravedly. Allegedly.

Emotion. Tamp it down. Prejudgment. Erase it. So difficult.

Dana has already considered and weighed the attorneys' descriptions of the evidence and arguments in their motion papers. That gives her some basis in fact for what she feels about this defendant. But the strongest jab to her gut is the impression he exudes right now, sitting in her courtroom.

Doctor Underwood smugly leans back and sideways in his chair, propped on an elbow, taking in the proceedings with half-lidded contempt. He's not a bad looking man, apparently more vigilant about his own health than that of his patients. Young middle age, neatly organized features, clean shaven and impeccably groomed. He wears a fine-tailored suit, expensive but not exorbitantly so. His choice of attire shows some level of respect for the court, no doubt on the advice of counsel. Throw him in a time machine, set it back twenty years, and he comes out as the ivy league brat his wealthy parents were proud to put through medical school. The parents are not here this morning, nor have they ever shown up in Judge Hargrove's courtroom during the previous proceedings in this case.

The jury box is empty. Voir dire will start after Dana has ruled on the defense motion at hand. Perhaps the defendant will wipe some of that smugness off his face when the trial gets underway. It would do him well to sit up straighter and widen his eyes in earnestness for the twelve people who will decide his fate. His attorney is running out of time to finish schooling him on his most effective, wordless performance.

Pamela Louise Grimes is an intelligent attorney with a manner and personality particularly suited to this case. She's tall and stately, with an air of grand magnanimity. Not a firebrand or a soapbox orator, she's a dogged debater who works at getting her way with smooth, well-reasoned persuasion. She sits next to her client like they're good friends, balancing out his cold arrogance with her warm, relaxed, understated demeanor.

At the prosecutor's table, the assistant district attorney puts on a different show of energy and intensity. ADA Sylvan Quince, mid-thirties, with nearly ten years' experience, is considered one of the finest trial attorneys in the Manhattan DA's office. He's articulate and clever, exuding an animated foxiness with his small, wiry frame and multi-racial features of universal appeal. Dana is hoping he'll be at his best today and avoid playing the ace up his sleeve, the emotion card. She's already feeling it and would resent any allusions to the defendant's smarmy character as a means of making up for the shortcomings in the People's case. The law is not solidly and squarely on Quince's side. Appeals to human nature aren't beyond him, but he's known to advocate right up to the ethical line, without ever crossing it.

As is customary for a murder case of this importance and complexity, Quince is aided by a younger attorney. Sitting next to him is ADA Carol Leipsig, with maybe five years of felony prosecutions under her belt, on the cusp of being promoted to the homicide chart. She will have little to say during this trial, with, perhaps, a chance to conduct direct examination of a non-consequential witness or two, while gaining invaluable lessons on how to prepare and present a big case.

Henny sits at his small desk to the side of the judge's bench. Zola has stayed in her office, working. If the judge needs her in the courtroom, Henny will call her. Captain Len Rankel and Court Officer Sheila Delano, the most junior officer assigned to Judge Hargrove, are on duty in the courtroom today. Both officers are armed, although they have no reason to be on high alert. Doctor Underwood kills slowly, if at all, with poisonous pills, not physical violence. He is currently free on bail and has never broken the terms of his pretrial release. A knowing eye can spot the distortion under his left sock when the pant leg is pulled up slightly as he sits. The telltale silhouette of an electronic tracking device.

A few minutes after nine, the hearing is underway. Judge Hargrove clarifies the scope. "We're not here to relitigate the search warrants for the defendant's office and the contents of his computer. My previous ruling covered that part of the motion. The warrants were issued on probable cause and were properly executed."

Attorney Grimes stands and says, "Conceded, Your Honor. The only issue outstanding is the defense motion, *in limine*, to preclude any evidence pertaining to patients other than the two named in the indictment, Franklin and Veskovic. The doctor is *not* on trial for his general medical practices or for anything to do with other patients."

Quince jumps to his feet and starts right in, "But...," and as he talks, an image flashes quickly through Dana's mind. A boxing ring. On opposite sides stand the ADA, five six and a hundred thirty pounds, and defense counsel, five ten and one sixty. Gloves raised, Quince bobs on his toes and dances up to Grimes. She stays solidly planted, tall, silent, grinning, undaunted. She extends an arm and easily parries her opponent's left jab, holding him at bay with a palm on his forehead as he twitches and jabs around her in the air.

Dana grins to herself. Meanwhile, Quince has continued, "...the defendant *is* on trial for murder committed with depraved indifference. The jury will need a factual basis to infer his mental state. His daily practices show that Mr. Franklin and Mr. Veskovic were mere numbers to him. He wrote thousands of lethal prescriptions for hundreds of patients. He knew that ten other patients died from overdoses, but he kept prescribing. I have Detective Vargas here now, waiting outside, ready to testify. The evidence of depravity is vast and stark." Quince gestures broadly, sweeping the whole universe into his case. "We're entitled to prove it. Indeed, it's my obligation to prove the defendant's mental state."

"Not with acts outside this indictment." Grimes lifts the paper from the table and nonchalantly raises her eyebrows. *Gee whiz, no debate here.* "Your Honor, the law is crystal clear. There's no need for witness testimony. I'm asking for a ruling in our favor on my papers alone. Mr. Quince is trying to prejudice the court against my client with irrelevant information. If he clears this hurdle, the second hurdle is a lot lower and easier to jump over. He's going for a conviction by defaming my client to the jury with this mumbo jumbo."

Dana doesn't like the implications in her argument. "I usually don't have much trouble distinguishing between mumbo jumbo and relevant evidence, Ms. Grimes."

"I wasn't suggesting—"

"Nor do juries, in my experience, have that difficulty."

"If I may, Your Honor," Quince breaks in, "the People feel it's imperative to give the court an idea of the scope of this evidence today, a preview of what we plan to prove at trial, to illustrate its relevance to the issue of mental state."

"Yes, and I'm inclined to hear it."

But Grimes, with her usual persistence, isn't ready to give in. "Then I would ask the court to excuse my inept phrasing a moment ago and to consider this. My point, simply, is that the court has all it needs right now to rule on the motion without taking testimony. Even if Mr. Quince could establish all his allegations of patient overdoses and lethal prescriptions, Doctor Underwood is not accused of those acts. He's on trial for the deaths of Franklin and Veskovic. Period. Anything else is irrelevant and unconstitutionally prejudicial and must be precluded."

"All right, counselor. I understand your position. You've met your initial burden on your motion papers, and the burden shifts to the People. Mr. Quince, I'll allow witness testimony. I need to hear at least some of the disputed evidence to judge how a jury might take it. If need be, I'll curtail the testimony as we go along. Call your witness, Mr. Quince."

"Thank you, Your Honor." Quince catches the eye of Officer

Delano, who steps out of the courtroom to summon the witness. Grimes resumes her seat and dips her head toward her client for a private word. As the doctor listens, his smugness flickers into a new alertness. He straightens his posture as Detective Aurelina Vargas walks into the courtroom and takes the oath.

Another challenge for the blindfolded lady. Judge Hargrove mustn't be swayed by her affection and high regard for Detective Vargas. "Lina," as she is known to close friends like Dana.

It's been a long time, but the bond these women forged two decades ago is unbreakable. Dana hasn't seen Lina since 1995, when she testified in a murder case against Niels Van Leeuwen. A complicated situation, involving Dana's Dutch au pair Anneke, the young woman who cared for Travis when he was two years old. Lina was the young cop who pursued the investigation when others had given up, uncovering key evidence. That's Lina. Dedicated and determined, a fighter for the victim from the very beginning of her career, when she was young and green. She's not green anymore after two decades with the NYPD and promotion to detective first class.

Has it really been that long since they've seen each other? Dana thinks back. No. The last time was in 2001, when they spoke about Ramón Pineda, an incarcerated felon seeking his release by post-conviction motion. Although Lina and her partner collared Pineda in 1992, she wasn't called to testify at the hearing in 2001, as Dana recalls…

Leading to another thought. Today, on cross-examination, will Grimes try to undercut the detective's credibility by dredging up that single incident in her past? It shook Lina up, so early in her career, to be taken off the beat pending an internal investigation into the discharge of her service Glock in the line of duty. If Grimes goes for it, Dana will be quick to cut her off. That incident is completely irrelevant to today's hearing. Moreover, Lina was cleared of any wrongdoing.

The judge's eyes meet the detective's as she takes the stand. They exchange subtle nods and smiles. Lina, now in her late forties, hasn't changed much. She's petite, no more than ninety-five pounds, and wears a gray pantsuit with white blouse. Court clothes. Her hair is still shiny black, but the pert ponytail is gone, replaced by a fashionably short hairstyle, one side longer than the other. Wouldn't it be nice to get out of this chair right now, pull off the outer layer, the black robe, and go out for coffee with Lina? They could talk about old times, when their jobs seemed so tough that they couldn't imagine things getting any tougher. Like this.

Fantasies aside, even the briefest *ex parte* communication between a judge and a witness during ongoing litigation is a no-no. They'll have to wait, and maybe, someday down the road, they'll go out for that cup of coffee.

The prosecutor quickly establishes Lina's background and training, including her status as lead investigator on this case. Then he launches into questions about the paperwork and computer records seized from the defendant's medical office. To speed things along, Quince takes shortcuts through the procedural foundation for the evidence. Grimes could object, but she doesn't. Clearly, she's more worried about substance than procedure, and she'll gain little by objecting. Detective Vargas maintains a solid chain of custody, and any objection will only lengthen the day for the negligible benefit of technical perfection.

Trial is another matter. If Quince decides to cut corners in front of a jury, Grimes might even forgo an objection. Juries can resent attorneys for nitpicking, and she might chance leaving the mistakes on the record as potential grounds for appeal. But Grimes, with no previous experience in Judge Hargrove's courtroom, would adopt this strategy at her peril. The judge is vigilant to the purity of the trial record and doesn't allow mistakes like this to go uncorrected. Dana will make Quince jump through all the right hoops.

But…her thoughts are getting away with her, wandering ahead to trial. Does this mean she's already closed her mind to the defense motion? The prosecutor wants to smear my client with this evidence, Grimes says. It's unduly prejudicial, she says. Unconstitutionally prejudicial.

Keep an open mind.

An hour in, Quince has managed to get a thick ream of patient charts into evidence, marked as People's hearing exhibits A-1 through A-254. He claims this is a small fraction of the documentary evidence and wants to introduce more, but Judge Hargrove cuts him off. Second-seater ADA Leipsig's primary duty thus far has been to keep the paperwork organized. She asks Henny to mark the documents, hands out copies to Grimes and the judge, and gives the original to Quince to inquire of the witness. Without her, this whole process would creep along at a snail's pace.

ADA Leipsig hands ADA Quince the exhibit marked A-22. He asks the witness to explain.

"This chart," Detective Vargas testifies, "shows that the defendant saw patient Barry Sorvino on the afternoon of June 10, 2014."

"Does the chart note Sorvino's complaints?"

"It's handwritten here." Indicating on the paper. "Only three words. 'Pain and anxiety.'"

"Any further symptoms or complaints noted?"

"No."

"Any diagnosis?"

"No."

"Any treatment noted?"

"Yes. Doctor Underwood prescribed Xanax, 0.5 mg, 30 pills, with one refill, and OxyContin, 160 mg, 30 pills, with one refill."

Grimes gets up and says, "Objection, Your Honor. This witness is not a medical professional. She has no clue whether these dosages fall within the standard of care."

"That's right," says the judge. "Detective Vargas is not qualified to give a medical opinion, but she isn't doing that. She's simply describing the exhibit. What is your objection?"

"That this kind of evidence should be precluded at trial. It's not related to the two counts against Doctor Underwood and doesn't show *any* kind of impropriety in his medical practice. Mr. Quince wants to introduce these prescriptions to a jury of lay people, with no medical support, to invite speculation that this dosage is too high for, quote-unquote, pain and anxiety."

"Not so," Quince tells the court. "Ms. Grimes knows that I plan to call a medical expert at trial, but there's no need at this hearing. If the court will permit me to continue, it will become clear why."

"Objection overruled. Go ahead, Mr. Quince."

"Thank you." He glances over his shoulder at Grimes, who responds with her typical aloof look and sits down. The doctor has resumed his sideways lean, but his eyes betray a hint of anxiety under the foggy gaze.

ADA Leipsig hands Quince a document marked People's hearing exhibit B. "Detective Vargas, showing you People's exhibit B, would you please identify this document."

"It's a police report from my precinct, the Fifth Precinct, concerning the investigation into the death of Barry Sorvino on June 11, 2014. It notes a telephone contact on Friday, June 13, between Police Officer Tadeo Montoya and the defendant, Garth Underwood."

"Objection." Grimes rises to her feet again. "Hearsay."

"It's a business record," Quince explains, "offered for the information provided to the defendant, not for its truth, but relevant to the defendant's knowledge and state of mind."

"I'll allow it in evidence for the purposes of this hearing," says the judge. To Grimes, "Overruled."

Grimes remains standing a moment too long, as if considering another objection. Dana knows where her mind is going. Where is Officer Montoya? "In the interest of expediency," the judge says, "I'm waiving proper foundation. If I allow any of this evidence at trial, we'll deal with the technicalities then, either by stipulation or witness authentication. Clear, counselors?"

They acknowledge their agreement.

"After I make my ruling, you'll have to hammer out a deal before we're in front of a jury. Proceed, Mr. Quince."

"Detective, does this document record the purpose of Officer Montoya's call to the defendant?"

"Yes. Here, under 'Comments,' it's noted, 'Informed Dr. Garth Underwood of the death of patient Barry Sorvino by overdose on June 11, 2014.'"

Again, ADA Leipsig is quick. She keeps it moving by passing around the next marked document.

Looking at her copy, the judge says, "Mr. Quince, I assume you don't have the medical examiner or records custodian here to authenticate this?"

"Correct, Your Honor. I beg the court's indulgence in that regard for this hearing."

Dana glances at Grimes, whose face says it all with her familiar insouciance.

"Received in evidence as People's hearing exhibit C," Dana says. "And counselor, you needn't have the witness read from the document. We can all see what it says."

Cause of death: Toxicity, Oxycodone Hydrochloride, Alprazolam.

How injury occurred: Oral ingestion.

Manner of death: Suicide.

At three forty-five, Dana calls a recess. It's her usual time. They come on like clockwork. Why is that? She's flashing, in pain, about to boil over.

"Ten minutes," she says, and steps down from the bench. Henny gives her a knowing grimace as she heads for the door. In most things, his understanding of her is complete, intuitive, and sensorial. Personal, but not creepy. Dana is okay with it.

She swishes past Zola's open door, seeing only the law clerk's back and hearing the contact between fingers and computer keyboard, a furious rattling. Inside chambers, behind the closed door, Dana pulls the row of snaps apart in a single, decisive rip, grabs the two sides of her black robe, and flaps them for air circulation. When she first went on the bench, she ordered a style of robe in the lightest possible weight and most breathable fabric. She wears a sleeveless blouse and skirt underneath. Still, it's strangling her.

And so thirsty. She opens a water bottle and drinks half the contents in continuous gulps.

There. Better.

Is this condition exacerbated by querulous attorneys and tedious proceedings? Undoubtedly. It all contributes to her need to get up and move. They've been in that courtroom since nine this morning, with only forty-five minutes for lunch.

Pacing around her desk, she thinks. Where is this going? Does she need to hear any more? Quince has given evidence of three patients who suffered the same fate as Sorvino. For six other patients, he's asked the court for leave to offer detailed proof: dates of patient visits, prescriptions Underwood wrote, dates of death and official notice to Underwood of their deaths. Quince then picked specific time frames and took Detective Vargas through office records showing the astronomical number of patients Underwood "treated." The records confirm that every patient left his office with a prescription for tranquilizers or narcotic painkillers.

Six months before the deaths of Franklin and Veskovic in November 2014, the office records became spotty and inconsistent. Four of the other ten deaths, including Sorvino's, occurred within that time period. Maybe the good doctor was finally getting nervous about someone noticing what he was up to. For those months, ADA Quince made a different evidentiary proffer. He has records from pharmacies within a twenty-mile radius, establishing that Underwood kept writing prescriptions at an even higher rate.

And *this* really stood out: No office records within the last five years that he received any medical insurance payments for patient visits. Cash only, and incomplete records of that, as well. Another proffer: "We're prepared to introduce evidence of several bank accounts owned or controlled by the defendant, each funded with cash only, showing an income of more than ten million dollars in the past five years."

This trial could easily whirl out of control. Judge Hargrove isn't going to allow that. Let the DA indict Underwood for drug dealing and forfeit his assets as criminal proceeds. Let the feds prosecute him for income tax evasion. Let the state AG prosecute him for multiple controlled substances regulatory violations. Let the AMA sanction him.

Instead, we have a test case for "murder." Two victims, not two plus ten. Why didn't Quince get an indictment for the other ten deaths? Dana understands it now. The evidence isn't as strong. The first six were spread out in time and much earlier in his career, the oldest one occurring fifteen years ago. The most recent four victims, including Sorvino, died within six months of the deaths of Franklin and Veskovic in November 2014. But all four of those patients were new to the doctor, a single appointment for each. No prior history to prove that the doctor was aware of their drug problems. Compare that to Franklin and Veskovic, who each saw the doctor three or four times and received steadily increasing doses of their pills, with no medically indicated reasons.

This case is close enough as it is, and Quince picked the two victims with the strongest evidence.

The other deaths, the official warnings, the number of patients and prescriptions, the millions in cash: Allow none of it, all of it, or some of it?

Suzy Suburbs gets Man One. Berto Barrio gets Murder.

Now, why did that pop into her head? It's a warning to avoid special treatment for privileged whites like Spinnaker and Underwood. Unlike Spinnaker, a girl who evokes some measure of sympathy, Underwood twists Dana's gut into knots and puts a bad taste in her mouth. A word comes to mind. *Despicable.* It's the impression she's been suppressing since this morning, when she reminded herself to rein in her emotions. It has only gotten worse. He's a person who corrupted his innate intelligence and advantage, laying waste to his potential for good in pursuit of material wealth. He's a person devoid of humanity who doesn't care if his patients live or die. Yes, he's depravedly indifferent.

The other side to this case is weightier and more comfortable. Rationality and the rule of law. Constitutional rights for everyone, this defendant included. The lofty ideal of due process.

There's a less comfortable consideration as well: An appellate court's authority to reverse a conviction and rebuke her in writing if she's wrong. Appellate judges look at the case on paper without having seen the depravedly indifferent person sitting in the courtroom, day in and day out, glowering in half-lidded contempt. Something to worry about? The specter of appellate rebuke, a permanent, public record for the entire legal community to see. Judge Dana Hargrove. Wrong. Media fodder.

But when did that ever stop her?

It's four o'clock. Past time. She doesn't need to hear any more evidence. An outline of her ruling is taking shape. It's time to go back to the courtroom, listen to closing arguments, rule on the motion, and wrap this one up. Tomorrow, they begin jury selection.

Dana snaps up her robe, feeling...fine. She goes into the robing room, eyes herself in the full-length wall mirror, and grabs a tissue from the box on the little table. With a pat of her gleaming forehead and a final self-evaluation, the judge balls up the tissue, clenches it in her fist, and makes her way back into the courtroom.

An altogether satisfying day, Detective Vargas thinks as she leaves the courthouse. A long time on the witness stand but well worth the effort. It's a difficult case, a test case, and Dana, a woman Lina has always admired, is handling the trial well.

In the courtroom, Lina had no problem thinking of her as Judge Hargrove, addressing her as "Your Honor." Twenty years ago, everyone could foresee where ADA Dana Hargrove was headed. Her talent was obvious, her career path predictable. Lina wishes there'd been a way to keep in touch with her and develop a closer friendship, but that's how it is with two busy women pursuing careers in criminal justice. No time. And in a town as big as Manhattan, it's the luck of the draw whether a particular prosecutor in the 500-attorney DA's office will land on the same case with a particular cop out of thousands in the NYPD. After 1994 there'd been no such luck of the draw, and then, in the early 00's, Dana moved north to Westchester County, out of the city all those years.

A small regret, but things could change. It's been a long time, and Dana is different. A bit colder maybe, but that could be the outward appearance of authority that comes with being a judge. Or it could be the contrast with Lina's image of Dana from the extremely emotional experience they shared on the Van Leeuwen case in 1994. That night is vivid in Lina's mind, like a noir film she's watched dozens of times, every line of dialogue emblazoned in memory. The luck of the draw. Dana was on the homicide chart. In the middle of the night, Lina picked her up in the squad car and drove her to the crime scene. It's a feeling you don't forget, a cop and a prosecutor riding to the crime scene in the dead of night, radio squawking, hearts beating, exhausted but alert, a body awaiting their inspection.

Lina's head is in that squad car now as she makes her way along a crowded street near the courthouse, zigzagging and shuffling more than walking a straight line. It's almost five o'clock on a Wednesday, the busiest workday of the week, and the streets are jammed with people leaving their offices. She comes to an intersection and stops at a red light. The usual din. Car horns honk, people chatter with coworkers or seemingly to themselves, their earpieces connecting them to family or friends.

As Lina waits at the corner, the throng grows. People press in, the decibel level rises, words are mashed together, a few break through. The woman standing next to Lina complains to her friend, "Can you believe it?" She's irate about her rough day at the office. The surrounding voices are speaking English, but then a single Spanish word comes through, some distance behind her, standing out because it's different. "Cariño," Lina hears, and then, "Pissed me off!" from that woman next to her. Still the light hasn't changed to green. "Querida pequeña." A man's voice, the same man. Strange. Is he trying to get someone's attention with these endearments? No one responds. Lina looks right and left and over her shoulder. The light changes.

"Bang bang!"

The masses surge.

Lina spins around and scans the hordes, looking for the man. People are coming straight at her, frowning at the obstruction, pushing around her on both sides.

The man who said that is the same man who uttered the

endearments in Spanish. She's sure of it. *Bang bang.* But in this confusion of faces, she sees no one likely to be him.

Ridiculous. She turns around again, and like the other pedestrians, weaves through the cars in the crosswalk that didn't make it through the yellow light before it changed to red.

That voice. Imagined or real? It's a voice she's heard before.

Looking straight ahead, focused on her destination, she awakens to what was instinctive only a moment before. Under her right palm she feels the steady, fast beat of her heart. The fingers of that hand are lightly wrapped around the butt of her gun, in the shoulder holster, concealed under the left lapel of her jacket. At the ready.

12 » AVOIDANCE

EVAN IS HOME, setting the dinner table, when Dana comes in at six thirty. Court is never in session past five. This means, as usual, that Dana has stayed after the attorneys and court staff have gone home, working in her chambers, thinking, talking, and maybe writing about the law. Tonight, not so bad. Six thirty is, for her, on the early side.

He hears the soft "thud" of her briefcase as she lets it drop to the floor in the foyer of their apartment. She walks into the dining room and pauses at the table. Evan looks up from the saltshaker in his hand. It's been a while since their homecomings featured hugs, kisses, or caresses. "Hello," is always nice, but she doesn't say it tonight. Instead, from across the table, she gives him a brief but warm half-smile and a distracted look, a sign that her mind isn't entirely here.

"How's everything down at the pill mill?"

She rolls her eyes. "I've hit nirvana."

"Sounds thrilling. I hope you got a prescription for me too. I could use some of that."

"Come see the doc tomorrow and he'll oblige. Just tell him you're in pain."

Is he? Evan is still convinced this is a phase, even if it's starting to stretch on a little too long. But she meant it as a joke, of course, and he can't help bursting into a big smile at her wry sense of humor. He loves this woman so much.

In response to his beaming face, Dana's half-smile inches up slightly. "I'll go freshen up, as they say." She turns away from him and heads for their bedroom. The first thing she does when getting home these days is to change into loose-fitting, lightweight clothes. It's been a warm day, and Evan has prepared their home environment ahead of time, hitting the down arrow on the AC several notches.

"Chilled pasta salad on the menu," he calls out after her.

A faint, "Yum," from down the hall.

Their conversation at dinner is sparse, polite, superficial. Dana gives him the highlights of the hearing, nothing too specific.

"It must have been great to see Detective Vargas again," Evan says.

"Mm-hmm."

"She did a lot for us. Went the whole nine yards. An amazing detective and compassionate person."

"That's Lina."

They're silent for several minutes. Dana has not revealed how she ruled on the defense motion, and Evan is hoping she will spontaneously tell him. He's dying to know because the case interests him. The legal issues are nuanced and fascinating. But the reason he doesn't ask directly and hopes she'll volunteer the information has to do with the strain that has come into their conversations.

He doesn't know when or how this started. Not exactly, but the earliest signs may have been two years ago, at the beginning of their big changes. Dana's father had just died. They were both in flux with their careers and considering the move back to the city. Dana's insomnia and night sweats started about that time too.

But how did it get to this point? He tiptoes around her, hesitates to ask what he wants to ask, anticipating the inflection in her response or his need to interpret a deeper level to it. The words she uses are fine, but there always seems to be something behind them. His desire to read her mind has grown overwhelmingly strong. If her voice and manner seem surly or indifferent or even condescending, he's left wondering if that's merely his own take on it. Or is that the real Dana, the new Dana?

An enigma. She was less so at the start of their relationship, but never entirely an open book. The part of her that he can never know may have been what attracted him. What still attracts him, and now, frankly, scares him. He wonders how a woman like this ever fell for him. He worries that, maybe, she never did, at least not as completely as he fell for her.

Does she still love him? Did she ever love him?

A vital and consistent element of their relationship seems to be slipping away. They were always close buddies, able to talk easily and fluidly about anything. Family, the kids, cases they worked. They used to call each other during the day, couldn't wait to get home at night to tell each other what had happened since the last phone call. That's love, isn't it?

The little silences crept in slowly and weren't noticeable at first. Now, they're deafening.

Is she angry at him? The few times he's asked that question in the past year, she's denied it and said, "Don't be silly."

Does her position on the court exhaust her more than her previous jobs? It seems unlikely. Every job she's held has been tough, but she thrives on the stress. Any hint that she needs rest is vehemently denied. Stubborn pride, but that's how she plods through the worst challenges and comes out stronger.

Is she no longer interested in hearing his opinions? A handful of times, in the past twenty-seven years, she's praised his intellect and legal strategies. Has said he's the smartest lawyer she knows.

Between those handful of times, he's believed in the permanence of her esteem. Now, that belief is slipping. Last Friday, for instance, she seemed disparaging of his suggestion that Suzy Spinnaker had already been dealt a break by the jury and, perhaps, didn't deserve any more leniency. He wonders if this is only his perception, skewed by emotion. Did she think he was criticizing her impressions of the case? Disagreements like this are no reason to shut down their communication. She values honesty and says she needs to hear conflicting points of view. Doesn't want to be surrounded by yes-people.

So, if he happens to approve of her ruling in the Underwood case, will that make him a milquetoast in her eyes? And if he happens to disagree with her, will he get one of those enigmatic looks with the flashing eyes? Something to read into. Proof positive of a dismissive or irritated or skeptical attitude. Or evidence of intellect, pensiveness, and gratitude for his honesty. Or anything else he wants to imagine!

Damn it! He wants to know.

"That's a tough issue in Underwood. How did you come out on it? Are you allowing the evidence?"

She puts her fork down, pats her mouth with a napkin, and places it on the table. Her plate is clean. She raises her eyes to him. The look is long and contemplative.

"Tough is right." A pause. He feels like a panting puppy, begging for a doggie treat. She gives in and tosses the bone. "I was conflicted, as you can imagine. This man has done despicable things. Hundreds of uncharged crimes that would take months to try. But the DA is going for the top, no compromise, that's it. Two counts of murder. I might not agree with the charging decision, but that's the DA's call. He can't have his cake and eat it too. He can't have a trial about uncharged crimes. He has to prove an act, causation, and mental state for each count of murder. That's it."

Evan is beginning to worry, to get angry even. She's precluding the evidence? All of it? How are they going to nail this bastard? He sees a way, a constitutionally correct way, to show the evidence of uncharged crimes to a jury.

But then, she goes on. "The DA has objective facts to prove the criminal acts and causation for the two murders. This case is all about mental state. I can't let the jury see this man through an antiseptic lens. Everything he does, how he conducts his medical practice, is relevant to his mental state. So, I came up with a compromise."

Evan releases his held breath. "You're allowing some of it?"

"Right. Out of the ten additional patients who overdosed, I'm allowing evidence of four deaths that occurred within the six months preceding the crimes in the indictment. I'm also limiting the timeframe for the other evidence. The cash payments, the number of patients he saw, and the number of prescriptions he wrote. I'll instruct the jury that the evidence is to be considered only on the issue of whether he acted with depraved indifference with respect to the two victims."

Evan nods and smiles. He agrees completely with her ruling but says nothing in the three seconds it takes him to absorb it. After that, there's no time to speak because she stands up from the table, picks up their two plates, and walks into the kitchen.

Leaving the scene. That, in itself, could be evidence of dismissiveness. *Your opinion isn't needed.*

Or, it could be evidence that she's finished with this topic after a long day in court. *Time to unwind.*

He goes for the second interpretation. There's nothing to debate. And it's time, maybe, to cut himself a break. There's evidence to support this too. When he nodded and smiled in agreement with her ruling, she responded in kind, warmth shining from her eyes, before she rose from the table.

* * *

They're together in the kitchen, cleaning up.

"How did your day go?" she asks for the first time.

He's not sure if she's aware of his schedule. If she pays any attention to it. Today was the first day of the study period before final exams next week. "Nice to finally have a break from teaching, but office hours were jammed with students worried about the exams, asking questions." There was also another disturbing interaction with Prescott, who wanted to know if the professor had read his "extra credit paper." Evan reported the incident to the dean and asked for family contact information, thinking he should call Prescott's parents. The dean said she'd take care of it.

Evan doesn't mention the incident to Dana. There's something more important he should tell her while she's still receptive. "I also got a call from Travis. Kind of surprising to hear from him now, when he's hitting the books so hard, but he wanted to ask me something about our lunch yesterday. About a person he saw in the deli."

This news grabs Dana's attention. She rarely calls Travis anymore and gets much of her information about him from Evan. It's another symptom that has worried him, this pulling away from the children. Evan mentions them as often as possible, to kindle the connections: his connection to her, as partner-parent, and her connection to the children, as mother. Her pull to them is there, indestructible, underneath her gradual change, the distance, the avoidance. He made the mistake of suggesting to her, once, that she was grieving the empty nest. She scrunched her brow, judge-like, and said, "Why would you think that? It's time for them to go off and start their lives."

True, but the avoidance in her answer only confirmed what he was thinking. This is painful for her, as much as, or more than, it is for him.

Last night, when they were sitting quietly in the living room and Dana wasn't forthcoming about her workday, Evan filled the airspace with a report on his lunch with their son. He told her about the incident with Prescott and about Travis's bashful admission that he and Ginger are thinking of moving in together. Dana adores Ginger. The news put a smile on her face.

She turns to him now and says, "You mean, he was asking about that student who came up to your table? What's his name again?"

"Prescott. No, Travis was calling about someone else. He described a middle-aged man, a little thick around the waist and an odd-shaped face. Fat jowls, a little stubble on his chin. He had longish, dark hair, streaked with gray. And some other details. He asked if I remembered seeing the man. I had a vague memory of someone who looked like that but couldn't be sure."

"Why was he asking?"

"He thought he saw the man again last night, when he was at a restaurant with Ginger. The man was smiling at them oddly."

Dana moves into high alert, her protective instincts kicking in. "He thinks the man followed him?"

"It crossed his mind, but he couldn't be sure it was the same guy. He was wearing the hood of his sweatshirt over his head. Travis ended up supposing that he was wrong, or if he was right, it was pure coincidence."

"Hmm."

Dana says nothing else, pensive as they finish cleaning up. Evan starts the dishwasher, and they go into the living room, lulled by the comforting white noise of rushing water.

Dana takes the easy chair. She could sit on the couch, but then, Evan might sit next to her. He plops down on the couch by himself and extends one arm along the back, one leg along the cushions.

She picks up her novel on the side table but seems distracted and gazes off into space, not opening the book. Finally, she says,

"Travis gave quite a detailed description for just a casual observation. What else did he say about the man?"

"Something about his clothing. Baggy, out-of-style jeans with that sweatshirt. Too heavy for the warm weather. And something about his nose. It was unusually prominent."

"Very observant. Makes me think it isn't a coincidence at all. It was the same man, in the deli, and at the restaurant."

"*Outside* the restaurant, looking in, he said."

"Really? That's odd."

"Yeah. The man was across the street, looking at them through the window. But the whole thing lasted a second or two. Mostly he was worried about Ginger. She bumped into the man when she left work a few minutes before."

"Oh!" Dana's eyes flash with alarm. "That's one too many coincidences."

Evan now regrets bringing it up. It all sounds worse than it is. "Really, he ended up thinking it was nothing."

Silence.

"Like you said," Evan goes on, "our son is observant, and he'll keep an eye out. He has good judgment. He'll be okay."

"But Ginger?"

"He's looking out for her. Walked her home last night. Didn't see the guy again. I'm sure it's nothing. You know how it is, Dana. The city is full of kooks, but Travis is vigilant and knows how to avoid them. We have to trust him on that."

"Right. We had to accept that the minute we sent him to college in the city."

Evan nods and laughs quietly, wanting to lighten the mood. "Just think how impressed Natalie would be with her brother's powers of observation! Travis sure has an eye for detail. Maybe we should call her and let her know."

"Too late."

"Too late? It's only seven thirty."

"I mean, it's too soon to call again. I just spoke with her."

"That was Saturday."

"No, after that."

"You spoke with her again?"

"Yesterday... No, maybe it was Monday night. Around eight or nine. She called me, out of the blue."

Evan is puzzled, trying to remember where he was on Monday night when Dana got the call. He knew nothing about it.

"How is she?"

"Fine. Just fine, she says."

Nice to know, and what else has Dana "forgotten" to tell the man she never talks to anymore?

But a moment later, she says something that makes him forget the resentment he doesn't want to feel. "I'm looking forward to having her with us this summer, aren't you? I miss her."

13 »   GIRLS

CHERYL ASKS CAITLIN, "What do you say we get your cousin Natalie over here?"

"Tally! Yippee!" The girl jumps up and down, clapping her hands.

"I'm gonna try, my little one. But I can't guarantee anything. You know how busy she is."

Hands on hips like a scolding parent, Caitlin says, "Busy, busy, busy."

A natural-born actress. Cheryl laughs in delight, pulls her daughter into a warm hug, and smothers her in kisses. If Cheryl were one of *those* kinds of mothers, Caitlin would be the next Drew Barrymore, a child star taking the world by storm. Raking in the coin so that Mom could retire early.

Never. Protect, nurture, love, embrace. Family. Cousin Natalie is Caitlin's favorite family member. She missed her on Saturday when Dana, Evan, and Brenda were over and has been asking about her.

Natalie may be a young woman now, but she still needs some mothering. Cheryl has noticed the subtle changes in the relationship between Dana and her daughter. What the hell has gotten into Dana? Former mother, now exclusively Judge Hargrove, 24/7. From the time Natalie started college, Cheryl has invited her to Dovecote Lane for meals and sleepovers. This is Natalie's childhood home. It's only an hour drive from Vassar College, closer and easier to get to than her parents' apartment in the city. Aunt and niece have always been close, and the circumstances make it ever more important to maintain that closeness. Cheryl reviews her calendar. They're due for another girls' night. It's a tricky time of year for her niece, but why not? What could be better than a brief rest and a little laughter before the real crunch starts? It's also a Friday, when every teenager is at least *thinking* of knocking off for the weekend.

At noon, Cheryl calls. She isn't sure of Natalie's schedule and is pleased to hear her niece's voice after the second ring. "Hi, Cheryl!"

"How's my favorite college sophomore?"

"Good. Classes are over for today. I'm sitting outside, having lunch."

"A beautiful day for it. Listen, Caitlin is dying to see you and so am I. We were wondering if you want to come for a sleepover tonight. I'll barbeque something, and we can all watch a Disney movie together."

Natalie laughs. The Disney movie suggestion is a joke, but actually, she wouldn't mind it at all. Those movies are still her favorites. "I'd really love to, but I have to finish a term paper and study. We have only a few more days of classes next week, and then finals start the week after that."

"Okay. Then we'll skip the Disney movie and just have dinner. You have to eat, don't you?"

"Sure. I'm tired of the dining hall."

"Barbeque sounds better, right? And a few laughs."

"You make it sound very tempting."

"After dinner, at eight o'clock sharp, I'll send Caitlin to bed and *you* will go upstairs to your old bedroom to write your paper."

Their connection is silent for a moment while Natalie thinks it over. Is Cheryl being selfish? The girl is a straight-A student. A few hours of laughter won't change that.

"Doubly tempting. I'm getting tired of studying in my dorm

room or the library."

"Great! Let's do it!"

They seal the deal. Natalie will be on her way over later this afternoon.

Renee watches Caitlin while Mario drives Cheryl to the grocery store. He waits in the parking lot for her. She has resisted Mario's repeated suggestions that he shadow her, or at least come inside, whenever she's in a public establishment. A bodyguard tagging along? She absolutely forbids it. "Please. I'm just a person going shopping."

This high-end grocer stocks the freshest produce and meats and has an on-site bakery, gourmet deli, and catering section with a wide selection of prepared salads, sandwiches, and meals. The place is always busy. Inside, a few of the employees smile big when they see her and say, "Hello, Ms. Hargrove." As she walks through the aisles, she gets a few doubletakes and shy smiles.

But Cheryl doesn't stray from her mission, mentally preparing her menu as she shops. Will Natalie be in the mood for hamburgers or hotdogs, steak or chicken? Maybe salmon. That would be lighter and healthier. Potato salad, macaroni salad, couscous, orzo, green salad, or five bean salad. Cheryl picks two. She's hosted many meals for her niece and knows what she'll like. She also knows that Natalie is trying not to overeat.

After making food choices for dinner and the next few days, Cheryl goes to the checkout and calls Mario while standing in line. "Almost done," she says into her cell. She pays the cashier and helps the bagger stuff her three reusable sacks, then declines his offer to carry them out for her. She wheels the cart outside to the loading zone, where Mario is waiting next to the Town Car, trunk open.

While Mario loads the trunk, Cheryl steps toward the

passenger door. Before opening it, she hears, "Are you Cheryl Hargrove?" She turns. A man is walking toward her from the front of the car.

Despite herself, an automatic smile brightens her face. She looks at him and says, "Hello," but, almost at once, regrets the warmth of her greeting. The man is approaching fast. A ray of sunlight glances off a diamond stud in one of his earlobes, a sparkle that matches his excitement. "I watch *Plain Justice* every week. I'm crazy about that show!" He reaches into his back pocket and digs for something. "Can I get your autograph?"

Mario's head bobs up from the trunk. In two blinks, he's on the man. "Hold it there!" A Neanderthal arm springs out straight from his body into a flat-palmed warning.

The man halts. His enthusiasm crumples. "Just want an autograph." He's holding a small notebook with attached pen.

"It's okay, Mario." Cheryl smiles at her driver. Smiles at Mr. Diamond Stud. He's harmless, isn't he? "I'd be delighted to give you an autograph."

"Wow, thanks!" He hands her his notepad.

Without asking his name, she signs a page of notepaper and draws a happy face next to it in lieu of personalizing the message. She feels safe with Mario at her side, but she's anxious to get going.

"Thank you, Miss Hargrove!" The man is chipper again, but when Cheryl waves and turns away from him, he uses the moment to give Mario a subtle scowl.

A bit shaken, Cheryl gets into the back-passenger seat and locks the door. What's wrong with her? Things like this never used to rattle her. Mr. Diamond Stud is an overeager fan, nothing more. Maybe all the needless drama with Hunter this week has put her on edge.

Looking out the window, she sees that a few onlookers have gathered. The autograph seeker waves the notebook, beaming with pride at his accomplishment. She feels the vibration of a big thud as Mario forcefully slams the trunk closed. He comes around to the driver's seat and starts the Town Car.

"You oughta choose your fans more carefully," he says, searching for a reflection of Mr. Diamond Stud in the passenger-side mirror. "That guy doesn't belong here."

"What do you mean? He's a person. A fan. Someone who watches the show."

Mario is still looking in the side mirror. "I don't like him. Why would a guy like that shop here? I don't see any shopping cart or groceries."

"He didn't go inside yet. Just drive, Mario." But she glances back too, over her shoulder. As Mario pulls out of the parking lot, Mr. Diamond Stud is still standing with a few of the onlookers, talking up a storm.

Natalie's lime green Volkswagen Beetle with the Vassar College sticker on the back window pulls into the driveway an hour after Cheryl gets home. Caitlin has been sitting on the ledge of the bay window, pretending to play with a dolly as a cover for her real game: keeping an eye out for her cousin. She sees the VW and squeals with glee. "Tally's here!"

Cheryl and Caitlin go outside and down the sloping front walk to the driveway. Natalie steps out of the car to their hugs and kisses. Cheryl grabs her niece's heavy bookbag, and Natalie hefts her little cousin into the air.

"Ugh," she grunts, "you're *way* too big for this." She puts her down again.

"Piggyback!"

"Okay. We can try that. Here." Natalie sits down on one of the wide, deep steps on the front walk and lets Caitlin climb onto her back, then grabs her thighs. Caitlin drapes her arms around her neck and presses in close, catching Natalie's hair underneath as she stands up. "Ow! Lean back a little." With one hand, the other hand still on Caitlin's thigh, Natalie pulls her long hair up and slings it in front of her shoulder. Cheryl helps. As they walk to the front door, Caitlin buries her nose in the thick, sandy-colored softness. Certain people in the family, those who know, have said that Natalie's hair is identical to Evan's, back in the day—when he had any.

"You smell so good, Tally!"

"Not me. My shampoo."

"You always smell like that. It's you."

Inside, Natalie squats, puts her cousin down, and kneeling at eye level, tells her, "Ride's over."

"That was so fun. I love you, Tally." Caitlin throws her arms around her neck, kisses her cheek, and runs off.

"Caitlin's love is fleeting but real," Cheryl says. "Come on. I'll get you some lemonade." They walk into the kitchen.

"Where are Renee and Mario?"

"Sent them home." Cheryl puts two glasses on the counter-top where her cell phone announces itself with a loud vibration against the surface. She touches the screen to look at the text message. "Let me edit what I just said. Mario has gone home but he's forever with us. That's him, reminding me to set the house alarm tonight. He also said it three times before he left."

"He worries about you."

"That he does." She gets the lemonade from the fridge.

"Everywhere you go, people recognize you now. It's so exciting."

"Not always."

Natalie picks up the undertone and looks at her aunt hard. "You look worried too."

"Not at all!" Cheryl laughs and ducks her head as she pours the lemonade. She didn't mean to inject foreboding into this conversation. "It's great to be recognized, but some fans can be a little annoying."

"Like what? Tell me some things they do."

"They can be very persistent in asking for an autograph. Like a man today, at the market." Cheryl hands her the glass.

"Describe him. What did he look like and what did he do?"

"I see I'm being interrogated by a cognitive scientist."

"I'm just curious."

"Okay. I was about to get into the car when he asked if I was Cheryl Hargrove. He walked up quickly, came very close, and was trying to get something out of his back pocket. Mario jumped in the way and said, 'Hold it there, buddy,' right when the man pulled out a notepad. I told Mario it was all right and signed the paper. The guy was so excited, he didn't want to leave. I wasn't about to hang out with him, so I got in the car."

"What did he look like? What kind of hair and eye color? How big was he?"

"Details, details." Cheryl thinks for a moment. "Hmm. This is hard."

"See what I went through? I bet you were a little nervous. It affects your perception and memory."

"I remember a few things. He was about my age, mid to late forties. He had three days of stubble on his face and a diamond stud in one ear. He looked like an aging hippie."

"Oh, but that's not a description. The 'hippie' part, that is. It's an opinion or a judgment. Or maybe your definition of a social classification."

"Everyone knows what a hippie looks like."

"He had long hair?"

"Actually, it wasn't too long."

"See? We have different opinions. 'Hippie' isn't a description. That's like when I asked Cee Cee to describe this man we saw, and she said he looked like a 'hard-working father.' It's an assumption based on his physical looks and what he said and did and how her own background and experiences influence her judgment."

"What man are you talking about?" Now it's Cheryl's turn to be curious, and she's glad to turn the conversation away from Mr. Diamond Stud.

"This man we saw on campus. On Monday. Kind of like what happened to you, coming on too strong. He was suddenly behind me, asking about Vassar. He said his daughter was thinking of applying. It was almost night, kind of dark outside. I told him to come back when the admissions office is open, but he said he couldn't visit campus until after work."

"I'd say that's where Cee Cee got her impression that he was a 'hard-working father.' What did the man's daughter say?"

"She wasn't with him."

"That's strange."

"I thought so too. And his eyes were unusual. See? I'm also giving an opinion because they're hard to describe. Deep-set eyes with a kind of dead or vacant look."

"He creeped you out?"

"A little."

"You thought he was giving you a line."

"I was worried about that, and it didn't help that Cee Cee was acting so friendly. After he was gone, we talked about it. I remembered way more details about his face than she did." Natalie looks off into the distance and shrugs. "But it didn't matter."

"Why not?"

"Turns out I was wrong, and she was right about him."

Cheryl sees the depth of Natalie's disappointment in herself. She takes this stuff so seriously! "Why do you think you were wrong?"

"We saw him again on campus this morning. He said he took a day off work to come back. He was smiling and so happy that he recognized us—just like that fan who wanted your autograph! But he looked a little different. His eyes are actually light brown, not dark and empty like I remembered. Just goes to show you how so many things affect your perception, like the time of day and perspective and mood."

So much in life isn't what it seems.

Cheryl nods in agreement, wanting to understand her niece's intensity and drive. Wanting to reach out and grab this lovely young woman and shake her and hold her close and whisper in her ear, "Relax. Live. Enjoy." Instead, Cheryl says, "But why do you think you were wrong? Just because he looked a little different in the light of day…"

"He was with his daughter! He introduced us. She's a junior where I went to high school." Natalie shakes her head, as if disappointed in herself.

Cheryl sidles up and puts an arm around Natalie's shoulder. She refrains from suggesting that it's never wrong to be wary or careful, realizing that she hasn't been the best example of prudence and caution in her own life. She also refrains from giving her niece a full bearhug. Something about that would come too close to justifying the depth of Natalie's unfounded despair. A simple squeeze on the shoulder says, *I love you, and that's all that matters.*

Aunt Cheryl did exactly what she said she'd do. At eight o'clock, she sent the two girls to their rooms.

Of course, Cheryl went into Caitlin's bedroom to read her a bedtime story. Everything in there is white lace and pink fluff. A dream world of unicorns and princesses. But that's not all. The décor also features images of female astronauts, scientists, divas, athletes, mathematicians, lawyers, and businesswomen of all shapes, sizes, and colors.

Natalie did notice, during their conversation about the man on campus, that Cheryl stopped short of praising her for being distrustful and cautious in dealing with him. Natalie's mother would have said something positive about her behavior to reinforce it, but Aunt Cheryl is different. She's carefree, and sometimes, nearly blind to life's perils.

When it comes to her daughter, however, Cheryl is cautious. She's protective of Caitlin, doesn't show her off, and doesn't even like to be seen with her in public unless it's absolutely necessary. To poke a few holes into this protective shell, she lets the world into Caitlin's living space, decorating her room with images of places and people from all over the globe and reading her stories about them.

In a way, Natalie's a little jealous. But when she enters her own girlhood room down the hall and shuts the door, she soon forgets that this is now the home of Cheryl and Caitlin. A step into this bedroom is a step back in time. At Natalie's insistence, Cheryl has preserved the room like a museum exhibit, a little cocoon full of her high school accomplishments, hopes and dreams. Mementos, photos, and awards cover the walls and shelves. Debate Team, Honor Roll, Stone Ridge HS Swim Team, prom photos, yearbooks, stuffed animals, a photo of BFF Maggie, arm-in-arm with Natalie, on Spirit Day. A bulletin board with dozens of hand-annotated photos of friends, each one cut into a shape: a heart, a circle, a daisy, a trapezoid, a cone. A photo of Natalie in cap and gown, with Mommy and Daddy on graduation day, formally displayed in a silver frame.

Only two years have passed since high school, but the mental images are smudged and fading, mere memories of memories, reinforced by these artifacts. How fast things change! Perhaps the day will come when she clears this room out and puts all this stuff into storage, in recognition of her new life. A more serious life.

But not yet.

Natalie's trip down memory lane, the one she takes every time she comes "home," lasts only a few minutes. She sees the trip for what it is. A short-lived distraction but useful. Cheryl did the right thing, luring her out of her dorm room and back home today. This is exactly what she needs. An intermediate step between college and living with her parents this summer. A grounding, a reminder of who she was, social to the nth degree, always with friends, her way of forgetting moments of self-doubt. A reminder of who she is now. Still social but reined in, struggling to make sense of things, a resolute student of cognitive science, single-minded in her mission to become a scholar in the field.

She's in a good spot at school, ahead of schedule. Most of her classmates seem to be scrambling, but Natalie's on top of her assignments and knows the material cold. She's ready for final exams. This term paper is nearly finished, but there's always room for revision and clarification. The theme is objective reality. She's focusing on the incongruities between so-called "facts" and subjective perception, exploring a hypothesis that objective reality does not exist. She's using several case studies in the required reading, but ultimately, she keeps coming back to examples in her own life.

It's eight fifteen when she powers up her laptop and gets underway. She finds areas in her analysis that need expansion and explanation. The concepts are so elusive. By ten thirty, her paper has grown from twelve to fifteen pages.

She stops typing and takes several minutes to read the entire paper. She's hardly aware of the house around her. All is quiet, so different from her residence hall at school, and even the library, with the ever-present background noises. In the dorm: voices, laughter, music, doors closing in the distance. In the library: footsteps, whispering, papers rustling, computer keyboards clacking, chairs scraping the floor.

Her paper is polished. She supports every assertion with

examples and sound reasoning. She's read it twice through, once to herself and once out loud to the room, or rather, to her photo of Maggie, which stares back at her from the wall over her desk. Maggie goes to a college in Virginia. They got together a few times last summer but haven't seen each other or talked since then.

If it's that easy to fall out of touch, it's possible they were never truly BFFs in high school. She loves her memories of Maggie and the things they did together. They were so close, weren't they? But nothing lasts forever. Events, interactions, and emotions occur in a nanosecond and are gone. Nothing lasts at all, except in the mind.

Maybe she'll find out if Maggie is back home this summer. They can create new nanoseconds together.

The digits in the lower right corner of her screen say 10:44 PM. Natalie turns off the desk lamp, leaving her laptop screen the only light in the room. She gets up from the desk and goes to the window overlooking the backyard. There's a moon tonight, and she can see the shapes of trees, the railing of the deck, and the outline of Caitlin's play structure.

So quiet. Caitlin must be asleep, and maybe her aunt too. Natalie should go to bed. But it's too early for that. She'd rather see if Cheryl is still up. They could talk. Despite this new life of ideas and theories that Natalie has carved out for herself, she still loves to talk. And talk and talk. They talked without pause, from four to eight o'clock today, and still there's more to say.

She opens the door and peeks into the dark hallway. Is Cheryl in her bedroom or downstairs? No light from the crack under her closed bedroom door. She's either asleep or downstairs. The door to the bathroom is open, and the nightlight illuminates the hall enough to see the way.

Natalie goes to the top of the stairs and looks down at the foyer. She needn't turn on a light. It isn't pitch black. Cheryl has left some of the outside lights on, the one at the head of the driveway where it meets Dovecote Lane, and the one at the side of the house, over Natalie's VW Beetle parked next to the garage door. The light seeps into the house around edges of curtains and blinds. There may also be a low wattage lamp left on in the living room. Mario is always telling Cheryl to keep lights on when she goes to bed.

Natalie starts downstairs. After two steps, she hears a rattling noise. Stops and listens. Nothing. Silence.

Down a few more steps, the rattling starts again. It's coming from the back of the house.

More rattling, growing in urgency. It sounds like—

Whoot, whoot, whoot!

Natalie jumps at the sudden noise and retreats backwards up the steps. Behind her: "Tally!" Cheryl is rushing down the hall in her shorty PJs. She doesn't look sleepy at all. She must have been awake.

The alarm blares intermittently, and now the telephone starts to ring.

Cheryl is next to Natalie at the top of the stairs. In a raspy whisper she says, "That's the alarm company. Wait here!" She takes a step down, and Natalie says, "No," in a rasp of her own. "I'm coming."

"Mommy!" Caitlin, hugging her dolly, is coming toward them from behind. "What's that noise?"

Cheryl turns to Natalie. "Would you please…"

"Sure." Natalie picks up Caitlin in one easy swoop. It's not like before. The girl doesn't feel heavy at all. Both their hearts are beating fast. Cheryl creeps to the bottom of the stairs and answers the phone in the hallway. She gives the passcode and says, "This is not a false alarm… No, no, we're okay… Thank you." She hangs up, goes to the keypad near the front door, and punches in a code. The alarm stops. "Everything's okay," she calls up the stairs. "Wait there. I'll just go check."

A minute passes. Two minutes. Caitlin is talking incessantly in a sleepy voice. "Where's Mommy? What's she doing?"

"Let's just wait and see." Natalie is scared and doesn't know how Cheryl could be so cool.

It seems like a very long time, but Cheryl eventually re-appears at the bottom of the stairs. "Coast is clear," she calls up. "Come on down."

Natalie puts Caitlin down and holds her hand as they descend the stairs and follow Cheryl into the kitchen. Cheryl has turned on the outside light over the deck. Natalie focuses on the glass French doors that open on the deck. "Just a sec." She grabs the European-style door handle and wiggles it up and down. "That's what I heard."

"Makes sense," Cheryl says, but nothing more. Opening her eyes wide, she looks at her niece, lifts her eyebrows, and gives a subtle nod in Caitlin's direction. That protectiveness. *Let's not say anything more in front of the little one.* Nothing to indicate that someone was trying to break in through this door. With another subtle nod of Cheryl's head, Natalie sees what she's indicating, something else awry. The intruder bumped into a chair on the deck and tipped it over while making a getaway.

Cheryl picks up Caitlin and holds her close.

"What happened, Mommy?"

"The house alarm went off. That's all. We're not sure how it happened." A half-truth.

"Is it broken?"

"We'll find out, honey. Some police officers are coming pretty soon to check and see if it's working."

And check on a few other things, no doubt. Through the window on the other side of the kitchen, they see the flashing red lights of a police cruiser. A minute later, the doorbell rings.

14 »   THREATS

DANA'S FIRST REACTION is anger. How could Cheryl wait so long to call her? It's Sunday morning, more than a whole day after an intruder set off the alarm.

And why didn't Natalie call? Another sign of the growing distance between them. When Dana resolved not to be a helicopter parent, she didn't mean to sever the cord completely. Natalie should know to call her mother about something like this.

With cell phone to ear, Dana glances at Evan, sitting across from her at the breakfast table. When he heard Dana's reaction to Cheryl's news, he raised his eyebrows at her, as in, *What happened?* Could he have gotten a call from Natalie about this and not told her? Not possible. The silences between them have been long, but this is something he would have mentioned.

Dana gets up and walks to the easy chair in the living room to continue the conversation with her sister.

"It wasn't a break in," Cheryl insists.

"So, he didn't get in. This time."

"Yeah, and that's why I have an alarm system. Everything turned out okay. No need to go ballistic."

"You were lucky. Some intruders wouldn't stop at the sound of an alarm."

"This one did, but it isn't stopping Mario from turning this place into Fort Knox. Yesterday, he got a security company over here at the crack of dawn. I'm now the proud owner of a video surveillance system. Make sure you wear your lipstick next time you come over. You'll be on camera. I've held him off for now on the ten-foot electric fence around the property. I'm not going there. No way."

"Well, too bad you didn't get the video camera sooner. We would know who was trying to break in."

"Mario is floating the idea that it was a man who asked for my autograph that afternoon at the market. He made me give a description of him to the police." She laughs.

"What?"

"Your daughter prepared me well for my interview with the police. Unwittingly. I was telling her about the man, and she tested my perception and memory of him. She is *so* into this!"

"Tell me about it."

"When I described him, she pointed out that I wasn't giving factual observations but a judgment or an opinion. She compared it to the way her friend described a man who took them by surprise on campus."

A small jolt of alarm. Another incident Natalie failed to mention? "What man?"

"Just some guy asking about the college. A father of a high school student. It seemed odd he was alone, but then they saw him again with his daughter. Turned out to be totally nothing. Just like my autograph seeker. Nothing to worry about. The guy was a little intense, but no way was he a burglar. I mean, follow me home and wait around for hours until it's dark? Come on."

"He didn't have to follow you. The whole world knows where you live. It's on the Internet."

"I'm not going to move, Dana. This is your house as much as mine. No one can see it from Dovecote Lane anyway. It's private."

Only the mouth of the driveway is visible; the house is shrouded by a dense thicket of bushes and trees at the front of the property.

"It's a safe neighborhood. No break-ins anywhere. I've never had a problem."

"Until now."

"You too, in all the years you lived here. No break-ins, no problems. Nothing worse than teenage pranksters with Crazy Foam on Halloween."

"Did the police dust for fingerprints?"

"Yeah, but they haven't gotten back to me about it. The only clue so far is something a neighbor saw, a couple doors down. She turned on her outdoor lights and came out on her porch when she heard the alarm. A car drove past her house, toward the main road. She couldn't say much about it except that it was a very old model, not in the best shape, and 'didn't belong' in the neighborhood."

"Could have been a coincidence."

"Could have."

"There could have been other cars the neighbors didn't see."

"Could have. What are you getting at?"

"Maybe the intruder is someone you know."

Cheryl sighs. "As in the one person you have in mind."

"You said you were going to talk to him. What happened last week? Did you go over to his house?"

"Yes. I told him he couldn't see Caitlin anymore. We argued, and I said I would sue him. He didn't take it very well, and then…"

"What did he do?"

"Got a bit irate and physical. Mario had to rescue me."

"Cheryl!"

"It wasn't that bad. But he kept calling me after that. Daily in fact. Tuesday, Wednesday, and Thursday. Meanwhile, I was getting the court papers together and had him served on Friday."

"That could have been the tipping point. Have the police questioned him?"

"They went over there. His brother vouched for him. Says he was home all night. I really don't think it was him. He's a little scary when he doesn't get what he wants, but he's no psycho, and he's no fool. He wouldn't break into the house in the middle of the night."

Dana doesn't agree. She starts to say something and stops herself. Cheryl has an answer to every question. She looks on the sunny side and finds the positive in every situation, the humanity and goodness in every person. It's not a bad way to be, but it always worried Dana, from the moment Cheryl, at age nineteen, moved to Manhattan, when Dana was twenty-six, just starting her law career in the DA's office.

The silence lasts only a moment until Cheryl fills it with chatter meant to be reassuring. To herself. To her sister. Lulled by the pleasing sound of her sister's voice, Dana glances around her clean, contemporary living room. The furnishings are sparse but comfortable, the color scheme a mix of medium tones, misty fog, walnut, taupe, caramel. A few original paintings on the walls, nothing overly expensive, artists she and Evan discovered upstate while vacationing. The most prominent piece is a square painting with a cubist flair. Against an ivory background, squares and rectangles and trapezoids in shades of gray, burgundy, and rust overlap in a deliberate pattern teetering on the brink of chaos.

Life does not fit neatly into boxes. People are capable of anything.

Cheryl pauses for air, and Dana says, "Be careful," nothing more.

Too carefree? Vulnerable? Her beautiful little sis Cheryl and niece Caitlin, the sweet baby girl. Dana's own baby girl, Natalie, now a young woman.

"Be careful" won't go very far. Mere words are no protection, and Dana takes no comfort in faith. God bless and watch over them? Of no use. Maybe she'll give Mario a call. He seems to be quite persuasive.

When the mosquito is buzzing incessantly around your head, you can't think of anything else. When it's suddenly gone, there's no memory of it ever being a problem.

That's how it's been for five or six days now. Forgotten, with a subconscious thought: The dean fixed the problem. Did she contact the family? Evan doesn't know. But whatever she did, the result is satisfactory.

Out of sight, out of mind. Until now.

What the hell is this? Another reportable incident. And this time, Prescott has gone too far.

The strange-looking letter in the afternoon mail, addressed to Professor Goodhue at the law school, has no return address, but the message easily identifies the sender. It's another demented cry for help from his troubled student.

One mistake. One judgment. Ruin a life.

The meaning of the words jumps out from the page. Prescott's mistake: He missed the makeup midterm. One judgment: Evan gave him an incomplete. Ruin a life: Prescott's. The "I" instead of an "F" is a beautiful gift, but the boy doesn't see it that way. He's obsessed with ruination.

What a strange note. Examining it, flipping it over and back again, Evan is baffled. Why did Prescott use an old typewriter? Is the kid an antique collector?

As doubts form in Evan's mind, his cell rings. The display says "Travis." He answers and asks, "How's the studying going?"

"It's going okay. My first exam is tomorrow. Contracts. But, Dad. Something weird just happened."

At home that evening, they put off dinner, place Evan's letter on the dining room table, and pore over it, standing next to each other. This is not a conversation made for sitting down or relaxing in any way, shape, or form.

"I was sure that Prescott sent this. The message fits his situation exactly. But then I compared it to the essay he gave me and started to have doubts. If he's going to send me a letter like this, why not use the same computer he uses to type his schoolwork?"

"Because it isn't from him," Dana says.

Evan knows that look. When Dana is sure of something, she's sure of it. "What's your theory?"

"It's from the same person who sent *me* a note. The typing is very distinct."

"You got a letter like this today?"

"About a week ago."

"Oh." Evan tamps down a new wave of frustration. He could ask why she didn't mention receiving an anonymous letter, but there are so many things she doesn't tell him now that it's fruitless to analyze. This is the new norm with them. He's going to fight it, and fight hard, but this isn't the moment for that fight. They've got a new enemy to face together. "What did your letter say?"

"Suzy Suburbs gets Man One. Berto Barrio gets Murder."

"Sounds like you memorized it."

Dana's face twists into a small grimace-smile. She isn't admitting or denying that she's worried about the letter she received.

Evan doesn't need long to think about the memorized message. "It's a reference to Suzette Spinnaker. What else could it be?"

"That's what we think."

"So, the letter writer is also trying to get to you through your family. If that's so, why didn't he or she mention Suzy in my letter? And why is the note tailor-made for Prescott's situation? Travis's note also fits Prescott."

Evan brings up a photo on his cell phone. Travis snapped

two pictures and sent them to Evan. One shows a disturbing letter he received, and the other shows the envelope it came in. The photos aren't the best quality, but the paper and typewriting are unmistakable.

Evan puts his cell on the table. They stare at the words: *Child of Privilege. I could have been you.*

Dana looks back and forth between the cell phone and Evan's letter. "It's obvious they came from the same typewriter. Your message fits Spinnaker more than Travis's. The 'mistake' could be Suzy's defense at the trial, which was kind of a hybrid between self-defense and mistake. She claimed she never intended to kill Connor. The 'judgment' in your letter could be Suzy's judgment of conviction that's 'ruining' her life. Travis's note could also be about Suzy. He's being compared to her. Travis and Suzy are both children of privilege."

"Then why does the mystery person say, 'I could have been you'? It sounds like a disgruntled Prescott to me. When he saw us together at lunch, he made a snide comment to Travis like, 'Oh, so you're the Goodhue kid.' Really nasty."

Dana swipes the screen to the photo of the envelope. "It's sent to Travis at his dorm." She shakes her head. "This is outrageous. NYU shouldn't be giving out personal information."

Evan picks up his phone. "I don't think that's the case, but the alternative is almost worse to think about. The letter writer could be stalking us. It's easy enough to follow Travis around. He has three places on his daily itinerary. His dorm, the law school, and Ginger's apartment downtown."

Evan is still holding his cell with the envelope on the screen when a call comes in. He glances at Dana before answering. "It's Travis."

Into the receiver, he says, "Two calls in one day. I'm honored."

"It just got really weird," Travis says.

"Can I put you on speaker? I'm with your mom."

"Sure."

Evan touches the icon and sets the phone on the table. "What's up?"

"I'm with Ginger, having dinner. She got a letter today too, at work. She thought it was from one of her clients who's a little off. He's been accusing her of —"

"Just a sec." Ginger cuts him off.

"Hi, Ginger," Evan says. "Tell us about your client. We're trying to figure this out."

"I can't tell you what he said to me. It's confidential. The therapist-client privilege."

Evan gives Dana a knowing look. Ginger is reluctant to divulge client confidences even though, apparently, she has already told Travis. But then, that's to be understood. Evan and Dana always share everything, don't they? Rather, they *used* to share everything, back when full disclosure was as vital to them as eating and breathing.

Ginger's right, of course. And whenever Dana and Evan shared confidential information from work it wasn't always professionally permissible, but there were bigger things at stake. Mutual support, legal advice, physical protection. The law sometimes treats a married couple like a single person. The marital privilege protects the sanctity of their communications. Does that privilege extend to a young couple planning to move in together? This thought, the last in a split-second flash of thoughts, makes Evan smile in spite of himself.

Dana says to Ginger, "If you can give us the context, it might help."

"Okay. The problem we have is about my personal experiences and qualifications to be a substance abuse counselor."

"Okay, and…"

Travis cuts in protectively. "I'll take a picture of the letter and send it to you. The weird thing is that it looks just like my letter. Why would the same person write to both of us? It doesn't make any sense. My note came from Prescott, but Ginger's must have been sent by that guy in her group therapy session."

"Your mom and I have been brainstorming, and we think your note isn't from Prescott. We think, maybe, someone else wrote it."

"Just send us Ginger's note," Dana says. She's impatient, anxious to solve this mystery. Immediately. "We'll figure it out and let you know what to do."

Sure. They'll figure it out.

"Okay," Travis says. "I'm hanging up now and taking the picture."

A minute later, Evan receives the photo. He enlarges it on the screen. They stare at it. Same kind of paper. Same typewriter.

These words stare back at them: *I've been there. You haven't.*

Evan shakes his head. "I don't see anything about Suzette Spinnaker in this one."

"But we can guess why the kids think this came from Ginger's client. He must have accused her of not being qualified as a counselor because she's never been an addict."

Evan nods in agreement. "Right. If it's her client, he's telling her that *he's* been through it, and *she* hasn't. That message has nothing to do with the Spinnaker case."

"But it isn't her client. Don't you see?"

"It's our person. The same person."

"It doesn't seem to be about Spinnaker, but we shouldn't limit ourselves to what the writer left out of Ginger's note. The writer has a personal agenda. This person said to me, 'Berto Barrio gets murder,' and now he tells Ginger, 'I've been there.' Berto Barrio is either the person or a pseudonym for the person who wrote these. Or maybe a friend of the person who has this agenda."

"If it is, what does he get out of telling Ginger that she's never been convicted of murder? Or that she's never been to prison?"

They lapse into silence for several seconds. The puzzle is only getting more complicated.

Finally, Evan says what they're both thinking. "Trying to get to you through your family. Even through Ginger."

Dana nods in agreement.

"One thing is clear," Evan says. "Our stalker is very clever, coming up with messages that relate to things happening in our personal lives."

"Clever, yes, but worse than that, he's done his homework. He knows who we are, the places we go, and the people we contact. He's watching us."

Another pause. Suddenly, they talk at once: "Maybe…" and "What about…?"

Dana speaks first. "You called it, Evan. 'Our stalker.' I don't think Travis imagined him."

"The man he saw in the deli and again that evening."

"There's a good chance it's him."

"I wish I could remember the guy."

"And what if… No, that doesn't seem possible. Could the same man have gone up to Cheryl's house?"

"It's a stretch. That would take a huge effort."

"Not impossible. We have to get something more concrete from Travis. More details about the man's appearance."

"He already gave us quite a bit, remember? Middle-aged, the hair, the nose, the clothes, some other things."

"Let's call him tonight. The longer we wait, the less he'll remember."

"Dana. He's got his first exam tomorrow."

"Is that more important that our safety?" She stares at him hard. "He has time to eat dinner with Ginger."

Evan does *not* want to call their son again. Wants to give him his few hours with Ginger. Does not want to burden his mind with this any more than it already is. Travis is at the start of the most important week of his school career. He already gave them a description, and several days have passed. That was last Tuesday. This is Monday. What more could Travis possibly remember? And Travis hasn't seen the man again since then, as far as Evan knows.

"Tell you what," Evan says. "I'll write down every detail I remember about the description and call Travis tomorrow, after his exam, just to confirm and see if he remembers anything else. I'll try to catch Ginger too, separately. But for now, let's give them their time together." Evan will work all this around his own schedule. He's giving an exam to his students tomorrow morning.

"Right. Ginger saw the man too, didn't she?" Dana's face softens and she gazes into the distance. "Okay, then. Okay." She looks at him to ask, "Can you fit that into your schedule and call me during lunch break?"

Her question signals some consideration, a small thought of him. His schedule. "Yes." Dana, he knows, has much more on her plate. "You have a heavy day on the bench tomorrow."

"You said it. I can't cancel."

They seem to be done with this conversation, despite the lack of resolution. The air around them vibrates with nervous tension. They're still standing next to each other at the table, a few feet of space between them. Now would be the right time for a hug. Closeness. Reassurance. If they were the way they used to be together.

He looks at her and inches closer, touches her shoulder lightly. She gives him the same grimace-smile she gave him earlier. Her vibe is pensive, walled-off, but cordial. *Please*, says the body language, *just give me some space. A lot of it.*

The wheels are turning. "I'm going to have to get some people on this," she says and walks away.

15 » *VENDETTA*

DANA HASN'T SLEPT well and worries it will affect her concentration on the bench this morning. After discussing the letters with Evan last night, she spent another hour puzzling over the problem, coming to a decision that she needs to enlist the help of a few key people. People who know her past. The more she thinks about it, the clearer it is that the stalker is a person from her days as a prosecutor.

Targeting her family? It's a personal attack, driven by a personal motivation. A deep-seated grudge, an obsession, a vendetta. Payback for something Dana did or is perceived to have done.

It's unlikely that she attracted this enemy in the year and a half that she's been a judge. In that time, the news services have run a few negative op-eds about her, but nothing sensational. She has presided over many felony cases, resulting in guilty pleas, convictions, and a few acquittals. A handful of defendants charged with murder pled down to manslaughter, but Spinnaker and Underwood are the first defendants who've taken their murder cases to trial in her courtroom.

The first anonymous letter mentioned one of those controversial murder cases, but only by way of comparison, making a social statement about class and ethnicity. *Berto Barrio gets Murder.* Free speech? Abstract social commentary? Maybe the writer is a political activist, a radical revolutionary, or a random nutjob.

None of the above. He's an individual with a personal agenda, as shown in his message to Travis. *I could have been you.* And in his message to Ginger. *I've been there.*

Their stalker is Berto, or a friend or relative of Berto, whatever his real name may be. And Berto "got murder." They're dealing here with a murderer or his friend. He or she. Slim chance it's a she.

How many murderers has Dana prosecuted? A number does not come to mind. She never regarded her cases as numbers but as human beings. She will have to comb through two decades of her career, from the time she was promoted to the homicide chart in the Manhattan DA's office, through her years as a bureau chief supervising homicide ADAs, and subsequent years as elected District Attorney of Westchester County.

Time to pull out the old case files. But she doesn't have access to them.

Last night, when the enormity of the task hit her, Dana spent the rest of the evening on the phone. She texted the people she works with every day, her staff and Captain Rankel. That part was easy. For people from her past, the effort was more involved. She had a list of several names. One name, Detective Aurelina Vargas, was scratched off the list as temporarily untouchable. Some of the phone numbers were out of date. Luckily, after getting the correct numbers and leaving messages, the two most important people on the list called her back. She hadn't spoken with them for a long time, so they had some catching up to do. By midnight, Dana arranged a meeting to be held today at one o'clock, during her lunch break in the trial.

After the phone calls last night, her nemesis struck. Insomnia. An optimistic estimate puts her total sleep time at three hours, with a soaking night sweat thrown in for fun.

Bleary eyed, headachy, and on edge, Dana walks into Henny's office at nine. He looks entirely too perky. "We're on board for one o'clock, Judge. Zola, Captain Rankel, and me. Anyone else you need to be here?"

"I'm expecting Gilbert Herrera and Indigo Raines. Please make sure you're in the office a few minutes in advance to receive them. I won't need you in the courtroom."

"Okay." He's jotting notes. "So that's six people altogether."

"We can fit around my conference table."

"Will do. I'll get the space ready while you're on the bench."

Dana can rely on Henny to provide the creature comforts. Six water bottles, coffee service at the ready, maybe even some cookies in the center of the table. "Water is probably enough. Don't need to overdo it."

"Judge." He looks at her like she's lost her mind. "It *is* lunchtime. We can't send them away hungry. I'll get a few finger sandwiches."

"Okay, Henny. But don't forget the most important thing."

"What's that?"

"Photocopies of all the anonymous letters, a set for each person."

"Of course."

Dana's head still pounds when she calls a long lunch break at ten minutes to one. They'll reconvene at two thirty. It's been a hellish morning, trying to stay focused on Quince's questioning, Grimes's objections, and Lina's testimony.

In the robing room, Dana removes the black layer and shrugs into a light business jacket. She takes a few extra minutes in front of the mirror before going to Henny's office to greet her guests. Her heart is pounding from the frazzled state of fatigue and tension she's created for herself with the help of an unknown stalker.

On top of everything else, the past is flooding relentlessly through her brain. Gil and Indigo are the two law enforcement professionals she worked closest with for big chunks of her career. They're exceptional at what they do, and more than that, she loves them dearly.

And maybe they love her too. How could she ask for better friends? Very busy people, but they've dropped everything to come help her on this. She's asking for their help as a personal favor, a matter with no official obligation attached. Last night on the phone, they needed no time to think about it and made no excuses.

Gil: "Anything for the Dane."

Indigo: "Didn't I always have your back? Let's find the scumbag and bring 'im down."

The mirror is not so friendly. A strand of hair is loose and threatens to fall from Dana's twist at the back of her head. She smooths the bubble, pushes the strand back, and pins it in place. Disheveled, borderline, close to paralysis. She could turn to stone right here, a fixture in a hidden recess of the courthouse, never to move again, but her eyes are moist, a sign of internal heart and flow. She blots the corners with a tissue and looks at it. Little spots of wetness.

Straighten up. Take command. We're going to talk about it and devise a strategy.

Dana walks out of the robing room into her office and sees that Henny has set the conference table with small paper plates, napkins, water bottles, sets of photocopies at each spot, and an appetizing tray of sandwiches and cookies in the middle. A side table holds soda choices, ice, a fresh pot of coffee with cups, real half and half, and sweeteners. Hopefully someone will eat something. She has little appetite. This isn't a party. But when she opens the door to Henny's office, she can't help bursting into a sunny smile.

She needs only an instant, a single image of Gil and Indigo

together, to complete the movie in her head of what they've been doing these last few minutes while waiting for her. They're tuned into an exciting tale of criminal pursuit, engrossed in rapid-fire tall talk, or rather, Indigo is talking up a storm while Gil listens, nods, and occasionally injects a well-placed expletive or facial expression. He's a man of few words and decisive action. She's a woman of many words and equally decisive action.

Indigo dwarfs everyone in sight, physically and vocally. Six feet tall and solid. A rich voice and a unique brand of verbal acuity. Formerly the confidential investigator to Westchester County DA Dana Hargrove, Indigo is currently the Chief of Police, City of Mount Vernon.

Gil has aged in a nice way. In his early sixties, he's now the most senior detective-investigator on the Manhattan DA's Squad. Undercover work has fallen into a distant past, so he's gotten rid of that greasy little ponytail and unkempt appearance. His hair is cut close to his head, thinning, almost full gray now. The pock-marked face with the strange, asymmetrical features gives him a distinctive and distinguished mien instead of the scary, mobbed-up look that was once his pride.

Gil and Indigo turn away from each other and give their eyes to Dana the moment she walks in. Gil's mouth twitches up into one of his signature crooked smiles and he shyly accepts her hug and kiss. Indigo, to her credit, shows impressive restraint and, in deference to her seniors, waits patiently before pouncing on Dana with a bearhug. "It's Madame DA, all grown up! Where's the black robe, sister?"

"I didn't want to intimidate you."

"No worries here. I paid all my parking tickets!"

In the midst of the small talk, Zola enters though the door connecting her office to Henny's, and Captain Len Rankel enters through the door from the public corridor. Introductions are made. Meanwhile, Henny has been standing behind his desk, nervously rocking, toes to heels, trying to catch the judge's eye. She tells the others, "Go on into my office, everyone, and grab a sandwich and something to drink. I'll be right there." As they file out, she pulls Henny aside. "What's up?"

"We got another letter in the morning mail." He pulls the letter and envelope out of the folder he created for mail from the public on the topic of *People v Suzette Spinnaker* and lays them on his desk. "I made copies for everyone."

Dana leans over the desk surface to examine the letter. The typing is distinctive and unmistakable. Two lines, separated by a carriage return, stare back at her.

The first line: *"I didn't mean it." "That's okay, Suzy."*

The second line: *"I didn't mean it." "Fuck you, B.B."*

"Quote marks around each sentence," Dana says.

"Like a conversation."

"Like two conversations. One with Suzy, and one with Berto Barrio."

"This doesn't look good, Judge."

"Another one to add to the list, Henny. Let's see what everyone thinks."

In Dana's office, the lunch plates have been filled. Indigo holds the top spot for number of calories on her plate, followed in descending order by Captain Rankel, Gil, and Zola. Dana guesses that Indigo ordered the seating arrangement. In an act of deference, she reserved the seat at the head of the table for Judge Hargrove, facing Gil on the opposite end. Indigo and Captain Rankel sit on one long side of the table, and Zola sits next to an empty chair for Henny on the opposite long side.

Indigo, food in mouth, extends a hand in Dana's direction, indicating the place reserved for her. Around a mouthful she says, "We don't have to stand up, do we, Judge? This is damn tasty."

"Len, did you forget to say, 'All rise'?"

"Sorry, Your Honor."

"Then you don't have to arrest her."

"Especially not while I'm eating." Indigo takes another large bite and talks around it. "Grab some food, Judge. You look peaked."

Henny takes a quick look at his boss and knows she isn't going to eat. "How about a ham and cheese, Judge?" He uses the tongs to put a sandwich on her plate and sets it in front of her as she tells the group, "Enjoy your lunch while I bring you up to speed." Henny passes out copies of the new letter.

It takes Dana about ten minutes to summarize the state of things. She gives the background behind each photocopy: the first letter to her, the anonymous three-page letter full of vitriol against Suzy, the letters to Evan, Travis, and Ginger yesterday, and the letter that arrived today. Dana explains why her husband and son thought their letters were sent by Evan's troubled law student Prescott Covington, and why Ginger thought her letter was sent by a belligerent client at her substance abuse clinic. Dana also lays out Travis's description of the man he saw twice in the same day last week.

Floating in the back of her mind is the incident on Dovecote Lane. She isn't going to mention it, when Indigo, having cleaned her plate, pipes up, "What about the break in at Cheryl's?"

"That isn't in your jurisdiction. How did you know about it?"

"I've got my sources. Anything Hargrove in Westchester, they call me. Force of habit."

"It doesn't seem related."

"All due respect, Your Honor, we can't rule out anything hinky involving your family right now." Indigo sends one of her big laughs into the room. "Didn't mean it that way of course. No skeletons of *any* kind in the Goodhue-Hargrove closet."

"No, but you're right. Let's throw that one into the mix. The police didn't recover any usable fingerprints or other clues. It remains a mystery whether the person trying to break into the house on Friday was a random burglar or someone targeting Cheryl, either the father of her child, or perhaps a mentally unsound fan." A knot of emotion invades Dana's throat. She clears it and says, "Natalie was in the house at the time."

Mild looks of concern pass over the faces of her staff. This is the first time that Henny, Zola, and Captain Rankel are hearing about the incident at the judge's former Westchester home.

Time to get this on track. Dana throws out the theories. "Best case scenario, there's no physical threat. The attempted break in and the man Travis saw are unrelated coincidences. The letter writer has a social or political agenda and is using my family to pressure me into giving Suzette Spinnaker the max because she's a, quote-unquote, child of privilege who already got a break. Or the writer is a friend of the victim, Connor Davidson, and that's the motivation for pressuring me into giving her the max. The person who wrote the three-page letter identifies himself this way and could be using the other letters as additional subterfuge and pressure."

Dana can't help noticing Gil's raised eyebrows and skeptical grin. She knows that face.

She goes on. "Worst case scenario, this is a personal vendetta against me. The letter writer is someone I prosecuted. He was convicted of murder. He's dangerous. Not only is he sending the letters, he's also following my family around. Between these two scenarios are hundreds of variations."

The laconic Gil can stay silent no longer. "Always go worst case. Don't want to miss anything."

"As an investigative strategy, but what's your gut instinct, Gil?" So many times in the past, Gil's gut instincts saved her life and reputation.

"Sorry, Dane. Worst case. Murderer. Dangerous. Could be Hispanic, but Barrio might be a ruse. His defense was justification or accident. He lost at trial. He did a long stretch and he's out, or he's still in and his friends on the outside are helping him."

A pall descends over the table and lingers.

Dana says, "My sense is that the list is very long if we include every person sent up for murder, still incarcerated or not, every ethnicity and socioeconomic class. We could shorten the list to Hispanic ex-cons who've served their time. But you're right, Gil, we could miss someone. The letter writer uses 'child of privilege' inconsistently. He first implied that he wasn't in that category by setting up a contrast between Suzy and Berto. Then he tells my son, 'I could have been you,' implying that he's also a so-called 'child of privilege' who didn't make it. One thing we do know, Berto Barrio isn't his real name, right, Zola?"

All eyes go to the judge's law clerk. She nods. "I researched the name and a lot of possible variations. Humberto, Roberto, Heriberto, Egberto, and more. Also, variants of the last name. I found no one named Berto Barrio convicted of murder. There were two murderers with similar names, but they weren't linked to you, Judge. Their cases were in different counties. There *is* one thing, though..." Zola hesitates, with a sheepish look on her face.

"You found something else?"

"Not in my research. But a minute ago, when you mentioned the attempted break in and the man Travis saw, I remembered something. I didn't tell you before because I thought, well... This seems less likely now, but I thought I imagined it. The day we got that first letter, I left the office late after doing research on Berto Barrio. It was on my mind. I was walking past the Tombs and I heard a voice behind me, very close. A man's voice. He said, 'Berto Barrio,' in kind of a loud whisper."

"Did you see him?"

"No. I stopped and turned around, but no one was behind me. There were people all around and ahead of me, but I couldn't be sure it was one of them. I really thought I imagined it."

"In light of everything that's happening, I don't think it was your imagination." Dana stops short and sucks in a sharp breath. This is too much. Dana and her family are the logical targets, but now she shoulders an added burden. Whatever she's done to anger this person is putting her staff at risk too. "We're all going to have to keep an eye out," she says. "No more late nights. Make sure you're on a busy street, never alone." Dana turns to Rankel. "Len. Have you seen anyone? Anything out of the ordinary?"

"No, Your Honor. My team is on the lookout, but so far, no one suspicious in your courtroom or the hallways. I've alerted the NYPD and put extra security on you and your staff here in the courthouse. You can be confident of one thing. Anyone who comes in through the public entrances goes through screening. If this man gets inside, he'll be unarmed."

Indigo takes the cue and can't resist. "When there's a will there's a way, my mamma always said. Murderers are a creative bunch. A belt, a piece of rope, a key fob, a cell phone. Two hands. Can't chop *them* off at the door."

Unfamiliar with Indigo's wry sense of humor, Len is put off. He looks askance at the large presence, sitting next to him. "No guns, knives, explosives, or bludgeons are getting in. Pretty hard to kill with a key fob."

"Can do some damage. How many entrances to the building besides the public doors?"

"Six," Len says, still a bit miffed.

"Never have any problems with people slipping in with employees, avoiding security?"

"Happens all the time," Dana says. "If I wanted to bring you in through the judges' entrance, I could do it, and your concealed piece wouldn't set off any bells and whistles. But we trust the judges and their staffs to use good judgment."

"We have security cameras at every entrance," Len says. "I work with the people monitoring the cameras. We've had a few incidents of undesirables getting in, but it's been worked out.

We're double cautious now, with these threats to Judge Hargrove." He looks directly at Dana. "When you have it, I'll need your list of suspects and their most recent mug shots."

"Thanks, Len. That's what I need from you two," looking at Gil and Indigo, one at a time. "I didn't keep records of my cases, and Zola's research covers only published case reports. Not every guilty plea and trial disposition is reported. Gil, I need someone on the inside to access the Manhattan DA's case records and get my full case list with dispositions. Same up in Westchester, Indigo. Once we get the list with NYSIS numbers, we'll check their incarceration status. Can you do that for me?"

"On it already," Indigo says. "I can have that by tomorrow."

"Same here," Gil says.

"And I know this isn't foremost on your mind, Gil, but would you humor me and look into this three-page letter? It's very caustic. The person who wrote it drops clues to his identity, things like when he was at MIT with Suzy and Connor."

"My pleasure." But his eyes are twinkling.

"Thank you. I'm so grateful for both of you! Top of your heads, who comes to mind as the person behind this?"

"Batman's crazy enough to do this," Indigo says. "Got twenty-five years, so he's still in, but he could be paying some of those musclemen at his old gym."

An unforgettable murderer. Perry Rigger, the bodybuilder who bludgeoned his wife to death with a baseball bat. "Doesn't quite fit our anonymous notes," Dana says. "The jury surprised us and came in with manslaughter instead of murder on his defense of extreme emotional disturbance."

"Just sayin', that man likes to fly off the handle. How about Yusuf Nashid, the man who killed his brother? He's either out or close to getting out, and there's a connection to Ginger. Her mother, what's her name, was his attorney."

"Vesma Krumins. She represented Nashid in the civil case.

Evan represented his brother's widow in the lawsuit for reparations."

"There you go. Evan won, and Vesma lost. Vendetta against both of them."

"Possible. But Nashid doesn't quite fit the messages in these letters. He was charged with murder but pled down to manslaughter."

"His paranoid mind could think he was being targeted and wrongly charged with murder because he's *not* a child of privilege. And his lawyer on the criminal case was Hispanic."

"Hernando Ramirez. A really good defense attorney."

"Right. See? I've gotta check out Nashid, and a few others. Like Enrique Trujillo, the landscaper in Cortlandt who killed his boss. Grisly buzzing with the electric hedge trimmer." Shudders go around the table. "Got murder, twenty-five to life. Jury rejected his 'accident' defense. 'I didn't mean to do it.' Fits the anonymous letter."

"Yup. Better check that one out along with the others. What do you think, Gil? Who are the likely Manhattan murderers? A couple of them jump out at me. Guillermo Restrepo, Tyrone Marshall, Ramón Pineda, Grant Spellman."

"Colombian cartel, gangbanger, junkie, and abortionist butcher."

What a memory. No-nonsense Gil, in a few words, sums up these four men, their cases now decades old. "All were convicted of murder," Dana recalls. "And I'm guessing that everyone, except Restrepo, is either out or close to getting out."

"I don't think it's Guillermo. He's in for life, for narcotics trafficking and ordering the murder of your friend's cousin, Domingo, in '88. He's getting old, gonna rot in prison. This game with the letters isn't the cartel's style. If he wanted to get back at Mr. and Mrs. Goodhue, the cartel would've done something a long time ago."

"Evan," Indigo cuts in. "Shouldn't he be here, putting his mind to this? He was with you on a lot of these cases. He knows your whole life, Judge."

Dana blinks. Gulps. Evan. Why didn't she ask him to this meeting? He's giving an exam today, but that was this morning, wasn't it? Why can't she keep his schedule nailed down in her head like all the other details that plague her? "He's in the middle of giving law exams, but he's going to call me soon. Probably before you leave. He said he'd talk to Travis and Ginger to confirm their description of the man."

"I'll need that description, Judge," Len says.

"I jotted it down. I meant to have Henny copy it for everyone." She twists to look over her shoulder. "It's on my desk —"

"On it, Judge." Henny jumps up and goes to the desk to retrieve her handwritten notes.

"I don't think it's the good old abortion doctor either," Gil says, as Henny leaves the room to do the photocopying.

"Spellman was always vocal that he was wrongly convicted," Dana recalls.

"But, same thing. If he was gonna do anything, it would've happened by now. He was paroled three years ago."

"Okay. You're already on top of these people."

"Just things I've heard. The other two, the gangbanger and the junkie, I'll have to check 'em out. Not sure if they've been paroled."

"They both had contentious post-conviction motions. That's why they stick in my mind."

"They're top of the list, but your list is longer than this table. You remember how it was."

"Bodies everywhere." In 1992, when she was promoted to homicide chart, the crack epidemic was still raging. The murder rate peaked in 1990 and stayed near that level for five years, finally starting a decline in 1995, going into a dramatic improvement with the new millennium.

Gil continues to reminisce. "Homicide detectives and lawyers were working their asses off. The Colombians were still king, but everyone was into it. Processing, selling, or using, or all three of the above. I can find plenty of names on your list, people likely to make a statement about *el barrio*."

"Okay. Whoever you come up with, the prime suspects, send recent photos to Len and me. I'll show them to Zola, just in case, right?"

Zola nods.

"You might remember seeing the person on the street. And we've got to show them to Travis and Ginger."

"Let me run forensics on the original letters," Gil says.

"You think we'll get anything?"

"No stone left unturned."

Dana's cell phone, on vibration mode in her jacket pocket, lets her know that a call is coming in. She pulls the phone out and looks at the screen. "Excuse me. This is Evan." She stands up and walks to the window.

"Evan. Thanks for calling. Everyone's here. What did Travis say?"

Behind her, Henny is handing out the new photocopies.

"He okayed the description. Doesn't remember anything else."

"Good. I'm handing it out now—"

"But, Dana. Something else important."

"What's that?" Behind her, the investigators and her staff are talking sotto voce. She hardly hears them. Evan's sunny voice has slipped under a cloud.

"Tally just called me. She got one of these letters. Today. Picked it up at the campus mailroom."

"How on earth…?"

"She texted me a photo. It's typed the same way. It says,

'Suzy had a Beemer. Natalie has a Beetle.'"

"Oh, my God." Dana's heart is in her throat. Her head pounds, the room swirls around her. She grabs a corner of the desk to steady herself, then finds her voice. "Send it to me."

"I am—"

"Now."

"The minute we hang up—

"Evan, we have to go get her."

"I'll tell her to drive down."

"In her Beetle? The one this man knows about?"

"I'll call the campus police and drive up myself to get her."

"No, I mean, yes, campus police, yes, but Mario is closer. He can drive to Poughkeepsie in less than an hour. I'm calling Cheryl and telling her we're borrowing her bodyguard."

"Okay, all right…"

But Dana has already hung up. She opens her contacts and frantically scrolls through the list, unable to find Cheryl's number with that little round photo, the TV headshot. Where is it? Her sister has disappeared. The phone vibrates with a text from Evan, sending the photo of Natalie's letter.

Suzy had a Beemer. Natalie has a Beetle.

Behind her, distant voices waft through the room, dreamlike. "Judge, what is it?" "You okay?" "Can we help?" "What's going on?" Indigo is by her side, putting an arm around her shoulder.

"I'm okay, it's all right, just give me a minute, please. Natalie got a letter. I have to call my sister."

She can't seem to operate her own phone. As she fumbles on the screen, Len's phone makes a sound. "Got it," he says to the group.

"The letter?" Gil asks.

"Mr. Goodhue sent it."

She hears this behind her back. Evan has every emergency contact on his phone, including Len's. He's taking care of this behind her back, and why not? His wife isn't thinking straight. Evan and everyone else can see it. All her strength and resolve are puddled at her feet, the sleeplessness and dread and tension taking their toll. It's shameful, but she can't seem to help it. She keeps her back to the group while she executes her plan.

Indigo has gone back to the table to look at the new letter. "Let's talk about Natalie," her voice booms in Dana's direction. "Let's figure it out, Judge."

Dana ignores her. She has found Cheryl's number and sees no other option. She wants Natalie with her. Now. Her daughter needs her. It isn't the same with Travis and Ginger and Evan. They're strong, resourceful, careful. A letter for each, a strange man seen twice, a mistake or coincidence according to Travis. All that was different somehow, but Natalie?

Dana makes the call and paces in front of the window as the phone rings in her ear, once, twice, three times, too long. Finally, Cheryl picks up.

"Can't talk right now, Dana. I'm getting ready to leave."

"To go where? I'm calling with an emergency."

"For you or for me? I'm getting out of here. I got a creepy letter today from Hunter. I can't believe that man! Didn't even have the nerve to sign it. I see now what's happening. He was the one trying to break into the house. He's harassing us instead of taking care of it in court like a civilized person."

"Hunter didn't write that letter."

"You haven't seen it. How could you know?"

"Please, just listen to me. Everyone's getting strange letters. Someone is targeting me and the family. Send me a photo of your letter."

"There's no question it's Hunter."

"What does it say?"

"Where'd I put it?" A pause. Cheryl is looking. "I don't even want to touch this thing. He says, 'Solve all your problems. Go to court and lock him away.' That's it. Don't tell me that isn't Hunter. I'm suing his ass. He's talking about the court case."

"I'm telling you, Cheryl, I'm the target. Your letter fits the pattern. It isn't Hunter. Take a photo of it and send it to me. And I need Mario to pick Natalie up at school. She got a letter from this madman. He's watching her."

Dana clenches a fist, her eyes skating the world outside her window. Cheryl doesn't seem to be listening. Fainter, away from the mouthpiece, Cheryl says in a singsong, "Come on, Caitlin. You have everything ready? Oh, that's so nice, sweetheart!" Into the receiver she says, "Gotta go. Mario's waiting. I'm not taking any chances with Hunter in the neighborhood. We can't stay here. Let him come and bang on the doors again! We'll catch him on camera while we're safe in the city. The doormen won't let him up to my apartment."

"You can't go anywhere yet. I need Mario to pick up Natalie."

"Mario? That doesn't make any sense. She can drive down herself. And you have every cop in the world at your beck and call. Mario is mine. I'll send you the letter, but I really think you're wrong about this, Dana."

Cheryl ends the call.

Dana freezes in a bubble of indecision. Slowly, she turns around. Five pairs of eyes regard her with compassion. Friends and colleagues, intelligent, rational people. Their respect is important to her. Just now, she stepped outside her professional shell and displayed the face and voice of a frantic mother. Out of control.

"Let's talk about Natalie," Indigo says again, quieter.

"Yes. Let's," says the judge. She straightens her spine and walks back to the table. In her hand, her phone buzzes. Cheryl is sending the photo of the newest missive from Berto Barrio.

16 »   HOME

FOR ONCE, DANA is home first. No more late nights, she told her staff. They all left at five. A court officer retrieved Dana's car, and she insisted on dropping Henny and Zola off on her way home.

Evan is still at his office, correcting the first set of exams. If he wanted, he could correct them at home. Dana wouldn't blame him if he gave this excuse to avoid her, to delay his homecoming. She's also finding it difficult to be in the same room with herself.

Inside the front door, she drops her briefcase, kicks off her shoes, and sheds her business jacket. She doesn't have the energy to change out of her skirt, blouse, and stockings, but goes into the living room and sits on the couch, the blinds closed, lights out. Still a few hours until sunset, and sunlight seeps in around the cracks, creating a filtered gray ambiance. Shutting out the light is the only therapy for her pounding head and the sharp pain behind her eyes. The ibuprofen she took does nothing but upset her stomach and bring on more flashing.

Cut yourself a break. An accomplishment. Somehow, she got through the rest of the afternoon.

The rational, clear-thinking people at the table helped her through the crisis with Natalie. Dana still isn't at ease, but she agrees with their theory. It makes sense. The stalker can't be everywhere at once. Manhattan, Westchester, Poughkeepsie. How does he know that Natalie Goodhue drives a Beetle? Would a (possible) murderer and ex-con have access to motor vehicle records? No way. How does he know that she attends Vassar? Does he have access to nationwide college and university records? No way. In the cyberworld, the names and ages of Dana's two children can be found without much difficulty, but there are limited ways to find the colleges they attend and the automobiles they drive.

This is what happened. The stalker was at Cheryl's house. The lime green Beetle has a Vassar sticker on the back windshield. He saw the car before he started rattling the handle on the French doors at the back of the house.

Of course. That's not to say that other possibilities don't exist. Could there be more than one stalker? Evan's student, Prescott. Cheryl's ex, Hunter. Maybe even one of Cheryl's fans, someone with a screw loose. Dana shudders to imagine it. But her rational side accepts the most plausible theory, posed by Gil and Indigo. There's only one stalker, and he's based in Manhattan. It's crazy to bring Natalie down to the city. She's safest right where she is.

The man mailed the letters in Manhattan and followed Travis, Ginger, and Zola around the city. He tried to break into Cheryl's house in a northern suburb, and likely drove there in the car that "didn't belong" in the neighborhood. Would he also take a longer trip, further north, to follow Natalie around the campus? It's possible, but not likely. He'd be out of place among college students. New York City is his venue. If Natalie comes to her parents' apartment, she'll be in the same town as their stalker. Not as safe, unless they lock her inside, and they aren't going to do that.

No, they've done the best they can. Local law enforcement is on alert. Indigo enlisted a friend in the Poughkeepsie Police Department, and Evan contacted the campus police. Natalie was with a campus police officer when Dana, during the meeting at her conference table, placed a call to them on speaker phone.

Natalie wants to stay at school, study for finals, and finish the term. Indigo, a strong and loving mentor from Natalie's high school days, advised her how to stay safe. Natalie agreed to go nowhere alone, to stay inside at night, and to limit herself to her dorm, the student union, the library, and the dining hall for the remaining ten days of the semester. It's a house arrest of sorts, but she'll stick to it.

This is the best we can do. The internal mantra does little to assuage the worry. Dana will not relax until this man is found. Self-reproach intensifies her unease. She's surprised at herself. Down on herself. Slightly ashamed of her all-consuming panic about Natalie. Why didn't she react this way when Travis got a letter? Because her son has a confident manner and maturity that Natalie is still developing. Because the situation was slow to build. A single letter to Dana, then a few more, then a stranger, a street person. A coincidence or a mistake, Travis thought.

The troubling facts crept up on them, delaying her realization of their gravity. That's one reason for Dana's meltdown today. But there's more. The threats to her family have awakened her to the changes in her relationship with them. With Natalie, especially. Regret is surging, responsibility is calling. It's all her doing, not her daughter's, and she doesn't feel good about it.

Pulling away from her daughter...*now?* An abrupt change isn't right for a girl who always leaned heavily on her family, hungry for contact and closeness, open to sharing feelings and moments, big and small. Nineteen, vulnerable, making a difficult adjustment to adulthood.

And what about Dana's stage of life? Complicated, self-absorbing, relentless. Fifty-three. Closer to the end than the beginning. There it is, over the horizon, but still a long way off. Years ahead with no children, the energy of youth sucked from the house. Years ahead with one person, a man she pretends to know so completely that there's nothing left to discover. Adjustment to a new professional status and public persona. The constant, useless, extreme physical discomfort. Heat, rising from nowhere, boiling her up to the brink of explosion. Insomnia, tension without respite. A roaming dissatisfaction with the world, its people, the lawyers and defendants in her courtroom, their annoying, predictable habits and whining and grandstanding and bad behaviors. Judgments and prison sentences on her plate, her call, her albatross. A criminal justice system that evolves at a snail's pace and never seems to get it just right. Will it ever get it right?

Children gone. When did they grow up? She misses them terribly and can never have them back. Not in the way it used to be.

Is any of that more important than what Natalie needs right now? No. And Dana is handling her personal list of miniscule crises abominably.

A sound escapes her throat, animal and aching. An involuntary reaction to a vivid image from the past. Their first apartment in the city, sometime in the nineties. Evan comes home, walks in the door, sees her, bursts into a smile, playfully grabs her and pulls her close. Their arms enclose each other in a private world, her nose pressed into his neck. She inhales deeply, his warm, human smell, skin, bristles, the collar of the shirt he's worn all day. The closeness settles and calms her to the core. When was the last time she had that feeling?

"Where's Evan?" Good question, Indigo. Why didn't Dana ask him to come to the meeting?

This is the best we can do. They've done what they can for all involved. They've given safety tips and warnings to Natalie, Travis, Ginger, Henny, and Zola. Young people, sharp, cautious and savvy. Dana will have to trust that everything will turn out all right.

She's lucky to have the personal attention and skill of Indigo and Gil on the case. The NYPD is on alert, but she can't expect a greater level of protection. A couple of strange letters? No physical threats in those letters? A man who might be following them but hasn't done anything to hurt them? This is nothing for the police to get excited about, even for a criminal court judge. Len and his staff will protect her in the courthouse and its immediate environs. She will not get 24-hour police surveillance for herself or her loved ones.

This is the best we can do. If she had the means, she would hire a "Mario" for everyone in her family.

People are capable of anything. *Whatever you're capable of, come and get me. Leave my family alone.* If she were face-to-face with this man, would she be strong enough to say that?

She squints into the grainy grayness, feeling down on herself for being down herself. *Lighten up.* Miraculously, by two thirty this afternoon, she was back on the bench, listening to the continued testimony of Detective Vargas in *People v Underwood*.

Already two full days with Lina on the stand, more to come. The list of People's exhibits is growing. Dana's ruling, allowing evidence from a six-month period and four patient suicides in addition to the two victims, encompasses a mountain of documents and computer records seized from the defendant's medical practice. Detective Vargas will be back on the stand tomorrow for more of the same, testimony and documentary proof of Garth Underwood's depravedly indifferent mindset.

Presiding over this criminal trial is the least of Dana's worries. Yes, she can get annoyed at the attorneys and their transparent games, can find it difficult to balance her bubbling anger at the despicable defendant against her duty to remain neutral. But the trial process is second nature to her, the realm of reason and intellect oddly comforting. She finds satisfaction in the intellectual games of strategy, legal issues, evidentiary rulings, organization and scheduling, movement toward the goal, the verdict. Her control over the process is a welcome distraction from Berto Barrio and the dread, anticipation, and uncertainty he induces. He skulks, somewhere, in the shadows. She waits, not knowing what he'll do next. The trial gives her a break from obsessing about it.

And a break from something worse. The difficult truth she's kept hidden until now: the mess she's making of her family life. Immersion in her professional life is an escape. It fills the empty hours that could be used for stewing over the mistakes she's made in her parenting. Mistakes she's made in her relationship with Evan. She replays every scene of avoidance and subtle insult and dismissal and isolation. She now sees her behavior for what it is, even understands where it originates. She's appalled at herself.

Sheer exhaustion. Her physical state is far beyond mere fatigue, carried to the point of shocked, wide-awake sleeplessness. She has no appetite, no thirst. She sits in the middle of the couch, cutting it exactly in half, even lengths on her right, on her left. The cubist painting stares at her from the opposite wall, its shapes gradually losing distinction with each ticking minute. Her hands are folded in her lap, her legs are pressed together, feet flat on the floor. Immobile, except for the tiniest rocking motion from her waist, forward an inch, back an inch. She breathes shallowly, her heart beating fast near the surface of her chest, making a flutter up in her throat. A quivering shell of air surrounds her. Sharpest are the two points of pain—a knife behind each of her eyes, open wide in the descending darkness.

Minutes. Hours.

Will he come home?

When Evan walks in at eight thirty the apartment is dark. Not a single light is on. He puts his keys and the mail he picked up downstairs on the little table, switches on the foyer light, and hesitates, guiltily.

Hiding is not, has never been, his style. Today, he poured

every ounce of Family Man he possesses into his phone calls and texts. Travis, Ginger, Natalie, Dana. Captain Rankel. The Vassar College campus police. A separate, private phone conversation with Indigo, who gave him the details that Dana would not. He was willing to drive anywhere, to do anything for Natalie and for Travis. For Dana. But the wisest plan, perhaps the only plan, is exactly what they've decided to do: keep to their daily schedules, exercise caution, let Gil and Indigo and Len do their work. He sees no point to a complete disruption of their lives. They will not drop everything, retreat to a bunker, and lock themselves inside. They won't let the stalker win. They are stronger.

So strong that Evan doesn't need to come home? It's not his style.

A few years ago, he would have said that the way Dana has been acting is not her style either. The panic in her voice today, the way she hung up on him, the way she's pushing him aside, time and again. He's grateful for Gil and Indigo, but he should have been there, with them, at that meeting. Last night, he knew that Dana was arranging something of the sort. He waited for her to suggest his participation. Who else knows her life work better? He waited in vain. Why didn't he speak up?

Whatever Dana is going through, it's changing him too. His moments of resolve, his plans to fight for her, to resist this new way they're interacting, seem to dissipate at the edge of action. And now, he's acting strangely, not himself. Why this? Avoidance, procrastination. He postponed his homecoming, not eager for the unpleasantness of the next act of rejection that's sure to come.

A record for him. He read and graded forty out of seventy-five essay exams for crim pro in one long afternoon and evening. Nothing to be proud of on a day like this, with everything that's happening, yet there wasn't much else for him to do. Might as well work, he told himself. He's done what he can for his wife and children, everything he was expected to do, and still, he doubts that Dana will want to be with him tonight.

He lingers another moment in the foyer, looking through the mail. Not a sound. Has she gone to bed already? A pinch of alarm heightens his senses. In a fleeting, terrifying second, he imagines she didn't make it home. He's lost his anchor. She's out in the world, an unknown place, taken or hiding or wandering. The Family Man's pride is a lie. He *hasn't* done everything he can for his family. He should have been here, making sure she made it home safely.

In the next breath, that terrifying doubt is gone. He senses her nearby. Like an intruder, he creeps into the living room and says, softly, "Dana?"

No answer. The light from the foyer does little good, and he's about to flip the switch when he sees a shadow on the couch.

"Evan. Please don't turn the light on. My head is pounding, and I can't bear to have you look at me."

He walks over to her. She stands up, sways and nearly topples, quickly sits down again.

"Dana!" He drops to the couch and puts an arm around her shoulder.

With her head drooping over her knees, she says, "I'm okay. A little lightheaded."

"Have you eaten?"

"No, I'm not hungry." She sits up straighter.

He puts a hand to her forehead, like a parent checking for fever. "I can't see you in the dark. Maybe you need a doctor."

"No, I'm fine. Not *fine*, really, but a doctor can't help."

"This has been too much."

"I didn't sleep last night is all."

"You're probably dehydrated. I'll get some water." He jumps up, runs to the kitchen, returns with a glass of water.

She takes a few sips and puts the glass down. They sit next

to each other in silence. He's not sure if she wants his arm around her shoulder again. "Better?" he asks, finally.

"Yes."

He regards her profile. Even in the near dark he knows this woman, her essence. Her mind is working. Something momentous is about to happen.

She turns to him, her face caught by the faint light emanating from the foyer. Her dark, liquid eyes glow softly. "I don't know where to start. I'm sorry, Evan. Truly, I am."

He could ask what she's sorry for, but he won't pretend. They both know what she means.

She puts a tentative hand on his knee and looks into his eyes. "I've been pushing you away. We could analyze it to death, but excuses won't move us forward. Today, this past week, everything that's happening..." Her voice is breaking. "It makes me see..."

"How important family is."

"Yes. Especially, how important you are to me." She fights to keep her composure and pulls it together for the critical part, the words he's been waiting to hear. "If you'll forgive me, I'm ready to come back, to be a true partner again."

He puts a hand on her shoulder, she lifts her hand to his shoulder, and they pull each other into an embrace, an awkward, side-by-side hug, as close as they can get, sitting on the couch. She buries her face in his chest and starts to sob. He strokes her head and some of the pins come loose, her hair half down and half up.

When her shuddering and tears stop, he pulls a handkerchief out of his breast pocket and hands it to her. "Clean," he says. "No hay fever, no cold germs."

She smiles, takes it, and blows her nose. The fabric of his shirt is soaking wet. In his mind, he travels back to 1988, to Dana's tiny office at the Manhattan DA, the day he saw her cry for the first time. His shirt was wet then too.

"Do you remember," he says, "about two years ago, when I was going through my mini career crisis? I was at the end of my rope. I couldn't stand the thought of another day at my firm. The depositions, the paperwork, the settlement conferences with nasty lawyers, all of it."

She smiles. "You surprised me. My sunny optimist, at the end of his rope."

"I was a different person for a while."

"That you were."

"You supported and encouraged me, even though it meant disruption to the family and lower pay. All for greater job satisfaction. You said the most important thing to you was my happiness. You were there for me, one hundred percent. I want to be here, for you. All the way."

"You are. You always have been. I'm the one who built the wall. I've been rejecting your gifts."

He touches her face, traces a line from her forehead to her temple, her cheek, her chin. He kisses her nose. He laughs a little. "You always had a way with words. If you don't mind, I'll keep that one, even if it's hyperbole. Gifts."

"You *are* a gift, Evan. The greatest gift I've ever gotten. I love you."

"I love you more than anything." His look lingers, and then he sees it. "You're completely wrung out. Exhausted."

She sighs. "I'm so wiped out, I can't move."

"Let's see." He takes a wrist in each of his hands and loops her arms around his neck. "Hold on tight. I can still do this."

"Be careful of your back."

"I have no back problems."

"There's always a first."

"Light as a feather." He puts one arm behind her upper back, one arm under her thighs, gets into a half-squat, and lifts her, then straightens up. "Piece of cake."

"There will be no cake tonight."

"You know what I mean."

As he carries her down the hall, he uses an elbow to hit the toggle on the light switch. "Impressive," she says, and kisses his cheek.

In their bedroom, the hallway light is just enough to see. He sets her down, sitting, on the bed. She makes a slow-motion roll onto her side and curls up in a ball.

He pulls the remaining pins out of her hair and puts them on the bedside table. "Dana. Let's get you out of those clothes."

"You'll have to help," she says into the pillow. "I'm too tired."

Gently, he pulls her up to sitting. Together, they take turns unbuttoning, unzipping, twisting, pulling, lifting, bunching, getting the blouse and skirt and chemise and stockings off.

"Can I wear one of your undershirts?"

"Sure."

He goes to his drawer for an undershirt while she takes off her bra. She holds her arms up, and he slips the shirt over her head. "Stand a sec." He helps her up with one arm and pulls the covers back with the other hand. She falls into the bed and curls up again. He tucks her in.

It's only nine o'clock. He won't be able to sleep yet, and he needs something to eat. But he'll stay with her for now, to see that she's delivered safely into dreamland.

On top of the covers, he lies down behind her, spoons her, and strokes her crown. He whispers in her ear, "We'll fight this together, my love. We'll get through this." It feels good to talk like this again. He hasn't called her "my love" in a very long time.

In return, he hears a word she hasn't used in many moons. "Darling," she whispers. "Thank you. Thank you for everything."

In ten seconds or less, she's sound asleep.

17 » INVINCIBLE

THE NEXT MORNING, Dana is invincible again. Loving and loved, well rested, she's fortified by a big, healthy breakfast and Evan's hug and kiss before he leaves for work.

Mr. and Mrs. Goodhue are in tune again, a team, two sides of a coin. Dana needs no prompts to know Evan's schedule. He's off to an early morning meeting at his firm to consult on trial strategy with a partner and an associate before they leave for court. Then he goes to NYU to grade more exams and hold office hours with students. He doesn't proctor another exam until tomorrow.

Before leaving for the courthouse, Dana calls her children. It's seven thirty-five, an iffy time for young people, but Travis is up and stoked.

"How was the contracts exam yesterday?" Dana asks. The question is a subterfuge for the ones she doesn't ask. Are you okay? Did you see the stalker again or receive another strange letter? She's a mother but no longer a panicked mother. She's a rational mother who knows that Travis would have called if something like that happened.

"It went well. Don't worry, Mom. I'm watching my back. I'll be studying all morning for my torts exam, tomorrow at two. Oh, and your investigator friend called me. Gilbert Herrera. He's coming here to show me some mug shots at eleven."

"Great. He's on the job. You remember Gil, don't you?"

"How could I forget him?"

Interesting. The craggy-faced investigator makes an impression on everyone, even young children. Travis was about eight or nine the last time he saw Gil, very briefly. "He *is* unforgettable, and he's a top-notch detective. Sorry we have to interrupt your studying."

"It shouldn't take too long."

"How's Ginger?" Another subterfuge for the unasked questions. The biggest unasked question is whether the lovebirds can temporarily halt their nocturnal rendezvous to avoid the subway, Travis going downtown, or Ginger going uptown.

"She's fine. I'm not going to see her today or tonight, but we'll talk later. I made sure that one of the counselors at her clinic is with her. He's actually going to pick her up and drive her there in the morning and take her home again after work."

Dana smiles to herself and shakes her head in awe at her twenty-two-year-old son. He knows how to humor his mother, and better than that, his pragmatism and caution are exactly what they need right now. "Good plan," she says.

"Don't worry about us. You have enough to worry about."

An extra brownie point for that. Concern for Mom. "Thanks Travis. You do me proud."

When they finish up, she dials Child Number Two, who likes to sleep late. It's a quarter to eight. Is she up yet?

"Hi, Mommy."

"Hello, sweetie. You sound like you're raring to go at this early hour."

"I knew you would call."

Another opportunity to smile. "You did?"

"You're checking up on me. After yesterday, I knew I'd be getting a lot of calls."

"We'll keep it to no more than once every ten minutes."

"I'm fine. Did you get that sicko letter yet?"

"I haven't seen it, but I'm sure Gil has it by now." As part of his plan to run forensics on all the originals, Gil had a member of his team drive up to Poughkeepsie and get Natalie's letter from the campus police. "So, what are you up to today?"

"Studying. No classes. This is the first day of study week."

"Okay. Study hard and stay safe. Stick to everything that Indigo told you to do."

"I will."

"That's my girl." Is it demeaning to use that word? In this context, Dana doesn't care about political correctness. Tally will always be her girl. "I love you."

"Love you too. You know what?"

"What?"

"You sound different today. I thought you'd be freaking out more."

"I got a good night's sleep. Everything's rosier when you're well rested. But actually, you could be right. I *am* different today."

"Sweet. I don't mind. It's okay by me."

And maybe she'll play out that difference in everything she does today. Why not? It's a good luck day, Wednesday, May 13, the day her family welcomes her back into the fold. She'll pick up where she left off, in the roles she nearly forfeited. Provider, protector, pillar. Loving wife and mother.

Another thing. Enjoyer of life. The external threats to her happiness and wellbeing feel less ominous today. The word "threats" sounds like an exaggeration. Someone out there has an issue with her. Doesn't like her or something she has done. Holds a grudge. Wants her to sweat and worry. She has the best investigators in New York working on the problem. The man will be found and dealt with. Meanwhile, it's a new day to be enjoyed.

He holds no power over her.

She abandons her usual habit and does not call the garage attendant in the basement of her apartment building to request her car. She will not drive to the courthouse today, to the judges' entrance where a court officer always meets her to park the car for her. She's a working woman, a professional, a commuter, one of the millions on the streets of this city. A pedestrian, an MTA customer. Just like Henny and Zola. Just like Evan and Travis. Well, maybe Evan took an Uber.

It's also a beautiful day. Bright blue sky, seventies, no humidity. Flowers and trees abloom in city sidewalk wells. Gorgeous. She looks forward to today's routine, the intellectual challenges of the law and evidentiary procedure. She's a servant of the people. The professional aspects of Dana's life add to her deeply felt contentment, right along with her enjoyment of family and the spring flowers.

Swinging her briefcase, she strolls the four blocks to the subway station at 72nd Street on the West Side. The sidewalks are crowded. She feels slightly reckless but hasn't lost her perspective or turned off her radar. By no means has the stalker left her mind. No doubt, he knows where she lives. He could be on the street, close by, stalking her now. He could be following any member of her staff or family, right now.

But if he's following anyone, it should be Judge Hargrove, shouldn't it? *Leave my family alone.*

The dare plays at the back of her mind. Is that what this is about? Daring him, out in the open? She's strong again, a fierce mother, a lioness. If they were face-to-face, right now, would she have the grit to deliver the dare? *I'm the one you want. Leave them alone.*

Dana has no time to contemplate the level of truth in that fantasy as she deals with commuter reality. Metro card machine, turnstile, underground platform at rush hour. The throng presses around and behind her, shoving her into the subway car packed with human beings of every color, age, height, and shape. In the bowels of the city she's one of them, an anonymous worker bee, jammed into the cracks and crevices between her fellow straphangers.

Emerging from the subway station a few blocks from the courthouse, Dana wonders if she'll encounter any reporters. On Monday, the first day of testimony in the Underwood trial, news vans were parked outside the building. The collective consciousness of the city has already forgotten Suzy, the bankrupt dot-com murderess, tucked away in her twelfth day of lockup. Grant Underwood is the new story in town, a chance for creative journalists to vie for the snappiest nicknames and headlines. The Oxy Don, I'm Bien Man, The Perco Saint. The Doctor Is In, Gulp and Go.

Monday's six o'clock news ran a clip of Underwood's attorney, Pamela Grimes. She recited her usual pat phrases about "Grant's innocence," as she stood in front of the courthouse with her GPS-cuffed client, before he headed back to his luxury Upper East Side apartment for another night of house arrest. Detective Vargas, who had just finished her first full day of testimony before the jury, successfully ducked the reporters on her way out, but they mentioned her in the newscast in appropriately melodramatic tones, while showing a sketch artist's rendering of her in the witness chair. The distorted perspective of the drawing placed her much too close to the pasty, sunken-cheeked Underwood, looking like one of his drug-addicted patients.

Monday and Tuesday were long days of tedious testimony, mountains of documents and computer records entered into evidence as People's exhibits. The press is already bored, and Aurelina is back today for more of the same. Dana guesses that the reporters won't be bothering them today but will return later in the trial when ADA Quince ramps up the drama and emotion.

His prospective witnesses include employees and clients of the defendant, who personally observed the assembly-line operation at the clinic, and family members of the victims, who discovered their loved ones dead from overdosing on the drugs Dr. Underwood prescribed.

As the courthouse comes into view, Dana sees that her prediction proves correct. No news vans. It's eight forty-three when she walks in the south entrance of the Criminal Court building, one of the two public entrances. She passes the security line for the public with its metal detector, conveyor belt, and wand-wielding guards, remembering the days when anyone could just waltz right in. She also bypasses the separate, quicker line for attorneys with proper ID. She's wearing her NYS Supreme Court Justice ID on a chain around her neck, but the security staff do not need to look at it. They know who she is, and they're flabbergasted, eyes opening wide in surprise as she walks up.

"Good morning, Judge Hargrove."

"Good morning, Bill."

The judge smiles at the others and takes her sweet time traversing the enormous lobby, drifting over to the elevator bank. The public elevators. *Are you here, Berto?*

Upstairs in the public corridor, she uses her key card to open Henny's door. She says her good mornings to Henny and Zola and goes to her office. A minute later, Henny announces Captain Rankel.

"Send him in."

Len strides in and gives the judge his sternest look. "I was waiting for your call at the back door when they said you came in the front."

"Sorry, Len. I should have given you a heads-up."

"All due respect, Your Honor, this is *not* the time to be using the public entrances."

She gives him a genuine smile. She simply feels happy today.

"I appreciate your concern. I'm keeping my antenna up, and the security crew in the lobby is very good at what they do."

She sees the thought behind his eyes, the one he isn't going to say out loud: Caution is one thing, stupidity another. "All right, Judge. Be extra careful."

"I'm adjourning the trial at four thirty so we can all get out of here early."

"I like that part of the plan." He glances at his watch. "It's a little after nine now. I'll let you know when the jury and the parties are here, ready to go. Herrera said he'd have some mug shots for me this morning. We'll be checking the halls and courtroom, and I'll show the mugs to Zola."

"Thank you, Len."

After Rankel leaves, Dana's private office line rings. Henny does not pick up or screen calls from this line. Indigo and Gil are among the few people who have this number, as well as her mobile phone number.

It's Indigo. "The three I mentioned yesterday are off the list," she says, and summarizes the results of her search. Perry Rigger, a/k/a "Batman," while in prison, strayed even further into the deep end and was moved to a hospital for the criminally insane, where they keep him heavily medicated. Yusuf Nashid served his sixteen-year sentence and was released to parole supervision this year but never reported to his parole officer, who believes he left the country to join a jihadist group in the Middle East. ICE had a hold on Enrique Trujillo and deported him to Ecuador before he completed his sentence in New York.

"No worries from those three," Dana says.

"They're still evil as sin, so I'm sending the latest prison ID shots to Len, just in case. I'm also about to e-mail you my whole list. All the Westchester cons and where they are. The ten names at the top are the likeliest. If any of 'em jump out at you, let me know."

"Will do."

"And one more thing, Mommy. I'll give Tally a call today and have my Poughkeepsie people check up on her too."

"Sounds like a rock group. The Poughkeepsie People."

"They rock, believe me."

"Thanks for everything, Indigo. I spoke to Natalie this morning and she's expecting a lot of attention."

"That girl!" Indigo lets out a belly laugh. "She always did need the love. Gives it back too."

After ending the call, the receiver rests in the cradle for less than a minute before her private line rings again.

"Dane."

"I've been hearing what you're up to."

"Yeah. I just sent some mugs to Rankel and I'm meeting your son at eleven. I'll try to catch Ginger after that."

"We've told her all about you, Gil. I didn't want her to worry that you're another stalker."

"Hah. Dana Hargrove, always the cut up."

Dana smiles. In her mind's eye, she sees Gil deadpanning that bit of irony. What a wonderful friend! "Send me the photos too."

"The minute we hang up."

"Who are they?"

"A couple of Bred Nation bad guys for starters."

"Stain and Bounce?" Dana will never forget the street monikers for Tyrone Marshall and Brendon Hayes.

"Nope. They're both still inside. These are their gang friends on the outside. They could have arranged these little treats for you, but I rate that possibility very low. A few other killers are higher on the list. They've all been released within the last year. John Sweitzer, Rodrigo Alarcón, Gus McKenzie, and Ramón Pineda. Since you mentioned him, I contacted his parole officer. Anthony Belaggio. Pineda has a job and he's adjusting okay since his release in February."

"As far as Belaggio can tell."

"Yeah, well, we'll take his word for it. For now. Slight chance the arresting officer keeps tabs on Pineda out of personal interest, but I know she's testifying in your trial right now…"

"Yes, please Gil, don't jeopardize my trial. You can't talk to her until it's over. She could finish testifying today or tomorrow, but there's also a chance she'll be recalled later on."

"No worries. I'm just as anxious as you are to slam the Oxy Don."

On her way into the courtroom, Dana stops at Zola's door.

"Len showed me all the photos, Judge. I don't recognize anyone. Sorry!"

"It's okay. We didn't think you would, but it was worth a shot."

"I wish I'd seen who it was. The more I think about it, the more I'm sure I wasn't imagining that voice."

Dana pauses to consider her law clerk's face. In contrast to her own calmer mood today, Zola seems to be unnerved after yesterday's meeting. "Take care and keep an eye out. I'm sending you home at quarter to five. No late nights." She's about to suggest that Zola get an escort to and from work for a while, perhaps her boyfriend. But then Dana remembers that Vadim is studying for his LLM and goes to school in the evening.

Maybe it's better not to say anything. She doesn't want to play to Zola's fears and exacerbate them needlessly. Zola is sensible and will take caution. Even so, Dana would like assurances…

But then, Zola solves her boss's momentary dilemma. "Thanks, Judge. I'll tell Henny to get Reggie to the courthouse at quarter to five. The three of us are leaving together. They're going to drop me at my apartment first, then go on together."

At ten o'clock, the morning session is underway. Aurelina is prepared for another day in the spotlight. She's not sure how much longer ADA Quince will keep her on the witness stand. The past two days have been grueling, but Lina doesn't mind. She's committed to using every lawful means available to shutter the pill mills in town and prevent this particular "doctor" from ever returning to his "professional" duties.

It's been a week since Lina testified at the pretrial hearing, before the jury was empaneled. In a week's time, the defendant, once regarded as GQ handsome, has noticeably declined. Today, his eyes are even deeper in their sockets, and air is circulating inside his suit jacket. The I'm Bien Man needs two things that his house arrest and bail conditions won't allow: a prescription for Ambien to relieve his insomnia, and a shopping trip for a new suit in his reduced size. Lina can barely stand to look at him, but when she does, she projects rational coolness instead of icy vengeance. Her demeanor must not signify a personal crusade. The evidence will speak for itself.

While testifying, Lina frequently looks directly at individual jurors. An even split of men and women, twelve in the box, two alternates on the side. The attorneys and Judge Hargrove did well in picking this panel. All fourteen are still awake and attentive. That could change at any moment, and that's why Lina likes to catch their eyes, one by one, to show her sincerity. She *is* sincere.

This is tedious. Grimes hasn't caved on a single procedure. No stipulations or concessions. She lost her motion, her chance to exclude a lot of this evidence, and now she's playing a game of subterfuge. Defense by procedure, defense by sheer weight of minutia, a cover for the underlying substance, the real truth. The prosecutor and witness, Quince and Vargas, do their best to draw the jury into the big picture without driving them nuts with the details.

At twelve forty-five, Quince isn't finished with Detective Vargas, but everyone's getting antsy for lunch. "Let's stop here," says the judge. "We'll adjourn until two o'clock."

Dana isn't going to skip lunch today. Henny has carefully wrapped and stored the leftovers from yesterday's meeting in their little fridge. The judge sits at her desk with a sandwich on a paper plate in front of her. She's alone, the doors closed. On the wall to her right, beyond the dirty window, the spring day shines on.

No better moment than now to call Evan. Just like old times. There were so many telephone conversations over lunch. Almost every day. But then, besides their mutual interest in the law and the cases they were handling, they also needed to discuss the children.

Raising children takes as much teamwork as running a small corporation. You go in with the ideal of staying ahead of the curve and find yourself in an endless game of catch up, a continual state of adaptation to the children's lives, barely understanding one stage when they've already entered the next. Instead of getting easier, the teen years are harder. More uncertainty. When Travis and Natalie were young, Dana and Evan dealt with illnesses, doctor appointments, playdates, and babysitters. When they were in high school, it was academics, extracurricular hobbies, friends they were hanging out with, online activities, college visits and applications.

Was this the glue that broke down between her and Evan? Their joint project has moved into a phase of semi-retirement. If that's part of it, she will resist. The children still need them, but in a different way. And as a couple, they stand apart from the children, in a union greater and stronger than their role as parents.

Evan is at his desk and picks up immediately when she calls. "What's on the menu today?"

"Leftovers," she says, "but very yummy. I was in no mood yesterday to enjoy the food. What are you eating?"

"The usual."

"Let me guess. A carton of yogurt and a banana that has less than a day before it turns to liquid."

"You know me too well."

She asks about his meeting at the firm, and they have fun, for a few minutes, debating a knotty legal problem in the civil case that Evan's colleagues are litigating. When Evan asks how her morning has been, she tells him about her calls to Travis and Natalie. "I'd love to call them again today. What do you think? Is it too much?"

"How about I call them this afternoon? That makes it one time each, Mom and Dad."

This settles her into a soft landing, back down to her comfortable flotation. No need to bombard the kids. That would be counterproductive. She called them once. Evan will call them both in the afternoon. Gil is going to visit Travis, and Indigo is going to call Natalie.

Dana gives Evan all the investigative updates, describes her morning session in the Underwood trial, and says that Detective Vargas is back for more of the same this afternoon.

"What time will you be home?"

"Hard to predict exactly. I'll leave at about five, but you know how the subway is."

"You took the *subway*?" He sounds just as shocked as Len and the rest of the security staff.

"It's such a beautiful day, I wanted to walk a little bit."

"Right. It *is* a beautiful day. How about we walk together this evening? I'll meet you at the courthouse."

Subtle. Okay. She'll let the men in her life take care of her. Evan can pick her up, and she'll tell Captain Rankel about the new plan. He'll be happy to know that the judge has regained her senses. "Sure," she says. She predicts, however, that Evan will suggest taking a cab when he gets here. Walking and the subway are less fun after a long day at work.

"It'll be about six thirty," he says. "I have meetings with students until six."

Good. Dana can use the extra time. She's behind on her other cases. Zola promises to deliver several draft decisions on motions for her review. They seal the plan and end the call.

A few minutes later, Gil calls. He met with Travis, then Ginger. They don't recognize any of the men in the mug shots. He also reports, "We know who wrote that long letter to you. Richard Theodore Flagg. He was Connor Davidson's roommate at MIT. Flagg left us a lot of hints in his letter, and the paper itself was a help. High-quality bond with a watermark."

"Really? I didn't see it."

"Very faint. The initials of the trading firm where he works. I'll e-mail his professional headshot in case you want to keep an eye out. I'm sending someone to talk to him now. He's a rich sonuvaprick. Before he made it big, he used to party with those Video Junkie brainiacs when they were in the money. From the sound of his letter, Flagg was closer to Connor than Suzy."

"Any chance he also wrote the other letters, just to throw us off?"

"Yeah. I hear they keep old typewriters next to the ticker tape machine down on Wall Street." That deadpan again.

"Right. And the cow jumped over the moon. Anything else, Gil?"

He gives her the status of the forensic analysis. He's been pushing the lab since yesterday, trying to cut the line, and finally succeeded this morning. They've completed the DFO processing for latent prints and came up with a "mess of partials." Gil isn't sure whether they're any good, but he's on it, running them through the database.

"And surprise, surprise. We got a DNA sample. But you're gonna have to wait for processing. Fingerprints are one thing, DNA another. Some people I'm dealing with don't think your secret admirer is more important than the murderers and rapists they're trying to find."

"Too bad for you he hasn't murdered me yet. What kind of DNA did he give us?"

"A single hair, about an inch and a half long, very thin. Inside the envelope to Natalie's letter."

"A good find."

"Guess what color it is."

"I'm on the edge of my seat."

"It's red."

"Bright red like Bozo the Clown?"

"Dane. You know what I mean. Did you ever prosecute Bozo? It's red, like a person with red hair."

"Okay, so, remind me of all the redheads I prosecuted for murder."

Silence. They're both thinking.

"It'll come to me," he says, finally.

But already, it's too late. Gil never needs this long to think about anything. If there were any redheads, he would have remembered them by now.

Ending today's court session proves easier than Dana anticipated. At four twenty-five, Quince says what they've all been waiting to hear: "I have no further questions for this witness, Your Honor."

"Thank you, Mr. Quince," says the judge. "Given the late hour, we'll continue with your cross-examination tomorrow, Ms.

Grimes."

Then, the truly unexpected happens.

Pamela Grimes stands up with a cake-eating grin on her face and says, "That won't be necessary. I have no questions for this witness."

Happy day.

Grimes sits down again, very pleased with herself. Garth Underwood seems mildly puzzled.

Lina doesn't understand at first, and then she gets it. From the start of the trial, Grimes has been interrupting left and right with procedural objections and technical arguments in a sarcastic tone implying that ADA Quince flunked criminal procedure in law school. She's done what she can with this strategy of distracting the jury from the substance of the documents and records, and now, she doesn't want to risk calling their attention to any documents again by letting Lina expound further. "No questions" is the defense attorney's way of saying that three days of testimony and a mountain of People's exhibits are inconsequential, not worthy of the jury's further consideration.

Judge Hargrove turns to Lina and says, "Thank you, Detective Vargas. You may step down." The judge takes off her glasses, and the women exchange a look with the slightest glimmer of recognition, a connection. Lina will not forget to reconnect, one of these days, when this is all over.

Only four thirty on a beautiful spring day, and Lina is free to do whatever she wants. Run some errands, walk in the park and smell the flowers, go home and relax.

Instead, she heads back to the precinct. To work. This is her life. Hard to avoid when the station house is only a five-minute walk away.

But she's in no big hurry. In front of the courthouse she runs into a colleague from an uptown precinct who just testified in another case. They grab coffee from a truck outside and shoot the breeze. A couple of other detectives she's friendly with join them. The party lasts longer than she realizes, but it's still early. She hasn't given up on her plan to get some work in.

She walks into the station a few minutes after five, heads straight for her mail slot, and collects a small pile of papers and envelopes. Not much. Almost every communication comes over the computer now. She finds something interesting sandwiched between an NYPD circular and an invitation to a retirement party. A sealed envelope with a first-class stamp, postmarked from a Manhattan post office downtown. No return address. Her name, the precinct address, and "Personal and Confidential" are typed in an old-style font in faded, irregular ink.

The best hope for the contents is an anonymous tip on one of the many cases she's working. But everything about the envelope screams "hate mail" to her.

Lina is no stranger to the occasional letter from a disgruntled witness or victim or ex-con. Anything sent by an incarcerated felon would be screened by Corrections and mailed in a prison envelope. This one couldn't be that.

This one is from a person walking the streets of New York.

Her mind goes to the anthrax scare of 2001. Everyone was nervous, everything was screened, and a sealed letter like this would never end up in her mailbox. Things have slipped considerably since then. She has no idea if this one was x-rayed or sniffed.

She puts on latex gloves and opens it with a letter opener. Inside is a single sheet of paper, three words and a question mark, typed on the same old typewriter.

She knows exactly who sent this.

Well, maybe not. It isn't always the obvious person. There are proxies and copycats and people with their own agendas who dredge up old cases with emotional baggage and use them to harass. There are people who concoct bogus new "evidence" in sensitive cases that can ruin a cop's career, looking for a chance to blackmail. There are people who do this sort of thing out of base hatred of the police, or maybe hatred of a particular detective, a very effective and successful detective.

But she thinks it's none of these. She thinks it's the person who first came to mind. And it's sad, more than anything else.

Lina doesn't consider this a serious threat, but she isn't one to sit back and wait. She'll run forensics on this paper, and before she goes home today, she'll do a few things to check on it.

She looks at the letter again and whispers the three little words written there: "Who shot first?"

She stares at it, the background noise in the station house fading into nothingness. In her head, she hears that voice again, the man who followed her last week, taunting her on a city street corner.

Bang bang.

18 »   SEVEN SHADOWS

ZOLA IS IN her office with the door open when she hears the electronic beep. The door to the courtroom opens, and the judge sweeps by in her black robe. She hears the judge enter the robing room and close the door behind her, and a minute later, the faint noise of the toilet flushing in the restroom on the other side of the robing room. Then, she hears the equally faint noise of the door between the restroom and the judge's office, opening and closing.

Five minutes later, Zola's office phone rings. It's the call she's expecting. The judge wants her to come in and drop off her work. The judge doesn't like to read on her computer screen and prefers paper. Zola gathers the copies of motion decisions she drafted in eight cases and goes through the narrow passage to the judge's door. She knocks once, announcing her presence, and enters without waiting. This is the way to do it when the judge has called her to come in. If the judge hasn't called first, anyone seeking entry should knock and wait for an answer. It's a matter of courtesy, privacy.

Zola walks up to the desk and hands the draft decisions to the judge.

"Thanks for these. I'll look them over tonight."

A knock, and Henny enters from his door. The judge has called him in too.

"Anything I need to know before you leave, Henny?"

"Here's your updated calendar and a few phone messages, nothing urgent." He hands the papers to the judge. "One of these is from Cheryl. She says you don't need to call back, but she wants you to know that she and Caitlin are at the Manhattan apartment and doing fine."

"Thank you. Okay, you two. Time to pack it in."

Henny turns to Zola. "Reggie is on his way. We'll meet him downstairs."

"Good plan," Dana says. "I'm sorry to put you through all this worry, but it doesn't hurt to be cautious for a while. This is going to turn out to be nothing. Unhappy people have been saying and writing nasty things to prosecutors and judges from time immemorial."

"Have your investigators come up with any leads?"

"They're closing in. We have some partial fingerprints, and maybe even a DNA sample."

Henny and Zola nod but don't make a move to go. They're stock-still, looking at the judge, waiting for something. Perhaps reassurance.

She smiles. "Your concern is duly noted. You'll both get a commendation in your personnel files. I'll be fine. Evan's coming to pick me up later. And the court officers are buzzing around me like the queen bee."

Zola collects her shoulder bag and meets Henny in his office. Together, they walk out the door into the public corridor on the thirteenth floor. People are milling around and spilling out of courtrooms. Attorneys, defendants, spectators, witnesses, and court personnel. Proceedings in the eight courtrooms on this floor are in the process of finishing up for the day.

"This is so bizarre, leaving when people are still here," Zola says. "It's only a quarter to five."

"It's the time of day we're *supposed* to leave, Zolita. Almost everyone does. Sadly, we're employed by a workaholic."

"Takes one to know one."

Henny laughs and answers his ringing cell phone. Zola can tell he's talking to Reggie. There seems to be some confusion about where Reggie should meet them, in front or in back, on the north or the south side of the monstrous Criminal Court building.

They stop walking as Henny tries to concentrate on the call, covering his ear and pressing his mouth to the phone. This is not a quiet place. Any public corridor of this building is a theater of human drama. Has a defendant just been acquitted? Is another one waiting for the jury to come in? Does a mother wail in despair after seeing her son pronounced guilty and led away in handcuffs?

Zola sees a half dozen dramas unfolding around her in the pockets of energy along this corridor. Each one is a mystery, with an unknown story behind it. Her eyes dart from one to the next. In a corner, a middle-aged woman embraces a sobbing woman half her age, holding the hand of an impatient toddler. To Zola's right, an attorney and client stand very close to each other in serious conversation, goosenecked over something in the attorney's hand. Behind her, she hears whoops of joy and laughter. Glancing over her shoulder, she sees three teenage boys high-fiving and cavorting.

By her side, Henny is still on the phone, but the topic seems to have changed. Zola doesn't mind if he needs another minute to discuss whatever he wants to discuss with his husband. She's fascinated and emotionally moved, just standing here, watching people. It's a contrast to her workday in the office, dominated by research, writing, scheduling conferences with attorneys, and occasional visits to the courtroom to watch the proceedings. Every day, she's close to the human drama, yet so far away. The cases she works on have lasting impact on so many lives, but she doesn't always get to see or feel it in a personal way, firsthand.

A voice intrudes into her zone. "Excuse me." A man in a suit and tie is walking up to her. "I have to file these papers by five. Do you know where Judge Brentwood's courtroom is?"

It's right behind them. She turns and points. The attorney thanks her and walks on. Henny says, "Come on. Sorry that took so long. Reggie was still walking, and he had a block to go. He's out front now, north side."

They continue down the corridor to the public elevator bank, as more dramas are enacted around them. Only when they're pushed into the back of an elevator, ten bodies in front of them, does the oddity of the man's question strike Zola.

She didn't get a good look at the folded papers in his hand but assumed that he was talking about filing a motion. It's not unusual for attorneys to drop off their motion papers at a judge's chambers. It's also not unusual for them to try to make a deadline at the last minute before the close of court. But it does seem unusual for a seasoned defense attorney not to know the location of the judge's courtroom where he's filing a motion. By that point in the case, he should have already appeared in the courtroom for an arraignment and a scheduling order.

Was he an attorney? She's never seen him before. Seasoned, was her impression based on his age and how he was dressed. Maybe he's new to the case and was appointed as substitute counsel. Maybe he's taking the unusual tack of filing a motion to dismiss in advance of the arraignment date. Maybe he isn't an attorney at all but a paralegal from a law firm.

Oh well. There are a thousand explanations. It doesn't matter. The elevator doors open on the ground floor, and Zola is glad to be going home and to have a little more downtime than usual tonight. She's been working on a new poem.

* * *

At ten to five, Dana goes into Henny's office, grabs a few case files from his cabinet, and returns to her desk. She leaves the door open, as she always does when Henny isn't around. It gives a bit more air circulation, or the illusion of extra air and space. Her office is stuffy, especially after hours, when the full building HVAC, which is really only a fan, goes into conservation mode. She puts the files on her desk and goes to the AC unit in her window. "Bye-bye," she says to her friend, a cooing pigeon that struts around on the air conditioner. The heightened buzz sends the bird on its way. She takes a moment to glance down at the mess of miniature cars and pedestrians on Centre Street, thirteen floors below.

She's wearing a sleeveless dress today, a summer style with deep pockets in the skirt. The matching jacket has remained on a hanger in the robing room all day. She sits down to read Zola's first draft, consulting the case file as needed. She doesn't change more than a word or two. Damn near perfect.

She hears a faint beep from a key card opening the door from the courtroom into the narrow passage to her office. Then she hears the distinctive sounds of a court officer approaching her door: the clatter of items on a utility belt and the squeak of rubber-soled shoes on linoleum.

There's a loud rap, rap, rap at the door. "Judge Hargrove? It's Len."

"Come in, Len."

He opens the door, and without moving out of the doorway, says, "The courtroom is tightened up. Too bad there's no way to lock this door." He's looking down at the bald doorknob in his hand. "And maybe that door too." He nods at the door between Dana's and Henny's offices. These two doors have no locks on them.

"Maybe we should put some bars on the windows too?"

"I'm just saying it would be nice. A little extra protection."

"The outer doors are locked, Len. Seems like plenty of protection." The only doors in their inner sanctum with locks are the doors to the robing room and private restroom, which Dana can lock and unlock manually from inside. But the inner sanctum is protected from the outside world by electronic key card entry wherever people might be able to get in from the public corridor, through the doors to Henny's office and the courtroom, and through the courtroom door into the narrow passage back to chambers.

Len glances around aimlessly, then closes the door to the passage behind him and walks through Dana's office toward Henny's office. "All right. I'll test the other lock on my way out. I'm about to go off shift. Lieutenant Yankova is in charge, and Officer Delano is here. Give Sheila a call when you go downstairs to meet your husband."

"Will do, Len. I've got Sheila on speed dial." Dana nods to the multi-buttoned apparatus on her desk, the dependable landline.

"Have a good night." He stops inside Henny's office. "Want this closed?"

"No thanks. Please leave it open."

Another aimless look around, and Len walks away, going out into the corridor through Henny's outer door. A moment later, Dana hears the beep of his key card as he opens the door again from the outside. He closes it and rattles the handle a couple of times.

All secure, Len? She smiles to herself.

In her pocket, Dana's cell vibrates with an incoming call. She looks at the screen.

"Hi, Gil."

"Dane." Car horns. Cursing. "Sorry."

"Are you in the car?" She walks to the window and looks out as she talks.

"Yeah. I've been doing a little legwork. Visiting a few parolees. Are you home? I called your cell 'cause I wasn't sure if you'd left."

"Still here. Evan's picking me up at six thirty. Anything new?"

"Nothing solid. We looked at all those partials. None of them are usable. And no one's looked at Bozo's hair yet. Sorry. Maybe tomorrow."

"Whatever you can do, I really appreciate it."

They talk a while longer, reviewing all that Gil and Indigo have done so far and the times that various people have checked on the wellbeing of the "children" today. Dana mentions Cheryl's message that all is well with her. They toss around ideas for things to follow up on and debate the order of the suspects on their list, most likely to least likely.

Suddenly, it all seems like too much. Dana is monopolizing the time of two very important people, the chief of police of a large suburban community and the senior supervising investigator on the Manhattan DA's squad. "Did I say how much I appreciate this, Gil?"

"Let me think." He clears his throat. "We're on the tenth Hallmark moment."

"Don't take time away from your other cases for me."

"Why would I do that?"

No way will she get him to back down now. When Gil starts a job, he finishes it.

They end the call, and Dana notes the time. Five thirteen. She puts the phone in her pocket and stands at the window, not ready to return to her desk. An hour and a quarter to go, and she's already finished three of Zola's eight perfect drafts. She isn't motivated to work on something else after she finishes the other five, and now she wishes that she hadn't agreed to Evan's plan. It's still beautiful outside. It would be nice to pack up, get out of here, and forget about everything. Walk a bit. She should have suggested walking up to NYU to meet him instead of the other way around. Doesn't make sense. All because of a few anonymous letters.

She mentally reviews the day. How bright everything was at the start of it! The euphoria. The little bit of recklessness. That feeling is still with her, but in a tamer form. A rational form. She recognizes now the silliness of the fantasy that played at the back of her mind this morning. What did she think she would accomplish with her adorable, ineffectual backlash? *Come and get me.* Did she really think that openly walking around in a city of millions would magically draw him out of the shadows? That she would lure him to her and away from her family? And if he suddenly appeared, did she think she would be strong enough to stand up to him?

It's been a different kind of day, filled with an underlying appreciation of everything that's important to her. Even now, as she momentarily plays hooky from her desk, she's aware of that difference. There've been so many nights in her eighteen months on the bench when she fervently plunged into the case files after the close of court and stay glued to the desk until seven or eight o'clock, giving all of herself to her work. *Not* giving enough of herself to Evan and Natalie and Travis. How wrong was that? How misguided was that?

Oh well. She can only go on from here. And now, with each minute lasting an eternity, her joy overflows at the thought of being with her husband tonight, like a teenager in her prom dress, waiting for Mr. Popular to arrive. If only the clocks in this city would magically speed forward, landing both hands on the six, digital numbers on 6:30. She'll rush downstairs, see Evan waiting at the judges' entrance, and pull him into an embrace, right there, out in the open, in front of any court officer or passerby caring to look.

Gazing out the window, her eyes glaze over and a smile graces her lips as she daydreams of the evening to come. But a blemish mars the image, a faint electronic sound at her back, announcing the key card entry of an intruder, a court officer buzzing into the chambers of the queen bee.

The next part plays out in slow motion, a delay before the jolt. Dana pivots gracefully, expecting to greet Officer Sheila Delano. She stops abruptly, her eyes seeing and recording, but the synapses lagging, a one-second postponement in the delivery of the message to her brain.

Sheila isn't there. A man in a business suit is in Henny's office. He grabs something from the desk and walks quickly toward her, crossing the threshold, entering, coming close. "Don't make a sound."

The jolt arrives with a sudden intake of breath, almost an audible gasp, but not quite. She understands this much. *Don't make a sound.* She nods and goes into an aftershock. She couldn't speak even if she wanted to. Something is happening to her lips. They're moving, or maybe it's only a quiver. Her throat is clamped shut. No sound escapes.

"Sit down. Over there." He jerks his head toward her desk chair, but she isn't looking at his face. Her eyes are drawn to a silver, sharp object in his hand.

She wants to move, wants to do what he says, but her feet are still glued to the floor.

He grabs her arm, turns her around, pushes her in the direction of the chair. "Go on. Sit. We have to talk."

His push does it, forces her to move. *Yes,* she's thinking. *We have to talk.*

She sits down and dares to look up into his face again. The look confirms her thought, her agreement with what he just said.

Yes, they have to talk. There's a lot to say, a lot to find out because she has no idea who he is. She doesn't know this man at all.

19 »   OUTSIDE

CURIOSITY AND INTUITION won't leave Aurelina alone. A minute after opening the strange-looking envelope, she stares hard at the three-word question, her eyes burning through the surface in search of its underlying significance. To him. What he wants or needs or plans to do. Whether he's sickly obsessive or merely provocative, vengeful or merely heartbroken. Why he hasn't let this go and hasn't moved on. The consequences.

First things first. She's ninety-nine percent sure who sent the letter, and ninety-nine percent sure he was the person mouthing "endearments" behind her back on a crowded street corner last week. But she needs to eliminate the one percent chance that it's someone else. It won't take long, and once she confirms his identity, the next thought is this. If he's following her and sending her letters, he must know that she's been testifying in Judge Hargrove's courtroom. It's a connection she cannot ignore.

Lina goes to her computer, logs in, and brings up the Inmate Lookup page on the Department of Corrections and Community Supervision website. She doesn't know his NYSID number off the top of her head, but his full name and date of birth are forever recorded in her memory. That's enough to find out his status.

The information pops up quickly. Ramón Pineda, d/o/b April 22, 1970. Released to parole, February 10, 2015. Three months ago. He's out, and everything fits. It must be him. *Bang bang.*

DOCCS takes a photo of each newly released inmate in the month prior to parole. Lina brings up Ramón's most recent photo, taken in late January of this year. The face is familiar, close to the way she remembers him. He's still lean, with sunken cheeks and a pear-shaped head, rounded near the bottom where it disappears into his collar. A long, protruding nose. Little gray puffs for eyebrows that rise up in peaks. A shaved head, a couple of days grown in, mostly gray stubble. He's forty-five. A gray wolf.

She reconstructs the timeline using information on the Inmate Lookup page and her own computer file, hoping to find clues to his current state of mind. She remembers the morning she arrested him all too well. July 25, 1992, three in the morning, a steamy pre-dawn in El Barrio. Lina was a rookie, barely a year into the job. She was riding with her partner Sergeant Dean Habberly when they were called to the scene of an armed robbery in progress at an all-night bodega.

Confrontation. PO Vargas discharged her service Glock, Sergeant Habberly did not. A bad ending. Store owner Felipe Bedoya, husband and father of three, shot dead by a bullet from Pineda's gun. Pineda shot and wounded in the shoulder by a bullet from PO Vargas's gun. *Who shot first?* An internal investigation cleared Lina of any wrongdoing. She acted properly in discharging her weapon.

After recovering from his wound, Pineda was held without bail pending trial, convicted of felony murder, and sentenced to an indeterminate term of twenty years to life. Admitted to Green Haven Correctional Facility in February of 1993. Denied parole twice, in 2013 and 2014, before he was paroled this year.

Lina should have known he was out, but she pushed this case to the back of her mind more than two years ago. In 2013, the parole board solicited her comments a few months before his first parole hearing. She wrote to the board, giving her recollections of the armed standoff, the arrest, and the trial, but she remained neutral on the issue of parole. She didn't give an opinion because she didn't have the information to form an opinion. How had he fared in the past twenty years? Who was he today? He was twenty-two when he committed a crime that was driven by heroin addiction. Certainly, he was no longer a junkie. Could he return to the community and be a law abiding, contributing member of society?

The Bedoya family was adamantly, emotionally, and vocally against parole. A mere twenty years for killing a respected, hard-working family man, husband and father of three? The wife and children have suffered. Parole was denied, and the case slipped to the back of Lina's mind. The board did not solicit her views in 2014 or 2015. Once was enough. She had nothing new to say.

On her computer screen, Lina brings up Pineda's institutional record. Model prisoner, no infractions, big or small. After a couple of denials, the parole board must have found that the strength of his institutional record outweighed the family's objections and warranted giving him a chance on the outside.

Then, why this? *Who shot first?* Remorse and acceptance of responsibility are key to winning parole. Pineda must have snowed the board because the three little words on this note prove that he's stuck in a losing refrain, his failed defense at trial. "I didn't mean to fire my gun." He claimed that he fired his gun accidentally when Lina fired first, hitting him in the shoulder. The physical evidence disproved his defense. And ADA Hargrove argued that, in any case, it didn't matter who fired first. Under the felony murder law, the robber is responsible if someone is killed during the commission of an armed robbery. Period. Doesn't matter how it happened.

In 2001, having lost his direct appeal and served almost nine years of his time, Pineda hoped to win his freedom. A lawyer with an innocence project picked up his case and filed a motion to vacate his conviction on the ground of prosecutorial misconduct.

ADA Hargrove allegedly concealed evidence that would exonerate him.

Again, it ended badly for Pineda. His lawyer happened to be an ex-ADA with a double agenda: a jealous grudge against Hargrove and a plan to enhance the creds of her innocence project to win the release of an incarcerated felon dear to her. But the lawyer used fabricated evidence on the motion, and the allegations against Hargrove were disproven. Pineda stayed right where he was for another fourteen years.

Lina assembles these facts and imagines how they might have played on the mind of a beaten man, living in a prison cell for twenty-three years. False hopes of release and a devastating disappointment in 2001 exacerbated his skewed perception. The law is unfair. The murder conviction is unjust. If he didn't mean to fire his gun, and if he didn't mean to kill Bedoya, why is he doing hard time? Decades of his life wasted by an unjust system.

Lina's views on incarceration have fluctuated over the years. She's seen some success stories but many more failures, if rehabilitation is one of the goals. She's come no closer to understanding the formula for surviving the hell of prison and coming out better on the other end. What causes some felons to take the path of remorse, acceptance, self-forgiveness, and redemption? What causes others to take the path of denial, perceived injustice, resentment, and a life of blaming others?

Apparently, Pineda has taken the latter course, and it's sad, more than anything. He's forty-five, still young enough to make a life for himself, and here he is, risking it all with a three-word letter and taunts aimed at an NYPD detective on a noisy street corner. Sad that he thinks he'll get away with it by leaving his signature off the letter and ducking into a crowd before she sees him.

But she knows it's him, and she also knows her duty to report this.

She goes into the system again and finds the name of his parole officer. Anthony Belaggio. She picks up the phone receiver, starts to dial, hesitates, puts the receiver down. Maybe this should wait. She could give Pineda another chance. She might never hear from him again. This could be the only thing up his sleeve. A few words, a pathetic bit of payback to the woman who shot him and got him convicted in an unfair system. A quick tongue-lashing for the small satisfaction of having the last word. And she would be sending him back to prison. For this. A few words. His opportunity to fly straight spoiled by a whim, something trivial.

She thinks again. There are parole violations, and then, there are parole violations. Drinking a few extra beers on a Saturday night? Something like that she could forgive. Taunting a police detective? That falls into the realm of the serious. She cannot ignore it.

She picks up the phone receiver again and looks at the time in the lower right corner of her computer screen. Five minutes to six. There's a good chance she'll catch Belaggio in his office. He's hardworking and dedicated. He cares about his parolees, looks for the good in them, and does what he can to nurture it. Maybe he's too optimistic and naïve, but isn't that better than always assuming the worst in humankind?

Tony picks up, and they exchange brief pleasantries.

"I'm calling about Ramón Pineda. What can you tell me about him?"

"He's doing all right. Lives with his sister. Keeps his appointments. Tox screens are all clean. He got a job working graveyard shift at a homeless shelter. He's a monitor but also does some light janitorial stuff."

"When did you see him last?"

"Ten days ago. But today, after Gilbert Herrera called, I swung by the apartment. He works nights, so I thought he'd be sleeping and I could rouse him, but no one answered the door."

"Detective Herrera? What does he have to do with this?"

"Oh, that's right. He said he didn't contact you because you were in the middle of testifying in Judge Hargrove's trial. She's leery of anything that looks like she's contacting a witness through a middleman. Doesn't want to jeopardize the trial."

A little over-the-top, but that's Dana. Beyond ethical to the point of avoiding anything that could even suggest a bogus accusation of unethical conduct. But wait a minute. Why would anyone think that Herrera was contacting her on behalf of Judge Hargrove? "Is the judge worried about Pineda?"

"There've been some anonymous letters to her and her family."

What?

"Herrera thinks it might be someone Hargrove prosecuted. If you interpret the letters a certain way, you *could* possibly think that Ramón wrote them, but I don't think so. He's been doing so well."

"Tony. I got a letter too. And it's definitely from him."

About quarter after five, Gil ends the call to Dana. He's driving back to his office in the DA's wing of the Criminal Court building, all the way downtown, after a visit to Pineda's apartment, all the way uptown. Traffic is bad. Rush hour. He won't get back until damn near six.

He didn't want to give Dana every detail on the phone. No need to bother her with it yet. He has a few things to check on before he's sure.

From the get-go, Pineda was high on Gil's list. This morning, the first thing that didn't sit right with him was Tony Belaggio's laid-back attitude. Gil has nothing against the smiling fairytale believer, and if everything is A-OK with Mr. Ramón Pineda, he'd like nothing better. But Gil needs to check it out. The anonymous letters raise too many red flags, messages that seem to fit Pineda's story. Tony's "investigation" falls short. A single unannounced visit to the apartment in the morning, when it's practically guaranteed no one will be there. Graciela, an RN at Columbia Presbyterian, doesn't get home until about four. And her brother Ramón, if he's their guy, probably doesn't spend much time at home during the day. He's out shadowing his victims.

Gil got to the apartment at about four thirty and spent some time talking with Graciela in Spanish. She opened up about her brother and showed Gil his room. There was nothing remarkable on the surface. It looked exactly as one would imagine the bedroom of a sixty-seven-year-old woman, their late mother. Graciela said some unsettling things about Ramón, ensuring his spot at the top of Gil's list. But one thing doesn't fit. In such a small apartment, if her brother is typing letters, Graciela should have seen or heard a manual typewriter. She claims to have no knowledge of a typewriter, and Gil believes her.

He almost started searching the bedroom, then thought better of it. It's iffy whether she can give legal consent to the search of her brother's private space, and Gil doesn't want to risk having the incriminating evidence suppressed. Tony, as the parole officer, might have the better legal right to show up for a warrantless search, but Gil needs a warrant. Tonight, he'll call a judge (other than Dana!) to get that piece of paper. He'll also contact the lab about that strand of hair. Even though it's after hours, and even though the lab hasn't gotten to the DNA analysis, he'd like a technician to, at least, look at it under a microscope.

At six, he's back at the office, walking up to his desk, when Detective Vargas calls. "The Dane will kill me if she knows we're talking."

"I know. Tony Belaggio told me."

"You talked to Tony?"

"I got a letter too. Typed. Unsigned. From Ramón Pineda.

I'm sure of it." Lina describes her letter and the incident on the street last week.

"It's him, no question," Gil says. "I'm about to call the night judge for a warrant to look for the typewriter. I also need to contact forensics."

"Good. I'll call Dana. We have to tell her who it is so she can keep an eye out."

"I talked to her forty-five minutes ago. She's in the office working late, until six thirty. Maybe I should call — "

"I'm done testifying, Gil. This is urgent. No way is anyone going to think I'm calling her about Underwood."

"Just watching my Ps and Qs."

"You're off the hook. Go get that search warrant."

"Okay. There's one more thing you should tell the Dane when you call her…"

20 » INSIDE

SHE SITS IN the leather executive-style chair behind her desk, and the man stands over her, holding the sharp, silver object by his side. He isn't pointing it at her, but one quick move could send it into her heart.

"You look confused, Dana Hargrove. Don't you know who I am?"

Her hands clutch the ends of the armrests. Her spine is straight, an alert posture. Her legs are pressed together. Her feet, in low-heeled pumps, are planted on the ground. But her voice still doesn't work. She frowns and moves her head slightly in a way that could mean "no."

"Have I changed that much?" He smiles. "It's been a while."

A synapse sparks a connection, and she recognizes the object in his hand. Henny's letter opener. It's a high-quality instrument made of pewter, very heavy, the handle thick and round, the blade substantial and sharp. Dana appreciates her administrative assistant's many talents: his precision, organization, neatness, and more. He uses the sharp edge of that tool to open all her correspondence without tearing the front or back of the envelope, preserving the information that can be gleaned from the outside. Like the originating post office and date stamp. Henny used that tool to open the letters from this man, whoever he is.

Indigo's voice speaks in her head. *Murderers are a creative* bunch. *A belt, a piece of rope, a key fob, a cell phone. Two hands.* A letter opener. Weapon of convenience. No doubt lethal in the right hands.

"Did you ever, even once, look at me? Take a good look at this face?" With that, he juts out his chin and throws his empty hand up to his face like he's about to slap it. The hand lingers in the air for a moment. "All those days we were together in court. Most of the time, I was over at the other table, sitting down. But you. You got to sit or stand and walk around and put on your show, whenever you wanted. If I even tried to stand up, there'd be someone pushing me down. An armed guard. Kind of like what I might do to *you* if you try to get out of that chair right now."

She's beginning to see through the transformation. The age, the weight, a couple of weeks' growth of facial hair shaved into a semicircle along his jaw and chin, longish thin hair, and the natural-looking color on all of it, his head, beard, and eyebrows, recently dyed, no dark roots. He wears a business suit and tie. Cheap fabric, imperfect fit, an odd color, almost brown, closer to eggplant. Folded papers stick out of a jacket pocket. His nose is familiar, long and protruding, but the pear-shaped face is much fatter, his lower jowls ballooning out over the sides of his collar.

More than two decades ago, she looked into those eyes, very briefly, off and on, as Pineda testified in his own defense at trial. But did she ever really see the man? She's looking at him now. It's the face of a wolf.

A lot has changed since his latest photograph, taken about four months ago. He bears little resemblance to it. She inhales deeply, hoping to calm her pounding heart. "Mr. Pineda." Her voice has returned. She tries to make it strong… "Your parole photo doesn't do you justice." …but the words come out shaky.

"So, you like me as a redhead? My first time. Amazing how good the dye kits are these days."

"It suits you."

"*Guapo, no*? And the suit suits me too, don't you think? I needed some new clothes for this meeting, my day in criminal court. I'm up thirty pounds since I got out. Couldn't eat that crap at Green Haven. My sister, Graciela, is a good cook." He looks down at the jacket and lifts the lapel on one side. "Would have been Brooks Brothers, but they didn't give me that fifty-cent raise on my minimum wage." He laughs bitterly. "I got a BA and a master's in prison, but my résumé got me shit. Cleaning toilets at a homeless shelter."

The harshness of his laugh brings back a memory of his voice and what he said, the last time she saw him. It was 2001, at the very end of the hearing on his failed post-conviction motion, when Gil was arresting his attorney. "My lawyer!" Pineda yelled, struggling against the hold of court officers. "She said she'd get me out!"

Unfortunate that Pineda got caught up in that mess. He was deceived and fed a menu of false hopes, but was any of that Dana's fault? "What do you want from me?"

"We're going to have a long talk. Then we'll see."

"You could have called for an appointment."

Another laugh. "You would have given me an appointment? I like that. No. It had to be like this. I made my own appointment."

"Like this, they'll revoke your parole and send you back."

"They will, will they? You're wrong about that. The fan mail means nothing. The letters can't be traced, and *you* aren't going to turn me in, are you?" He steps closer, lays his free hand on her shoulder, and squeezes it. Her entire body shudders, an involuntary recoil. He's so close, she feels the heat escaping through the openings in his suit jacket. Smells the nervous body odor and bad breath. She tries not to show her revulsion and straightens up quickly. He smiles down at her. "How's that feel? Now you know what it's like to be touched by a man holding a lethal weapon. Touched, like I was, when you don't want it." He takes his hand off her shoulder. "You're not going to move out of that chair now, are you?"

She shakes her head.

"That's a good judge. I'll go sit down, and we'll talk." He walks around the desk and sits in the guest chair, facing her. They're going to talk. They've been talking. Her head is a white buzz of unreality, but she's speaking and making sense. How, she doesn't know, but there've been years of training in the theater of the courtroom, where every performance is fueled by nervous energy, the catalyst for effective persuasion. She needs to give a strong performance here but doesn't know how she'll pull it off, when the pressure is mortal and blinding.

He doesn't suffer under the same weight. He's intelligent and articulate and it surprises her. She remembers a volatile young man, newly weaned from the heroin but still with the mindset of a junkie, the eyes alternately focused and clear, narrowed and spiteful, doleful and downtrodden, glittering and manipulative. The man before her today is well spoken and measured. He has the slower, steadier energy that comes with middle age, a different kind of package for the toxic anger and resentment burning inside.

Her only weapon is intelligence and language. She needs to compete but can't match him while she's fighting the fear. A new shockwave hits with the incongruous sight of this man settling into her guest chair in this office, her place of respect and purpose and professionalism. Her mind can't process the scattershot messages. Escape, control, peril, why, blood, rescue, Sheila, scream, don't, trick him, play him, you're smarter, is this real? Cell phone, in her pocket. She feels the hard, plastic rectangle next to her hip. What can she do with that?

He smiles and says, "This is so worth it. I've been waiting a long time to see that look on your face. How does it feel to be helpless?"

Control is the word, one of the million that flash in her mind. She needs to know more about him to gain the upper hand. "How did you get in?" Perhaps he's concealing another weapon under that suit jacket.

"Like everyone else, through the main door. Oh, but I see what you're thinking. I'm one of the people you put away for murder. Killers don't walk nicely into public buildings. I might have wasted ten officers on the way in. Bodies everywhere."

Was it only yesterday? At her conference table, Dana and Gil reminiscing about the crack epidemic. *Bodies everywhere.*

Pineda could be lying about the main door. He could have used the same key card to avoid security and enter the building in back. But even if he was screened, it's not much of a relief. The letter opener is bad enough. *Two hands. Can't chop them off at the door.* "I meant, how did you get a key card for my door?"

"You should tell your law clerk to be more careful. She puts her card in that little pocket on the outside of her handbag. Very convenient for her. Very convenient for me too. Just slip it out, easy as can be. I've seen her do it a hundred times."

"Zola. Where… What did you—?"

"I didn't touch her." He's enjoying Dana's angst. She isn't hiding it very well, putting on a poor performance in her quest for control. "We had a quick chat in the hallway, that's all. She's probably home by now. Doesn't even know I have this." He pulls the card out of his breast pocket, shows her, and puts it back. "I couldn't pass up the chance. It was too easy. I've been waiting for a day like this."

A day when Dana sends her staff home early, making them easy targets in crowded public areas.

He glances at the open door to Henny's office and over his shoulder, at the two doors on the wall behind him. "Speaking of getting in, who can walk in here, right now?"

"Any of the court officers on duty."

"Who are you expecting?"

"No one." It's half a lie. Sheila might come to check on her, but she's not obligated and might think it's not necessary. Before going off shift, Len would have told her that Judge Hargrove is locked up tight. For the first time, Dana prays for Officer Delano to make an unprompted visit. She usually doesn't appreciate interruptions after hours, when it's quiet and she's concentrating on her work. The court personnel have picked up this vibe from her body language and curt replies whenever they knock on her door. She will never, ever act that way again. *Buzzing around me like a queen bee.* How arrogant that sounds to her now!

Pineda gets up and closes the door to Henny's office. "No lock," he mutters to himself, grabs a chair from Dana's conference table, and places it against the door at a tilt, with the chair back under the handle. He goes to the door next to the conference table, opens it, looks left into the narrow passage, and glances back at her, over his shoulder. "Where's this go?"

"The courtroom."

"Key card entry from the courtroom?"

"Yes."

He walks into the narrow passage, turns right, disappears for five seconds, and reenters her office through the restroom door. "Very cushy. Judge's *baño* and changing room. My prison cell wasn't much bigger than that, but I had a tiny window, way up high." He motions to that imaginary window, then closes both doors and pushes chairs against them, like he did with Henny's door. "Now we can talk." He sits down. "If someone comes in and tries the door, you're going to yell out that everything's fine, and they're going to believe you." He points the letter opener at her and stabs the air.

She stares at it, her mind abuzz with the suggestion that someone is going to come and knock on one of those doors. When that happens, there's no way she can yell, "Everything's fine," and make it sound believable. Or if she manages to pull it off, maybe she can add a few words in code, something they can see through, so they know she's in trouble.

"You're gonna say, 'Don't come in. I'm getting dressed,' or 'I'm on the crapper,' or however you like to say it."

Good one. *I'm on the crapper.* Code for Judge Hargrove has lost her mind. In spite of herself, her lips curl up in a half smile. Immediately, she suppresses it, afraid it will set him off. And it does.

He jumps up and thumps his fists on the desk, the letter opener pointing straight up. The butt of the tool bangs loudly on the wood. "You think that's funny."

"No. I think I'll say, 'Everything's fine.'" And hope they don't believe it.

He backs off and looks at the chair tilted against Henny's door, rethinking his plan. He talks as he rushes around the room. "If they knock, you say you're busy, in a private meeting." Chair removed and returned. "If they come in, you say, 'This is Mr. Johnson, an attorney. We're in a private meeting.'" Two more chairs removed from the other wall and returned to the table. He pivots around and declares, "*That's* what you'll do. Understood?"

"Yes."

"Why do you think I bought this suit? I'm a lawyer." He sits down. "No one in this building knows me anyway. I even passed your main man. The old guy, Rankel. He doesn't know me."

Pineda narrows his eyes at her through a moment of silence, when the only sounds are the hum of the air conditioner and a rhythmic pulsing she can't quite place... It's her heart beating fast and high up in her chest. His sudden agitation has triggered another rush of adrenaline. The blood rushes into the distended veins behind her eardrums in a whoosh-whoosh sound. A hot flash starts in her belly and geysers upward, making a fireball of her head. A trickle of sweat drips down the back of her neck. She levels her own narrowed eyes at him and demands, "Why me and my family?"

"Why, yes, why, why, why? Why did I spend twenty-three years in prison while you had all this?" He waves his arms around the room. "Everything organized and neat and black and white. You and the law books. Doing your job. Following the law." Mocking, "'It doesn't matter what you really intended.' Isn't that what you said? If someone dies, the robber is a killer. Doesn't matter if it was an accident or a mistake or I didn't intend to kill the man. Why would I want to kill that man? Do you think I'm happy about it? But you, no, you were just doing your job, following the law."

"I'm not the only one. Police officers, the judge, the jury. But you picked me and my family."

"Well, that's interesting. I did think about those people. But the jury only did what *you* told them to do. The judge only had the case because *you* charged me, and *you* got an indictment in the grand jury. That policewoman shot me and arrested me and lied about me shooting first. I'd like to have a talk with her too. She's on my list of seven. But it's a little trickier getting close to someone wearing a piece. You don't have a gun, do you, Judge? Maybe I should come over there and pat you down?" He jumps up and takes a quick step toward her. She startles. He laughs and sits back down.

Through her fright, Dana feels sad for him. After all these years, he's still in denial, still claiming that Aurelina shot first. He was high during the robbery, his perception skewed. A bullet from his gun killed Bedoya. He had no defense, regardless of who shot first. The felony murder law is tough. It's been criticized, yes, but this isn't the time for social debate. The law assumes that a killing during an armed robbery is foreseeable, never accidental, a mistake, or unintentional. It's second degree murder, not manslaughter, and certainly not self-defense from a cop on the scene, trying to prevent a tragedy.

"So, you have a beef with me and the policewoman. Not my family. Not my staff. Why all the letters? Even my son's girlfriend. And driving up to my sister's house." His face, the knowing smile, confirms the truth of her accusations. "My family has nothing to do with this."

"Oh yes, they do. Maybe not your staff. They're the icing. Your law clerk was too easy. But your family has everything to do with this. Your sister lives your life on TV. Your husband teaches the law but doesn't change it. Your kids have everything handed to them. That VW Bug. College. Careers. The girlfriend for your boy. He's the same age I was when you put me away."

He pauses to stare at her, looking for a reaction. She keeps a neutral face.

"He's going to be a lawyer just like mom and dad. I could have been him. I could have had a career like that." He searches her face again. "You don't believe me. You don't know anything about me, do you?" He shakes his head. "I was just another perp with a drug problem, stealing money to get my fix. The police came, started shooting. That guy in the store is dead, and *I'm* the one who goes down for it."

His voice starts to break, his lower lip quivering with emotion. "But what did *you* ever try to find out about *me*?" He slams his chest with an open hand. "You know nothing!"

She senses his shame. The aggression is meant to replace the effeminate weeping. This new energy is dangerous. The air is charged and pulsating.

She isn't a psychologist or a mind reader. She doesn't know if it's better to acknowledge his emotions or ignore them, speak or remain silent, look at him or keep her eyes averted. She's operating on pure instinct and intuition. Twenty-three years of pain is bottled inside this man, ready to explode. His foot shakes, sending the jiggle up into his knee and thigh. His eyes glisten with tears, pain, and excitement. A frisson of energy jags his body. This is his moment. He's been planning this, dreaming of it, working the details out in his head countless nights while lying on a hard bunk in a cement prison cell.

Did you ever, even once, look at me? He's punishing her for not seeing him. Is this what he wants? To be seen and heard, known and understood.

She *did* see and hear him, didn't she? Judged him by his actions on that single night in 1992, informed by the evidence and the law. It isn't wrong to view his actions through the lens of the law. But it isn't enough. *It isn't who I am,* he's trying to say.

And then, he starts to explain.

When Ramón grabs and squeezes the shoulder of the woman who destroyed his life, red lights flash and alarms sound. It's ecstasy, making the almighty judge cringe, reducing her to a state of helplessness. Almost too much for him. It's what he's been craving for years. It's what he wants right now, more and more of it, until she's on her knees, begging.

But the bitch is strong, and he's a bigger man than that. He'll restrain himself and prove his greater strength that way. Losing control won't serve his purpose. Since 1992, he's been on a steady path, working on his self-restraint, notch by notch. A twenty-three-year course of self-study in controlled behavior. His state prison record proves his success. In Green Haven, where everyone is out to get you, he dodged and avoided and sometimes just took it, never resorting to violence or verbal abuse. Planning and deliberation propel the Judge Hargroves of the world ahead of everyone else. He's learned that lesson, and now it's her turn to learn from him.

He's no criminal. He isn't a murderer or even an armed robber. He's burdened with a conviction record of larcenies and one "murder," that miscarriage of justice. But the rap sheet isn't him. It covers six months of his life, when he was twenty-one and twenty-two. He's not a perpetrator but a victim, a man who's been wronged. This woman will be made to see it and regret it and change because of it.

They'll talk. He'll make her understand, and then he'll leave her alone. For now. He'll find a new hiding place for his typewriter, keep it handy in case he needs to send her another warning. Fear and uncertainty will keep her from doing anything about their meeting today. He'll see to it. Forever, if he needs to.

This is only the beginning. He'll teach her the feeling of powerlessness. Throw her into a reality she can't control for as long as possible. Make her live in daily subjection, like he did. Helpless, vulnerable, and weak. Frantic with frustration.

That squeeze of her shoulder! He felt her fear. Almost felt sorry for her, but a few extra things are hard to resist. She flinches whenever he takes a step toward her or waves the letter opener in her face. Little signs of his power over her. Confirmation that he's chosen the right way, the only way. Call her office for an appointment? Ridiculous, but he supposes he could have done that. He could have been sitting here in the same suit and tie, having a sedate, businesslike discussion with her, all on the up and up. She'd plant the old guy, Captain Rankel, right behind him, to look over his shoulder in case he tried anything.

Worthless. It would be giving her control over him, all over again.

Frightening her is less about pleasure and more about control. It was the reason he carried a loaded gun with him to the bodega that night. To scare, not to shoot. Not to kill. He didn't want to kill anyone. He was desperate for money. The smack was fucking with him, and if he'd been straight, he would have known not to put bullets in that gun. Hell, he wouldn't have had any reason to rob a bodega owner in the first place.

But that's the smallest part of the reason he's here. Dana Hargrove never took the time to find out anything about him. She can do the same thing to anyone in her courtroom. He can't let that happen. She's no longer a prosecutor recommending sentences. She's a judge with the authority to lock people away for as long as she wants.

In 1993, after the jury found him guilty of felony murder, he was processed like every other convict. A probation officer interviewed him and prepared a presentence report for the judge. The report had a pathetically inaccurate summary of the interview, a single sentence to describe the event that consumed his life:

"Mr. Pineda states that he fell into heroin addiction when he was grieving for the loss of his girlfriend."

ADA Hargrove probably read the report, but that's all she knows about him. He remembers her standing up at the sentencing hearing and recommending the max. The judge showed some compassion, giving him twenty to life instead of twenty-five to life.

Now, eye to eye with Dana Hargrove, Ramón is testing her knowledge. She doesn't believe him when he says he could have had a career like her son. She knows only one thing about him, the crime he committed on July 25, 1992. "That guy in the store is dead," Ramón says, "and *I'm* the one who goes down for it." He's surprised to feel the emotion creeping into his voice, the sting in his eyes. He hadn't planned on it. He hates himself for showing it. He summons the willpower to overcome it. He slams his chest with an open hand. "But what did *you* ever try to find out about *me*? You know nothing!"

She sits dumbly, shell-shocked, because she knows he's right. She judges men for their crimes, discrete acts she plugs into the framework of the law. Words on a page. She doesn't investigate the *people* she's locking up. Is it a millionaire white girl from the suburbs or an impoverished Latino from El Barrio? Why do these defendants act the way they do? How are they the same or different? She doesn't know and doesn't care.

He'll tell her. He'll make her see how uninformed and false her opinions really are.

"What do you know about Roselia Morales?"

A blank look. She hasn't a clue.

"Roselia was a smart and beautiful girl, better than you or me. We grew up in the projects. Tough neighborhood. We were raised by single mothers, but we were doing okay, living at home, going to community college. Big dreamers. We were getting good grades, were going to transfer to SUNY, apply for scholarships, work our way through college, whatever it took. That was our life, Roselia and me. The night she died, November 10, 1991, she was twenty. I was twenty-one. She was on her way home at midnight and walked through the wrong place at the wrong time. Caught in a turf war between crack dealers. Gunfire. The man who killed her was Jeff Thrasher. Now do you remember Roselia?"

Judge Hargrove is pretending to think. "I'm afraid I don't."

"Your office, the Manhattan DA, fucked up the case, that's why you should remember it. Roselia was nobody to your people. Nobody." He stops and breathes. Hargrove's blank look proves what he just said. Roselia was nobody to her.

Damn, this is harder than he thought. He squeezes the pain into his lower gut. He won't break down in front of this woman. He stands up and paces the room as he talks.

"A deal was made with the shooter, Thrasher. Your office wanted his testimony against crack dealers and murderers. He turned state's evidence and pled to assault against the guy he was trying to kill and reckless manslaughter for killing my beautiful Roselia. The sentence for that is *nothing*. The murder charge was dropped. The DA thought that was a fair deal because he didn't *intend* to kill her, did he? She happened to get in the way of his bullet."

He pauses to examine Dana Hargrove's face. Not a flicker. She's too smart not to know what he's getting at, but she doesn't care. Doesn't want to give him an inch. He'll lay it out for her, and he'll say it better than any lawyer could. "Sound familiar? Some people get felony murder when they don't mean to kill anyone. Other people get a slap on the wrist when they *do* mean to kill someone and end up killing someone else instead. Someone nobody cares about. Thrasher got a sweet deal, only ten years. He finished his time, long ago. He's out on the streets now, living his stinking low life."

Ramón halts behind his chair and turns away from the woman sitting at the desk. A moment to compose himself. He puts the letter opener in his jacket pocket, sharp end down, the handle sticking out. He drops his head into his hands, pretending to massage his temples as he wipes a tear away and sniffs up the snot in his nose. He inhales deeply, rebuilding his strength to go on.

Everything that happened to him back then is on her, this judge, a cog in the machine that disrespected Roselia and treated her life like dirt. Drugs and crime happened to Ramón for a brief time in his life. Why? Dana Hargrove doesn't care. Lawyers and judges like her process people like him every day, packaging them into neat containers and running them through the system. She doesn't know this kind of pain.

He turns around to face her. "I had to push it away. I needed a fix, an escape from the pain. The guy who murdered Roselia started it, but you and your people pushed the knife deeper and twisted it. The Manhattan DA is worse than the murderer. You're in the business of helping killers if it suits your needs."

He pauses, looking directly at her, but a loud noise jars them both. The desk phone is ringing. They look at it. He takes two steps to the desk and reads the display. A string of numbers, no name. She tilts her head up at him, as if waiting for instructions.

"Let it go," he says. "You have a message machine, don't

you?"

"Yes."

As it rings a few more times, her eyes tell him something. She knows the number. The ringing stops abruptly. "Who's calling you?"

The answer should be on the tip of her tongue, but she hesitates a moment too long. "It's my husband."

The hesitation. She must be hiding something about her husband. "What does he want?"

"He's supposed to meet me here."

Bitch. "You lied." He wants to grab her again. Scare her good.

"No," she protests. "He's not coming here. I'm supposed to meet him later, downstairs, at the back of the building."

"When?"

"Six thirty." She's processing another thought. He sees it behind her eyes. "Mm, maybe I should call him." A little stutter. Is she putting on an act? "He might wonder why I didn't answer."

"We're not done here. We won't be done at six thirty." Ramón has no idea what time it is, but he's only just begun. "There's a long way to go."

The phone starts ringing again. He looks. "Is that the same number?"

"Yes. It's him."

He thinks for the duration of one ring and says, "Answer it. You're working late. You'll meet him at home later. Make it sound real." For emphasis, he tilts the handle of the letter opener toward her, keeping the blade in his pocket.

"Okay." She picks up the receiver.

He's regretting his decision even as he tells himself it's better this way. He paces in front of the desk as she talks.

"Hi, Evan," she says into the receiver. A pause and, "Mm-hmm. I have a lot of work to do... Yes. I'm sorry... Yeah, it's kind of bad, but I have to get this done. No need to meet me here... It's not like that... Okay. I just have a lot more to do. I'll be home late. I love you."

She hangs up and looks at him. For what? Approval? He's not a hundred percent happy with the way it sounded but can't put his finger on the reason. He wasn't thinking clearly and now regrets not finding a way to listen in. Twenty-three years of slow planning isn't the same as quick thinking on the spot.

"Was that some kind of secret message..."

"No—"

"...telling him to come?"

"No, he won't. I told him not to."

The air between them has changed. Ramón's rhythm is interrupted, his advantage slipping away. He steps closer to the desk and leans over it, toward her.

"Please," she says. "Go back to what you were saying. About needing something to help the pain. I want to know."

So smooth, pushing back with words, edging into a new role. The therapist, poking around for vulnerable spots. Tell me your story, you pathetic wasted man. He resists. "You'd like that?" He returns to his chair. "We'll sit here until you know what it's like, not getting what you want."

Much of the story about Roselia and Thrasher is news to Dana. During Pineda's telling of it, he paces with that letter opener in hand, his volatility growing. Dana slows her breathing to calm herself, to be ready for the next unpredictable emotion. A brief reprieve. He pockets the instrument, sharp point down, and turns away, trying to hide his tears. Even with his back turned, she can feel the emotion.

He's right, in a way. At the time of his trial, she knew some of his background, but none of these details. She remembers reading something in the presentence report about his girlfriend's death, but she never knew about Thrasher or his plea deal.

Should she have investigated, found out everything she possibly could about this man before recommending a sentence to the judge? It wasn't possible in those days. She relied on the probation department to put the facts together in a report for the judge. She was inundated with work, one murder case after another. But is that any excuse?

Now that she's a judge, her sentencing decisions weigh heavily on her. She gives herself no excuses. She needs to know everything she can find out. But back then...?

It's too late, of course. In Pineda's mind, Dana Hargrove is the cause of his woes, indistinguishable from that evil office with hundreds of attorneys, the Manhattan DA. She can guess the next part of his life story. His fall into heroin addiction isn't his fault either. What good did twenty-three years in prison do for this man, for any of us, if he can't move past the blame?

He composes himself and turns around again. She keeps a neutral face, sensing that it's dangerous to react or comment on his emotion. She's a blank slate as he talks. Let him get it out.

And it's what she predicted. The DA's plea deal with Thrasher was the cause of Pineda's need to "escape the pain."

As he talks, she feels the hard rectangle of her cell phone in her skirt pocket. She fiddles with it under the desktop. If she could manage to touch a few icons without him seeing, she could send a text to Evan. They have an emergency code. Text "Z" for trouble. Or maybe she could try something out in the open, tell Pineda that her husband expects her at home, and if she doesn't call, he'll worry. Evan knows her well enough that he'll sense trouble the minute he hears her voice.

"The Manhattan DA is worse than the murderer," Pineda is saying. "You're in the business of helping killers if it suits your needs." He pauses, trying to gauge her reaction.

But a loud noise startles them. The desk phone.

At once, Dana hopes for an opportunity but sees the risk.

The light on the panel is the public number for her chambers, the one that Henny would pick up first and screen, if he were at his desk. The caller ID does not display a name but a string of ten numbers.

"Let it go," Pineda says, looking at the number. "You have a message machine, don't you?"

His choice of words dates him. The confusion of entering a different technological age after twenty-three years in prison. "Yes," she says. After four rings, the call will bump to the court's automated voicemail system.

She doesn't recognize the long number, even as it tugs at her memory. The person on the other end is someone significant, someone who could help.

Maybe he sees this in her face. Abruptly, three things happen at once. The ringing stops, Dana remembers the number, and Pineda asks, "Who's calling you?"

If the caller's name had been on the display instead of the number, what would Pineda have done? He doesn't know that it's the personal cell phone number of Detective Vargas, the woman who shot him in 1992. He also doesn't know that, as a witness in an ongoing trial, Lina should *not* be calling the judge. Her call can mean only one thing. She knows.

A split-second decision, and it's out of her mouth. "It's my husband."

"What does he want?"

"He's supposed to meet me here."

"You lied."

"No. He's not coming here. I'm supposed to meet him later, downstairs, at the back of the building."

"When?"

"Six thirty." She hesitates slightly before daring the next move. "Maybe I should call him. He might wonder why I didn't answer." She could press redial and have a fake conversation with "Evan."

"We're not done here. We won't be done at six thirty. There's a long way to go."

But then the phone starts ringing again. He asks, "Is that the same number?"

"Yes. It's him."

She sees him thinking, considering his options. "Answer it. You're working late. You'll meet him at home later. Make it sound real." He's clutching the handle of that letter opener, twitching it toward her.

"Okay." Dana's sweating. How easily he could order her to turn on speaker phone. His preoccupation saves her. And maybe also his backwardness, the years shut off from society.

She picks up the receiver. "Hi, Evan."

"Dana." Aurelina lowers her voice to a whisper so she can't be overheard. "Someone's there?"

"Mm-hmm." Pineda is pacing in front of the desk. Dana keeps her voice loud as a distraction. She doesn't want him to hear Lina. "I have a lot of work to do."

"Pineda?"

"Yes. I'm sorry."

"Is he armed?"

"Yeah, it's kind of bad, but I have to get this done. No need to meet me here."

"We're on our way. If you hear us, drop if you can."

"It's not like that..."

"Duck and dive."

"Okay. I just have a lot more to do. I'll be home late. I love you."

Lina hangs up. Dana is unsettled. *Duck and dive*. Does she think Pineda has a gun? But Lina didn't ask, and Dana could only hint.

Pineda doesn't seem happy with her performance. "Was that some kind of secret message…"

"No—"

"…telling him to come?"

"No, he won't. I told him not to."

Her captor seems more agitated than ever. She senses that the defensiveness in her voice is feeding his angst. She needs to be proactive, to lead him.

He steps close to the desk and looms over it.

"Please," Dana says in a smooth tone. "Go back to what you were saying. About needing something to help the pain. I want to know."

But she's wrong again. Her words tick him off. He refuses to go on and returns to his chair. She's made to sit in silence, so he can teach her a lesson that she's not going to get what she wants.

Ramón is hardly back in his chair when he hears a faint electronic beep and the sound of a door opening in the outer office.

His eyes flit to his captive's, reading them. Will she stay cool?

Someone is clattering through the office of that man, the judge's secretary, or clerk, or whatever she calls him. The intruder comes to a halt at the closed door. There's a knock. "Judge Hargrove?"

He flashes a warning look.

"Hello, Sheila," she calls out. "Still here. I'm in a meeting."

But "Sheila" doesn't listen. She opens the door a sliver, and with her hand on the doorknob, sticks her head in and glances at the judge. The officer senses another presence, opens the door wider, and turns to Ramón. "Oh, hello." As if she didn't hear the judge say that she was in a meeting. The officer's eyes linger on him too long, moving up and down, subtly sizing him up. Nosy ass court officer.

"This is Mr. Johnson, Sheila. He's an attorney on one of my cases."

The officer turns to the judge again. "Sorry to interrupt. The captain didn't say you had company."

"It's okay. I forgot to mention it."

The officer nods and inches back into the doorway. "Call me when you're ready to go downstairs." She closes the door. Ramón hears her clatter through the neighboring office, open the outer door, and leave.

Two interruptions already. How many more? His time may be shorter than he thinks.

"How'd I do?" Dana Hargrove asks.

Flippant, almost. It angers him, adding to his mounting panic. "Won't win an Oscar."

"It's the best I could do."

"Like all your lies. 'No one's coming,'" he mocks. "Then it's your husband and a court officer."

"I didn't lie. I didn't expect her. But maybe you should leave now. Officer Delano is good at reading people."

"Oh, is she? That's right. I have the look of a killer. You put me away for murder, didn't you, ADA Hargrove?"

He evaluates. The officer didn't challenge him. She left them to finish their "meeting." But he feels pressed for time and needs to accelerate the pace. He'll drive the point home quicker and leave Dana Hargrove something to think about. Until next time. They will meet again.

He stands and says, "Let's see how good *you* are at reading *me*. Get up."

She doesn't move. He's scaring her a little bit and likes it.

"I said get up before I pull you out of that chair!"

She stands.

"Come here... Come on. Now."

She sidles around the desk.

"Let's take a little walk to the *baño*."

"Why?" But she starts walking. He follows, a hand on her shoulder. A little guidance. He bends past her to open the door and gives her a little push inside. A bit too much. She bumps into the sink.

He inspects the restroom doors, one to her office, one to the robing room, both with locks on the door handles from the inside. He closes the door to her office and punches the lock, then steps toward the robing room and stops. "You're not going to lock me out." He pushes the door wide open, grabs the clothes tree with her robe and jacket, and lays it down against the door, lengthwise, straddling the threshold. He steps on her jacket on his way to the other door. Same thing. It can be locked from the inside, preventing entry into the robing room from the narrow passage. He presses the button on the doorknob.

"Perfect," he says, taking three steps back to the restroom. "No way I'm letting you lock me out. We'll be cellmates for a while. Just like home." He comes very close to her. She's facing him, propped against the sink, her arms crossed, clutching the elbows. She jitters and sweats a little, more nervous than she was, sitting at her desk. He reaches around her, picks up the soap dispenser on the sink, and sniffs the nozzle. "Except *we* didn't have all this perfume. Pretty much smelled like BO and greasy prison food turned to shit."

She straightens up and tries for her therapist role again. "Mr. Pineda…"

"Shut up and feel it. You're nobody. For twenty-three years, you live in a place no bigger than this. I'd make it stink for you if I could." A dull thud. The plastic soap dispenser is on the floor. He kicks it under the sink. "Siddown! Go ahead. Do what I say."

The toilet has no cover to it. She's lowering her dainty ass onto the seat when he sees the outline of the cell phone against her thigh. He reaches into the pocket and pulls it out. "Sit." No messages on the screen in the last hour. "You're not calling anyone." He throws the phone into the robing room, where it hits the floor with a loud crunch. "You're cut off from the world. Every move you make is watched and controlled." He stares at her, daring a reaction. "Guards push and poke you when you don't want it." He jabs her shoulder.

"It must be terrible. I can imagine what you—"

"No, you can't, and I don't have twenty-three years to show you. But you're going to feel it, right now." In the tiny space, he paces around the toilet, circling his cellmate. He says nothing for a long time. He wants her to stew in it, like he did. They're both sweating, breathing the unconditioned humid air, laced with a mixture of lavender hand soap, old rusty pipes, and mildewed crevices.

But the strange thing is, *he's* the one who feels confined. He's back in his cell again, circling like a caged animal. *He's* the one feeling despondent, enraged, weary of the willpower it takes to control his emotions. He's unable to pull the same out of her, to squeeze her into a box of fear and dependence. It's not what he dreamed or planned. It's not the way he wants it.

He has to draw her into his hell, make her suffer the way he did, right now, in this cramped space. "There's pain, too much of it, and you need it to stop. Drugs are everywhere. You grew up with that shit all around, but you stayed strong. You always rejected that life. You weren't going to become one of those sick people in their stinking graffitied hallways and dark alleys. You were better than that. But then you're twenty-one, and something really bad happens. Life ends for you. You're in the worst pain of your life, and it's so easy to find peace. No one can take that kind of pressure. Your willpower snaps."

He halts and snaps his fingers loud, an inch from her face. Her head jerks back reflexively, but her eyes are merely sad and foggy. He wants to see terror and frenzy and isn't getting it from her. "You don't go for crack." He reverts to his erratic pacing. "Everyone was doing crack those days, but you aren't like everyone else. You're smarter than them. You go for dreamland, a heroin high. But you won't get hooked. You self-medicate under your own treatment plan. Just a week or two, long enough to move past the pain, to forget the way Roselia died. To forget the way those people downtown treated her like ghetto trash after she died. So, you shoot up one time. Then a second time. Maybe a third time, but now you can't remember the plan. You're hooked. Your life belongs to smack."

He stops, unable to look at his captive, but he senses the worst. She isn't cringing in fear or claustrophobia. She isn't frantic to get out. No. He's picking up something else. She's listening to him and starting to pity him. Miss Holier-Than-Thou pities him. Not what he wants. She's a caged animal, just like him, but still in control.

He swivels, right and left, looking up into the corners of their cell. His hand squeezes the handle of the letter opener in his pocket. "Don't you see? I was hooked, all because of you and your people. No money, sick as a dog, had to get it. So, you tell me. Who killed that man? You tell me, Dana Hargrove. Who killed him?" His face is wet. He's shaking, snot running into his mouth. He wipes his face with an open hand, then the other. He's choking and can't go on.

Marched into the windowless restroom, Dana loses all sense of time as she watches Pineda starting to lose it, checking the doors and throwing the clothes tree on the floor. It could be two minutes or an hour since that phone call. Lina should have gathered the forces by now. She should have called Gil… But no, Dana prevented that from the get-go. She told Gil not to contact Lina, so how would she know that he's working on this? But Lina must have found out. She wouldn't have called Dana to warn her about Pineda unless she and Gil were talking and figured out who sent the letters.

And Officer Delano. Is she getting help right now? Dana tamps down her disappointment in the young officer, not letting it turn into rage. Sheila is new on the job, much less experienced than Len. Still, she should have suspected something amiss and challenged this man. Why didn't she at least ask for his identification? Did she really fall for the "Mr. Johnson" story? Dana is a better actress than she thinks, or else her position of authority lends a seal of veracity to her words. Perhaps Sheila is awestruck or cowed by her, willing to believe whatever she says.

But Pineda is far from impressed. Her status as a judge holds no sway over him. Quite the opposite. Dana needs to keep up an act without knowing the best role to play. They're seesawing on the balance of power. Is it better to be weaker or stronger than him? Or on par?

Draw him out. That's what he's here for. To tell his story. To make her accept the blame. To make her feel helpless. To teach her about his life, twenty-three years living as a pawn, controlled by others. Watched and prodded and marched around with the herd, locked up in a tiny space for hours on end, going mad.

He wants her to be helpless, but her helplessness is fueling him. Should she stay silent? Should she challenge him, tell him he's ruining the chance he's been given? He's burying himself at the age of forty-five, much of his life still ahead. She could promise not to turn him in if he leaves right now. Promise to keep up the "Mr. Johnson" ruse if Sheila ever asks again. But he'll see it as a trap, an attempted manipulation to get him out. And he's already told her what he expects. She is to remain quiet about this after he leaves, if he leaves, whenever that may be. His call.

She hopes he doesn't snap before then.

A quick decision. She'll commiserate, show him that she

understands. It feels more like herself, not a stage role. She *does* feel his pain. He's shaking and crying now, but he's also clutching the handle of that letter opener in his pocket. The situation is delicate, sad, terrifying. She's walking a tightrope. One false move and…

How has he fallen to this point? The sobbing has taken him. He's crashing in front of this woman. He can't go on, has failed miserably in taking control of her. Not what he planned, and now something else. He's letting her walk right into the opening. She starts talking, and despite himself, he listens.

Despite himself, she's drawing him into the velvet of her voice, the smooth comfort of it. It's a therapeutic tone and he resents the underlayer of arrogance, but still, she's sucking him in, like her words hold the cure to his despair.

"I understand now what you meant about my son," says this woman who's a mother and a judge. It's calming, soothing, forgiving. His tears are nothing to be ashamed of. "You could have had a life or a career like my son. But then tragedy struck. You fell into addiction." *Not your fault.*

A cleansing wave rises, begins to crest. Did he hear her correctly? She admits that he isn't to blame!

"You were grieving for your girlfriend," she goes on. Dana Hargrove, the woman with the golden voice. A fleeting thought. The tug of memory. This is the woman he has reviled for almost half his life. "It was a senseless death, pure chance the way your girlfriend walked into the path of a stray bullet…"

The wave breaks in a violent crash. A desecration and defilement. Dana Hargrove hasn't heard *anything* he's said. His blood rises. "My 'girlfriend'? You can't even say her name. She has a name. Roselia is her name!" He grabs the judge by her shoulders and shakes her hard. "*You* made her worthless! Not the stray bullet. *You* treated her like nothing!" He crushes those soft upper arms, lifts her off the toilet seat, and slams her to the floor.

Bone against tile. The back of her skull. He hears it.

He looks down at her and waits a second, two seconds.

She isn't moving.

Panic rises in his chest.

Her eyes are closed. She's very still.

Is she breathing? Yes. But why doesn't she move?

What should he do now? Flee, and be quick!

A grave mistake. Her last thought before the shock of that change in his eyes. The crush of his hands. The violence. The ground coming up to meet her.

She hears it more than feels it. The crack of her skull.

The room goes dark.

When Dana and Cheryl were children, growing up in suburban New Jersey, they had a cat named Cinnamon. One day, when Dana was about ten and Cheryl was five, Cinnamon put on a fascinating show for them. The girls were downstairs in the finished basement, inside a makeshift playhouse, when they heard curious noises. A series of thuds, very faint, like something soft was hitting something else soft.

They pulled the curtain aside and looked out. Cinnamon was batting at a dead mouse. The cat kept at it for a minute or two, using one front paw, then the other, tilting her head from side to side, getting different angles on her prey. Was Cinnamon going to clamp that mouse in her jaws, carry it away, and eat it? Dana had once seen Cinnamon chewing on something dead in the backyard. Later, she saw a pile of tiny broken bones.

But this time, the cat seemed to lose interest, or else she got distracted and just walked away. For a moment longer, the girls watched the dead mouse, feeling sad and almost angry at their beloved Cinnamon for her cruelty. But to their surprise, the mouse abruptly bounced up and darted off, very smart and very alive.

Dana's tormentor is breathing hard, muttering under his breath. She senses him looking down at her, considering his next move. She keeps still and breathes shallowly, her eyes closed.

In the robing room, her cell phone vibrates against the floor.

21 » CONVERGENCE

WHY DOESN'T DANA answer? Gil says she's working late, until six thirty. She could be in the other office, the ladies' room, whatever. Maybe she doesn't answer her office phone after five.

Lina doesn't want to leave a message about something like this. She doesn't have the private office number, but if she digs, she might find Dana's cell number from years ago. Most likely, she's changed it by now. A matter of personal protection.

Lina waits a few minutes and calls the main office number again. Thank God she does.

She hears "Hi, Evan," sending her headlong into crisis mode. She lowers her voice, saying barely enough to get the basics. The man could be standing over Dana. Could be doing any number of things… Lina can't let him overhear.

Readjustment. Spontaneity. Always at the ready. "Hi, Evan" catches her off guard for a split second. She was expecting to deliver a warning, to recite the details that Gil learned from Graciela Pineda about her brother. Convey the news that, since his release to parole, Ramón Pineda has gained a lot of weight and has let his hair and beard grow. He recently became a bottle redhead and spent his meager wages on a cheap suit he doesn't need. After so many years in prison, Ramón is a bit of an enigma to Graciela. Her car went missing one night and miraculously reappeared, along with Ramón's admission that he had "borrowed" it. Some of his behavior seems odd, but that could be the shock of his reentry into society.

"Hi, Evan." In that split second, Lina readjusts. Dana doesn't need to know the new details about Pineda's appearance and behavior because she can see them for herself. Doesn't need to know that Gil is calling the after-hours judge for a search warrant, hoping to find the typewriter in his apartment. Gil won't be doing that now. He's needed for other things.

Lina prays the man hasn't harmed Dana. Nothing in her voice hints at physical pain or injury. She sounds slightly nervous, but overall cool and composed. She's a tough one, that judge. If anyone can get through this without permanent emotional damage, it's Dana. Physical damage is another thing. Lina can't let that happen.

The moment she hangs up, she jumps into action. With a quick look at the time, 6:09, she gets moving, her mind abuzz with the possibilities and unknowns. She's wearing her court clothes. She throws off the suit jacket, switches to the belt holster, grabs her vest, and sprints out the office door, cell phone in hand. Yells at the desk sergeant: "Criminal Court building. Thirteenth floor. Send two units. *Now.*" Can't flood the area; would be counter-productive. The DA's squad is in the building and will get upstairs faster. Court officers too. And one more thing. She yells over her shoulder on her way out: "Alert the captain! Judge Hargrove held hostage." It's Fifth Precinct's jurisdiction. Can't bypass the captain. She has no idea where he is at the moment.

She's dialing Gil, feet moving, jogging, mind active. A failure of security. Somehow, Pineda got into that office without anyone noticing. But how could he bring a gun into the building? *Is he armed? Yeah, it's kind of bad.* A firearm? Damn! She should have asked. A failure in questioning. But he's armed with something dangerous. *It's kind of bad.* He has a weapon and got around security. He avoided detection, and that means the weapon could be a gun.

Gil picks up. Between panting breaths, she tells him enough of what he needs to know. Thank goodness she's kept up her cross training. These short little legs are fleet. "I'm two blocks away," she says, still running.

"Grabbing my crew and going upstairs," Gil says into her ear.

She jogs past the street vendor where she enjoyed a long coffee break after her tedious day on the witness stand. When did Pineda get into Dana's office? Was he holding the judge captive while Lina and friends were trading jokes and war stories? Half an hour wasted. Too late now to get that time back. Can only go forward. And fast.

Sheila rushes away from Judge Hargrove's door to prevent any chance that "Mr. Johnson" can overhear the squawk of her two-way radio. She calls in an emergency to her supervisor, Lieutenant Teodora "Dora" Yankova.

Twenty-four years old, top of her class at the academy, less than two years at the court, Sheila's been doing a top-flight job here, but now, she isn't so sure. She may have just sabotaged her career, but that's the least of her worries.

This is the first real dilemma she's had to face. Situations in the courtroom are always clear cut. Spectators who shout obscenities from the audience. Defendants who jump out of their chairs and threaten to run. Something different just happened in Judge Hargrove's office.

Sheila goes over the scene in her mind, evaluates, and comes out fifty-fifty. Even odds. She either did the right thing or left the judge in danger.

Which is it? She doesn't know.

Her instincts are tingling. The man sitting in Judge Hargrove's office looks nothing like any of the mug shots that were circulated today. But her gut says there's something off about him. She's never seen him in the courthouse before, but she can't expect to recognize all the attorneys. The place is swarming with hundreds of them every day.

On the two-way, Lieutenant Yankova asks, "What's up, Sheila?"

"There's a man in Judge Hargrove's office. I don't have a good feeling about him."

"How so?"

"The explanation she gave —"

"Hold on. I'm getting another call about this."

A call about *this*? Sheila paces and weighs conflicting thoughts.

This isn't the first time Judge Hargrove has met with attorneys after the court is closed. Usually, there are two of them at a time. *Always* two or more, right? That's the tip off. *This is Mr. Johnson, Sheila. He's an attorney on one of my cases.* It doesn't look good for an attorney and a judge to hang out alone together in chambers, discussing an open case. Smacks of possible bribery or collusion.

Is Judge Hargrove in the middle of negotiating a payoff? Not nice to think. She doesn't seem the type.

So, it was a legitimate meeting, like the judge said. Or maybe not. Maybe the man is threatening her and told her what to say. Sheila brings the judge's face and voice to mind. Controlled, a bit uptight. She looked pale, but not abnormally so. Stressed and tired, like everyone else around here.

"May I see some ID?" she should have asked. Should have walked right up to that man and given him another look. She could have pretended it was the usual protocol when visitors are in chambers after five o'clock. Nothing personal. "Thank you, Mr. Johnson. Sorry to interrupt."

How would that look? A junior court officer challenging a respected judge twice her age. Doubting the judge, checking up on her. Arrogant and disrespectful.

Lieutenant Yankova is back on. "Hostage situation. Clear the corridor. DA's Squad and the Fifth are coming. Meet in front of Judge Brentwood's door. I called EMT to send two ambulances."

Sheila's heart skips a beat and starts racing. *Two ambulances.*

She turns and looks at Judge Hargrove's door, fifty yards distant. What is going on in there, right now? How could she have missed this? She's armed and wearing her bulletproof vest. It's regulation. She's trained and equipped to rescue, to fight, to save. How did she miss this?

Helpless to do anything now except follow directions.

Sheila's aimlessness lasts a single second, and then she's on the move. It's six twelve. The courtrooms are all locked, some staff are still behind closed doors. The area is quiet, but not empty. Three, four, five people are scattered in the corridor. All but two people are walking to the elevators, on their way out.

Sheila strides up to the two loiterers, a man and a woman, talking. "Clear the area. Immediately." They give her a startled look and do as they're told.

The seconds tick too slowly, an eternity, less than a minute in real time. Then they start arriving, singly and in batches, within seconds of each other, all of them smarter and faster and braver than Sheila. Lieutenant Yankova, six court officers, Gil, his two men, Lina, and four from the Fifth. "The captain is fifteen minutes out," Lina reports.

They assemble at the end of the corridor near Judge Brentwood's courtroom. While they talk, Yankova stations two court officers outside each of Judge Hargrove's doors: the courtroom door and Henny's door. Just in case the man emerges and magically surrenders.

The lieutenant orders Sheila to join the assembly. She's the only one here who saw the man. She may know something that will be of help.

May know. Something. What Sheila knows is that she failed miserably in her chance to save Judge Hargrove.

Ramón backs away from the prone body. She isn't dead, he's sure of that much. She's unconscious.

He can't understand how this happened. He self-trained against anything like this happening. An unconscious judge ruins everything. The years of planning. The years of pride in his self-control. The lessons he was going to teach this woman.

He hates himself for letting her set him off. It enraged him, her denseness, but he knows her better now. She's all show, only pretending to listen and understand. She will never comprehend him or her part in all of it, but he has to keep trying. There's still a chance, if he leaves now.

She won't talk. She'll wake up and remember him and fear him and know that she can't possibly reveal what happened here. She slipped on the tile. An accident, that's what it is.

He'll leave, but he'll be back. Not for a while. He'll have to wait, again, for the right moment, but it will come. This meeting is only the beginning.

Her unconscious body blocks the door to her office. He turns away from her to leave through the robing room. There's a noise, five feet away. That broken piece of plastic is vibrating against the floor. He picks it up. The screen is a spiderweb, but he can still read what's underneath. There's a little picture of her husband Evan, and next to it, "OMW. ETA ten mins."

The time is now six sixteen.

He's still thinking straight. He still has a chance. He puts the mobile phone on the restroom floor, closer to the unconscious judge, where it will blend into the scene of the accident.

* * *

Suggestions are flying. Everyone has an idea.

He has a gun. Impossible. But the judge said he's armed. A weapon of some kind. Could be a gun; there are ways to get it into the building. Check security footage. No time. Hours of video to review if he got here this morning. Smoke him out with teargas. Get the bullhorn. Is there a PA system? Through the fire alarm. Call in a hostage negotiator. It will only rile him. Better to take him by surprise. What kind of man is he, Detective Vargas? You arrested him. What is he capable of? What did you see, Officer Delano? Their faces, words, body language. Is the judge hurt or scared? Did you see a weapon?

Meanwhile, Gil's tech crew has quietly threaded snake cameras and mics under Henny's door, the courtroom door, and from the fourteenth-floor window down to Judge Hargrove's window. They give report. Nothing at all. No sign of the judge or Pineda. No voices in conversation. Faint sounds of shuffling feet and muttering. A man's voice.

Only a few minutes have passed, but there's no time for debate.

"Enough," Gil says. "Let's get her out. We're going in now."

"We'll each head a team," Lina says. "Come at him from both sides."

"IT disabled the security locks," Lieutenant Yankova says. "The doors are unlocked. There's no electronic sound, but he's going to hear you. This place is old and creaky." She taps a few icons on a tablet she's holding and shows Gil and Lina the layout of the offices.

The plan is set. Gil and his two men from the DA's squad, plus Sheila, will enter Henny's office. Lina and the four cops from the Fifth, plus Lieutenant Yankova, will enter the courtroom. Yankova and one uniform will cover the courtroom while Lina plus three go into the narrow passage. The remaining six court officers are stationed in the corridor, three and three, outside the two doors.

Lina looks up from her phone. "Captain gives the go-ahead. My team needs a head start." The courtroom is much larger than Henny's office. Gil's team will wait five seconds. Pineda won't be able to hear Lina's team when they enter through the main courtroom door, but he'll be able to hear them when they open the door into the narrow passage. At that point, Gil's team will be at the judge's office door.

Where is he? The possibilities are these: Zola's office, the robing room, the restroom, the narrow passage, or a corner of the judge's office, out of camera range. Where is she? Any one of those places, and they hope to God she isn't hurt. They still can't hear her.

"Surprise is on our side," Gil says. "We go in quickly, firearms drawn. Fire *only* if he's about to use deadly force. Do *not* fire if he's holding the judge."

"I warned Judge Hargrove what to do if she hears us," Lina says. "Duck and dive, if possible. You are *not* to shoot if she's anywhere in range."

All heads nod.

"Let's go!"

Ramón straightens up from his crouch near the prostrate judge on the tile floor. He feels the letter opener, heavy in his jacket pocket. He cannot have it on him when he walks out of here. There will be people outside, in the hallways, not nearly as many as before, but there will be officers and attorneys and employees wondering why a thick metal handle is sticking out of his pocket. He'll put it back on the desk where he found it. Fingerprints don't matter because the judge will say nothing and her assistant will know nothing.

The folded papers are still in his other jacket pocket. It seems so long ago now that he was in the corridor, waving these papers at the judge's law clerk, distracting her with them while he pulled out her key card with his other hand. He was proud of that maneuver. A good trick, like a magician. The ease of it assured him that this meeting was meant to be. How could everything have gone so wrong?

So easy at first. Wait until no one was looking, wave the card over the reader, and walk in. The letter opener was an unplanned bonus. When Dana Hargrove thinks about their time together this evening, she'll see the irony of it, the way her handpicked staff helped him out. The court clerk with his meticulous habits, the precision, high-end tool he uses to open letters. Far more than needed. A thick, dense handle and a long sharp blade. The law clerk with her predictable habit, never straying from her system of storing her key card in the slender outer pocket of her handbag. Thinking only of her own convenience.

Ramón will return the letter opener, but should he return the key card? He slips a finger inside his breast pocket and feels the top edge. He wants to keep it, even if there's no hope it will ever work again. No doubt they'll deactivate it. But he has a fondness for the little piece of plastic, a symbol of his act of cunning. When he leaves the building, no one will see that he has it, deep inside his breast pocket.

He walks into the robing room, puts a hand on the doorknob, and pivots back for a final glance at the judge. He wishes it hadn't ended like this. She hasn't moved, but she's not dead. He knows she's not dead. How long can someone stay unconscious and not die? A long time. Maybe she's bleeding out in her brain. Impossible. He didn't throw her hard enough to kill her.

What has he gotten out of this hour with her? She will be changed, he has to believe that. She'll wake up and remember their time together. If she can't fix what she did to Ramón Pineda, if he's beyond saving, there will be someone else. She'll think twice the next time she's on her high horse, staring down at a blameless man at the defense table, considering how badly she can ruin his life.

With his left hand on the doorknob, his right hand circling the handle of the letter opener, he hesitates. Why? It's time to go. His stomach churns with quickening dread. The spiderweb floats in front of his eyes, cracked over the face of that bald man, smiling and saying "OMW."

Walk out of here. Now. It's as easy as one, two, three. As easy as how he came in.

During the years Ramón served his time, Department of Corrections policies on the treatment of prisoners changed at a glacial rate. Entertainment was always a big issue with inmates. Confinement, once the claustrophobia wears off, is mind-numbingly boring. There are chores and crappy meals and exercise yard, but the intellect needs stimulus. There's school, if you choose it, but more is needed. Art and entertainment and lightness, otherwise the mind will spin its own creations and drama, a cesspool of intrigue and evil scheming.

Censorship. The library had certain books, not others. Movie night featured films not much more violent than *Bambi*. Better not give these dangerous men any ideas. Better not show them films about serial killers or clever financial schemes or mafia hits. No need to give them advanced degrees in criminality.

The entertainment policy seemed to exclude any film with gun violence, no matter how removed from reality. Ramón had a friend who was incensed by the lousy lineup. Tico, doing time for armed robbery. He made a list of his all-time favorite flicks and started a movement among the prison population to pressure the administration into showing them.

Partial success, a few victories. One of the films that came in was *Butch Cassidy and the Sundance Kid*. Armed robbers in the 1890s. Rated PG. It was a good flick. Ramón liked it, and afterward, he and Tico had a good time with it. "Warden's gonna get slammed on this one," Ramón said, "teaching us how to hold up a train on horseback!"

Tico laughed and shook his head. "And how to go out in a blaze of glory. Fuck it, man, that's how I want to go. It's the only way." Tico quoted Paul Newman's famous last line, "'For a moment there, I thought we were in trouble.' Then blam!"

They lapsed into silence, imagining what it would be like. Ramón and Tico, crime partners, badly wounded in a gunfight, surrounded by the Bolivian *federales*, no possible escape. Nothing else to do but accept it and leave this world with a sense of humor.

"Yeah," Ramón agreed. "That's the way to go." Too quick to feel it.

Ramón turns the doorknob and pulls the door toward him. He hears something, and for a moment, he thinks he's in trouble. He dismisses the thought and steps into the narrow passage.

The rest of it is a flash and a blur, his confusion, his reflexive reaction.

People are moving inside the judge's office. Then they're moving in the courtroom. Maybe they're both places at once, he doesn't know.

The doors open, a split second between the two.

The courtroom door. A woman two-arms a gun at him.

"Freeze!"

Startled, Ramón steps back, thrusting his right arm out in defense.

"Drop it!"

Drop what?

The office door opens. A man's voice. "Drop it!"

Ramón turns. He stares down the barrel of another gun.

Reflexively, his right arm swings out at the man.

Bang.

Something falls on the floor amid the deafening explosion.

Dazed, Ramón looks down at the fallen object. His thoughts flow and converge in a swirling universe.

I know these people. The old guy. The little woman at the other door. I know her very well.

Ramón is suddenly very tired. He leans back against the wall and crumples slowly into a sitting position on the floor, next to the letter opener.

He's staring down at the sharp silver point when the black curtain rises up from his belly and shuts out the world.

22 »   *SHOCK*

TWO AMBULANCES ARE parked behind the courthouse. The EMTs are busier in one ambulance than the other. They close the back doors and pull away from the curb, with siren and flashing lights.

Dana sits on the back ledge of the other ambulance, pressing an ice pack to her head. She's trembling, almost imperceptibly, from head to toe. She refuses to acknowledge the visceral tremor. This is nothing.

No one agrees with her self-diagnosis. Gil and Lina have already checked on her and thrown in their two cents. Evan is with the EMT attending to her.

"We should take you in and run some tests," the EMT says.

"I'm fine, really. I was never unconscious."

Evan strokes her cheek, puts a finger under her chin, and slowly tilts it up to look in her eyes. "Do this, Dana. For me. For the kids. You hit your head hard on a tile floor. They should scan you."

"It's a bump. My hair cushioned it." The goose egg is at the back of her head, under the half-fallen French bun in her thick hair.

With more coaxing, she relents. Evan rides along with her to the hospital. She lies on the gurney with her head propped up, and Evan sits next to her, holding her hand. The EMT gives them as much privacy as possible in the cramped cabin of the ambulance. The driver has not engaged the emergency lights and siren.

"Thanks for doing this," Evan says. "We have to be sure you're all right."

"I have a hard head."

"That, you do. Always did have a hard head. And a beautiful one."

"My skull and brain are fine. If anything is hurt, it's this." Her free hand forms a fist over her heart. Does Evan understand? Her soul is hurting for a man who was dealt a bad hand in life but then thought he could bluff his way to a win. A man who denied his own responsibility and then squandered his chance to move forward, to try and start fresh in this world despite its pitfalls. She's thinking of that man now and feels sick for him. She'll be thinking of that man for a long time to come.

More than that, in this very moment, she's worried if he'll make it. Would she have felt this way, twenty-three years ago?

Upstairs in the narrow passage, the EMTs were working furiously on Pineda. Dana saw a lot of blood before they whisked her away. No one could tell her anything about his condition. A moment ago, at the back of Dana's ambulance, Gil was vague and jocular about his part in the rescue. She's not sure if Gil even knows how badly he wounded Pineda. Of course, Gil is also worried for himself, although he will never admit it. Like every law enforcement officer in this position, he faces an investigation into the discharge of his weapon in the line of duty.

History was not repeated. Lina will be spared an inquiry this time.

Evan's eyes are glistening. "I can't even imagine it. Must have been terrifying."

"I was scared, but not every minute. It went back and forth. When we have the time, I want to tell you every detail."

"You need to rest now. I'm here, whenever you're ready to

talk." He looks down at their intertwined fingers and up again, into her eyes. "You're a tough one, taking this so well. I'm a basket case. I could have lost you. I wish I'd done more to prevent this." There's helplessness in his eyes and voice.

She loves him so much.

She squeezes his hand. "You did everything you could. We all did. This man was determined to come and talk to me." She smiles. "I told him he should have made an appointment."

Evan laughs and kisses her cheek. "Yeah, where did those days go, when people dropped in for coffee, uninvited?"

It *is* kind of funny. She'd like to think they could have done it that way, without the threats or the letter opener or the inevitable consequences: parole revocation and return to prison. Wouldn't Mr. Pineda like her to testify that way at the hearing on his parole violation? *He made an unscheduled visit, Your Honor. Just dropped in for a chat, not a kidnapping.*

Or maybe, she could characterize it as a CLE course, continuing legal education for improved judging.

Ramón Pineda dropped by today to remind her what it's like to stand behind the defense table, hearing the words that redirect your path, forever. She could have told him that she didn't need reminding, especially now. The onus of pronouncing sentence weighs heavily on her. She looks back on her career, and whatever her failings, can say that she never objectified the men and women who got to their feet behind that table when the judge said, "Please rise" at the end of the case. Her perspective has been, and always will be, from the outside. There's nothing she can do about that. Ramón has brought her a step closer to the inside.

But it's the inside of only one man's reality. Thousands of days form a life before a man gets to his sentencing day. What's done is done. For him. How he comes to this point, how he views his path, and what he does with it, differs from the next man. And the tipping point, the point of no return for every person who commits a crime, happens long before the sentencing day, before the verdict, the indictment, or the arrest.

Ramón's path changed forever the minute he targeted Felipe Bedoya's store and stepped inside with a loaded handgun. What's done is done. What he did today was a matter of choice. Ramón had his uninvited visit, and now it's Dana's turn to drop in on him, if or when he's well enough to talk. Evan won't like it. Gil and Lina won't like it. But she feels she must. There is yet unfinished business between them.

The story of Pineda and Hargrove, in distorted form, is trending on the Internet before she gets to the hospital. News vans and reporters were already clogging the area when her ambulance pulled away from the courthouse. Now, the air is alive with tweets and headlines and special reports. "Hostage Crisis in Lower Manhattan." "Kidnapped Judge Escapes with her Life." "Hostage Taker Shot in Criminal Court."

While a doctor examines Dana, Evan is busy on the phone, trying to contact everyone in the family before they hear the sensationalist reports from the mouths of TV personalities. He mans two cell phones at once, his and Dana's. Calls are coming in and going out.

He starts with the people closest to them: Natalie, Travis, Cheryl, his mother Brenda and brother Albert. Gil calls him to say that he updated Chief Raines on the situation. Between scans and tests, Dana asks Evan to call Henny and Zola.

Although Evan knows enough of the story about the key card and the letter opener, he doesn't mention those details on the phone. He'd like to relieve Dana of as much stress as possible, but she should be the one to convey any information that could affect her employees emotionally. He simply reassures them that the judge is all right, and she expects to see them tomorrow.

By ten p.m., Dana is given a clean bill of health. No concussion, no subdural hematoma, a single dose of Tylenol with codeine for the pain. Back home, the drug eases her into complete escape, eight hours of black, dreamless sleep in Evan's arms.

By six thirty, she's up and getting ready for work. No one will see this knot at the back of her head under a well-positioned French bun. The Underwood trial must go on. A small crisis at the courthouse is no reason to interrupt it.

Evan sees her getting dressed in work clothes and asks what she's up to. "You need rest, Dana. I can call and arrange an adjournment, at least for a day."

She won't hear of it. Is she still in shock? Later, she will recognize the possibility. This has been the pattern in her life for every traumatic event. She goes into automatic pilot, ignoring the odd haze around the edges, a sign that this isn't a day like every other. A robotic acknowledgment of a subliminal thought. Something life changing may have just occurred, but it's still business as usual, the daily routine. Nothing should stop.

A few days later, it will hit.

But today, a monkey wrench is thrown into her machine. Len calls at seven fifteen. First, he wants to know if she's all right. Satisfied with her assurances, he tells her not to come in. Her courtroom and offices are off-limits for the day. Crime scene investigators are finishing their jobs, and after that, a cleaning crew and painters will be taking care of the blood. It wouldn't be a nice reminder upon her return to the office. "Do you want me to call your staff?"

"I'll handle that, Len. I need to talk to them."

"Good. And I'll be talking to Officer Delano."

She gets the drift. He's clearly unhappy with his subordinate's performance. "Len, don't go hard on her. We'll talk about this later. Basically, she came into my office, and I convinced her I was in a meeting. I'm grateful she notified her supervisor, and I don't blame her or my staff for anything."

He clears his throat and says, "You're being very forgiving, but, all right. We're still going to be conducting our internal investigation."

"What about my jurors, Len?"

"Already on it. We're notifying the attorneys and the jurors of a postponement until tomorrow. We're telling the jurors not to read or watch news reports about any incident at the courthouse last night."

She laughs. "Good luck with that! I'm sure most of them have already seen the news."

"Does this mean a mistrial?"

"Absolutely not! This has *nothing* to do with Garth Underwood."

"All right, Judge. Rest up. And one more thing, if you're interested. I have an update on the health of your attacker."

"I'm very interested."

"Took a bullet to the upper right chest, missed the heart and lungs. Underwent surgery last night and is said to be stable." He lets her know where to find Pineda, under guard, in the prison ward at Bellevue Hospital.

She thanks Len and calls Henny next. He's effusive with expressions of concern. She assures him of her good health and says that the court is closed today for reasons unrelated to her wellbeing. Tomorrow will be business as usual. They'll meet with Zola in chambers at nine o'clock, before the trial starts.

She hangs up without mentioning the letter opener. Crime scene bagged it as evidence, and Henny will notice the absence tomorrow morning when he's deprived of the means to open the mail. Use a finger? Impossible. Dana predicts that he'll go nuts when he finds out that Pineda could have killed the judge with his beloved letter opener. Better to deal with this at the meeting tomorrow.

Dana is about to call Zola when her law clerk beats her to it.

"Judge, are you all right?"

"Completely fine, thank you."

"Last night when your husband called, I had just clicked on a news report but didn't know it was you. Thanks so much for having him call me. He's very comforting!"

"Yes, he is, isn't he?" This makes Dana smile. "I was about to call you now. We are all taking an unscheduled vacation day. Investigators need the place to themselves."

"Okay. Thank you for letting me know. Just one other thing… I saw a news story with a photo of the man." She stops, tries to go on, and stutters a bit, very unlike her.

"What is it, Zola?"

"I wanted to ask you… I'm sorry if it's hard to talk about what happened, but I've been so worried! Does the man look different now? Maybe heavier than he is in the photo, with reddish hair? I think I saw him when I was leaving last night. I don't know, but now I can't find my key card. Could he have…?"

"Zola, please don't worry about it." And Dana tells her, in the gentlest tones, exactly how it happened. Zola is reduced to tears.

Dana's heart goes out to her. She does not blame Zola for anything that happened and tries to convince her of that. They will all need time to heal. A lot of this is going to take time.

There's only one thing that will take no time at all, and it's on the agenda for tomorrow's meeting. New rules for the handling of key cards.

Some things cannot be put on hold. Evan is proctoring a law exam this afternoon and will have to leave the apartment at noon. They make the most of their morning together, taking a long breakfast, making conference calls to the kids, first Travis, then Natalie, and after that, hours of nonstop talk in the living room.

They sit next to each other on the couch, alternately holding hands or absently touching each other, faces, shoulders, forearms, knees, in the rhythm of their customary closeness. Dana is ready to tell him every detail she can remember, from start to finish. As best she can, she also tells him how she felt and what she was thinking at each stage of the encounter. Evan listens raptly, asks questions, throws out his psychological analysis of the offender, and utters his exclamations of awe, admiration, and empathy.

Their conversation has returned to the easy flow they always had together. They enjoy and revel in it, their exchanges of intellectual and emotional intimacy. She's holding nothing back. Except... There *is* a thought at the back of her mind. Should she mention it? He will have a very strong opinion if she reveals what she's planning to do when he leaves for work.

But before they know it, the clock shows eleven thirty, and it's time for Evan to get ready to go. He starts by clearing the breakfast dishes and coffee cups, taking them into the kitchen. Dana uses the opportunity to check her work e-mail. "Nice try!" she exclaims loudly.

"What's going on?" he yells over running water in the kitchen.

"Pamela Grimes just sent a motion by e-mail attachment. She's asking for a mistrial and a new trial before a different judge."

Evan comes back to the living room. "Nice try is right!"

"Pure stalling tactic, asking for a redo. It'll take six months or a year before a new judge gets up to speed and coordinates everyone's schedules again. She hopes the prosecutor will lose a few witnesses in the meantime. Motion denied."

"Without a hearing?"

"Oh, I guess I'll let Grimes and Quince debate this a little bit tomorrow morning before I bring the jury in. But her argument is ridiculous. Listen to this: 'The hostage crisis in the chambers of the Honorable Dana Hargrove on Wednesday, May 13, 2015, is the top story in every newspaper and online news source in New York City. It's the reason the court closed on Thursday, May 14, 2015. The jurors cannot avoid hearing this news. Given Judge Hargrove's background as a prosecutor and the understandable human compassion that her ordeal will generate in the hearts of the jurors, this incident indelibly prejudices the jury in favor of the prosecution.'"

Evan laughs and walks up to her, his arms outstretched. "She has a point. I'm feeling that understandable human compassion for the judge in my heart right now."

She stands and accepts his embrace. "You're feeling compassion for the blindfolded lady of justice, not the prosecutor."

"Righto. Let that jury be prejudiced in favor of our honorable criminal justice system."

"Maybe it'll make them listen more carefully to my instructions on the law."

With Evan off to law school, Dana phones Cheryl for a long sisterly talk. She gives the short version of her ordeal and receives her sister's heartfelt expressions of love, relief, and awe at her moxie. The conversation turns to Cheryl's plans. She and Caitlin are still at the penthouse in the city, but they'll return to Westchester this weekend if all goes well tomorrow, when Cheryl has her first court date with Hunter. "We'll see how he behaves." She has scrapped her idea of accusing him in open court of stalking her. One good thing in all of this ("sorry, Dana!") is Cheryl's relief that Hunter didn't write that letter or try to break into the house. The man who did those things is now in custody for the long haul.

Dana ends the call feeling heartened and steered more directly toward the road to renewal. She's enjoying her unexpected vacation day, having the time to talk at length with the people she holds most dear. A huge weight is lifted knowing that, whatever she went through, they are safe.

Now, her thoughts return to Ramón Pineda. Her plan falls well outside the box, and maybe the DA's office and the NYPD wouldn't approve, but the law doesn't forbid it, and she's compelled to follow through. She *will* drop in on him today, despite what, most assuredly, would be her husband's misgivings. But she will do this sensibly, wisely. She will not go alone, by car, taxi, or subway. She will go under chaperone.

Whom should she call? Not Len. He's keeping an eye on her courtroom and offices today.

Not Gil. He's under scrutiny. How would that look, bringing him along? She almost smiles at the thought, hearing his deadpan voice in her head. *Right, Dane, let's go visit the man I just shot.*

Not Lina. Another person who shot this man. No need to orchestrate another face-off, reminding them both of 1992. Besides, it's best to avoid extended contact between witness and judge until the Underwood trial is over, in case Lina is recalled to the stand. Last night, when Lina paid her a brief visit at the back of the ambulance, Dana expressed her heartfelt gratitude. More of that to come after the trial is over.

The logical person to call is a very busy and important woman, but maybe she'll take another few hours this afternoon for an old friend and former boss. Dana could use Indigo's lively personality and unique sense of humor right now. And when the visit with Pineda is over, Dana will have a chance to turn the tables and ask Indigo how everything is going in her life.

An hour later, Dana sits in the front passenger seat of the official vehicle of the Chief of Police, City of Mount Vernon. A hulking, Darth Vaderish Chevrolet Suburban.

"Just like old times, isn't it? Hauling Your Honor's you-know-what around town." As Dana's confidential investigator, Indigo used to drive her to every official event of the Westchester DA and every crime scene that could benefit from her investigative acumen.

"Except this car is five hundred times bigger and we're not in Westchester. We're in Manhattan, where you won't even find a place to double park this thing."

"Darlin', they make room for Chief Raines wherever I go. And with last night's judge hostage in the front seat, I'm set. We're royalty. Did you alert the press?"

"A low profile might be best for this adventure." Even as she says it, Dana knows that six-foot-tall, booming-voiced Indigo is not a person who goes unnoticed.

Her friend has a huge smile on her face as she gazes into traffic from behind the wheel. "I wore my lipstick, didn't you notice? We'll look good on tonight's news."

"And I wore my sunglasses. On second thought, maybe we ought to turn around. There's no way I want the press to get wind of this."

"No worries, Judge. Sneak attack. They won't know what hit 'em, but if anyone notices, you'll be out of there before Tanya Jordash can say, 'Live from Bellevue.'"

"Okay, it's a plan. I'm going to keep this short."

"I'll be right there with you. I brought my six-shooter in case he tries anything." She pats her hip. Dana looks at her askance. Indigo quickly darts a glance and bursts into a belly laugh. "Just pulling your leg, Judge. Seems right to talk Wild Wild West, seeing as your friend was shot by a Manhattan cop in 1992." The NYPD was notoriously behind the times, failing to switch from revolvers to semiautomatics until well into the nineties.

"Actually, Lina was in the pilot program then. She had a Glock semiauto."

"A modern girl."

"You won't have to use your six-shooter. He'll be on pain-killers, and I only have a few things to say to him. He might even think they're nice things."

"A few *nice* things. You're something else, Judge Dana Hargrove. That man had more than a few *not*-nice things to say to you, not to mention slamming your head on the floor."

"The tile was slippery."

"Now we're sounding like the battered wife."

"The point of my visit is this. I don't want the next and last time I see him to be in a courtroom, testifying at his hearing on the parole violation."

"How about at his *new* criminal trial for kidnapping and assault?"

"I'm not pressing charges."

"You're not." Deadpan. "This fella must be a real charmer. What *really* went on in your office last night?"

"He came in, saying he just wanted to talk. He was desperate to explain himself. His life started on a good track that went wrong. He didn't want to kill that store owner, and he blames me and the system. After twenty-three years, he can't reconcile what he did and needs to externalize the blame. I don't think he wanted to hurt me physically. He was trying to scare me to make a point."

"Other ways to make a point, Judge."

"Yeah, well, this is the thing. State prison. How can that be the right punishment for every felon? Prison did a number on him, twisted his mind in a strange way."

"Prison twists some minds and not others. We've all seen a few of 'em come out and make a good life. This one did not. You're not responsible."

"But I don't see the point of laying it on thicker than it already is. I'm not leveling any new charges, but he'll be sent back on the parole violation. Nothing I can do about that. His max on the original sentence is life. It'll be up to the parole board whether or when they let him out again."

"Can't be too soon in my book."

"He has to feel there's some hope, if he's going to move on from this. Maybe he'll get another chance and make good next time."

"Well, isn't he lucky that he kidnapped you instead of me! Since we're being all nice about it," she flicks up her wrist and checks her watch, "do we have time to pick up flowers? Maybe one of those cute 'Get Well' balloons too."

They convince the police officer to leave them alone. After all, Indigo has her six-shooter. But the officer makes sure that Pineda is handcuffed to the bedrail before he allows them inside.

As they walk in, Ramón's head is turned to the wall. The top bedsheet is pulled down to waist level. A hospital gown covers the left part of his chest, and the right side is bandaged. An IV runs into the arm farthest from them, the arm that isn't hand-cuffed. His pulse, respiration, and blood pressure are displayed for the world to see.

Surreal. That's how this feels. Dana's vision is still enclosed in the hazy outline of shock. Why is she compelled to do this? True to her character, there's a rational underpinning to this radical plan. Her unannounced visit evens things out between them. Yesterday, Ramón stood over her, rendering her physically, but not mentally, helpless. It wasn't until the end of their encounter, when he lost control, that he attempted to strip her of dignity with a violent act. Now, *he* is in a position of physical helplessness. She will stand over him, but she will not try to erase his dignity. She wants to give some of it back.

He's physically, but not mentally, helpless. The painkillers do not kill his abilities to comprehend and remember.

This is how she knows.

She comes up to the bedside and says, "How are you doing, Mr. Pineda?"

A small current of recognition ripples through his body the minute he hears her voice. She can see it. He turns to her, and his half-lidded eyes pop open. He's alert and listening.

Indigo stands at attention next to the judge. Together, they form an imposing presence, but Ramón isn't cringing or cowering. He lifts his eyebrows in an expression of self-mockery. "I'm alive." His voice lacks the crispness and drive it had last night.

"I wanted to let you know that you didn't hurt me when you threw me down. I have a bump on my head, that's all. I don't plan to level any new charges against you."

She pauses. His eyes have grown wider in surprise.

"But the state is charging you with a parole violation. There's nothing I can do about that. I'm an officer of the court and must tell the truth at your hearing. I'm a witness, not the judge. It's not up to me whether you're sent back on your original sentence. And if you're sent back, it's not up to me whether you're paroled again."

Another pause, a longer one this time.

"No," he says. "Not up to you." There's no sarcasm in his voice. Only shame. He turns his head away and looks at the wall. *Me.* Did she just hear that word? Wishful thinking. It's what she hopes for him, an assumption of responsibility. A first step in moving forward.

She comes closer. "I also want you to know something very important."

His head is still turned away.

"It's my duty to judge each case in my court on its own merits. To consider each defendant as a unique individual. But I want you to know that I carry with me everything you told me yesterday, about your life and experiences and views of the law.

I'll remember every word of it. And if there comes a day when you're out of prison again, I hope you'll do one thing."

She waits, hoping he'll turn to face her again. He does.

"I want you to come talk to me. I'll listen to you. We'll have a conversation. I promise you."

He nods, just slightly.

"But make an appointment first," she adds. She's not trying to make light of it, nor does he take it that way. His expression remains somber.

"All right, Mr. Pineda. Until we meet again."

Dana turns. Indigo turns.

They're halfway to the door when she hears his voice again. *I'm sorry.* Real or imagined?

Either way, his thoughts and feelings are out of her hands.

It goes as scripted. Automatic pilot for the rest of the day at home and all day at work, Friday. Professional. In control. Meeting with staff. Defense motion for mistrial denied. Resumption of jury trial. A day of testimony. Trial adjourned until Monday morning. "Have a good weekend." Bang of the gavel.

True to her usual pattern in dealing with trauma, Dana compartmentalizes her mind, holding onto her routines, her intellect and rationality for two full days. It's time now to feel the full impact of her terrifying ordeal.

Saturday brings the letdown, the haze lifted, the crash, the giving in to extreme emotion.

Dana spends the day at home, crying, in Evan's arms. She cries for Ramón Pineda, for his bad luck and self-sabotage, for the world's cruelty and unfairness, for the dichotomies of randomness and choice. She cries for herself, for the vulnerability and strength she showed that man. She cries for her biases and insight, for her coldness and warmth, for her selfishness and transformation.

At the end of the crying comes a long sleep and a bright Sunday. Every thought, purpose, and desire is imbued with a dazzling clarity and crispness. It's a day for family. For Evan, Travis, and Natalie. Her wonderful children are still hard at study, but she takes time for them, and they for her, in long conversations on the phone. They express their joy and relief that their mother emerged from her ordeal without serious injury.

While talking to Natalie, Dana nearly breaks down. Tears of joy spring to her eyes and her throat clogs with emotion. Natalie can hear it in her voice and teases her. "You're a wreck, Mommy."

"I know."

"But totally fine."

"I'm more than fine. I'm ecstatic." Does Natalie know why? More than anything, Dana is looking forward to renewed closeness with her daughter.

"Not as ecstatic as me. I get to come home soon."

"And quiz me about my perception and memory of being held hostage?"

"Only if you want to and it isn't too traumatic."

"Oh, I want to. But mostly, we're going to have fun. We're going to go places and do things. It will be a fantastic summer."

"Woohoo! I love you, Mommy."

"I love you more."

JUNE

SENTENCING DAY HAS arrived. Judge Hargrove gives herself a final appraising look in the mirror before leaving the robing room. Without a glance, she passes the freshly painted wall on her way through the narrow passage to the courtroom.

"All rise," Len bellows as the judge enters. The din of a hundred people recedes into a cacophony of stray murmurs and whispers, rustling papers, coughs, scuffling feet, and chairs scraping the floor at counsel tables. "Hear ye, hear ye…"

Dana strides up to the bench and scans the audience as Len finishes his proclamation. "The Honorable Dana Hargrove presiding. Be seated and come to order."

Every seat is filled. The two camps dug into opposite sides of the courtroom, as they did during the trial. The side behind the prosecutor's table is muscled with angry, indignant supporters of Connor Davidson. The mother, father, and brother of the victim sit in the front row. The mother grieves openly, her handkerchief ever available. The father and the brother puff out their chests, fit to burst the buttons of their suit jackets, as their eyes intermittently hurl daggers at the murderer.

Behind the defense table, the pews are filled with the less belligerent followers of Suzette Spinnaker. There's a feeling of resignation and weight on this side of the audience. Surprisingly, the mother and the sister (but not the father) sit in the front row.

The Spinnaker family did not attend a single day of the trial, but Dana gleans their identities from the family resemblance, the trappings of money, and Suzette's needful glances over her shoulder at her mother. In a fit of parental remorse about her poor showing, Mrs. Spinnaker sent a letter to the court a week ago, begging for mercy on behalf of her daughter.

Young men and women in their late twenties are scattered throughout the audience. Presumably, these peers of Suzette and Connor have chosen their respective sides of the courtroom according to their loyalties. Dana recognizes a few faces from the trial, including one that's now very familiar, although not quite as handsome as the photoshopped image on his professional headshot. Richard Theodore Flagg. Dana seems to recall a day during the trial when Flagg sat on Suzette's side of the courtroom, but she could be mistaken. Today, he sits behind the Davidson family.

Undoubtedly, many of the other people in the audience are relatives, associates, and friends of the victim or the defendant, but Dana also senses that some of these people are mere gawkers and curiosity seekers. A few sketch artists and reporters are present, but no cameras are allowed.

At the last minute, Evan slips into the courtroom and squeezes into the back pew. The judge catches his eye, then she studiously avoids him. He's sitting on the Davidson side, but that could be only because it has the larger sliver of available space. She hasn't revealed her proposed sentence to Evan. In a way, she hasn't revealed it to herself. She's been waffling within a certain range of years. Something important to her decision hasn't happened yet, and she's keeping her mind open until the last minute, when she will say, "I hereby sentence you to..."

Suzette sits next to her high-priced, daddy-financed lawyer. She's noticeably nervous. During the trial, she consistently maintained her façade of pert confidence in her attractiveness and charismatic draw. That demeanor is drastically beaten down. Her eyes are red rimmed. She's pale and thin, lost in her clothing. She's been given a reprieve from prison garb for today's proceeding, but the outfit she picked, a chic designer skirt suit from happier days, no longer snugs her form. At Rikers, no online shopping is allowed.

Judge Hargrove talks to her directly. "Ms. Spinnaker. We're here today for sentencing. You've had a fair trial, and the jury found you guilty of manslaughter in the first degree. The probation department interviewed you and many people in your life. I've studied this thirty-page presentence report in detail." She lifts it to indicate. "This court also received more than a hundred letters from people in the community, including your family and friends, and those of Connor Davidson. I've read and considered every one of those letters." Dana looks at the family members in the audience, one by one, as she speaks.

This reference to their letters may trigger thoughts of other letters that have been in the news: Ramón Pineda's correspondence to Judge Hargrove and her family. The letters themselves were never released to the press, only watered-down descriptions. One news service claimed, without support, that Pineda was obsessed with the Spinnaker case and wrote to the judge about it.

Suzy Suburbs gets Man One. Berto Barrio gets Murder. In a few words, Ramón expressed his opinion on class, ethnicity, bias, and the felony murder law. But he was implying more than abstract commentary. He was comparing two people who both said, "I didn't mean to kill." Dana has recently studied another person who, in a sense, "didn't mean" it, a man who was depravedly indifferent to whether his victims lived or died. Last week, a jury found Garth Underwood guilty of two counts of second-degree murder. How do the crimes of Suzy, Ramón, and Garth compare?

Garth Underwood's sentence, Dana's new albatross, will be

a source of vexation and distress for many days to come until his court date next month. As with Spinnaker, verdict day brought an end to Underwood's freedom. House arrest revoked, ankle bracelet removed, remanded to custody. Quite likely, the I'm Bien Man will not fare well in Rikers this month, or in state prison after he's sentenced and sent up the river.

Ramón's message is indelibly etched in the judge's memory and thrown into the mix with the hundred-plus letters and the presentence report, which chronicles Suzy's background and the influences that led to her crime. Hers is a singular story. Like everyone else, she's unique. Thousands of days formed her life before she got to this point. Comparing her to other people can't be the measure of a prison sentence.

Besides the letters and the report, Dana's head swims with the rubric of the law, principles engrained in her from the first lessons in law school. How does a court arrive at a sentence? Through the exercise of discretion after weighing the gravity of the crime, the circumstances of the offender, and the goals of sentencing: deterrence, rehabilitation, retribution, and isolation. A balancing act and, voilà, the magic number appears.

Does Suzette Spinnaker need to be deterred and isolated, to spare society from the danger she poses? Her crime was specific to a relationship and unlikely to be repeated. Is the community entitled to retribution, to appease an emotional desire to punish? Prison is the community's condemnation of the defendant's behavior, and the taking of a life begs a serious sanction. Does Suzy need rehabilitation? Yes, but how well does our prison system deal with that?

We've all seen a few of 'em come out and make a good life. This one did not.

Programs and therapy and education are available in state prison, but so much depends on the individual. In her interview for the presentence report, Suzy clung to her story. Her mind dwells on an irrational mixture of mistake and self-defense, at odds with the physical evidence that she repeatedly stabbed Connor. She's unable to own what she's done.

She has another chance, here, today, and Judge Hargrove will be paying close attention.

First, the judge invites the prosecutor to offer the People's recommendation. The ADA stands and gives a short, well-reasoned argument for the maximum sentence of twenty-five years. He mentions something that reminds her of what Evan said on the night of the guilty verdict. The evidence fully supports a conviction of murder, but the jury exercised compassion and lowered the crime to manslaughter. A mercy verdict. She's already been given a break.

Dana cannot ascribe to this view. What goes on in the jury room is secret. Yes, juries ignore the law sometimes and make emotional decisions. But Dana takes the legal view of the verdict and will not assume otherwise. The jury had a reasonable doubt as to the defendant's intent. They believed she had the intent to seriously hurt Connor, not the intent to kill. The court respects that decision.

And now, the moment is upon them. Will Suzette take this opportunity to speak?

"Ms. Spinnaker, please rise."

The depleted young woman rises into a slumped posture, with head bowed. Very quickly, she straightens up and regains an ounce of her characteristic defiance. She stands tall to hear the words that will redefine her path forever. But the tipping point, the change in her path, happened long before the verdict or the indictment or the arrest. What's done is done. How she views her path to this point, and what she does with it from here on out, are important to the judge deciding her fate.

"The law gives you an opportunity to speak at your sentencing hearing. You have no obligation to do so, but the court will listen carefully if you choose to speak. Would you like to say anything before the court pronounces sentence?"

Suzette parts her lips but freezes in a gap-mouthed daze, speechless. Throughout her public life, she's been known for her loquaciousness, even at her trial, when she took the witness stand in her own defense. The judge can't believe she won't open up now and give them a piece of her mind.

Everyone waits.

She isn't going to speak.

But then, a dark cloud passes over her face. With an air of haughtiness, she projects loudly from her slight frame, in a voice at once bold and whining. "Jail is unbearable. The cruelty and dehumanization are unimaginable to all of you." She swivels and gestures. "I've been stripped of my dignity and given no respect for my intellect or my accomplishments."

Judge Hargrove is sorely disappointed. Is this going to be nothing but a rant by a selfish, spoiled girl?

That girl's voice softens a bit and takes on the quality of an actress in a melodrama. "Now that my freedom has been taken away, I truly know how precious our freedoms are."

A switch to soapboxing on human rights by Suzy, the martyr.

"I'm saying all this because I want the court to know, and I want the Davidson family to know," she turns briefly to them, "that I *am* being punished. This is true punishment. It's torture. It's excruciating. I'm paying double for a tragic mistake. I loved Connor Davidson with all my heart. I admit that we fought. I did not mean to kill him. I did not even intend to seriously hurt him. I miss him every minute of every day, and on top of this agony, I'm paying double with the indignity of incarceration and wasted years of my life. I will be paying for a very long time, whether Your Honor sentences me to five years or twenty-five years. I'm paying. Believe me."

She is unrepentant. Audible sobbing rises from the Davidson

row, where the mother sits hunched behind her wadded-up hanky. The Davidson men are livid, chomping at the bit to lash out.

"Five years is payment enough, Judge Hargrove. It's more than enough, more than I deserve for having an argument with a man I love and making a tragic mistake. Ten or fifteen or twenty or twenty-five years won't bring him back to me or the Davidson family. The minimum, five years, is pure torture. Go ahead and have at it. Tie me to the rack. But don't do it for longer than five years."

She sits down in a huff, arms crossed over her chest. Her attorney, out of his client's view, directs a subtle raise of his eyebrows at the judge. She invites him to speak. He stands in his thousand-dollar suit and clears his throat. He has done well by his client in convincing the jury that she isn't guilty of murder. But he doesn't mention this. After the defendant's petulant rant, he keeps his comments short, imploring the court, simply, to exercise compassion and mercy.

At the finish of this, the last speech, the judge is ready.

"Ms. Spinnaker, I'm prepared to pronounce sentence. Please stand and face the court."

Sulkily, with a roll of her eyes, Suzy gets up again. Her face betrays a new inkling of insecurity. Did she manage to bury herself with her words?

Dana is now confident in her decision. The high end of the range she's been considering fully accounts for every mitigating circumstance in this unique case. Suzy's speech has failed to add anything more in mitigation. Still, the judge decides to come down a year from the high end of her range for whatever symbolic value the number may hold.

"A jury has found that, on November 27, 2014, you intended to cause serious physical injury to Connor Davidson, and thereby caused his death. You have committed a grave offense, taking a life that can never be restored. I heard all the evidence in this case, and contrary to what you have said here today, the jury's verdict is fully supported. After considering your statement and all the other statements and materials before the court, I hereby sentence you to a determinate term of incarceration of twenty-one years in state prison."

Twenty-one, the age of majority, adulthood, hoped-for maturity.

Judge Hargrove turns to Len. "Take charge." She bangs the gavel.

On Saturday, Cheryl and Caitlin welcome the family to Dovecote Lane for a barbeque on the deck. The whole gang is here. Dana and Evan drive up from the city separately from the "kids," Natalie, Travis, and Ginger, who take the lime green Beetle. The Westchester residents, Evan's mother Brenda, brother Albert, and sister-in-law Christine, come in Al's car.

It's the first time the family has been together in one place since the harrowing events of the spring. Life is good as they look forward to summer. The suspicions and fears of a month ago no longer control them but will never fade from memory.

Ginger's client Jack, the one who gave her such a hard time, returned to group therapy only once to spew more vitriol, but she hasn't seen him since. She wouldn't be surprised if he's back in the bottle. He wasn't ready to make a change. Cases like his come and go, but Ginger perseveres. The success stories on the job remind her of her father and give her the reward she needs.

Evan's "stalker" Prescott is another story. A sad one. The law school dean expelled Prescott and spoke with his parents, suggesting that they get help for their son. A week later, the boy attempted suicide. His cry for help landed him in the hospital, where he's currently receiving psychiatric treatment. Evan still gets spooked when he remembers the eerie coincidence of Prescott blurting, *"People versus Pineda"* in criminal procedure class, mere days before the letters started coming.

Cheryl has been making court appearances in her lawsuit to terminate Hunter's parental rights. Her case is strong, and Dana predicts she will eventually prevail. Although Hunter doesn't have a leg to stand on, he hasn't given up his fight. The one good thing is that he's behaving himself, abiding by an order of protection and staying away from Cheryl and Caitlin during the pendency of the case. He's been cowed into submission. Whether it's Mario's influence or the court's authority, Cheryl isn't sure, but those forces, working together, are doing the trick.

Dana was called to testify at the hearing on Pineda's parole violation. Her time on the witness stand was short. The court didn't need every detail. Even one of those letters Pineda sent would be enough to justify revoking his parole and sending him back to the place he'd left only five months before. Ramón was doleful and silent at the hearing. Does he regret what he did to Dana and her family, or is he merely sorry that things didn't go as he'd planned?

Their eyes met several times in the courtroom. Dana could not read whether his mood reflected self-pity and false righteousness or enlightenment and remorse. She's still haunted by visions of him, standing over her, wielding the letter opener. Other times, she thinks of his face and his words and feels compassion, not fear. She believes he's good at heart but mentally unsound in his struggle to comprehend and overcome the reasons for his nightmare. Bad luck, a distorted perception, skewed responsibility, the wrong choices.

Dana breathed a big sigh of relief when Gil was cleared. The confrontation with Pineda was fraught with uncertainty. Gil saw the glint of steel, and in the split second allowed for choice, he reacted. Dana is deeply grateful to him and Lina and the other fine officers who came to her rescue.

True to their mutual promises, Dana and Natalie have already embarked on their summer of "fun" which, for them, includes the intellectual game of analyzing the events of May 13, 2015. A fascinating case study in memory and identification. Natalie has pored over every available photograph of Pineda and questioned Dana at length about her initial failure to recognize him. Facial recognition should have been stronger, Natalie thinks, even factoring in the passage of time, the stress of the moment, and the changes in his appearance. Mindboggling. Dana admits her own fascination with the mysteries of perception and concedes at least partial responsibility for Natalie's overwhelming interest in the subject. But she's also mindful of the need to lighten up Natalie's life with engaging distractions. They've already had a shopping spree and a night at the ballet with Cheryl.

Travis seems the least scarred by the days of fear in May. But that's quintessential Travis, outwardly confident and almost stoic, even though he feels every emotion—love, anger, compassion, and fear—very deeply under the surface. In these ways, he's like his mother. For him, it was business as usual through the stressful times. He kept a level head and scored high marks on his exams. He recently started his summer internship at Legal Aid and moved into a one-bedroom apartment with Ginger.

Healing from the trauma, with challenges met, goals achieved, resolutions made, the family looks forward to a sunny summer.

At four o'clock, people start rolling into the driveway at Dovecote Lane. First to arrive are Brenda, Albert, and Christine. Cheryl greets them warmly. "Welcome, welcome! The city folks are going to be a little late. They're hung up in traffic."

"That's city life for you," grumbles Al. He wouldn't live in the city for anything.

"Can't wait to see Dana, Evan, and the kids," says Christine.

"What horrible times they've been through. I haven't seen them since Christmas."

"We're fortunate everything turned out the way it did," Cheryl says.

Al helps Brenda out of the car. "Hello, my sweet girl." Brenda reaches her short arms up and Cheryl stoops down to her level for a hug. Cheryl and Brenda share a special affinity as the de facto babysitters of Natalie and Travis when they were young.

Everyone is settled on the deck with drinks when the kids arrive. Cheryl and Caitlin go out to the driveway to greet them. Natalie immediately scoops up Caitlin for the customary piggy-back ride. In TV-star glamour mode, Cheryl welcomes Ginger with a big hug and kiss that leaves lipstick on her face.

"Thanks for inviting me," Ginger says, a bit abashed. She's still in awe of Cheryl, even though they're not strangers. Now that Ginger has moved in with Travis, she's officially part of this family, if she wasn't already. She and Travis were high school sweethearts their senior year, and Ginger has been to the house on Dovecote Lane many times.

Travis accepts his own hug from Cheryl and uses his thumb to smudge the bright pink off his girlfriend's cheek. True to character, he jumps into a matter of business right off. "Ginger's going to spend the night at her mom's. I'll take her over after dinner and come right back."

"Sorry I won't stay the whole evening," Ginger says.

"My goodness, of course you have to go see your mom! I'm honored you're taking the time to stop here first." Coming from Cheryl, this sentiment is completely genuine.

As they talk in the driveway, Evan and Dana drive up, and the party is off and running.

By eight thirty, Travis has taken Ginger to her family and

returned, and Evan's side of the family has just left. Brenda was tuckered out, and Al and Christine have an early morning planned for tomorrow, setting out on a trip to visit their daughter and grandkids.

The days are lengthening, and the air is warm and fragrant with the promise of a hot summer ahead. In two weeks, the longest day of the year will be upon them. Cheryl lights four citronella candles and puts them in each corner of the deck.

Like everything else she does, Cheryl's choice of deck furniture is unrivaled. She has an eye for luxury and comfort. They each sit in a cushioned chair that molds perfectly to their backs. No one wants to move. The night is magical. They linger outside through the slowly descending gray of dusk, not caring if the mosquitos bite.

Five chairs are lined up closely, all facing out to the backyard.

On the left side of the deck, Caitlin sits in her mother's lap, snuggled up against her shoulder. Cheryl strokes her baby-soft hair and hums a quiet lullaby.

On the right side, Natalie and Travis sit together. They've had enough time tonight to catch each other up on their lives, and now they're content to enjoy the evening in silence, feeling the warmth of home.

In the middle are Dana and Evan, their lounge chairs placed with enough room between them to dangle two arms. Does anyone see? She dangles her right arm over the side, he dangles his left, and their fingers touch, play, intertwine, and release. His hand is large, sensitive, warm, and dry. In this moment, Dana is brought back to every summer evening she ever spent with her family on this deck, overlooking the backyard and its border of tall, majestic trees. Oaks, maples, tulip trees. A large lawn set against a wall of green. Natural, comforting, private. Expansive, yet intimate.

Why did she ever fear the thought of living here with Evan,

the two of them alone, tucked away in their secluded nest? "I love this house," Dana says to everyone. "It's so comfortable, especially with the addition and improvements you made, Cheryl. Promise me you'll give the house back to us someday."

"No need to ask. It's yours and Evan's whenever you want it."

For another few minutes, they let the darkness and quiet envelope them. "Just listen," Dana says. Nature is starting to turn up the volume. Tree frogs and crickets. An owl hoots in the distance. Not yet, but later in the summer they'll see fireflies and hear the lusty swell of the cicadas, their vibrating tymbals rising to a crescendo and receding, only to rise again.

Evan is tickling her palm. "It's been a long week," he says with an audible yawn.

She tickles back. "I'm exhausted."

His whole hand covers hers, circles it, and squeezes. "Shall we?"

She squeezes back, and their hands disengage. She places her hands on the armrests to help push herself out of the chair.

Dreamy and woozy, Dana stands up with a little wobble and reaches back for Evan's hand. They take a step, and Dana stops in front of Cheryl, momentarily confused. It's dark, and her sister's chair seems to be in the way.

"Don't worry," Cheryl says. "There are ways to work around it."

Dana shuffles a bit, pulling Evan along, and finds a way around the chair. "Good night, all," she says. "I love you."

Good nights are said all around.

Inside, Dana leads her husband up the stairs and down the hall into the private guest room at the far end of the new addition.

"That was an odd way to say it," Evan says.

"What was odd?" She closes the door behind them.

"There are ways to work around it. The chair."

Dana smiles and drapes her arms around Evan's shoulders. "Darling, in a minute, I'll show you exactly what that means."

Their lips meet in a kiss.

———

AFTERWORD FOR LAW BUFFS

YOU DON'T NEED to be a law buff or lawyer to enjoy the Dana Hargrove novels, but if you like legal stuff, here is some info with a few citations for further reading.

In my legal career in criminal justice, I've worked on both sides of the aisle and at center, for the courts. My experience includes law clerk to appellate judges, assistant district attorney for the Manhattan DA, assistant deputy attorney general for the New York State Organized Crime Task Force, court-appointed appellate counsel for criminal defense, and principal court attorney and supervisor for the Appellate Division of New York State Supreme Court. So, while the cases in the Dana Hargrove novels are born in my imagination, they are always based on real legal principles, New York statutes, and caselaw.

In *Seven Shadows*, Spinnaker, Pineda, and Underwood are imaginary defendants, each charged with murder in the second degree under different theories found in NY Penal Law Section 125.25.

Suzette Spinnaker was charged with intentional murder under subsection (1) of Section 125.25: "With intent to cause the death of another person, [s]he causes the death of such person." The jury acquitted her of murder and found her guilty of the lesser included offense of manslaughter in the first degree under NY Penal Law Section 125.20(1), on the theory that she only intended to cause serious physical injury.

Ramón Pineda was convicted of felony murder under subsection (3) of NY Penal Law Section 125.25. A person is guilty of this crime if "he commits or attempts to commit robbery [or a list of other felonies]…and, in the course of and in furtherance of such crime or of immediate flight therefrom, he…causes the death of a person other than one of the participants." Intent to kill is not an element of the crime, so lack of such intent is no defense. Ramón's failed defense was that Officer Vargas, not he, caused the death of the store owner.

In 2001, Pineda moved to vacate his conviction under NY Criminal Procedure Law Section 440.10(1)(g), on the ground that: "New evidence has been discovered since the…verdict of guilty after trial, which could not have been produced by the defendant at the trial even with due diligence…and which is of such character as to create a probability that had such evidence been received at the trial the verdict would have been more favorable to the defendant." Pineda's post-conviction motion is central to the plot in the third Dana Hargrove novel, *Forsaken Oath*.

Evan posed an interesting question to his class about post-conviction motions in the *Hypotheticals* chapter. If a defendant admits the crime under oath as part of a guilty plea, can that defendant later move to vacate the conviction on the ground of actual innocence? The New York statutes do not expressly allow this. In January of 2014, a New York Appellate Division held that a "freestanding" claim of actual innocence could be raised in a post-conviction motion after a jury trial (*People v Derrick Hamilton*, 115 A.D.3d 12), but did not decide that question with respect to a conviction based on a guilty plea.

In January 2015 (before Evan's lecture), a New York trial court in *People v Natascha Tiger* (County Court, Orange County Indictment. No. 12-00215) dodged the issue by simply assuming that such a claim could be raised but denied the defendant's motion on the ground that she could not prove, by clear and convincing evidence, that she was actually innocent. In 2017, a New York Appellate Division reviewed the case and decided that a claim of actual innocence could be made on a post-conviction motion taken after a guilty plea (*People v Natascha Tiger*, 149 A.D.3d 86). But in 2018, New York's highest court, the Court of Appeals, with two judges dissenting, reversed the Appellate Division, stating that "a guilty plea entered in proceedings where the record demonstrates the conviction was constitutionally obtained will presumptively foreclose an independent actual innocence claim" (32 N.Y.3d 91, 102). If there ever was a compelling case for an actual innocence claim after a guilty plea, *Tiger* is that case. The facts are laid out in detail in the Appellate Division's decision. Take a look!

Fictional character Garth Underwood was convicted of murder in the second degree under subsection (2) of NY Penal Law Section 125.25: "Under circumstances evincing a depraved indifference to human life, he recklessly engages in conduct which creates a grave risk of death to another person, and thereby causes the death of another person." The imaginary Underwood case is similar to the New York case, *People v Stan XuHui Li*. The defendant Li, who ran a "pill mill," was convicted in December 2014 of two counts of manslaughter in the second degree under NY Penal Law Section 125.15(1), on the theory that he recklessly caused his patients' deaths. Li's conviction was upheld by the Appellate Division in 2017 (155 A.D.3d 571) and by New York's highest court, the Court of Appeals, in 2019 (2019 NY Slip Op 08544).

One significant difference between the Li case and my imaginary case is that Underwood was convicted of the more serious crime of murder in the second degree. The California case mentioned in *Seven Shadows*, *People v Hsiu Ying Lisa Tseng*, also involved murder in the second degree, but under the differently worded California law, which requires proof of "implied malice," defined as a "conscious disregard for human life." Like the Underwood case, evidence of uncharged patient deaths was introduced on the issue of Tseng's mental state. In October 2015, Tseng was convicted of three counts of murder in the second degree. On appeal, her challenge to the uncharged crime evidence was rejected by the California Court of Appeals, which affirmed her conviction (30 Cal.App.5th 117 [2018]).

Finally, a footnote [marked with * at the beginning of this book].

Empathy, although a non-legal concept, is vital to good judging. The quote from Azar Nafisi which appears at the beginning of *Seven Shadows* can be found in her appearance on the NPR podcast, *This I Believe*, July 18, 2005.

OPUS NINE BOOKS

All works published by Opus Nine Books are dedicated to the
nine members of the family headed by John and Kate
Swackhamer at 3 South Trail, Orinda, California — a large world
under one small roof.

ACKNOWLEDGMENTS

The author gratefully acknowledges the contributions of Emilya Naymark, Christopher W. Jones, Esq., Kevin Stamey, and Annette Swackhamer Drohan, who read earlier drafts of this novel and provided valuable insights, feedback, and editing suggestions. Thank you!

.

DEAR READER,

As I write the afterword for this updated edition, the sixth (and last) Dana Hargrove novel is on the horizon, to be published in January 2022. For more than a decade, Dana, her family, friends, and colleagues have been a big part of my life. I hope you'll get to know them well!

Each novel is a standalone, finding Dana at a different stage of her personal life and career. Here they are, with the years in which each story takes place:

Thursday's List (1988)

Homicide Chart (1994)

Forsaken Oath (2001)

Deep Zero (2009)

Seven Shadows (2015)

Power Blind (2022)

Let me know what you think! Now's the time to return to your online bookseller and post a reader review of any length on the webpage for *Seven Shadows*. Or, send me a message through the contact page on my website, vskemanis.com. While you're there, subscribe to my blog and take advantage of the free e-book offer for one of my story collections.

To keep up with the latest news about my books and life, look for V.S. Kemanis on Goodreads, BookBub, Facebook, Twitter, Instagram, and YouTube.

Thanks for reading!

V.S.K.

www.ingramcontent.com/pod-product-compliance
Lightning Source LLC
Chambersburg PA
CBHW030319080425
24770CB00005B/60